"SUPERCARRIER"

FRIES ENTERTAINMENT INC. Presents
"SUPERCARRIER"
Starring ROBERT HOOKS, KEN OLANDT,
CEC VERRILL, and RICHARD JAECKEL as Rivers.
Musical Theme by BILL CONTI;
Score by JACK ESCU.
Executive Producers CHARLES FRIES, STEVEN E. DE SOUZA.
Supervising Producer CHUCK BOWMAN.
Producer RICHARD MAYNARD.
Teleplay by STANFORD WHITMORE and STEVEN E. DE SOUZA;
Story by STANFORD WHITMORE.
Directed by WILLIAM GRAHAM.
Produced in association with
RICHARD MAYNARD PRODUCTIONS,
REAL TINSEL PRODUCTIONS, INC.

FRIES ENTERTAINMENT INC.

SUPER CARRIER

AN INSIDE ACCOUNT OF LIFE ABOARD THE WORLD'S MOST POWERFUL SHIP, THE USS JOHN F. KENNEDY

GEORGE C. WILSON

BERKLEY BOOKS, NEW YORK

All photographs not otherwise credited
are by the author.

This Berkley book contains the complete
text of the original hardcover edition.
It has been completely reset in a typeface
designed for easy reading and was printed
from new film.

SUPERCARRIER

A Berkley Book/published by arrangement with
Macmillan Publishing Company

PRINTING HISTORY
Macmillan edition published 1986
Berkley edition/March 1988

ISBN: 0-425-10926-7

PRINTED IN THE UNITED STATES OF AMERICA

10 9 8 7 6 5 4

To Joan—FOR EVERYTHING.

And to all the other Joans who silently and bravely suffer the anguish of waiting for their men to come home from the sea.

Contents

1 / Mishaps   1
2 / Departure   13
3 / Shipmates   28
4 / *Kennedy* Incorporated   47
5 / Steam   65
6 / Bear Hunt   71
7 / Rio—First Liberty   86
8 / Mishaps Continued   97
9 / Terrorism   118
10 / Bombing Raid   133
11 / Aftermath   155
12 / Christmas   168
13 / The Box   190
14 / Secretary Lehman   203
15 / "Smart" Bombing   220
16 / Antisubmarine Warfare   232
17 / Marine Pullout   243
18 / Riding the Tomcat   246
19 / Homeward Bound   264
       Epilogue   278
       Acknowledgments   284
       Index   287

1   Mishaps

NOTHING inside or outside his speeding fighter plane gave Frenchie any hint that he was about to crash into the Mediterranean Sea below. All the instruments, dials, buttons, switches, and gauges inside the cockpit of the F-14 Tomcat fighter looked good. No red warning light commanded his attention. He had plenty of gas.

Lieutenant David Pierre "Frenchie" Jancarski looked around the world outside the cockpit. Viz—for visibility—was excellent on this early afternoon of 11 November 1983. Beams of bright light shot down through the blue sky, virtually unobstructed by clouds. The sunbeams passed right through the scratched plastic of the F-14's cockpit and bore into the slightly rippled surface of the Mediterranean. This lit up the Med into a postcard blue. Frenchie looked straight down and saw he was responsible for the only dark spot on water. The arrowhead shadow of his F-14 raced over the waves at 400 miles an hour.

Off in the distance, Frenchie could see home, the USS *John F. Kennedy*, an aircraft carrier. She was one of the nation's supercarriers. President Reagan had changed her original orders to sail through the Suez Canal on the way to the Indian Ocean. Instead she was standing off Lebanon to help protect the U.S. Marines penned up at the Beirut International Airport. Frenchie and his radar intercept officer in the back seat, Lieutenant Commander Ollie Wright, had just pulled two hours of aerial guard duty in the sky around the airport. Nothing exciting had happened despite all the fears of Higher Authority.

Higher Authority was the convenient but unaccountable term for everyone from the admiral commanding the battle group off Lebanon to the President of the United States in Washington. Frenchie, Ollie, and every other aviator on the *Kennedy* had been told that Higher Authority was worried about another sneak attack on the marines. Three weeks ago—at 6:20 the morning of 23 October 1983—a lone terrorist had driven a truck filled with explosives into the marine compound, detonated the load, and blew up himself, 220 marines, 18 sailors, and three soldiers, most of whom were asleep in their racks. Higher Authority was worried not only about another suicide attack on the marines but about an outright invasion of their compound; about a Kamikaze bombing of the American ships standing off Lebanon, including the *Kennedy*; about a night speedboat attack against the ships in the battle group; about a hang glider assault on the ships close to shore by Lebanese tribesmen, laughingly called the Cruise Druze threat by the pilots. Higher Authority, it seemed, was worried about everything.

Higher Authority also had to prepare for the possibility that the so far supine Syrian Air Force might suddenly rise above the ridges of the Bekaa Valley and take on U.S. planes off Lebanon and sometimes over it. Some of the U.S. planes patrolling off Lebanon were unarmed, like the EA-6B Prowler electronic eavesdropper and signal jammer and the E-2C Hawkeye warning and control plane. But the F-14 fighter planes were armed with two types of missiles—the heat-seeking Sidewinder and the radar-controlled Sparrow as well as rapid-fire guns to combat the Syrians—or maybe even the Russians—if they decided to do battle at some point.

The two-hour combat air patrol mission Frenchie and Ollie had just completed was one part of the U.S. military response to all the "what ifs" Higher Authority had pondered when American troops were dropped into the whirlpool of Lebanon. The two naval aviators from the VF-31 Tomcatters squadron —who flew under the slogan, "We get ours at night"—saw nothing dangerous or exciting about flying along the edge of Lebanon. Their mission had been just another boring aerial patrol. They had flown up close to airliners coming into Beirut to make sure they were not bombers in disguise which could suddenly veer off from an innocent looking landing approach and bomb the marines at the airport or the ships offshore. Frenchie and Ollie also had to keep track of military planes all around them, but so far no Syrian MiGs had appeared to challenge them. Every aviator on the *Kennedy* itched for a kill to avenge the marines and to prove himself in combat. But this day the only non-U.S. military planes Frenchie and Ollie had seen in the skies were friendlies, either Israeli or French.

Three days earlier—on 8 November 1983—another F-14 from the *Kennedy*'s VF-31 squadron had raced by a French F-8 fighter from the carrier *Clemenceau* flying off the Lebanese coast. Lieutenant (junior grade) Cole "Bam Bam" O'Neil was piloting the F-14 and Commander John "Belly" Scull was working the radars in the back seat. It was a clear day like this one. Bam Bam, though a nugget pilot (the term for a pilot on his first cruise), was skillful and disciplined. Belly was an old pro who would have been watching the instruments one second and the F-8 the next. Suddenly and for no apparent reason, the French pilot to his horror saw Bam Bam fly smack into the water. Bam Bam and Belly went straight to the bottom of the Med still strapped into the seats of their plane. Nobody would ever know why the plane went into the water. It would go into the Navy record books as a "mishap." Flying high-performance jets over the water was dangerous business. Accidents happened. Yet Bam Bam and Belly had been real live people, with wives and other loved ones. They were alive one minute and dead the next. Nobody could take their deaths with the equanimity the Navy term "mishaps" implied.

While shocked and saddened over the deaths of his squadron mates, Frenchie deep down could not forgive Bam Bam for flying right into the water with a $40 million fighter in broad daylight. He could not imagine himself doing the same damned fool thing. Especially on a beautiful day like this. Frenchie's landing grades showed he was not the hottest pilot in the squadron as far as getting the 28-ton Tomcat down on the deck of the boat. But he believed his skipper who kept telling him his landings would improve with more practice. Today—on what would have been his 136th landing, or trap—Frenchie was determined to get the grade of OK. This was the equivalent of an A from the landing signal officer who stood at the edge of the flight deck and helped pilots land safely with radio warnings and commands. Only the grade of OK underlined—an A plus —was higher. The young pilot shook off the fatigue which had piled up from flying around-the-clock missions and concentrated on landing on the carrier dead ahead on the Med.

Frenchie could see that the skipper, Captain Gary F. Wheatley, was doing all he could to make the upcoming landings easier for the pilots. Wheatley was steaming at high speed into the wind. The churning from the *Kennedy*'s four propellers kicked a plume of green-and-white water out from her stern. The faster the carrier went into the wind, the steadier the wind would be pushing against the plane's flight control surfaces. This would make the plane more responsive to the split-second corrections fighter pilots made just before slamming their Tomcats down on the deck in a controlled crash.

But nothing can make a carrier landing really easy. Come in too low, and you hit the stern of the carrier. This was a ramp strike. You died. Come in too high, and your tailhook missed all four wire cables stretched across the flight deck to hold you down. This was a bolter. You roared off the front end of the carrier and tried again. Come in too far to the left or right of the center line painted down the canted landing deck, and you crashed into one of the planes parked on either side. This was a mishap. You burned up in the resulting fireball. Come in perfectly, and your tailhook snagged on the Number Three Wire and stopped you in the middle of a 150-mile-an-hour roll. This was "a nice pass." The landing signal officer would give you an OK. His grade would end up in color next to your name on the chart in the squadron ready room. No chart was studied with more intensity by the competitive fraternity of carrier aviation. The chart showed how good you were compared to the other pilots. Frenchie wanted to be higher up on the chart than he was. He did not mind being considered wild and crazy on the beach—he kind of enjoyed that—but he wanted respect for the way he behaved in the air. He already had one flying caper to live down.

Frenchie and a fellow pilot in VF-31 while warming up for the upcoming, long deployment of the *Kennedy* thought it would be spectacular to zorch in and out of staid old Washington National Airport in their Tomcats. Somehow, they received permission from the civil aviation authorities to make touch and go landings, meaning they would let their wheels kiss the runway and then zoom back up into the sky. Washington National is the domain of commercial transports piloted by men who fly in and out with the care of old ladies on walkers. It is not a place frequented by aggressive fighter pilots flying hot planes like the Tomcats.

Unfortunately for Frenchie and his buddies, an admiral sitting in one of those airless Washington offices overlooking Washington National was gazing at the runway when the two red-tailed Tomcats came roaring in. He could not believe his eyes. It was as if two black bears had galloped out of the woods into a crowded shopping center. The admiral complained about the touch and goes to every important person he knew—which was a long list of well placed people. The chain led back down to Commander John "Market" Burch, skipper of the VF-31 Tomcatters. Higher Authority told Burch if he did not discipline his aviators, it would. Burch had no intention of subcontracting out his command.

"You used poor headwork," Burch snapped when he confronted Frenchie and his three co-conspirators. Burch ordered all four to appear before him in a formal disciplinary proceeding called a Captain's Mast. Masts usually are held only for sailors, not officers. Burch also issued the aviators letters of reprimand. And he told them that their Washington National caper had cost them the privilege of flying their planes onto the *Kennedy* once she reached the open sea. The four aviators would suffer the indignity of walking aboard the carrier with the sailors and Black Shoe officers who did not fly. Carrier aviation held special responsibilities along with special privileges, he told the abashed aviators.

Burch admired high spiritedness in his fliers on shore, but he had to insist on deadly serious discipline in the air. Otherwise people would die and $40 million airplanes would be lost. Burch had a special fondness for Frenchie. He saw some of himself in the twenty-eight-year-old Nugget as he looked back wistfully from age forty. "That-crazy-son-of-a-bitch" was the one word term Burch affectionately used for Frenchie when he talked about him—which was often. He laughed at the stories about Frenchie on the beach.

There was the night, for example, when one of the young ladies partying at Frenchie's bachelor pad in Virginia Beach decided the time of the evening had come to play follow the leader. She would be the leader. She climbed the stairs. The aviators and other ladies—called Hooters—at the party followed. The giggling leader climbed out on the balcony overhanging the living room, slid over the railing and jumped with a whoop into Frenchie's couch in the living room below. Everyone but Frenchie followed her, making a perfumed jumble of laughing young bodies on the fabled Frenchie couch.

As much as he enjoyed such partying by night and playing sports—especially golf—by day, Frenchie said the only real highs he got came from flying his Tomcat. He put the feeling into words one day.

"The F-14 is such a beautiful airplane. I'm in love with the way the airplane looks. I'm proud to be flying it. You can escape the workaday world in it. On a bad day, like in the winter when it's cold and it's raining, we take off and beam right through it all. Then it's the clearest, bluest day you've ever seen up there. And you fight and you have fun. You win or you lose or whatever. But you get something out of it. Then you come back down. It's almost as if you get away from the world at work and go into a place that's always beautiful. It never gets bad up there. It does get cloudy up to 20,000 to 30,000 feet, but not very often. Most days you get a low layer. Once you go above it, you're golden and it's terrific. Then you come back down with the rest of the people in the world who have to live on the streets every day. They never get a chance to go up and enjoy this kind of thing. Flying a supersonic fighter, being the cream of the crop, being the lead protection for America. I couldn't go cruising without flying. If you don't fly for two or three days on a ship, you start to get irritable, pissed off. Then you fly and you're all right. *Fix* is a great word for it."

Burch as skipper of VF-31 wanted to preserve Frenchie's romance with his airplane but, at the same time, saw the need for placing a steadying hand on the young aviator. That is why he teamed him up with the veteran RIO (radar intercept officer), Ollie Wright. This combination was right out of the Navy management book for reducing risks: match young aggressiveness with seasoned caution. Frenchie was single, happy-go-lucky. Ollie was married, serious. Youth with age; Frenchie was twenty-eight, Ollie, thirty-eight. Inexperience with experience; Frenchie was on his first cruise, Ollie his sixth.

While a ten-year age difference is not a great gap in civilian life, it is a whole generation in the military where the cruel calendar is marked off by wars. Frenchie was a boy of thirteen when the North Vietnamese staged their Tet offensive in 1968. Ollie was a man of twenty-three who could have fought in it. That made them a generation apart in wars. Ollie also had

3,000 hours in the air and had seen almost everything a pilot could do to an airplane. And he was not shy about sending cautionary words from the back seat to nugget pilots like Frenchie. The word in the VF-31 squadron was that Ollie could be a pain in the ass but he could *save* your ass if you listened to him. This day, like every day and night he flew, Ollie was swinging his helmeted head from the instruments inside the airplane to the horizon, the sea, and the carrier outside it. He knew they were lining up for the most dangerous part of carrier aviation: setting the plane on top of a matchbox bouncing on the sea.

Frenchie aimed his Tomcat for the right side of the *Kennedy*'s island poking up from her otherwise flatiron profile. The landing pattern called for him to roar to the imaginary point in the sky called The Break, a few miles off the bow of the carrier; turn hard left without losing altitude; head downwind parallel to the ship; then start a 180 degree left turn across her wake to slip into the landing approach groove leading to the deck. Frenchie hit the break at 400 miles an hour, pushed the stick over left—you do not have to use the rudder much on the Tomcat —and felt the plane skid around the turn. He eased back on the twin, gray throttles with his left hand. The plane skidded around the turn on its momentum and then slowed to the desired 320 miles an hour. Frenchie pushed the button on the left side of the throttle near his left knee. This activated the mechanism which swept the Tomcat's wings forward to provide more lift and maneuverability at this lower speed.

Ollie looked outside and saw the wings start forward at the right instant. He looked inside again at the instruments. He did not like the way the altimeter needle was falling. They were dropping below 800 feet.

"Watch your altitude," Ollie warned Frenchie through the lip microphone.

The nose still did not come up. They were rapidly dropping below 600 feet. This was dangerously close to the water for a heavy jet flying slowly.

"Pull up! Pull up!" Ollie commanded.

The nose at last came up. But the plane was still mushing downward toward the sea. They would smack into the Mediterranean at 200 miles an hour unless the Tomcat could recover. Ollie saw white-caps out of the corners of his eyes. He had never been that low over the water before. He knew it was too late for the plane to save itself—and them. He reached between his knees for the yellow-and-black ejection loop. He pulled it up toward him, hard. This started a series of explosions. The first blew the canopy clear off the jet. The second blasted Ollie's seat straight up the rails and out into the open sky. The third explosion blasted Frenchie out of the plane a split second after Ollie had rocketed clear.

Ollie felt the explosion kick his butt. Then he felt the wind smack him hard in the face and chest. It twisted his head around like a rag doll's. Next came a big yank from above as his parachute opened. He would say afterward that "it was like God snatching you by the back of the neck and saying, 'Gotcha!' " The sudden braking action of the parachute straightened out Ollie's body. He felt himself swing sideways one time over the water. Remembering his Navy training given on shore in the swimming pool, he pulled the beaded loops of the life preserver straight out from his beltline and then down. He heard the hissing of his life vest filling with gas just as he hit the water. This meant the automatic system was working. Ollie would not have to pull the mouth tube out from under the front flap in his life vest to inflate it. The life preserver was also supposed to inflate once it tasted salt water if the aviator had failed to pull the inflation beads or if he could not inflate it by mouth. Ollie felt the preserver press against his neck as it inflated there. This would keep his head above water. The waist pockets of the life preserver would provide buoyancy for the rest of his body. Ollie snapped off the Koch fittings holding his air-filled parachute to his torso harness. The chute started to float away from him, a welcome sight. The chute was not going to live up to any of the horror stories all Navy aviators had heard. It was not going to fill up with water and pull him under, like an anchor. Nor could it now fall over his head and smother him. There were still the parachute shrouds to worry about. They could still entangle him. He felt a couple of shrouds around his legs. He gingerly moved them down his legs and out toward the chute being blown away from him. The blossom of nylon which had saved him scudded across the Med for a while, then sank out of sight. The water was a tolerable 70 degrees. Ollie felt fully conscious. He knew the ship was nearby. He dared think he would live through this—his first ejection into the open sea. He could not see Frenchie. He worried about whether the pilot had gotten out of the plane in time.

The explosive charge under the seat had fired Frenchie out of the cockpit 0.4 seconds after Ollie. That split second delay, designed to keep ejected aviators from colliding in midair, almost killed Frenchie. Only the guiding drogue chute had had time to open all the way before Frenchie slammed into the water. His big chute did not open like Ollie's to break his fall. The plane was flying forward and dropping downward when Ollie and Frenchie ejected. The upward thrust of the rocket helped Frenchie some. The drogue chute helped a little more. But he still hit the water at about 100 miles an hour. The impact would have killed most people. It knocked Frenchie unconscious and snapped bones. His automatic life preserver worked as advertised. It inflated by itself when it sensed salt water. This kept Frenchie's head above water even though he was unconscious. His head had hit something even with such force that his red-and-black helmet was pierced and dented. He probably had collided with the wreckage of the plane. The inner liner of his helmet against his skull was not broken. His left leg hung under him on threads of bone and bleeding tissue. Luckily his oxygen mask had been torn on impact, providing breathing holes. Otherwise Frenchie would have suffocated after running out of the short supply of oxygen from the bottle packed into his seat pan survival kit. Lady Luck had run out on Frenchie when it came to his 136th trap. She returned in the nick of time to keep him breathing as he bobbed unconscious in the Mediterranean. Frenchie was bleeding externally and internally. Help would have to get to him fast to save his life.

I hoped I would come to know men like Frenchie and Ollie by joining them on an aircraft carrier for an extended deployment designed to influence international events in some distant trouble spot.

Ever since World War II the United States has been without enough land bases overseas to project its military power. American presidents from Harry Truman through Ronald Reagan have turned to carriers to show the flag, express concern, and provide the launching pads for direct military action. This part of the carrier story has been told. The untold story is what life is like inside these instruments of national power; these floating cities of five thousand men nobody knows. I wanted to live in one of those cities for a full deployment in order to chronicle its life.

Secretary of the Navy John F. Lehman Jr. and Admiral James D. Watkins, Chief of Naval Operations, were persuaded that a faithful account of what goes on inside the steel walls of a ship of the line in this era of half war, half peace would give American citizens a better appreciation of the men who guard our security. After considerable discussion, Secretary Lehman, Admiral Watkins, and other Navy officials approved my going aboard a carrier as an objective observer. I would be free to tell the story as I saw it, the bad with the good. The only condition the Navy imposed was to review the manuscript for classified information which might help a potential adversary. Admiral Watkins was extremely proud of the post Vietnam, all-volunteer Navy of 1983. He urged me to see it all—to study the carrier from the engine room to the bridge, and everything in between. He suggested I take the flight physicals, survival training and tests required to qualify for flying in Navy jets. "I don't want you to have any excuse for not learning what goes on out there," Watkins said with a smile as we parted.

I needed no urging to become qualified to fly in jets. I had enthusiastically joined the Navy air corps as a seventeen-year-old high school senior who wanted to fly those lovely gull-winged Corsairs off carriers to help win World War II. The war ended after I had been accepted into the Navy V-5 pilot training program but before I could earn my "Navy wings of gold," as the recruiting posters used to say. By the time I did reach flight training, the Navy had a glut of World War II pilots on its hands. We young aviation cadets were given the choice of signing up for an additional four years or getting out of the Navy. Eight years in uniform with nobody to shoot at sounded like an eternity to an impatient nineteen-year-old. So, having missed the war, I opted to be discharged from the Navy in 1947 to finish college and pursue a career in journalism. I had to wait two decades to experience combat—and then it was not as a Navy pilot but as a civilian war correspondent in Vietnam for *The Washington Post* in 1968 and 1972. I never lost my love of airplanes and flying, though. I had to settle for a private pilot's license and light planes until the opportunity of going to sea on a carrier and flying in its jets came along.

Given my foreshortened Navy flight training, it was like walking back through time when I reported to the Naval Air Station at Patuxent, Maryland, in the spring of 1983—36 years after leaving the Navy—to listen to an instructor tell me how to live through an emergency ejection from an aircraft. After the classroom lectures and tests in the pressure chamber, the instructor directed me to the hangar-laboratory where a replica of a Navy fighter cockpit sat on the floor. I strapped myself into the cockpit, assumed the posture for ejection and waited for the command, "Eject!" On that command, I pulled the same yellow-and-black loop under the seat that Ollie Wright was to yank several months into my reincarnation. I felt the kick in the butt which Ollie was to tell me about, was hurled up the rail leading from the cockpit toward the roof of the hangar, and slid safely back on the deck. The instructor gave me a thumbs up. I felt young again and eager to fly. Life's best moments, for me, have been those on the edge.

From Patuxent, I went to the Naval Air Station at Oceana, Virginia, to join active duty naval aviators in taking water survival tests. In one test, we jumped from a tower into the swimming pool while dressed in full flight gear; snapped on a variety of rescue hitches on the cable dropped from the simulated helicopter above; and held on while the winch hoisted us up to the platform representing a helicopter door. In another test, we were dragged the length of the pool on a cable simulating a wind-driven parachute dragging us across the ocean. We had to flip over on our backs to keep the water from pouring into our mouths and then release the Koch fittings holding us to the runaway parachute. I worried that the cable would pull me into the concrete end of the pool before I could unfasten the confounded fittings. In another test, I found myself in the water with a parachute canopy stretched over my head. The idea was to keep the canopy from smothering you. I gently pulled the canopy toward me and over my head, one rib at a time, as instructed. I then felt for the shrouds dangling down into the water like the stingers of a jelly fish. I pulled the last shroud over and past me and swam clear of the chute. The hardest test for me was staying afloat in one place for ten minutes, as if waiting to be rescued. I had on full flight gear which made trying to stay up exhausting. A friendly pilot treading water next to me tipped me off to the trick of inflating the leg pockets in my gravity suit to provide buoyancy. Everybody was doing it. With that boost, I passed that and all the other water survival tests, along with the flight physicals. I was certified as qualified to fly in Navy jets. All I needed now was a carrier to fly off of, and, hopefully, land back aboard.

The Navy chose the USS *John F. Kennedy* for me to join for a regular deployment. I suspect the ship's outstanding performance record was one reason for the choice. The Navy wanted to put its best forward. Another reason, I suppose, was that the *Kennedy* was scheduled to sail into a peaceful area, the Indian Ocean. No one in the Navy knew President Reagan would make the story dramatic by ordering her, with me aboard, to change course and steam to Lebanon where her planes would go into combat for the first time. No one could know, either, that three of the *Kennedy*'s airplanes would crash into the sea, a fourth would be lost in a midair collision, and a fifth would be shot down over Lebanon. Nor could anyone predict that a small group of sailors would demand to be let off the carrier as conscientious objectors while we stood off Lebanon. Or that the ship and its aircraft squadrons would win one award after another for excellence. These and other events would all be part of the life I would experience and chronicle inside the floating city. I was told to report aboard the *Kennedy* in work khakis and black shoes the morning of 27 September 1983, if I still wanted to go to sea for seven months.

Like the thousands of others getting ready to board the *Kennedy*, my wife, Joan, and I tried to prepare ourselves for the long separation. She gallantly agreed to keep our house in Great Falls, Virginia, on the market while I was at sea, and, if it sold, move all by herself into the one we had purchased in Washington. Our children—Kathy, 24, and Jim, 23—were out of the house and pretty much on their own. Joan would also have to keep an eye on my ninety-year-old mother as well as her own, who was ailing; make the house shine for potential buyers; earn most of the money for the household by continuing to teach math at Cooper Intermediate School in McLean, Virginia; call the plumber; walk the dog; feed the cat; pay the bills; cook supper after supper for herself; and eat all alone night after night in a dark, empty house. Stores in Navy towns pass out shopping bags labeled: "Navy wife: It's the toughest job in the Navy." We were to learn this is no overstatement.

2   Departure

A BENEVOLENT breeze, soft and warm, blew over the marshy flats of the Virginia Tidewater as Joan and I drove toward Pier 12 at the Norfolk naval base where I was to board the USS *John F. Kennedy*. It was 27 September 1983 and the carrier was not due back until 2 May 1984. The sun ducked in and out of the clouds often enough to lighten the grayness of the huge ship rising up from the pier like a forbidding mountain of steel. We had gone over the business of running our affairs before this morning. I had given her power of attorney. We did not have much more to say once we reached the pier. Our focus shifted from our lives to the clutching couples around us. It was a heartrending scene familiar to Navy families but new and arresting to us. We tried to be considerate and not look at the anguished goodbyes as we threaded our way through the crowded parking lot and out to the flat expanse of blacktopped Navy pier, but the farewells proved too emotional to ignore.

There was the young officer and his distressed girl friend, or wife, standing alongside a low sports car in the parking lot. She was dressed well enough for a cocktail party. The tears had unloosed the mascara from around her eyes and her hair was twisted and wet. She kept her head bent hard into the khaki blouse of the young officer and implored, "Now you come back to me, hear? Take care of yourself. I love you." All he could summon up for the moment was, "I'd better go now."

Joan and I gained the pier where Navy families were gathered in small clusters. Tots often strayed from the nucleus and chased bubbles of white plastic packing which the wind drove around the pier. Conversation was stilted in the little family groups. A Hispanic chief, his net laundry bag over his shoulder, during each gap in conversation edged over to the foot of the aluminum ladder, called the brow, leading up into the maw of the carrier. He reached the bottom of the brow finally. He picked up one child after another, starting with the youngest. He looked each one in the eyes, said something I could not hear, kissed and set the child down, and picked up the next one. He shook hands gravely with a tall teenaged boy, presumably his son, and kissed an adult woman with a laugh, probably his sister. He then went into a tight embrace with his wife. Everyone had tears in his eyes by the time the chief abruptly broke off and walked resolutely up the brow. He turned back once for a limp wave and was gone inside the dark ship which was to take him to the other side of the world and God knew where else. Only then, with his father out of sight, did the son bend over and give in to the sobs which racked his thin body. The monster at the pier was taking his father away again. The boy could not bear it.

A twenty-year-old third class petty officer I would come to know as Joseph Daube of Huntington, Long Island, stood uncertainly near the brow with his Georgia peach, Terrie, nineteen, of Griffin, Georgia. They had hardly been together since their marriage eight months ago because Joseph had been to sea for five of those months. He and Terrie had rationalized the upcoming separation. They had told each other they would be happier than ever when the *Kennedy* came home in May, partly because of all the money they would save during her long deployment. They had pasted up a bar chart in their Virginia Beach apartment. It showed their current savings near the bottom at $400 and their May, 1984, goal of $5,000 at the top. Joseph stood at the brow trying to say goodbye to Terrie without breaking down. He told me later how he had tried to steel himself.

"I told myself it never would be over unless it started. I had signed the paper to go into the Navy. Going to sea was part of it. I wanted to get it over with. But it was hard saying goodbye to Terrie. We really didn't say anything. She said, 'I love you.' She is pretty worried that I have to work on the flight deck. Guys come around and say they saw this and they saw that happen up there. I told her I loved her. I figured I would be with her for the rest of my life. I could handle seven months. I kind of had to tell her to leave because I couldn't take it. I didn't lose it until I got on the brow and looked down to see her. Then I cried. Whenever I looked down and saw her, I cried. I tried not to look at her anymore.''

Rear Admiral Roger E. Box, who turned forty-nine on departure day, proved that pier-side goodbyes do not get easier, no matter how many you go through. He held his wife, Ruthie, stiffly at the foot of the brow and kissed her without breaking down in front of the sailors he would command. He confided to me later that this departure was the toughest one of all to struggle through. He said it suddenly struck him that, actuarially, he and Ruthie had fewer years ahead of them than they had already spent together.

The loudspeaker ordered guests to leave the carrier. The crowd on the pier was thinning out. I decided it was time for Joan and me to say goodbye. We clinched, said some mutually encouraging words and then I, too, walked away and up the brow. She wanted to stay on the pier to take pictures and see the huge ship leave the pier, ease down the Elizabeth River, and then grow small as she steamed into the Chesapeake Bay, through Hampton Roads, and out into the open sea.

I was dressed in work khakis, carried a camera, suitcase and typewriter, and probably looked to the young officer of the deck like a tourist. But he politely directed me to the cabin I was to share with an officer. It was across the cavernous hangar bay and down two flights of steel stairs called ladders, and located conveniently under the wardroom where I was to eat my meals as a paying member of the officers' mess. I entered a window-less, small cabin with walls of gray steel, side by side desks, and an upper and lower bunk. My roommate had staked out the lower bunk, as was his right if for no other reason than that he got there first. I felt claustrophobic in the tiny room. I wanted to get back out in the open air as quickly as possible. I found my way up the ladders to the flight deck and stood at the edge looking down at the people on the pier. After much searching I picked out Joan in the crowd. I caught her eye. We were now in two different worlds, I realized, symbolically separated by the oily moat of water between the carrier and the pier. The ship stood high and mighty like a fortress alongside the pier, with her men locked away inside. The ship seemed to mock the bereft family members stranded in the valley formed by the carriers *Kennedy* and *Independence* tied up on either side of Pier 12. I understood suddenly why so many Navy families said their goodbyes at home. Several enterprising sailors reduced the separation between mountain and valley by climbing out on the catwalks nearest the pier. One sailor, who looked no more than eighteen, carried on a yelling conversation with his plump, giggling girl friend standing on the pier. "Take care of my bike, will you?" I heard him shout. She nodded her head. He folded up his white sailor cap into a frisbee and hurled it across the moat to her feet. She picked up the hat and clamped it with a laugh onto her brunette head. This inspired me. I tore a page out of my notebook, folded it into a paper airplane and tossed it down from the flight deck toward Joan. It flew true to the pier. A little girl picked up the plane and, after much hand directing by me, Joan retrieved it. "Your first airmail letter," my note began.

At 9:35 A.M., the sailor who in the next few moments would earn the nickname "Captain O.D.," made his dramatic entrance on the pier. His conveyance was a white Navy ambulance which beeped-beeped its way through the crowd, pulling up alongside the sedate black sedan of Admiral Wesley L. McDonald, commander of the Atlantic fleet. Earlier in the morning, Captain O.D. had triggered the first medical alert of the deployment by falling out of his car onto the pavement of the parking lot near the pier. His wife, fearing for his life, ran to the ship for help. Navy doctors, after examining Captain O.D., ordered his stomach pumped out at the nearby naval hospital. The *Kennedy*'s commanders ordered medics to return Captain O.D. to the ship so his last-night excesses would not get him out of the deployment.

I saw two white clad attendants jump out of the cab of the ambulance and snap open its doors in the back. One reached in to pull out Captain O.D. The woozy sailor could not stand. An attendant got on each side of him and dragged his limp form up the brow. His head was bent down low. His feet, shod only in white sweatsocks, dragged behind him as the attendants pulled him along. His wife, wearing a Navy jacket with the sailor's name emblazoned across it in white ink, followed behind her husband shouting, "You can't go to sea."

The sailors standing around me on the flight deck were drawn to the bizarre scene. They provided a running commentary uncluttered by any hard information about what really had happened to Captain O.D.

"Looks like he OD'd."

"Yeah," agreed his buddy.

"She's probably the one who fucked him up in the first place," said a third sailor.

Captain O.D. was soon out of sight as the attendants dragged him into the ship and down into sick bay, leaving his frantic wife behind. He told me later that he "tried to do a foolish thing" on the eve of our departure by drinking a combination of beer, wine, and whiskey to end his depression. He said that his wife had had a miscarriage, that he had been rejected for the state trooper job he wanted because of injuries he had suffered in a car wreck, and that he could not face the ordeal of going to sea for seven months. Whether Captain O.D. had really tried to commit suicide or just went out on a roaring last-night drunk would remain a mystery to his shipmates, the *Kennedy* doctors and me.

"Hi boys—you're late," said the sailor next to me as he noticed four sailors hurrying up the brow ninety minutes after their 8:00 A.M. reporting time.

"Atlantic Fleet departing," intoned the ship's loudspeakers to announce that Admiral McDonald had completed his ceremonial goodbyes to the top officers and now was heading toward the black sedan that would whisk him to his headquarters in Norfolk. It was 9:55 A.M. Departure was less than an hour away.

"Have you seen Wadsworth?" asked a worried chief as he scanned the faces of the sailors on the flight deck. "Wadsworth is UA." UA stood for unauthorized absence. Wadsworth and forty-nine other sailors would be punished for failing to report to the *Kennedy* before she left the pier. Some of the UAs would be flown out to sea to join the ship and be charged for the plane fare. Others would be court martialed. A sailor was supposed to catch his ship, drunk or sober.

"Please do not be alarmed," the ship loudspeakers said in a commanding tone. "Marines will be firing blanks."

A small rectangle of marines in jungle fatigues pointed their black M16 rifles at the sky and fired. They were rehearsing for burial-at-sea services to be conducted shortly after the *Kennedy* reached the open sea. Families of Navy men may request such burials but do not choose the ship.

I shifted my gaze from the marines back down to the scene on the pier. Hundreds of people were still standing there, including Joan. I saw her dutifully taking pictures. She could not pick me out from the crowd of sailors in dungarees around me. I spotted two little girls, evidently bored from hours of waiting for their Daddy's huge ship to pull out, chasing those same plastic packing bubbles the wind was still blowing helter skelter around the black macadam of the pier.

"Defense Comptroller arriving," announced the loudspeakers. "Attention Hangar Bay One." This was for Vincent Puritano, the closest version of Pentagon treasurer. He had been invited to watch the drama of the *Kennedy*'s planes flying from their land bases onto the carrier once we reached the open sea. The planes would put teeth back into the now toothless carrier. The Navy welcomed opportunities to try to persuade influential people that aircraft carriers were still worth buying, even though their price had risen to $4 billion each, not counting the price of their planes or of their escort ships.

"There will be an FOD walkdown on the flight deck," boomed the loudspeakers. I was to hear that announcement hundreds of times during the course of deployment. But I had no idea what it meant this first time. FOD, explained one of the sailors next to me, stood for foreign object damage—any hunk of metal or other crud that the engine intakes of the jet aircraft could suck off the deck. FOD could be sucked right into the multimillion dollar engine, breaking its spinning blades and perhaps ruining it entirely. The Navy looked for FOD with the fastidiousness of a royal housekeeper looking for lint on the queen's rug. Carriers are vacuumed, scrubbed, air blasted, swept, and searched regularly by hundreds of pairs of eyes in the bent heads of men walking slowly up and down the flight and hangar decks. The first FOD parade of the deployment started at the bow. The men walked shoulder to shoulder toward the stern. Every so often a sailor would bend down to pick up a stray piece of metal or a BB left over from when the steel flight deck was resurfaced with a tarry nonskid coating. He would drop the FOD in the plastic bag carried by the senior petty officer at the head of the slow parade.

"I want to go home," chanted a young sailor who went into a dance next to me on the edge of the flight deck.

"Aw, it won't be so bad," said his buddy feebly. They were eyeing the tugboat that had chugged up the Elizabeth River to help nudge the carrier into the channel leading to Chesapeake Bay.

"Ship is underway," announced the loudspeakers to the crew and their loved ones still waiting on Pier 12. Steam was turning the turbines geared into the propellers. The *Kennedy* cast off her lines and inched forward toward the channel.

With the help of the tug, she nosed into the channel and clumsily turned right—to starboard. She immediately picked up speed and glided away from the pier. I kept watching Joan from the flight deck. She soon blurred into the oranges, browns, and reds of the clothing worn by the people waving from the pier. I looked away from the tiny finger that was now Pier 12 and returned to my stateroom to unpack for the long voyage. My roommate, Lieutenant Richard "Rick" Titi, administrative officer of the medical department, had obviously settled in. His clothes were already stowed in the drawers and hung in his closet. I unpacked most of my stuff and then returned gratefully to the open deck once again.

The 83,000-ton *Kennedy* plowed through Chesapeake Bay and into the open Atlantic with hardly a quiver. She stopped briefly at 1:30 P.M. so the current generation of sailors could conduct burial services for two from the last generation. Clarence E. Rizer III, an aviation machinists mate, first class, shook the ashes of Seaman Gertell H. Balcom, his father-in-law, into the sun-dappled Atlantic. Lieutenant George P. Byrum, one of the *Kennedy*'s three chaplains, knelt at the edge of the flight deck to spread the ashes of Rear Admiral James M. Shoemaker on the open sea. The same marines who had rehearsed while the carrier was tied to the pier were now resplendent in dress blues. They formed the backdrop to the funeral services and fired the final salutes into the bright sky. One of them played "Taps." The ship moved on. The ashes swirled away from the giant carrier, sinking into an ocean which Balcom and Shoemaker knew well from their years in the United States Navy.

Skipper Gary F. Wheatley of the *Kennedy* wrote the Shoemaker family afterward that "it was the kind of bright, clear autumn day that brings joy to a sailor's heart. The ship's position was 36 degrees 51 minutes north, 75 degrees 39.8 minutes west, close to the Chesapeake Light, which is the seawardmost beacon that guides ships over the horizon and into the Chesapeake Bay and Hampton Roads."

While the ship steamed toward her rendezvous point for receiving her aircraft, farewells were being said in the squadrons based around Norfolk. A carrier's air wing is a conglomerate of squadrons which are rotated among the carriers rather than kept with a single ship. The *Kennedy*'s Air Wing Three for this deployment would consist of the HS-7 antisubmarine helicopter squadron based in Jacksonville, Florida—the Shamrocks who flew the Sikorsky SH-3H Sea King; the VS-22 antisubmarine squadron of Cecil Field, Florida, near Jacksonville—the Vidars who flew the Lockheed fixed wing S-3A Viking; the VA-75 and VA-85 squadrons of Norfolk—the Sunday Punchers and Buckeyes, who flew the Grumman A-6E Intruder medium bomber; the VAW-126 early warning squadron of Norfolk—the Seahawks who flew the Grumman E-2C Hawkeye warning and control aircraft; the VAQ-137 electronic warfare squadron of Whidbey Island, Washington—the Rooks who flew the Grumman EA-6B Prowler; the VQ-2 electronic intelligence squadron of Rota, Spain—the Skywarriors who flew the Douglas EA-3B Skywarrior (called the "Whale" because of its size); the VF-11 and VF-31 squadrons of Oceana, Virginia, near Norfolk—the Red Rippers and Tomcatters (also called the Bandwagons), who flew the Grumman F-14A Tomcat fighter. The Rooks had said their goodbyes back in Whidbey the day before to give them enough flying time to reach Norfolk and then fly on out to the ship. The squadrons from Florida timed their departures to enable them to fly directly onto the *Kennedy*. VQ-2, based in Rota, Spain, would wait until the ship got into the Mediterranean before flying aboard. The A-6E and F-14A squadrons from the Norfolk area were so close to the rendezvous point offshore that they could wait until afternoon before flying out. Many of the men from the Norfolk area squadrons brought their families with them to the ready room to hear the last minute briefings on the rendezvous procedures. Others said goodbye at home.

Dana O'Neil, a young bride who had been married to Lieutenant Cole "Bam Bam" O'Neil of VF-31 for only seven months, insisted on sticking with her husband until the last possible second. Friends told me later that she seemed to sense that she would lose Cole forever if she let him go to his plane. She cried uncontrollably in the ready room and sought privacy in the gear room across the hall. Bam Bam had remained in the ready room to hear the pretakeoff briefing by Skipper John

"Market" Burch of VF-31. Burch warned his men to push the emotion of the departure out of their minds and concentrate totally on flying the airplane. Otherwise someone was going to get killed. Burch finished his briefing, sought out Dana, tried to comfort her, and then left the upper floor of the hangar for his F-14 fighter on the tarmac below. Bam Bam followed. Dana still could not let him go. She followed Bam Bam right down the stairs and out onto the hangar floor, sobbing all the way.

"This can't be," Burch told her softly. "You can't come out here with us. You've got to let him go to his airplane. Don't worry, I'll bring him back to you safe."

Six weeks hence Burch would regret uttering those words he had believed so fervently on the day of departure. He would find himself in the bow of the *Kennedy* presiding over the memorial service for Bam Bam, dead at age twenty-six. "Life did not have time to corrupt Bam Bam O'Neil," Burch would say as everyone fought back tears.

Lieutenants Larry McCracken and Doug Miller were among the aviators already in the air and headed toward the ship when Bam Bam broke away from Dana at Oceana. McCracken and Millar of VS-22 were in a flight of four S-3A Vikings out of Cecil Field. Their flight leader checked in by radio with the ground control stations as the planes flew from Florida north toward the *Kennedy* in a gaggle. Millar got on the radio and called the carrier himself when he got within 50 miles of the rendezvous point.

"Strike," Millar radioed the controllers who sat in front of green radar scopes in a semi-dark room inside the *Kennedy*. "Vidar seven zero three. Checking in on Mom's 270. Fifty. State seven point nine."

Millar had compressed vital information for the controllers into the radio jargon of carrier aviation. The first word of such a radio message was always who it was to; the second and third was who it was from. "Strike" was the radio controllers monitoring the long distance air traffic. "Vidar" was the call sign of the VS-22 antisubmarine warfare squadron. 703 was the tail number on the S-3A talking with Strike and appearing as a green dot on the radar scopes. "Checking in on Mom's 270" meant that the VS-22 Vidars squadron had plane number 703 heading east toward the *Kennedy*, on the 270 degree radial emanating from the carrier, called Mom. The single utterance "fifty" meant Vidar 703 was 50 miles away from the ship.

"State seven point nine" told the controllers that the state of the plane's fuel supply was 7,500 pounds. This was enough JP 5, the fuel Navy jets burn—it has the look and consistency of the fuel oil that goes into home oil burners but is called "gas" by Navy men—for McCracken and Millar to reach the ship and make several passes, if necessary, to hook into one of the four steel arresting wires spread across the angled deck.

How much fuel Navy carrier planes have while flying over the open ocean—which cannot be used like a farm field for emergency landings—is always crucial information. If the pilot is low on gas, the carrier flight deck can be cleared for him so he can land ahead of any other planes in the area. If he cannot do that, the carrier can launch one of its flying tankers to refuel him in midair. If the carrier is near a coastal airport, Navy men aboard ship will calculate whether the plane could reach the field by climbing to the altitude that would stretch the fuel the farthest. If the plane has too much gas, it could be too heavy for the wire cables that catch its tailhook when it slams down on the deck at 150 miles an hour. In that case, the pilot would be directed to dump thousands of pounds of fuel in the ocean —something that is done almost every time the Navy conducts flight operations at sea. Gas is the live or die fluid when aviators are in the middle of the ocean with no place but their carriers to land.

McCracken set up his aircraft for a touch and go landing. His plan was to keep the tailhook up inside the fuselage of the S-3A so it would not catch one of the four arresting wires spread across the flight deck. He would let his wheels touch and roll on the deck, hopefully right in the center of the narrow runway, and then roar off into the sky and come around for a trap. It sounded simple. It did not turn out that way.

While the aviators were setting up for their grand entrances, I walked into the office of Lieutenant Commander Fred J. Major, the head of the ship's administration department. He warmly welcomed me aboard, told me how to respond to man overboard drills and went through the other procedures I should follow to fit in as a seagoing member of the *Kennedy*. I would find him as supportive and helpful and friendly the last day of the deployment as I did on this first one. He was hectically busy this first day, as he was to be on so many days, trying to figure out who was aboard and who was missing from the ship's roster of almost five thousand men. He was personnel director for the captain and executive officer in this role. I left Fred. I wanted to climb to the air control tower on top of the *Kennedy*'s island to watch the planes land. I felt as if I had climbed enough stairs to reach the top of the Washington Monument when I reached the tower, the eagle's nest of tinted green glass run by the Air Boss of the ship, Captain Mike Boston. He was sitting in a chair labeled Air Boss and barking one command after another into the microphone which carried his voice to every corner of the flight deck far below. Sailors in white sweatshirts stood behind the Boss to help him keep track of every move in the delicate ballet his crew must dance with split-second precision on the flight deck to keep themselves and the fliers alive. An aircraft carrier's flight deck is a million accidents waiting to happen. A plane crashing and touching off a fireball is just one of the dangers. A sailor can be standing on the wrong patch of the deck and be blown overboard by the blast from a jet engine yards away. Or he can make the mistake of getting close to a jet engine's intake and be sucked into it. Or he can be doing everything right and get his legs cut off as one of the arresting wires breaks and snaps down the deck like a whip. Or he can zig instead of zag and get run over by a plane taxiing to its parking space, or be struck down by a tractor zipping across the flight deck on one of its thousand-a-day errands. Or he can be standing under something heavy, like a 1,000-pound bomb, or even a wrench, when it falls from its resting place. And he can be in the way when something breaks, like the launch bar which hurls a plane off the deck. Boston had to worry about all these hazards while landing and launching aircraft in rapid sequence. He was busy getting ready to take on the first wave of planes when I entered his domain. He welcomed me effusively, and then, understandably, turned quickly back to his work.

One plane after another fell out of the sky, found the invisible landing groove astern of the carrier and slammed down on the steel deck with screeches and bangs so loud that on the highway they could come only from head-on collisions. The tailhooks sent up a shower of sparks as they banged along the deck feeling for an arresting wire. Once a plane was in a wire and stopped, it would be pulled backward slowly so the wire would drop out of the hook. This is called spitting out the wire. Once out of the wire, the pilot would follow the hand signals of a Yellow Shirt, a sailor wearing a yellow shirt, to the parking place picked out with great care by another intense group of people playing musical chairs with airplanes from a room in the island on the same level as the flight deck.

We watched with no special concern as McCracken came out of the sky and toward the deck in his wide-winged S-3A Viking. We heard the landing signal officer standing on a platform below the edge of the flight deck tell McCracken, "Right for lineup." The pilot was drifting to the left toward the parked planes the edge of the flight deck. McCracken's wheels touched the deck briefly before he roared off the bow for another pass. He turned left at the break, flew downwind along the prescribed landing pattern, got in the approach groove once again and set the plane down, snagging the Number Four Wire. He had come in a little high, causing his tailhook to pass above the favored Number Three Wire. The LSO (landing signal officer) gave him the landing grade of fair, or average, about a C. McCracken taxied to the side of the flight deck and changed seats with Millar. Millar, like McCracken before him, intended to do one touch and go and then make his trap. Then the plane would be parked for the rest of the day. Millar did his touch and go without any problem, went around to do his trap. He got in the landing groove, then saw the ball ride up above the cross-hairs of the lights in the Fresnel lens, meaning he was high. Millar brought the 35,000 pound plane down on the deck anyhow and caught the Number Four Wire by keeping the Viking in the proper nose up attitude. He rolled backward to spit out the wire and followed the directions of the Yellow Shirt to his parking space. A Navy jet is graceful and controllable in the air, but is like a cow on a wet kitchen floor when it gets down on the undulating flight deck. A wrong move can send the plane rolling across the deck and into the water, drowning the crew inside. Millar pushed the throttles in slightly to increase the speed of his roll toward the parking space. He pushed his feet against the upper part of the rudder pedals to apply the brakes for a turn on the deck. Nothing happened. The brakes were not engaging. This could be dangerous. Without brakes, he could go over the side or, when the ship pitched or rolled, he could crash into a parked plane, touching off a fireball. The Viking had a backup braking system for the very emergency Millar was experiencing. He flipped the toggle switch to engage the backup brakes. Still nothing happened. Neither set of brakes engaged. The Viking was loose on deck. Millar and McCracken in the front and Lieutenant (junior grade) Mark Lethbridge and Petty Officer

First Class Steven Whyte in the back would have to eject if the plane rolled toward the end of the flight deck.

Ejecting on the busy flight deck is risky. If the rockets designed to cut loose the S-3A's canopy worked, and the ones under the crew members' seats pushed the men high enough in the air for their chutes to open, there were still plenty of perils. The men might land in the water next to the carrier and be sucked into its propellers. Or they could eject so late as the plane went over the side that their ejection rockets would slam them into the steel side of the carrier, killing them on impact. Even if they were lucky, ejected into the sky and floated right back down on the deck, they could be run over by another airplane coming in for a landing or be sucked into the engine intakes of aircraft preparing to take off. Ejection was not very appealing to Millar and McCracken as they struggled to bring their loose plane under control.

Millar turned the Viking's navigation lights on. McCracken pulled the lever to drop the tailhook back down on the deck. This signaled the Air Boss in the tower and everyone on the flight deck that they had a runaway plane to stop. Millar put the Viking in a tight left turn in the hope it would stay in a controllable circle. His engines were at idle but still pushed the plane around at a fast clip. He was grateful for the fresh coat of nonskid that might keep the tires on the deck as the plane kept going round and round. If he shut down an engine, the plane would move slower. But he needed the engines to energize the hydraulic systems and to generate the electricity for the radios keeping him in contact with those outside trying to save the plane.

If the S-3A did skid out of its tight circle, Millar figured he could stop it by aiming for the jet blast deflector nearby—a steel wall which rose out of the flight deck to catch the flaming exhaust of planes as they were launched. But the fuel-laden Viking might go up in flames when it collided with the deflector.

Senior Chief William D. Griffin, forty-one, of Hernando, Florida, knew as he watched the Viking go round and round like a whirling dervish that he and the rest of his flight deck crew had to do something fast. He watched with awe as his kids forgot their own safety and did everything they could think of to capture the loose plane. Airman Apprentice Chad James, nineteen, of Middlebury, Vermont, ducked under the left wing of the Viking and threw a chock around its left main wheel. The 18-ton Viking ran over and out of it. Aviation Boatswain's Mate, First Class William R. Smith, twenty-nine, of Chesapeake, Virginia, picked up the rejected chock and slid it around the left wheel again. Aviation Boatswain's Mate Second Class Randy Reynolds, twenty-five, of Columbus, Indiana, was throwing a chock around the right wheel at the same time. The crew inside the whirling Viking felt the bump-bump each time the plane jumped over a chock. Smith and Reynolds decided at the same instant that the only way the chock would stay around the wheel would be if they held it there with their feet. They took the risk, each planting his foot against the beam of the chock to keep the plane from kicking them out. The chocks stayed in place. The Viking rocked against them and stopped. A Blue Shirt rushed his tractor with the long yellow tongue of a tow bar into position at the nose of the plane. He hooked the Viking onto the bar. The wild plane was captured at last. The crisis was over. The Blue Shirt towed the Viking plane to its parking space. Green Shirts chained it to the white stars of steel bars recessed into the flight deck. These anchoring points were called pad eyes. They looked like so many divots chopped out of the fairway of black steel.

McCracken, Millar, Lethbridge, and Whyte climbed out of the plane. They were relieved and grateful. They had dodged another of the bullets carrier aviation is always firing at its practitioners. They walked across the flight deck to the ladder that would take them down to the 03 level where they stowed their flight gear.

From the tower, I could see an officer rush up to Millar and engage him in what looked like a highly animated conversation. I learned later from Millar what happened.

"Admiral Metcalf wants to see you up on the flag bridge right now!" the officer told the pilot, who was still sweating from the tension of his struggle with the Viking.

Millar did not know what he was in for as he climbed the steep ladders toward the flag bridge where admirals stood in solitary splendor. He did not know whether he would be chewed out or commended. You never knew which way it would go around airplanes. There are so many different courses of action to take in an emergency. Vice Admiral Joseph Metcalf III, commander of the Second Fleet, which included the *Kennedy* while she was sailing in the Atlantic, swung around in the big upholstered chair on the left side of the admiral's bridge and fixed his eyes on Millar.

"That was good work," Metcalf said in extending a congratulatory hand. "I've never seen anything like that done before. What were you going to do if the chocks didn't stop the aircraft?"

"I was going to break off the circling and try to engage the arresting gear backwards," Millar replied. This would have required driving the Viking from the bow toward the stern in hope the tailhook would catch one of the four arresting wires stretched across the deck before going over the cliff.

"I wonder if it would have worked," Metcalf replied.

For their efforts in stopping the runaway Viking, the Navy would award McCracken and Millar Medals of Commendation; Griffin, Smith and Reynolds achievement medals; Airman Apprentice Chad James, Lieutenant Commander Steven G. Lewis, Aviation Boatswain's Mate Third Class Robert E. Dry, and Airman Recruit Lawrence H. Shapiro letters of commendation.

The other planes flying onto the *Kennedy* landed and parked without incident. The cruise was off to a good start, but there were 218 days to go. And the luck would not always run this good.

3   Shipmates

I KNEW from my previous times at sea—including crossing the Atlantic from Barcelona to Norfolk in a destroyer and sailing submerged for a week in the nuclear attack submarine Finback (of Cat Futch fame, the topless dancer who danced on the sub's deck)—that it is very easy to feel alone in the crowd on a Navy warship. The letdown and feeling of aloneness is particularly acute right after departure. Sometimes you feel the warmth of the last embrace or wake up in the middle of the night smelling the hair of your little girl or boy.

For once you climb up the brow and enter a Navy ship, you leave behind the entire support structure which helped sustain you ashore: family, friends, sex, sports, hobbies, music, dogs, current movies, live television, radio broadcasts, restaurants, bars, stores, telephones, newspapers, magazines, private bath and bed, long showers, cars, quiet, beauty, the fragrance of flowers or mown grass or burning leaves, vistas, variety, drinks at home at day's end, mobility, freedom. Especially freedom. You do not appreciate the freedom to go where and when you please until you become confined for an extended period in that special prison that a ship can be.

Besides this downside of a long deployment at sea, there is the upside: the sense of adventure that comes from not knowing what will happen during the long voyage ahead, who you will meet, what dangers you will encounter, how you will cope in the crucible, and what exotic places you will see. I was decidedly upbeat in the first days aboard. Besides the newness and drama all around me, I had hopes of flying off and on this tiny landing field in the jets I saw tied down on the flight deck and inside the cavernous hangar bay.

As I explored my new town, I peeked through open doorways into the cabins in officer country and noticed men hauling all kinds of earthly goods in the passageways as some of the officers made last minute changes in their rooms. I soon concluded that men who have been to sea before for extended periods are like soldiers who have been to war before in the mud. They bring along as many creature comforts as they can carry to soften the life out on the point. The combat trooper can bring only as much as he can carry himself, such as extra wool socks and candy bars. His seagoing counterpart has a ship to carry on *her* back whatever he can fit into his living and working quarters. Sailors had only a foot locker and a flat drawer under their mattress for storage, enough for clothes and writing paper but little else. Officers lived in rooms. Admirals, captains, and a few commanders had rooms all to themselves. Junior officers live in Boys Town—rooms crammed with up to eight people. But no matter what size the room, I saw extraordinary attempts to recreate the comforts of home inside it.

I spotted stereos, videocassette recorders and movie tapes, televisions, refrigerators, exercise bicycles, weight lifting sets, word processors, guitars, canned food, and books. I was told other rooms held fold-up Christmas trees with lights and ornaments to soften the big day we would spend on the ocean thousands of miles from home.

My tour brought home to me that I was at sea with a new breed of warrior—the post-Vietnam, consumer oriented, better paid volunteers of the 1980s. A Navy lieutenant flying planes off a carrier at the time of the Tet offensive in 1968 was paid $982 a month, including hostile fire and flight pay. His successor pilot of lieutenant rank on the *Kennedy* received $2,596 a month. The All Volunteer Force formed after the draft ended in 1973 was alive and well in 1983.

I looked around to see if there were the equivalents of miniplaygrounds in our walled city. I had always heard aircraft carriers were three times as long as a football field, but at sea the vast flight deck becomes a crowded parking lot for airplanes, trucks, and tractors, and the hangar bay below is transformed into a giant repair garage. Sailors told me that they could jog on the flight deck only when airplanes were not taking off or landing. For want of any other space, they jogged around the parked airplanes and tie-down chains in the hangar bay. The war machine's arms and accouterments took up so much room in our town that the most popular playground turned out to be the steel cubicle off the hangar bay filled with weightlifting equipment. It was used around the clock by sailors and officers. There was a crew's lounge for cards and movies, a small library, and video machines to one side of the long tables and benches where the sailors ate cafeteria style in two rectangular rooms. Many of the video games on this mightiest war machine of all were for playing war with flashes of green light.

After my tour, I returned to my two-man room wondering if the sea bag full of books I had brought along would be enough. My roommate, Lieutenant Rick Titi, was not in, as often would be the case in the brief time we were to live together. He was the administrative officer for the medical department and worked there at least 12 hours a day. I figured I would make him feel uncomfortable, certainly at first. Here was a reporter that somebody high up in the Navy had dropped on him. Right in his own room, for God's sake. Who the hell knew what this reporter would write down and put in the book?

Our room was just above the waterline. Its long distance from the flight deck muffled the sounds of the controlled crashes of carrier landings five stories above us. But even a room this deep inside the carrier was assaulted by the special noises of a live warship: the throbs and squeaks of pumps, the whir of fans, the clanging of machinery, the piercing whistles prefacing announcements over loudspeakers, the banging of doors, and the high-pitched screams of jet engines. Flight surgeons on board warned me that I was going to lose some of my hearing in the coming seven months, even if I remembered to wear my ear plugs in the noisiest places: the engine rooms, catapult work spaces, and flight deck.

I sensed that no amount of jogging, weight lifting, reading, or playing video games would be enough to make life for me and five thousand shipmates bearable. Lieutenant Commander Sammy Bonanno, the head landing signal officer for Air Wing Three on the *Kennedy*, confirmed this for me in our first meeting on the carrier. "You can't survive out here without friends," he warned with a concern which made me feel he would become a friend during our long voyage.

As far as making friends, I came aboard USS *John F. Kennedy* with special liabilities and special assets. I was from the hated Press. The liberal Eastern Establishment Press at that. And, for all my shipmates knew, I might be a spy for the Secretary of the Navy, the Chief of Naval Operations, or the Naval Investigative Service. Then again, if I really were writing a book about the *Kennedy*, which people back home would read, it sure as hell would be nice to be in it. Also, I was a curiosity—a real live reporter who could not escape. There would be plenty of time to bitch about The Press to this guy. I guessed my advanced age would be a wash. It would take a while for the young officers to accept me as an equal—I would have to earn their acceptance—but I figured the young sailors would welcome someone they could talk to and who reminded them of their fathers, uncles, or brothers.

I decided to ease into relationships and to do what my shipmates did as far as when I got up, ate, worked, and slept. Wearing work khakis with no insignia, I blended in with the officers and chiefs. I had the protocol rank of commander. The sailors stiffened when they saw my khaki but relaxed when they noticed I wore none of the hardware signifying that I had the authority to tell them to do something.

My first mornings dramatized that the Navy of 1983 was more gentlemanly—at least in dress—than the one I had known from the inside in the 1940s. I saw the officers flip-flopping their way to the communal heads on shower clogs, which was not new to me, and dressed in fancy bathrobes, which was very new. The uniform for this morning parade was no longer skivvie shorts and T shirts. Luckily I had brought along a bathrobe which, had I worn it during my previous incarnation, would have brought hoots of "fairy."

Reveille was another surprise. No more police whistles blown in the passageways or bugle calls broadcast over the loud-speaker. Personal alarm clocks and, for high ranking officers, telephone calls over the ship's internal system did most of the waking in officer country. I quickly saw why. Some men worked days, others nights, and some both, depending on their specialties and the demands of the constantly moving carrier. Officers slept in rooms holding from one to eight persons, each of whom might be working on a different shift. The same was true for enlisted sleeping compartments.

The standard day shift for sailors was from 7:00 in the morning until 7:00 at night, seven days a week. They often worked longer than twelve hours a day. Ship's company officers seemed to work from 7:00 A.M. to 9:00 P.M., often with a nap in the afternoon. They worked seven days a week, too, while the ship was under way. There was almost no pattern to the working habits of the officers and men in the air wing. Flight operations and the mechanical temperament of their airplanes dictated when the men in the squadrons worked and when they slept. A cranky airplane could keep men up all night getting it fixed and ready to fly the next morning. Squadrons felt under great pressure to have their airplanes "up," ready to be launched off the boat.

Officers ate cafeteria style in two different wardrooms, except for the evening meal, which was hosted by the executive officer, and on special occasions when white-coated sailors served as waiters. Except for breakfast, the officers had to wear the uniform of the day in the wardroom below the hangar bay. The second eating area, called the dirty shirt wardroom, located just below the flight deck, was where aviators could wear flight suits and others work clothes. I ate in both places. I bought meal tickets like my officer shipmates. Sailors ate free. I found the food for officers, chiefs, and sailors surprisingly varied and tasty. The offerings compared with those dished up by a generous college cafeteria.

At breakfast and lunch, I handed over my meal ticket to the cashier to be punched and then hunted for an empty seat at one of the long tables in one of the wardrooms. I noticed from the first that aviators would almost always sit in a phalanx with members of their own squadron. Their distinctive shoulder and chest patches identified each group. The aviators did not seem to mind my breaking into their ranks, which I often did at both breakfast and lunch. Sometimes I would sit with ship's company officers or with the tech reps. The tech reps were the technical representatives whom the Navy brought along to help maintain and fix the fancy gadgetry for 20th century warfare, everything from jet engines to radars to black boxes. The tech reps were shunned by many of the officers, partly because of the mistaken notion that these civilians were making piles of money to do what Navy technicians could do for themselves. I often sat beside a tech rep or one of the civilian college teachers on board, as well as the regular Navy officers. I figured everyone on board could teach me something.

The first mealtime conversations with the young officers were cordial but guarded. Many of the older officers I sat with would bitch about the way the press had covered the Vietnam War, whether they had been there or not. One antipress commander took great relish in telling me this anecdote about Nam as I lunched with him and half a dozen other officers.

"I was flying a TV camera crew in my chopper down to a town in Delta. The reporter told me:

" 'Now you sure be back to pick us up here at 2 o'clock.'

" 'Yes sir, 2 o'clock.'

"Well, I don't know how the hell they ever got back."

This provoked appreciative laughter all around the table. I could understand it. Television crews were often obnoxious as hell in Vietnam and other places. So were print reporters sometimes. But I have never felt apologetic about the way most of the press reported on Vietnam. The reporters I traveled with around the boonies in 1968 and 1972 passed on to the public what they saw and what they heard from those fighting the war. Army battalion commanders who were losing kids day after day at a time Cambodia and Laos were havens for the enemy provided me with eloquent testimony about the no-win nature of the war. I passed their testimony on to the public through my newspaper. I felt World War I would have been far less bloody if reporters had made the generals explain trench warfare tactics and held them accountable for the losses. But I made little headway in defending the press to my shipmates. Our arguments spiced the wardroom conversation on occasion, however.

Between meals, my routine on the *Kennedy* was like that of a reporter covering city hall. I would check in with the people who knew what was going on because they were at a vortex of information. The vortexes were as far apart as the air control tower at the top of the carrier island to engineering headquarters deep in the guts of the ship. One of my daily stops in between was Trouble Central, the offices of the three chaplains crammed between the ship's library and crew's lounge underneath the aft mess decks. The chaplains' biggest challenge was to help the hardworking serfs in our walled kingdom get through the long days and nights; to help them adjust to a life no American high school or suburban home could prepare a teenager to live. Many of the teenagers had not yet jelled. They had little inner strength for want of solid pillars. Relatively few were deeply religious. But religious or not, many sailors and a few officers sought out the chaplains.

"All I can do is try to stop the bleeding," Captain James E. Doffin, head chaplain, told me. He was a cherubic looking, down-country speaking Baptist from Charleston, South Carolina, who also happened to have earned a graduate degree at Princeton University. I was to hear and remember much of his sage advice, like this homily he gave to a sailor who kept having discipline problems with his superiors: "When you're in a hole, it's time to stop digging."

In one of my first stops to Trouble Central, Lieutenant George Byrum, a chaplain of the Plymouth Brethren faith, told me why he thought so many sailors had trouble adjusting to life on a Navy carrier, especially their first cruise:

"The kids we see are spiritually illiterate. One-upmanship is big out here. There is pressure on the new kid which says that we are going to see that you are properly initiated into manhood. For the kid who doesn't have a full sea bag, the big problem is that he can't get away. The bigness of the carrier intensifies the aloneness problem. You're constantly passing people on a carrier whom you never knew."

Lieutenant Commander Michael A. Walsh, the Catholic chaplain on board, was as dour as Doffin was bouncy. He told me he had heard a call from God to minister to men out on the sea in ships.

The opposite of Trouble Central was the air wing. The fliers and others attached to it specialized in irreverency, light heartedness, and constant needling of each other and anyone else who came into range.

"Here comes that damn Democrat!" Sammy Bonanno would say by way of greeting when I entered the CAG (commander of the air group) office where he worked as administrative officer in between helping planes land on the deck as LSO (landing signal officer) or flying F-14s himself. "Are you really stupid enough to stay out here with us for seven months?" was another standard Bonanno question.

I considered myself an independent politically. But Sammy in one of our first conversations had heard me criticize President Reagan for sending marines into the Beirut International Airport with no clearcut military mission. I saw it as a no-win, a mini-Vietnam. A word against the president was enough to label me "a damn Democrat" in the Reagan stronghold I found inside the *Kennedy*.

Guessing my age was a *Trivial Pursuit* pastime in the air wing from early on. I figured the records with my birth date were on my survival training records in the CAG office. But I would only say "more than fifty but less than sixty" to keep the game going.

I found the squadrons always doing something that interested me, like briefing for the upcoming mission or conducting "what if" quizzes in the ready room about emergencies in the air. Their ready rooms were congenial. There often was an intense acey deucey game going on in back. On the table up front in this seagoing substitute for a living room a tin of cookies or cake from someone's wife often was up for grabs. The unwritten rule was to bring the goodies out of your room and share them with the squadron. The aviators went out of their way to make me feel welcome and were intensely interested in seeing a book about themselves in print. "Maybe you can tell my wife what I do out here," was a typical comment.

Again, like a reporter covering city hall, besides visiting the centers of information, I talked endlessly to the Little People as I pounded my new beat. The green sailors, those who had not been in the Navy long enough to become a petty officer in charge of anybody or anything, were among the most appealing of these Little People to me. Their friendliness, innocence, dedication, fear, warmth, homesickness, determination, and modesty made me think of them as men-children. They seemed flattered when I stopped to talk with them. Here was somebody in officer khakis who just listened and did not order them to do anything. Sailors' faces visibly brightened whenever I wrote their names down on my yellow pocket pad. It got so I could hardly ever walk all the way across the hangar bay without a young sailor hailing me and pausing to chat.

"You're the guy writing the book about us, aren't you?" would be a typical opener.

"Will my name be in it?"

"Maybe. What is it? And where are you from?"

This would launch the sailor and me on a conversation. It might just be about the chances of the Washington Redskins winning the Super Bowl. I am a low key interviewer who leaves long spaces between my questions to encourage my subject to fill them in. I could tell in many of my interviews with the Little

People, and some of the Big People as well, that my interest in them personally increased their sense of self-worth in our often impersonal universe 1,051 feet long and 270 feet wide.

At some point in my daily rounds, I took the equivalent of what was for me a walk in the woods. I would go down to the hangar bay, stand at one of its huge open doors and study the sea and sky. The hangar bay was the lowest of the readily accessible viewing spots on the *Kennedy*. The flight deck and bridge were too high to make you feel close to the ocean. I could see the greens, browns, and blues of the sea from that spot. I could also look out to where the sea ran into the sky and wonder how Joan and all the other people living normal lives beyond the horizon were doing. I love the sea and the creatures in it from years of fishing and boating on the ocean. I scanned the water racing by and looked for porpoises or whales or even seaweed but seldom saw anything at all. Perhaps the noise of our huge ship scared the sea life away. Studying the sea, even without seeing any life in it, broke the grip the gray ship got on my psyche. I would often see a sailor staring out the hangar bay doors, too. Sometimes we would talk. Other times I sensed he sought solitude and left him alone.

Besides talking to sailors, I often went with them when they did their work. I sat in the duck-blind-type pit dug into the flight deck, for example, while planes were launched on either side of it. This gave me a sense of how the sailors felt who worked in the pit every day during launch. I doubt that I could ever feel safe or comfortable doing this job on the potentially murderous flight deck. The hot blast of engine exhausts washes over you and the grit pings against your goggles. You feel the closeness of danger. This makes you careful. Flight deck veterans told me the two most dangerous jobs on the flight deck, if not in the whole world, were those of hookup man and hook runner.

The hookup man is the last person to crawl under an airplane before it is launched. His job is to make sure the launch bar attached to the plane's nose gear is hooked firmly into the shuttle, the hook-shaped steel slide which yanks a plane down the deck when the catapult fires. Otherwise, the bar could slip out of the shuttle after the plane was going too fast to stop and too slow to become airborne. If anything breaks while the hookup man is under the plane, which is straining with engines at full power against the hold-back bolt, he could be run over and killed. If the hookup man moves the wrong way, he could be sucked into the engine intake and be sliced up by its whirling compressor blades. If he pops out of his duck walk at the wrong instant, he could be decapitated by the wings as the catapult snapped the plane down the deck.

The hook runner runs toward the airplane as soon as its tailhook snags an arresting wire upon landing. He signals the deck edge operator whether the connection is right for pulling the plane backward so that the wire will fall out of the tail hook. If the arresting wire breaks from the strain of 28 tons of plane slamming into it, the wire would most likely whip down the flight deck and sever the legs of the first person in its path—the hook runner. Arresting wires have indeed broken on carriers and cut off sailors' legs. Some of the men on the *Kennedy* had seen this happen.

I got to know a hookup man and a hook runner on the *Kennedy* well by putting on the required helmet and goggles and going out on the flight deck with them to watch their work at close range. I also talked to them between launches and traps in their work spaces. With the noise, nobody can hold a conversation on the flight deck during flight operations.

Boatswain's Mate Third Class Robert "Marty" Martell, twenty-five, of Burlington, Massachusetts, was a hookup man on the *Kennedy*. He represented one slice of Young America —the men and women who feel compelled to rebel against main stream society while they are growing up, whether they have a cause or not. They defy convention and become ostracized by the mainstream, pushing them closer than ever to fellow rebels. Marty and I talked about his life, about the Navy, about his future, about almost everything. Often we would stand in the catapult room below the flight deck where Marty and other Green Shirts hung out between launches. On days the planes were not flying, we would chat in the sun on the suddenly safe and quiet flight deck. Once in a while I would go to his "room"—one bed, one drawer, and one locker amid three tier bunks—to look at his letters and photographs.

"I couldn't find much in the way of jobs after graduating from high school in 1978," Marty told me in one of our many taped interviews. "I kept getting laid off and being broke. The winter of 1978 was a bad one for me. I lived in my car, a 1967 Plymouth Fury, in the Burlington Mall for about a month. I used to put on my parka and crawl under a blanket. But it was still cold as hell. I'd go to a friend's house in the morning to take a shower. Sometimes I'd go to my girl's house. But her dad didn't like me. He'd tell me to stay away. I couldn't go there too often. That was Sue. We kept going together and breaking up. I had her tattooed on my arm when we were hot and heavy. Then we broke up and I had to have another tattoo put over her.

"Things were so bad for me that my sister's husband said, 'Hey, why don't you join the Navy?' I said, 'Fuck off.'

"I was coming out of a bar in 1978 when this guy came barreling down the street in his car and hit me as I stepped off the sidewalk. He tried to drive away, but he was so drunk he smashed into two parked cars and stopped. I was messed up pretty bad. I had a big gash in my head and had to stay in bed for three months. I was back home then. The guy's insurance company offered to settle up for $14,000. I should have held out for more. I needed the money. I settled. Lying there in bed month after month made me do a lot of thinking. I realized I had to do something with my life, or I'd be dead from drinking or drugs by the time I was twenty-five.

"I joined the Navy in September 1980, when I was twenty-two. I told myself, no matter what, I'm going to make it. Splug and the boys laughed and set up a pool, each of them writing down the day and time I'd be out of the Navy and back home in Burlington.

"I got shit-faced on my ass on the way out to boot camp at Great Lakes. I was out of it when I arrived there. The next morning I heard this banging on garbage pails and guys shouting, 'Get up, you assholes.' Holy shit. For the first time it hit me. I said to myself, 'What have I done? I'm in the fucking Navy.'

"The Navy grew me up. I was twenty-two going on sixteen when I came in. They got my head out of my ass; knocked the chip off my shoulder. I've been in trouble once since I've been in. I took a little unscheduled five-day vacation. That was the summer of 1982. They took me up before the captain. That was really something. My legs were shaking as I stood there and felt him yelling at me. He gave me twenty days' restriction, twenty days' extra duty, and fined me $250 a month for two months. I'm not doing that again. Ain't worth it.

"Splug, Mumbles, and Froggie are still back in Burlington doing the same thing, hitting the same bars. They're pissed off about me staying in. I'd like to get out in a way. I like the work out on the flight deck, working with machinery, getting my hands dirty. It never stops getting exciting out here on the flight deck for me. It's hard to explain to somebody who hasn't been out here and done it. Every time I see one of those things go off the end of the boat, I know I done something. I've accomplished something for the first time in my life. I feel good about that.

"Can't see me in no office with coat and tie. But it is lonely, awfully lonely out here. I ain't married. I ain't in love. Privacy is hard to come by. I'd like to go ashore and buy me a Harley Davidson Sportster 1,000cc.

"I'm sending $300 a month home for my mom to keep for me. My dad, who never used to speak to me, writes me now. He told me people never knew he had a son until I got in the Navy. Now all he does is talk about me. I've suddenly appeared. I'm surprised he still talks to me after some of the shit I pulled. But he still loves me. I know that. I still ain't no angel. Deep down I know that staying in is the best thing for me."

One night I stopped to talk to Chief Bob Neely, Marty's immediate supervisor, who sat at a desk in a cubicle in front of the catapult room. Neely is a soft-spoken, reflective man who had known hard times himself on the outside before advancing within the Navy.

"You know," Neely told me, "kids like Marty—they don't even know what they missed. They don't expect nothing. They give their life for you. If I had a half dozen Martys, I'd stay in the Navy forever." I agreed. Marty was the kind of man I would want to share a foxhole with in a war.

The hook runner I got to know was Michael J. Goulette, nineteen, of Port Jervis, New York. He represented the type of young volunteer the admirals bragged about in talking about recruiting for the post-Vietnam, all volunteer force. No arrests; no drugs; no tattoos; no rebellion. Goulette was a main stream American teenager, not a temporary social outcast like Marty. He had other options when he joined the Navy "to see the world while saving money for college." That venerable Navy recruiting slogan still had draw in the 1980s, especially in America's small towns.

"I wanted to try to do something; see some place besides Port Jervis," Mike told me while we were sitting among the chains and other tie-down gear in his work cubicle off the catwalk which led to the flight deck. If he was going to sea on a carrier, he wanted to be outside, where the action was. He said he volunteered for the dangerous job of hook runner. I asked him what he thought about as he ran toward the controlled crash of a carrier landing.

"The only thing you've got on your mind up there is the wire," he told me. "If that goes, you go. And you have to keep looking out for jet blast. It can knock you over. In the beginning, I was a little scared up there. The impulse is to run away.

"The hours (at least twelve, often sixteen, a day) don't bother me. It's the being out from everywhere. When you're on a ship, it's nothing like being on land. You're enclosed. You can only go so far. That's the hardest part to get used to, knowing that you're going to get up every day and do the same old routine for 220 days.

"Been getting letters from people I never knew that well at home. My mother and father, they're always complimenting me on what we're doing up there. I read them, then ten minutes later I'm answering them. If you could run a telephone out here, it would be great."

Mike said he did not intend to follow his dad into trucking, but hoped to go to college on the money he saved in the Navy. "I don't think I was ready for college right after high school. I went into the military to try to get my act together. I'm glad I did it."

I could tell just by looking around the carrier that it was the young kids who did the heavy lifting, who made the warship run. I asked the Navy in Washington to give me a breakdown of the ship's company. The results confirmed my visual impressions from roaming the ship:

- Seventy-four percent of the enlisted people were age seventeen through twenty-five, meaning the Martells and the Goulettes did three-quarters of the work on the carrier.
- Only fifty-three people out of the 3,159 chiefs, petty officers and sailors in the ship's company—not counting the tenant Air Wing Three—were more than forty years old.
- Seventy-seven percent of the ship's enlisted personnel were white, 16 percent black, and the rest Hispanic, Native American, and Asian.
- Almost one third—1,033 out of the 3,159—of the enlisted people were married, substantiating that the sailors of the

1980s married young.
* Three industrial states with high unemployment sent the most sailors, with New York contributing 304; Pennsylvania, 231; Ohio, 200.

"Your ship is run by kids, your squadron is run by kids, and this Navy is run by kids," Captain Mike Boston, the Air Boss I had met in the tower the first day out of Norfolk, kept telling his fellow officers.

What neither Navy statistics nor impassioned reminders could project, though, was the anguish that many of the sailors went through because they had tried to do too much too soon on the assumption that once they were sworn into the Navy, they were automatically "men" with steady incomes who were ready for adult responsibilities, including marriage and father-hood. I came to know many of these kids and felt their pain.

Some were teenagers who suddenly found themselves alone thousands of miles at sea after marrying women they did not really know, purchasing cars and renting apartments they could not afford, fathering children they were not emotionally or financially prepared to raise and support. The women on shore caught in these situations often felt pained, abandoned, bitter, lost, and depressed. Some sought help from the Navy, which in turn worked closely with the American Red Cross. The Red Cross checked out a situation and then apprised the men of it through staccato cables like these:

... WIFE STATES NON RECEIPT OF CHECK ... STATES NEED FUNDS FOR RENT AND MAINTENANCE. REQUEST SVCMN (serviceman) DEPOSIT FUNDS TO AMCROSS FOR TRANSMITTAL TO WIFE ...

... BELIEVE WIFE HAVING NERVOUS BREAKDOWN. REQUEST THAT YOU TRY TO GET HOME ...

... SVCMN'S WIFE REQUESTING SVCMN'S PRESENCE ASAP (as soon as possible) DUE TO THEIR SON'S PHYSICAL AND EMOTIONAL PROBLEM. DR STATES (name withheld) IS HAVING SEVERE BEHAVIOR PROBLEMS AND MORE SERIOUS PSYCHOLOGICAL PROBLEMS WHICH HAVE ESCALATED SINCE FATHER'S ABSENCE. MOTHER UNABLE TO CONTROL CHILD ALONE ... FATHER'S RETURN WOULD HELP ALLEVIATE THE IMMEDIATE CRISIS. A

PERIOD OF LEAVE WOULD BE INSUFFICIENT AND WOULD PROBA-
BLY ONLY ADD TO THE PROBLEM. IF THINGS CONTINUE TO
ESCALATE AT PRESENT RATE CHILD COULD BE DANGEROUS TO
HIMSELF OR OTHERS. HIS BEHAVIOR IS OUT OF CONTROL AT THIS
TIME . . .

. . . AMCROSS CHAPT PORTSMOUTH VA REQUESTING SVCMN'S
PRESENCE FOR APPROX TWO WEEKS. DR HAS ADMITTED WIFE TO
PSYCHIATRIC HOSP. DIAG MAJOR DEPRESSIVE DISORDER. PROG
FAIRLY GOOD BUT NEEDS SVCMN'S PRESENCE . . .

The chaplains would recommend to the executive officer
whether the serviceman receiving such a cable should be flown
off the carrier. The XO and captain would make the decision.
Sometimes the serviceman was flown home and sometimes his
request for emergency leave was denied. The chaplains on the
Kennedy would do their best to console the anguished in their
uniquely challenging pastorate on the sea.

Any place with five thousand men living together would
experience many of the same problems portrayed by the Red
Cross cables. But there were far more relief valves on land. The
anguished would not be surrounded by a moat thousands of
miles wide.

"I can only apply the Band-Aids," Chaplain Doffin lamented
when I asked how he consoled the officers and sailors who
received cables about trouble at home. "I can't give a man no
damn pass to leave this base and go into town to see his wife or
kid. I can't go to see his wife. I can just talk to the man, pray for
him, loan him money, write letters in hopes of helping the
situation."

One day Chaplain Doffin was talking to a troubled sailor I
shall call Ben about problems at home. Ben had been deserted
by his mother and was raised in a Texas orphanage. He married
the first girl he ever dated, only to discover she was neglecting
his baby daughter and sleeping with other men. His first plan
was to kill his wife. The second was to kill himself. Chaplain
Doffin had so far talked him out of doing either. But Ben,
another hard-working sailor grateful to the Navy, could not
keep his mind off his situation at home. He wanted to talk it out
with somebody outside the chain of command. That somebody
turned out to be me.

Ben's dark eyes were afire when he entered the chaplain's
office for our one-on-one conversation. A small but muscular

man, Ben crunched my hand in greeting and then launched into a story which he said he wanted told in the book, with his name attached, so people would understand how pressure can build up inside a man, especially when he is isolated at sea. Some day, when he is older, Ben may feel differently about having his troubles attributed to him by name. But his story does give another insight into those who carry the burden of defending the country; it is often those who got the least from society on their way to adulthood. And Ben's story also explained to me why so many senior officers voiced variations of this quote I heard one of them say as I made my rounds on the *Kennedy:*

"Sailors have more troubles than anybody in the world. Their troubles are a real pain in the ass to deal with. But sailors will do anything for you if you show some interest. They're the kind of guys you want to go to war with."

Ben traced his early impoverished childhood, recalling the day his eldest sister, who was married, found him and his brother alone in the apartment. Ben was nine years old and weighed only 49 pounds. His sister could not afford to raise the boys herself, so she took them to the local police station. Ben and his brother wound up in a county orphanage in Texas.

"I knew what was going on. I was scared that I would never see nobody no more. The orphanage turned out to be a real nice place. I was always throwing up before I got there. I knew I was sick for some reason, but I didn't know why. After I got to the home, they kept us in the hospital for two weeks. Gave us shots and stuff. I didn't have shoes when I got there. At the home they gave you shoes and put clothes on you, you know. They had three meals a day. They had kids to play with. They had all the toys you could ever imagine. They had a swimming pool. They took us everywhere.

"We went to public school. The home had their own buses and everything. I didn't make good grades at first because I didn't know how to read. I was in third grade, behind two grades. I started learning how to read with special teachers and everything. When I got about twelve years old, they took me from the fifth grade and put me in the seventh grade.

"I graduated from high school in 1978. I got all the good citizenship awards from the home and a lot from the high school. I was pretty confused, but I always had wanted to join the Navy. All the kids at the orphanage, they didn't know what they was going to do when they left the home. They would say,

'I got no family, what am I going to do?' Most of them would join the armed forces. I have a lot of friends in the service.''

Ben put off joining the Navy. He worked at various jobs around Texas. He earned up to $9.45 an hour as an iron worker. He met a girl in Tyler at church, dated her steadily, and then was told by her father that he had to marry her or stop coming around the house.

"I was dumb, right? I had known her for six months—hadn't dated that many other girls. Her parents wanted her out of the house. She was pregnant. But I didn't know it. We got married.''

Ben traced how the marriage quickly fell apart; how he tried to save it by joining the Navy and moving his wife and baby girl to Norfolk; how his wife failed to care for the baby or clean up the house and ultimately flew to California where she became pregnant by another man. She refused to let Ben see his own baby daughter. He first decided to kill his wife. Then he went home on emergency leave to resolve the situation. Failing to do so, he took a rifle out to the Texas woods with the idea of shooting himself. He said he remembered the chaplain's advice to let his wife go and to build a new life for himself. Ben came back to the *Kennedy* and dug into his work in the fuel spaces situated deep in the hold. His wife's parents took the baby and were rearing it at the time we spoke.

"I'm so glad I'm in the Navy," Ben told me near the end of his long soliloquy. "I make $1,100 a month and send $500 a month home to my sister for my baby. I know she's mine. She looks just like me.''

I heard scores of other arresting stories from sailors and officers as I made my rounds. Some were positive; some were negative. I visited one sailor in the brig who had tried half-heartedly to kill himself by drawing a razor lightly over his wrists. He could not cope with the confinement and harsh one-upmanship of shipboard life. I also had long talks with some of the forty civilian technical representatives who lived on board. Their job was to help sailors and officers master the intricacies of the radars, electronics, and engines their companies had sold to the Navy. I concluded the tech reps would be needed in any war on our complicated warships. Congress should prepare some kind of emergency legislation in peacetime to make it legal to impress these technicians in wartime. A few of the tech reps told me that their superiors, living comfortably on shore, had told them to go to sea or lose their jobs. Many of the tech reps led unhappy lives on board. They were shunned by Navy officers and were too old to socialize with the sailors they instructed. They lived in two ghettos on the ship called The Homestead and The Cavalier.

I found the sixty-five marines on board separatists, too, but by choice. Their main job was to guard the special weapons locked deep inside the *Kennedy* and to respond to any radioactive accidents. The marines held themselves apart from the rest of the ship's company, believing they were among the "few good men" on board.

One group of shipmates sought me out and tried to convert me to their cause. They were the seven sailors who, after joining the Navy voluntarily, were trying to get off the *Kennedy* on the grounds that they conscientiously objected to war. I heard them out, but told them they would have to press for their conscientious objector discharges through Navy channels, not through me and my employer, *The Washington Post.*

I could understand why the Martys, Goulettes, Bens, and other young sailors I met had joined the Navy. They saw it as something different, promising, exciting, or as the only way to get a steady job. I had a harder time understanding why the ship's company officers with college degrees, who did not experience the excitement of flying planes off the boat, would stick with jobs that kept them at sea most of the time.

"Look," Commander Ted Smith, the *Kennedy*'s tireless supply officer told me one day: "Here we are forty-two, acting twenty-two. This is a nice club out here. We don't have all the problems of home. For a department head, the system is almost feudal. He has his own fief. We're spoiled; pampered really." Pointing to a white-jacketed sailor serving us dinner in the wardroom at the moment, Smith added, "There are guys in white coats like him to wait on us; to clean up. These aren't your high society kids out here. They are so malleable they'll do almost anything you tell them."

Commander Mike "Iron Mike" Fahey, engineering officer with enough degrees and training to bring him a high paying job on shore where he would get home every night to eat with his family, slept only four to six hours a night on the carrier. He seemed to be working all the time. His engine rooms gleamed like a prideful farmer's dairy. Why?

"I really like being around the kids," Iron Mike told me as

we wandered through his labyrinth below deck where the machinery hissed, clanged, throbbed, and chattered. "It keeps me young. I approach this thing from a coaching standpoint. It's a big sport. I get awfully tired, but I don't get burned out. I look at my contemporaries working at dull jobs on the beach and ask myself: 'What have you fuckers been doing all these years?'"

Lieutenant Commander Joel Geister, a tall, dark, John Wayne type of officer who ran the rough-and-ready deck force—the "deck apes"—said he loved the fraternity, drama, and responsibility of keeping the carrier alive. Taking a long drag on his cigarette, Geister told me, "Psychologists probably will say everybody who is in the Navy has a little boy syndrome."

The most uplifting change I noticed was the harmony between black and white sailors. I had sailed on Navy ships in the 1970s as a military correspondent, including a cross-Atlantic trip with the Mod Squad of destroyers, and found the races dangerously polarized. Blacks often handed me petitions charging their superiors with racism when I went down into engine rooms or walked through mess decks. Sabotage and muggings broke out in the post-Vietnam, racially polarized Navy. I found no such polarization on the *Kennedy*. "We're too busy to get into the race thing," was a typical response when I asked black sailors about it. I witnessed this marvelously healthy vignette one afternoon on the flight deck:

White sailor to black sailor: "Hey, you're ruining the neighborhood. You're the only black here."

Black sailor to white sailor: "Fuck you. Sell while you can get a good price for it."

Then, best of all, they both laughed.

4 Kennedy Incorporated

"THIS ship, this weapon, this oil tank, this town, this airport, this factory, this everything is unmanageable," I told myself as I marveled at what was going on all around me. The carrier was a million accidents just waiting to happen. I wondered how any one person could run this universe.

I climbed to the bridge many times to talk to Skipper Wheatley in hopes of finding out. He always greeted me warmly and never ducked a question. My first entries into his inner sanctum on the bridge caused some of the officers standing there to stiffen. But Wheatley's warmth eventually thawed everybody. I called him Captain, of course, and he called me George. Even though I wore work khakis, I was never quite in uniform, even on the bridge. I just could not give up wearing Wallabees. The biggest concession I made was to wear black ones.

Wheatley, as skipper of an aircraft carrier, was at once all powerful and powerless. He could fire his officers, send sailors to jail on the ship, work everybody to exhaustion or give slack, or allow a damaged airplane to land on his deck or order it to take its chances and try to reach a land base. He could forbid showers to save water, and issue a thousand other orders to make life better or worse on the ship. In that sense, he was all powerful. But he could not run everything on the ship. He had to trust his subordinates. In that sense, he was powerless. If they did something wrong, even when he was asleep, it would be Wheatley's fault. The captain of the ship was not really all powerful; he was all responsible.

"So how do you manage this unmanageable monster?" I asked Wheatley one day as I stood beside his big upholstered chair on the port side of the bridge. He answered the question as if he were giving one of the management courses he had taken at the Industrial College of the Armed Forces, at George Washington University and at Harvard University on his way up to his present prized command:

"Basically, the thing that has stood me in best stead from all the lessons set forth in management courses I took, was to delegate to subordinates and to trust them—trust them enough to make a mistake. Let them know they can make a mistake, almost to the point of saying, 'If you're not making a mistake, you're not trying.'

"My management challenge becomes one more of motivation and direction than crisis management and involvement in the day-to-day details of what goes on. I don't care how good you are, you can't do it. I've seen some people try that, to run the details themselves, and it's usually counterproductive, regardless of how talented they are."

Through the years, the Navy has developed a management structure for a carrier resembling that of a corporation. Specialized functions are clustered into departments, with a commander or captain in charge of each department. The *Kennedy*'s departments were Administration, Air, Aircraft Intermediate Maintenance, Communications, Dental, Engineering, Medical, Navigation, Operations, Supply, Air Wing, Training, and Safety.

Also, the Navy gave the carrier skipper a vice president to act as his son-of-a-bitch. His deputy, with the title of executive officer, ran around the *Kennedy* yelling at department heads and sailors alike to get the jobs done. The XO was much more visible to the sailors than the remote captain. I asked Wheatley if there was any danger that a super-active executive officer like his own, Captain John Anthony Pieno, would make it seem to the men on board that he, not Wheatley, was running the ship. Wheatley's smile crinkled his face all the way up and under his dark glasses. He took his eyes off the sea dead ahead of the carrier, turned to me and said:

"Very simply, the XO is the man who translates the

command goals into reality. I come up with the goals, the ideas. The XO makes them happen. In the final analysis, the man who makes the hard decisions is the captain. You don't get to be a captain by making the easy decisions. I am the man who must punish at mast. The XO may be perceived as being the bad guy because he has got to make things happen. He has to keep the pressure on. The tough decisions have to be made by the man who is responsible.''

The skipper of a carrier or any other ship does set the tone, color the personality, and dictate the style and philosophy of his ship. I concluded Wheatley's tone, personality, and style could be summed up in just one word: *correct*. He was proper, but not prim; cordial, but not warm; humorous, but not funny. His philosophy was that of the overachiever—the Middle America conviction that anybody could achieve his goals if he would just set them down and work hard until he reached them. He believed the United States Navy was still one of the places men and women could realize the American Dream of being judged by what they did, not where they came from or what social and political connections they had. He was a zealot when it came to working to get ahead. He told me in one of our chats on the bridge that it infuriated him to see officers or sailors waste their time in the Navy rather than seize its opportunities. I came to learn that this Navy overachiever, this grandson of Tennessee dirt farmers and son of a General Electric plant foreman, this Annapolis graduate—could sound like a missionary, a zealot even, on the subject of making the most of the moment at hand.

Shortly after leaving Norfolk, the sailors who had never sailed on the *Kennedy* before were summoned to the crew's lounge in the stern of the ship for orientation lectures. I decided to attend Wheatley's lecture to the young men to see whether he gave them fire and brimstone or gentle, fatherly advice from "the Old Man." I had been to the lounge many times before to talk to sailors during their off-duty hours. Usually the lounge was heavy with cigarette smoke, especially along the wall where President Kennedy's portrait hung over an artificial fireplace. Card tables were located there. These modern sailors did not play cards much, however. They most often played packaged games of war. This day the lounge was dressed up for the Captain. Its chairs were lined up in neat rows facing the lectern near the door where Wheatley would enter. After I had sat down among the sailors, several eyed me suspiciously. My khakis provoked alerts all down the rows for fear I was a chief officer who could give the sailors some grief. Then one of the sailors put his buddies at ease by saying, "He's the guy writing a book about us." The strained expressions turned into smiles and winks. Everyone still likes to see his name in print.

"Attention on deck! Attention on deck!" the chief at the front of the room commanded.

With a scraping of metal chairs, the room full of sailors rose from their seats and stood at the loose attention American sailors have perfected over the years. It is not the rigid attention of the Army airborne or the marines. It is a laid-back attention, as if the sailors were saying to themselves:

"All right, asshole, I'll stand up, but you better have something to say."

I stood up along with the sailors waiting for Wheatley's entrance. I was a khaki blob amid the dark blue dungarees and light blue shirts of the kids who did the heavy lifting on an aircraft carrier. They had already been told that the *Kennedy*, winner of several Navy E's for excellence, was a special ship that would demand their best.

The door snapped open. The young sailors saw their Captain close up for the first time. He was six-foot-three with a thickish, but not fat, build; thinning, reddish-blond hair, and the square chin and clean features of the man in the Arrow shirt ads. He wore a green flight jacket, the equivalent of the varsity sweater for aviators, to remind everybody that he used to fly A-6 bombers before he climbed to the heights of the Navy bureaucracy and won command of an aircraft carrier. He towered over the lectern. He told the sailors to sit down and then caught their attention by almost shouting:

"This is a capital warship, not a love boat."

He went on to explain to the now silent room of sailors:

"We have more destructive force on this ship than the entire Navy carried in World War II.

"We carry two million gallons of jet fuel and two million gallons of ship fuel and bombs, rockets, and bullets. And while we have an automatic sprinkling system in the magazines, we can't lean on them to protect our lives and let somebody smoke a cigarette.

"Every senior petty officer on this ship is a safety officer.

"I want you to stay alert!"

Changing the tone of his voice from warning to exhortation, Wheatley laid some of that missionary zeal on the confused teenagers sitting before him:

"My personal goal is that every man leaves the Navy with a crow on his shoulder that will represent some skill he can sell on the outside. I don't care whether you stay in the Navy or get out. I have a commitment that you go back as a petty officer and with a skill you can market on the outside. This doesn't happen automatically. Once you've done that, you've got a proven record of achievement. Go crow!

"Another personal reason I want you to advance is that I can't give you a raise. The only way I can give you a raise is to promote you. This is another reason I want you to advance.

"Responsibility." He said the word slowly and paused to let it sink in. "Each of us has responsibility. You have an absolute right to expect me to know my job—to feel confident that I'm not going to do something stupid or dangerous to put your life in jeopardy. What you know or don't know, or do or don't do, affects everybody on this ship. You wouldn't like it if I were high on booze or pills. There is no place on a warship for anybody who diminishes his capability by being on booze or drugs."

As far as getting along on the ship day by day, Wheatley continued in a voice less strident, "a recruit in the Navy only has to do three things. One: be at his place of duty on time; two: do a day's work for a day's pay; three: show mutual respect, not just to the captain, but to those above and below you. And remember that there's no such thing as a stupid question.

"Nobody can guarantee where you're going to be a day from now," Wheatley warned the young sailors as the *Kennedy* steamed south with a schedule that bore no resemblance to where the carrier would actually sail.

"This not knowing causes emotional insecurity. It's one of the personal sacrifices you have to make. But the flexibility is what makes the carrier such a great instrument of national policy.

"Don't ever forget that the only reason this ship is any good is the crew. The difference between a winner and a loser is the people right here in this room."

With that, Wheatley—perhaps to demonstrate that he could relate to the young sailors' personal concerns—asked for questions. He got only a few. Most of the young men were holding back. They saw no reason to risk getting in trouble with The Old Man so early in the cruise by asking stupid questions. The new sailors would be on this boat a long time. Their murmurs and lifted eyebrows to each other suggested that they had concluded the less they saw of this captain over the next seven months, the better off they would be.

Wheatley in his indoctrination address to the new sailors purposely made no attempt to be entertaining or brotherly. We discussed, in one of the many conversations I tape recorded on the bridge, the pros and cons of trying to be popular as a commanding officer. Wheatley had been a bit of a hell-raiser as a young pilot and still loved to party on the beach. But he believed it was a mistake to play to the crowd as a commanding officer, to go out of your way to be popular with your subordinates.

"You find your subordinates have an image of what they want their leader to be," he told me. "And in spite of what people say, they don't want you to be one of the boys. They don't want you to be a clown. They want you to be somebody they can respect—somebody they can look up to because they are in effect saying, 'If I'm successful, I'm going to be him.' So I push real hard both on the officer corps and the enlisted on this concept of mutual respect. I think it's very important."

"But," I pressed, "where is the fun in a job like yours where, as captain, you must distance yourself from the pilots and others with whom you would like to stay social? Where you often must eat alone? Where the demands are endless? Where you are away from your wife and children for months on end when you could be home, where, given your management background, you could be making more money than you are now? Where anything that goes wrong is your fault?"

"It's the unlimited nature of this job," Wheatley replied. "It's got to be the best job in the Navy. There are only thirteen operating carriers in the Navy and I command one of them. That is part of it. Put that together with the great elation one achieves from working with the kind of people I work with, the XO and my department heads. That has a synergistic effect.

"The fact that you say, 'Gee, I'm skipper of a carrier' wears thin after a while. That gets you seven months' deployment away from home. But what is really good is dealing with the individuals you work with, and that includes the sailors. There are some great young people in the Navy."

If that is the up side of commanding an aircraft carrier, of managing the unmanageable, of being captain, mayor, and father confessor for this weapontown hybrid, what is the downside of trying to be an effective skipper?

Wheatley usually responded to my questions quickly in whole, cogent paragraphs which sounded like written remarks rather than the spontaneous answers that they were. This time he paused and stared out to sea before answering.

"The hardest thing to deal with—and I hope you can find a way to explain it in your book—is the very arduous and deep emotional insecurity that takes hold of so many people on a deployment like this. The never knowing what is going to happen next. Are we going to get home? Are they going to send us through the Suez Canal because something happened in Iran? Is the admiral's staff on board going to be transferred tomorrow? Are we going to have a liberty port? If my wife comes over to see me (when the ship goes into port), am I going to get to see her or are we going to pull out too early for that, like that other ship did? Or like happened to me five years ago? Is there a problem at home, and that's why I'm not getting any mail? Or is the mail just slow?

"People like to be able to count on things. They like to be able to say, 'I'm going to see you in a week,' and count on it. If you could do that and say, 'Hey, this cruise is going to be over on May 1.' If you could believe that in your heart, then you could say it was a cruise."

But in Wheatley's view the *Kennedy* was on a deployment. He corrected anybody who called it a cruise because our duration, liberty ports, and destinations were all uncertain as we steamed toward Rio de Janeiro, despite the seeming specificity of our sailing orders.

I saw Wheatley in many settings as I roamed the ship. At dinner, he could be either the needling extrovert or the warm host. With department head officers, he could be the coach trying to teach. With sailors brought before him for punishment at captain's mast, he could be the ferocious judge or sympathetic captain willing to give the accused a second chance. He was considered a hard ass by the sailors I talked to. They feared going before him, which is the kind of deterrence to stepping out of line which warship commanders like Wheatley try to generate.

One afternoon when I was an observer at captain's mast, a

sailor who had been in the Navy for four years without moving up into the petty officer ranks was brought before Wheatley for failing to obey orders of petty officers. He told Wheatley at the outset of this disciplinary proceeding that he was jealous of petty officers who were younger than he. That was why he refused to take orders from them. The sailor was standing at attention on the platform below the ladder leading down from Wheatley's sea cabin off the bridge. Only a narrow lectern separated captain and sailor. The sailor's explanation offended Wheatley. His face reddened as he leaned within inches of the sailor's face and shouted:

"How come you're not a petty officer? You took the test only once in four years. You're not a petty officer because you don't want to be a petty officer. If you wanted to be a petty officer, you could be. Maybe you resent these other men who took the time and effort to study and take the test—who might be junior to you in time but senior to you in rank.

"You ought to be second class by now. Do you think when you get discharged from here and go out you'll be able to pick your own boss? What are you going to do if you've got a younger man, the boss's son, as your boss? Suppose you know more about the job than he does? Are you going to resent him, too?"

"No sir," the sailor answered meekly.

"Then why can't you respect the petty officer who has been appointed over you here? Because you know what's going to happen to you when you're a civilian and you act that way? You're going to get fired! Nobody out there is going to counsel you. You're not going to have a first class petty officer. You're not going to have a chief. You're not going to have a bunch of people who care about you—who are going to sit down and try to improve your performance—to try to keep you out of trouble. You're going to get fired! You're going to be out of a job. It's that simple. Is that what you want?"

"No sir."

"Then why the hell can't you improve your attitude?"

"I'm jealous of the petty officers, sir."

"You don't have to be jealous. You could be a petty officer. You're not a dummy. You're an intelligent, capable man. You could be a barn burner. Why don't you quit feeling sorry for yourself and get off your butt and be somebody! You've got the capability. You shouldn't be here at mast. You ought to be one of the leaders. What are you doing—screwing up purposely so you get some attention? I'll guarantee you, you're going to get plenty of attention. You don't have any business being at mast. There's absolutely no reason. You did this deliberately. You know better. There's absolutely no reason for behavior like this out of an individual like you. If you're jealous of people who are senior to you, that's your own fault. You could be senior to them. What are you going to do the first time you have a setback in civilian life—say those bastards are picking on me again and quit?''

"No sir.''

"That's what you're saying. The solution starts right here with you. You are a capable, talented man. And you're pissing away your talent, and you ought to be ashamed of yourself for that. You've served honorably for four years. You ought to be a superstar. It makes me sick to see a man like you who has to come to mast. You can't pick your boss, just like I can't pick my boss. You do the best you can. If you suffer a setback, you turn around and keep working. That's the only way you're going to make it in civilian life. You know that. I want you to be a success. I don't want you to be a failure.''

Wheatley leaned back from the lectern, brought his head back down close to the stunned sailor and let loose a thunderous summation: ''You're not a failure! Quit acting like a failure, God damn it! Act like the man you are! Understand me? Know what I'm saying?''

"Yes sir.''

"I find you guilty as charged. I award you a reduction in rate and a $200 fine. On the basis of your superior service, what your superior petty officers say about you, I'm suspending the reduction in rate for six months, which means you don't lose your stripe. Are you going to take that third class exam in March? I don't care if you're getting out of the Navy or not. I want you to take it and pass it.''

The chastened sailor mumbled something that sounded like, ''Yes sir,'' saluted and disappeared down the ladder under the landing.

I saw the same kind of Wheatley fury when he held mast for a repeat offender, a black fireman who on this occasion was accused of calling his black first class petty officer ''nigger, Uncle Tom''; of refusing to obey his orders and perform work assigned to him or stow his clothes and make his bed; of threatening to beat up the petty officer once the ship reached port. The fireman had also accused the petty officer of stealing money from him, triggering an investigation which had found the petty officer innocent.

"What do you have to say for yourself?" Wheatley asked at the outset of the captain's mast held on the same narrow landing.

Fireman G said the petty officer had double-crossed him at the last captain's mast by failing to speak up for him as promised and then made fun of him in the bunk room afterward.

"When we got back down to the coop, he just laughed at me. Him coming up here and cutting me down in front of all those high ranking officers puts more grief on me than I can bear. I didn't mean to go off like that, but it just happened. I won't lose my temper anymore as long as I'm in the Navy."

Wheatley asked the petty officer to give his side of the story:

"I thought he was pulling a prank when he accused me of taking his money off his bunk. The investigators cleared me and said he was trying to find a way to get back at me. G is working in the 03 head. He is a slow, plodding type worker. I've counseled him in regard to grooming, work habits. He tells people how to do the jobs they are trying to teach him to do. He needs constant supervision by me. He always questions me. I tell him I'll give him my answer after the job is done."

"Does he generally get to work on time?"

"No sir," his petty officer answered.

"What does the chain of command have to say about this man? Is he worth saving or should we kick him out of the Navy?" Wheatley went from one superior to another as they stood shoulder to shoulder on the landing between two decks in the carrier island.

"He doesn't play a straight game," complained one of G's superiors. "He says one thing to the leading petty officer and another thing to the division officer. I don't think he's playing a straight game or acting like a sailor."

Only Lieutenant Commander Joel Geister, head of the Deck Department where G was assigned, held out any hope for G becoming a productive sailor in the United States Navy. "He's somewhat immature," Geister said. "He blows hot and cold."

G, who had brought several sailors to the mast with him to testify that he did work hard, violated protocol for a mast by breaking into Geister's testimony to declare:

"Sir, no one has to stand over my back and supervise me since I've been in Deck Division."

"That's not what the chain of command just said," Wheatley shot back. "This is the third division you've been in now—two in Engineering and one in Deck. How many places do you have to go before you find your niche?"

G remained on the offense, a sharp contrast to most sailors who quake when they appear before the ship's captain. He said Chief S had transferred him out of the deck department only because he had not been trained to repair the launches and thus could not fix them when directed to do so.

"Do you expect me to believe that?" Wheatley snapped, his blue eyes blazing at G. "Do you want me to get Chief S up here right now? Do you want to stake your naval career on what you just said?"

Silence.

"Answer me!" Wheatley thundered.

G, finally on the defensive, mumbled, "Yes sir."

"All right," Wheatley snapped. "Let's get Chief S up here right now."

A ship at sea is a sealed city. Unlike cities on land, witnesses can always be found and summoned to court. They have no place to hide and cannot refuse a captain's request to appear before him. His power is absolute as far as who does what on his ship, in his city. The beefy chief, wakened out of a sound sleep, reached the landing breathing hard from the climb.

"Why did you transfer Fireman G from the boat shop?" Wheatley asked the chief.

"I had trouble with him. He was a malingerer. I had trouble with him in the berthing compartment—in keeping his rack clean. He was sleeping with the sea bag in his rack. I told him to put sheets on the cover, and no more sleeping with his uniform on. That wasn't adhered to. I also had trouble with him up in the work space where he would try to snow people that knew the rate. He was going to teach them, even though he had never worked with diesels before."

"G has just testified," Wheatley told the chief, "that there were two reasons he left the boat shop. One was because he didn't put his clothes away when they came from the laundry, and, two, because he didn't know how to fix the boat. And he implied that was because you wouldn't give him any help in teaching him how to fix the boat.''

"No sir. He went back to the main spaces because he did not want to conform to the standards we set. On a one-on-one situation, he was trying to tell them what to do when, in fact, he didn't know himself. He would not take outside advice.''

Wheatley had heard enough. He delivered a nonstop blast across the lectern at Fireman G. His words ricocheted off the steel walls, causing the marine aide standing in back of the captain to wince.

"You're obviously a sea lawyer and a liar! You're no dummy! You know what you're doing! You're manipulating the system every chance you get! You blow smoke! You prevaricate! Oh, you're just a damn sea lawyer! You don't care about your shipmates! I don't know what you're doing in the Navy. You know you've got a lot of capability. You're not using it. If you would expend one tenth of the energy you expended in being a sea lawyer doing your job and being respectful of your shipmates, you wouldn't be in any trouble. Any man who is too lazy to put his laundry away; who spends two hours gathering witnesses to talk about something that is irrelevant—who do you think you're kidding?

"You've got one champion left on the ship. That's Commander Geister. I'm not going to throw you out of the Navy today. But I guarantee you if I see your face at mast again, you're going to be a civilian so fast you can't believe it. Do you understand that? If you want to stay in the Navy, start being the man you're capable of being. You've got one person who wants to keep you. Do you want to stay in the Navy?''

"Yes sir.''

"Then you start acting like it! I find you guilty as charged. I award you a $500 fine, reduction in rate, three days bread and water. That's all.''

For the first time in the mast, G visibly flinched when he heard his sentence. He would be going to the ship's jail, the brig, for three days, and eating nothing but bread and drinking water.

G saluted the captain, turned on his heel and left the landing. Wheatley, just before leaving the landing, turned to the petty officer who had brought the charges against the fireman and said: "If he looks at you cross-eyed, I want you to bring him back to mast.'' Nobody moved until the angry captain was out of sight.

Wheatley's stern lecture and punishment did not take.

Fireman G would get in trouble again before the cruise ended and be kicked out of the Navy.

Wheatley's sympathetic side showed up at another mast where the question was what to do about a hard-working sailor whose urine indicated he had broken the rules and smoked marijuana. The Navy in 1983, along with the other services, called sailors into sick bay with no prior warning and ordered them to urinate in a bottle. The bottle was sent to a laboratory for urinalysis. If the test indicated marijuana, the sailor was called to captain's mast. A second failure of the urinalysis test often led to commanders discharging the sailor from the Navy. Sailors on the *Kennedy* believed urinalysis tests could not be beat. "If you smoke pot," one sailor told me in a typical reaction, "you get caught. Then you're out." The armed services were reluctant to crack down on drug abuse right after the Vietnam War when the draft ended. Military authority had been fractured. Military leaders could not find enough volunteers to fill their ranks in the early 1970s. I have always suspected one reason the Pentagon did not order a crackdown of drugs was for fear of losing too many soldiers, sailors, airmen, and marines in the thinned ranks of the 1970s. By the time the *Kennedy* sailed in 1983, all the services were attracting more volunteers than they could use, making it safe from a manpower standpoint to discharge anyone found guilty of drug abuse. The sailor standing before Wheatley at mast said he could not understand how he could have failed the urinalysis test because he had not been smoking dope. His superiors testified that the sailor was an outstanding performer on the ship.

"I'm going to dismiss these charges," said Wheatley after hearing out the accused and his witnesses. "If I've made a mistake and you're a drug user, what's going to happen is that you'll be caught, and I'll throw you out of the Navy. But based on what everybody said here, I don't think I'm making a mistake. I think the mistake was made someplace else. I'm going to take your word and the word of the chain of command that you're not a drug user and, accordingly, I dismiss these charges."

The sailor was jubilant. The lawyers who had prepared the charges and believed him to be guilty were deflated. Wheatley wiped the court cases out of his mind, left the podium, and climbed the ladder to resume the business of sailing the carrier and catching its airplanes on the deck.

Wheatley's son-of-a-bitch, Captain John A. Pieno, the executive officer, called XO by his officers, shared both Wheatley's working man's background and zealousness about the upward mobility the Navy provided to those who might otherwise be left by the wayside in 20th century America. I was to talk to XO Pieno almost every day we were at sea. We puzzled over the pattern of world events on the basis of what little information came into the ship, argued over politics, laughed at ourselves and the rest of the human comedy we were playing in out here on the open sea, and talked endlessly about the Navy generally and the *Kennedy* specifically. I would drop into his office after supper and conversationally hopscotch the world with him. He seemed to enjoy our arguments. I do not claim I was right. But I was different—a civilian with contrary views on many subjects we covered. I did not try to tell him what he wanted to hear. I was not trying to get promoted.

I learned from observing him day and night that Pieno, as XO, not only was responsible for implementing Captain Wheatley's policies through the chain of command, as the Navy management book said, but also for keeping the city part of the ship running. He was supposed to solve problems before they reached the captain's in-basket. In one of his many problem solving roles, Pieno was hotel manager for the congressman and other VIPs who dropped in by helicopter with little advance notice. They needed a room, preferably with bath, on the already crowded ship. Pieno's hotel duties for the regular crew on board extended to spot checks: bathrooms, called heads, on the theory that the top command owed the men aboard a clean place to live. Pieno listed the worst heads under the heading "Shit Holes" in the ship's printed Plan-of-the-Day to impel action. As XO, Pieno also was the morale officer. He decided when it was time to run bingo games and Monte Carlo nights for the crew. He was also the provisioner who made sure other ships kept giving the *Kennedy* her vital food and fuel while she was thousands of miles from the nearest store and diesel pump. He also decided on behalf of the captain when sailors should be allowed to be flown off the ship to reach the bedside of a stricken wife or child or parent.

Pieno's rank of captain often was not enough to move the ship's bureaucracy into action. In those cases, he often threw tantrums for effect. He confided to me that they moved junior officers but not department heads and other old hands in the ship's company. "The XO's banging the pots and pans again," an irreverent commander told me in response to one of Pieno's tirades.

In the privacy of his cabin, I sometimes found Pieno transformed from the flamboyant, shouting XO to a brooding man wondering where life was taking him. He complained about the Washington bureaucracy, worried about the crew being worked too hard, and wondered out loud if he had left something undone that would trigger a disaster on the carrier. I asked him one night to explain how he motivated homesick sailors stuck in a floating city thousands of miles from their parents and girl friends. How do you get them to work twelve or more hours a day seven days a week without resorting to the lashings and other punishments used by yesterday's captains on ships that stayed at sea for months at a time?

"I can see where a lot of these kids are coming from," replied Pieno. He said he had known America's left-outs while growing up in New Orleans. He felt many of these left-outs on the *Kennedy* undervalued themselves because nobody had ever told them they were anything special.

"The most effective thing you can do to motivate a kid is to make him feel part of an integral group that he is helping move toward a goal. The goal of the group becomes infectious. As long as the kid sees he is reaping some kind of benefits from it, he'll go right along to benefit himself.

"But before we can do anything for a kid in the Navy, he has to mature enough to want to do something to improve himself. This is the most important thing of all. He must be willing to take responsibility for what he does. If he doesn't want to do that, if he doesn't want to advance, he'll die on the vine.

"Some kids are perfectly content to be sweeping decks, cleaning heads their whole time in the Navy. They'll serve perfectly honorably and they will get out of the Navy without doing anything more than those type of jobs they started out doing.

"Then we get other kids in the Navy who work so damn hard to improve themselves and get ahead, but they just can't do it. They try and they try. But they never had the background, the exposure to formalized thinking so they could develop it for themselves, the education, the guidance to be able to get ahead.

They'll just never make it. This hurts me more than anything else when I see it because you know these kids will give their lives and limbs for you.

"The most important thing we can do for the health of the Navy is to get these young kids who *can* improve themselves to experience success. We may be giving them the first taste of success they have ever had. We want them to get used to success so they keep helping themselves and advance. They have got to learn early that they must swim upstream like the salmon to get where they want to go."

Below Wheatley and Pieno—manager and deputy manager of the plant in the corporate sense—there was a manager who has few parallels in private industry, the command master chief. He served as the liaison between management and labor, so to speak, by walking the tight line between the officers and enlisted people on the carrier. He was not an officer of the corporation nor was he a shop steward for the labor force on the ship. His job instead was to do what he could to make the officers and enlisted men mesh better. A sailor who went through the regular chain of command and failed to get satisfaction could send a chit to the command master chief. The chit would have a red line through it. The sailor was supposed to get an answer to his request within twenty-four hours. The command master chief was the first stop for the red line chit. He would read it and then send it on to the XO along with his recommendation on what to do about the grievance. The command master chief's office was next to the spiritual counselors for the corporation, the ship's three chaplains.

Stanley G. Crowley, a forty-nine-year-old high school dropout with a round face and an almost constant smile, was the *Kennedy*'s master chief, its ombudsman. He had climbed to the top of the enlisted ranks in his twenty-three-year career in the Navy. Crowley walked ceaselessly around the ship, trying to dispense good cheer and listening to the sailors who stopped him on his rounds. He had a deep faith in God and in the Navy but did not talk like a zealot for either. He did, however, emphasize the positive in his one-on-one talks with the sailors and on his nightly appearances on the *Kennedy*'s closed circuit "Fathom" television shows. Crowley, during my first days aboard, struck me as a cheerleader who did not get his hands dirty along with the other chiefs and sailors he was trying to inspire. I came to appreciate and admire his role as a vital link between sailors and officers, as trouble shooter, and as a rumor stopper.

One day on the bridge, the head of *Kennedy* Incorporated, Captain Wheatley, explained to me what Crowley did for him:

"One, he is a conduit to me of the mood and needs of the men; two, he is a great dispenser of information.

"He is the man who is the equivalent of the counselor in the old days. We get people like Stan Crowley, a mature person who has reached the top of his spectrum, who knows he is not going to be promoted to the officer corps. He knows he is not going to do much else. He is a man who, like the statesman philosopher, is able to give me advice in a non-personalized way. He doesn't have to do anything for his own personal benefit. He works for me. He also works for the XO. In industry, he would be like a board member who has already been a proved performer in another corporation and comes in and sits on our board of directors."

I talked with Crowley in his office, in the chief's mess where he ate regularly, in the television studio (where he started every show with, "Good Evening, *Kennedy* Men"), in the passageways as he made his rounds, in philosophical seminars (where he proved extremely well read), and out on the flight deck where we jogged. In all that time, in all those places, Stan Crowley never appeared down. He had the adrenaline of a politician, always able to get it flowing when communicating with another person. He was at peace with himself, with his Navy, with his family—wife and six children—and with his Mr. In-Between role on the ship. He could even look on the bright side of the seven month deployment, declaring the long separation would make him and his wife appreciate each other more when they reunited in May.

His turn at the lectern during the indoctrination of the new men on the *Kennedy* showed him to be part cheerleader, part salty sailor, part Dutch uncle.

"Are you guys *Kennedy* men?" he began in a takeoff on the Marine drill instructor meeting the new men in the film, *An Officer and a Gentleman.*

"Yes sir," they replied lamely.

Crowley cupped his hand around his ear as if he had not heard them.

"Are you guys *Kennedy* men?" he repeated.

"Yes sir!" they shouted back at him from their seats in the crew's lounge.

"That's a little hokey," Crowley told the green sailors. "We know it's a little hokey. But it proves something. It proves that we can do anything together."

5 Steam

CAPTAIN Wheatley, XO Pieno, and Master Chief Crowley could expound on their theories for managing a ship and inspiring its crew. But I wondered what life was really like below decks where the men often worked far below the water line and went for weeks at a time without seeing sky or sea. I had been taken on a guided tour of this world, of course, which revealed engine rooms, machine shops and carpentry cubicles packed tightly together. The complex looked like a sea-going version of the shops I had seen built into the walls of ancient cities like Jerusalem.

Iron Mike Fahey urged me to get to know the "pit snipes" down in the bowels of the *Kennedy* who made the steam. He told me about one of his first class boiler tenders, a big black man from the South named Thomas Brinson III. Brinson knew something about management, the practical kind practiced by some of the best petty officers in the Navy. He could kick ass in his special world of heat and noise to get the steam made. He also could be fatherly, even to the point of teaching some of the white cast-asides from American society how to read. Young sailors under him called Brinson "Daddy B."

I borrowed the thick blue Navy text, *Principles of Naval Engineering,* and interviewed some of the engineering officers before venturing into Brinson's domain deep down in the ship. The *Kennedy* was designed to carry nuclear reactors to provide heat needed to transform water into powerful steam, but former Defense Secretary Robert S. McNamara had insisted she be conventionally powered. So she burned fuel oil in giant brick boilers below deck. Iron Mike traced for me the path of steam from the boilers to the machinery it powered. Steam on the *Kennedy* turned the carrier's four propellers, each 21 feet across. It desalted sea water into fresh for drinking, washing, and cooking. It launched the aircraft by sending a tremendous blast against the piston which powered the catapult. It heated and cooled everything on the ship from the admiral's cabin to the kennel for Duke, the dope dog, who was riding along to sniff out any caches of drugs. And it generated the electricity to light the ship-city and heat the ovens which baked 6,000 hot dog and hamburger rolls every day.

With the textbook and Fahey's lecture in my head, I descended the steel ladders leading to Brinson's domain in Machinery Room Number One, called Main One. The noise got louder the deeper I went down into the ship. It also grew hotter. Everyone in the machinery rooms wears ear plugs against the noise but can only sweat to relieve the heat. I ended up on a narrow, silver-gray catwalk which ran over, under, and along pipes of varying dimensions. I spotted the glassed-in office, called the watch station, for Main One.

"What can we do for you?" Daddy B asked. He was standing behind a high, gray counter near a brass phone which kept him in touch with his men out in the noise and heat beyond the watch station. It also connected him with the central engineering control station for the whole ship. We talked for a while. Then Brinson slid a cup of thick coffee over to me. He seemed to appreciate my interest in the world few people visit unless they have to.

"Nobody bothers us down here," Brinson told me with a smile. "Too hot and too many steps."

He urged me to watch the lighting off of a boiler. The ritual turned out to be another microcosm of Navy management: break big jobs into little ones, one for each man, and have supervisors supervise the supervisors who supervise the kids doing the work. It was the human wave approach to managing the unmanageable. Any private shipping line would go broke trying to make the payroll for all this manpower. But Navy ships do not have to make a profit or pay overtime. The Navy relies on amateurs right out of high school, not master mariners, to run the most demanding and powerful ships ever built. The Navy can sail with amateurs as long as it has enough professionals like Brinson to oversee their work. But when key members of this management layer are missing, as in the 1970s, it becomes dangerous to take a ship to sea. The skipper of the *Canisteo*, for example, refused to take his oiler to sea in April 1980, because he felt he was dangerously short of experienced boiler technicians like Brinson.

Eggie Brashers and Steve Benoit were the two sailors designated to light off the boiler the day I went out onto the lower catwalk, called the fire alley, to watch this rite below the waterline. Brashers and Benoit knew from Daddy B's lectures that if they did the wrong thing, they could turn the huge steel box in front of them into flying shrapnel. Worse yet was what Daddy B might do to them afterward. A chief and an officer from Engineering arrived to help Daddy B supervise the lightoff.

Brashers, twenty-six, had entered the strange world of Main One from college where he grew tired of studying and of the tight supervision of his parents in Dayton, Ohio. Now, he strode purposefully down the alleyway between the squarish fire boxes. He stopped before an upright gray pipe filled with fuel oil. It held an iron poker like a rose in a vase. He withdrew the poker and lit with a cigarette lighter the band of oil-soaked cloth at the far end. The poker ignited into a torch of yellow, smoky flame.

Remembering Brinson's stern instructions and the Navy manual, Brashers gripped the torch firmly in both hands and walked down the fire alley to his twenty-year-old shipmate, Benoit. Benoit looked like a riot cop in his flame-retardant gloves and plastic face mask. He took the torch from Brashers and thrust the flaming end through a hole in the steel box in front of him. The torchlight revealed the insides of what looked like a cavernous brick fireplace with an A-shaped top. Row upon row of water pipes covered the sides and ceilings of this special seagoing fireplace called a boiler. The idea was to start a fire in this fireplace and keep it going. The hot fire would boil the water flowing through the pipes and turn it to steam. The steam, under continuous heat, would become frantic and press hard against anything trying to hold it back. It then would be directed against turbines, which would be turned by the pressure like windmills being twirled by the wind. The turbines, as they spun from the force of steam, would turn the *Kennedy*'s four propellers fast enough to push the 83,000-ton ship through the water at more than 40 miles an hour, as well as give life to the floating city.

"Torch still lit!" Benoit shouted to confirm to Daddy B that the flame was burning steadily inside the boiler 14 feet high and 12 feet wide.

"Hit it!" commanded Brashers.

Brashers, standing to Benoit's right on the fire alley, started to turn a wheel-shaped valve counterclockwise. This allowed fuel oil to rush out the end of a pipe and into the boiler. A steady stream of forced air would circulate droplets of fuel around the inside of the boiler, making an explosive mixture of oil and air for the flame Benoit was holding steady.

"One thousand one!" Brashers yelled over the noise of the blowers. He was signaling that the valve had been admitting fuel oil into the boiler for one full second. If his count went beyond three seconds, everyone on the alleyway would rush to shut everything down. Otherwise too much fuel could accumulate in the boiler and explode catastrophically, perhaps blowing the boiler apart and showering the engine room with flying brick and steel.

"One thousand two!"

Whump! the boiler issued.

"Fire's lit!" Benoit called out.

Clean white flame filled the boiler. The boiler soon would be assisting three others in sending steam through the ship's arteries and veins. Brashers and Benoit had done their jobs.

When their shift in Main One ended, Brinson, Brashers, Benoit, and other pit snipes would walk up ladders to their sleeping compartment—still without seeing the outdoors. They would go for weeks without knowing whether it was raining or snowing, or whether the sun was shining. They worked, ate, and slept in a world without natural light. Whether it was shared experience and respect, that misery loves company, or conditions which made everyone interdependent, the pit snipes became melded into a tight fraternity after a few weeks together. I went down to their domain many times and came to know Brinson well. The Navy could rightly claim him as one of its success stories.

Brinson, thirty-two, told me that the odds stacked up against him early in life. At age three, he saw his father shot to death during an argument with their landlord in St. Petersburg,

Florida. His widowed mother could not afford to raise both her boys plus her baby daughter. She sent Brinson and his younger brother by train to Cairo, Georgia, to live with their grandmother. Brinson's mother figured they would be better off there. The grandmother owned her own house. They ought to be able to find work eventually in the farms around Cairo to help for their food, his mother reasoned.

"I started working in the tobacco fields around Cairo when I was seven," Brinson told me. "I got $2.50 a day for a day that began at sunup and ended at sundown. I still remember how hard it was for me to walk over those big clumps of red dirt because I was so small. I never felt anything as hot as a Georgia tobacco field. I used to get 50 cents a bush for breaking okra. You had to be real careful not to get the fiber on your skin. It would really itch. You had to button your shirt up real tight, making you even hotter. But the stuff always seemed to get in there anyway."

As Brinson was preparing to enter his junior year at the black high school in Cairo, the white establishment of the town decided to bus him and four of his black schoolmates to the white high school. He felt uncomfortable in his new surroundings once again. But there was a bright shaft of light in the experience. His white English teachers assigned him novels to read. He had never read inspiring novels before. They transported him out of Cairo and fired his dreams. He resolved to go to college after high school, whether he had the money in hand or not. He applied to Fort Valley State College in Georgia and was accepted. He reported there in the fall of 1969 and felt gloriously free. Free of Cairo, free of his grandmother, and free to pursue his curiosities in classes that were exhilarating for him. He also met and fell in love with Linda Copenny of Columbus, Georgia. She was studying under the type of college loans which Brinson had been unable to obtain. They were married in 1970 and moved into an apartment off campus. They agreed she would stay in college until she earned her degree. He would remain as long as he could make enough money at part time jobs to pay for his college and their mounting living expenses. Brinson took every job he could find: night janitor, day laborer, foreman. He still could not make enough money to pay for everything. That is why a white Navy recruiter at Warner Robbins military base outside Macon, Georgia, saw a five-foot-eleven-inch black built like a linebacker filling up a chair in his office one day in 1973. Brinson said the exchange stuck in his mind:

"We can get you in as a cook," the recruiter said.

"I don't want to be no cook. What else you got? Something that pays a bonus."

"Only thing is boiler technician. You wouldn't like that. It's hot, dirty work down in the hold."

"There's no work the Navy's got for me that's any hotter or dirtier than that I've already done."

Brinson liked the idea of getting a bonus and also of volunteering for a job others were afraid to try. He saw boiler technician—whatever that might be—as a challenge. He experienced doubts when he arrived at the Navy boot camp in Great Lakes, Illinois, and found himself the old man amidst a bunch of teenagers.

"I kept telling myself I was going in a positive direction; that wherever I was going had to be better than where I had been."

Brinson watched the steam build up in the Alpha One boiler Brashers and Benoit had just lit. He knew there was no use torturing himself while he was at sea with the old question of whether he could make it on the outside. He and Linda would have to wait until May, when the *Kennedy* was supposed to return to Norfolk, to continue the debate.

Right now the skipper on the bridge was ringing bells for steam. He was moving south fast, trying to stay ahead of a storm. The ship had been ordered to steam across the equator to Rio de Janeiro for some updated gunboat diplomacy and then head east across the Atlantic to the Mediterranean. The Russians would be watching her all the way. The *Kennedy*'s planes would be watching back, sometimes in eyeball-to-eyeball confrontations in the sky six miles above the carrier.

6   Bear Hunt

WE drew abreast of Cuba on our way to Rio de Janeiro. Tension mounted all through the carrier. Cuba was Bear country. The intelligence community had alerted the *Kennedy* that Soviet Bear bombers might be passing overhead. The talk turned to Bear hunts, Russian pilots, and the eyeball-to-eyeball encounters *Kennedy* fliers had had with them over the years.

I knew from years of covering the military that the United States and the Soviet Union had been shadow boxing with their planes, ships, and submarines ever since World War II. One tactic employed by both sides is to provoke the other into activating its defenses to reveal how good or bad they are. American planes have been lost while thrusting at Soviet air defense, for example, to "tickle" their radars into action. The radar signals and capabilities are duly recorded during such electronic thrusts and parries of the Cold War.

I also knew before boarding *Kennedy* that Navy leaders were becoming increasingly concerned about the threat Soviet Bear bombers posed to their aircraft carriers. They were worried not so much about a Bear flying over a carrier and bombing it World War II style as about the bomber serving as a spotter for Soviet submarines loaded with long range cruise missiles. The Bear crew in a war could direct the fire of the submarine from the air the way a forward observer on the ground directs army artillery fire. One version of the Bear appears to be dedicated to this role, the Bear D.

The Navy response to the Bear threat to carriers has been to send its fighters aloft to intercept the Bears before they can fly close enough to do the carrier any harm. The intended message has been that in a war the fighters would shoot the bomber down before it could direct a submarine's cruise missiles or fire its own missiles at a carrier. The Soviets, for their part, keep trying to find a hole in a carrier's defenses and fly their bombers through it. This determination by both superpowers makes for intense competition in the skies over a carrier battle group. Each country through this one-upmanship reveals to his potential adversary some of the hunting and killing techniques it would like to keep secret. So Bear hunts are instructive as well as tense for both the hunter and the hunted.

The Soviet Bears which patrol the Atlantic where the *Kennedy* was sailing originate from a Northern Fleet base in Olenegorsk, near Murmansk, and fly all the way to Cuba in one hop. The Bears pass through North Atlantic Treaty Organization radar coverage, starting in Norway, so their movements come as no surprise to the Navy and to others plugged into the Western intelligence network. The Bears use Cuba as a launching pad for their reconnaissance of the U.S. Atlantic fleet. They often fly from Cuba across the Atlantic to Luanda, Angola. Then it's back to Cuba and home to Olenegorsk. The Cuba to Luanda leg would put them near us as we sailed along the South American coast to Rio.

What I did not know until I got aboard the *Kennedy* was how the confrontations between American and Soviet fliers over the years had generated a spirit of camaraderie; an aviator-to-aviator rapport that transcended the politics of the Cold War. There was a warm side to the Cold War after all when it came to the men out on the point of its spear. I felt good about this. The fliers' stories brought to mind the open cockpit chivalry of World War I, and tales of American and German soldiers exchanging Christmas presents across no man's land during a lull in the trench warfare. I detected a certain sadness and regretfulness in some of the pilots as they told about Russian pilots they had waved to across the gap of sky between the planes. Some of the *Kennedy* fliers said they wished the Cold War could be shut off long enough to bring the Russians into the O Club to throw down a few shooters and talk about their lives, their planes, and flying. Pure flying knows no political bounds.

One name that drew knowing smiles from many officers on

board was Lieutenant Viktor Belenko, the Russian pilot who flew his MiG 25 fighter to Japan in 1976 and defected. Belenko had been giving lectures to American fliers. *Kennedy* aviators who knew Belenko regarded him not only as a uniquely qualified instructor but as "A Player," an aviator who loved to fly hard in the air and play hard on the ground, to drink and chase girls. "Being in the Russian military is like being in a chicken coop," Belenko would say in his lectures. "You know you're going to be fucked. You just don't know when." Belenko made the fliers even more curious about the other Russian fliers they often saw up close during Bear hunts.

Belenko told his American hosts shortly after he defected that the two things he most wanted to see were an aircraft carrier in action and an Air Force base. The U.S. government accommodated him on both counts. Rear Admiral Roger E. Box told me during one of our conversations that Belenko was so fascinated with the flight operations on the carrier he visited that he refused to go to bed during his first day and night aboard. He could not believe the artistry of the ballet he watched on the flight deck. He told Navy officers that it was too complicated to stage just for his benefit. He said his political officers had been lying to him in ridiculing the carrier's capabilities.

One morning over breakfast one of the older fliers regaled me with the human side of Bear hunts he had been on or heard about over the years. The fliers, American and Russian, when the political climate allowed, went to great lengths to make each other laugh. One stunt pulled by the American fliers was to go aloft with those old man rubber masks and pull them over their heads when they came abreast of the Russian plane. One pilot out Bear hunting in the Christmas season had pulled on a Santa Claus hat and beard when he drew abreast of the Russian bomber. Not to be outdone, the Russians frequently pushed the centerfold pictures from *Playboy* against the plastic blisters of their bomber and toasted their American comrades across the sky with a can of Schlitz beer.

Other fliers told me that frequently when a Navy fighter flew alongside a Soviet Bear for an extended period the Russians inside would hold up fingers or signs telling the American crew to switch to the 333.3 radio frequency over which the two planes could communicate. Once connected, the first questions the Soviets asked the American fliers was how much money they made and where they lived. Another burning question was this one, coming through the air in broken English tinged with incredulity:

"It's really true you don't have any women on your aircraft carriers?"

"It's really true," came back through the earphones in the leather helmets worn by the Russians.

I thought this was a logical question. Why would it not seem strange for five thousand men to be kept out to sea with no women for months on end? I asked around the ship whether the Soviets carried women on their helicopter carriers and other warships. Nobody seemed to know. But the Soviets do have luxurious looking white hospital ships that go from ship to ship. I was to fly over them later in the deployment as they were tied to anchored Soviet warships in the Mediterranean. The scuttle-butt on the *Kennedy* was that these white ships are literally love boats as well as hospitals in which attractive women on board tend to all the needs of the sex-starved Russian officers and sailors in romantic surroundings. A floating brothel for the boys at sea. I could confirm with high ranking Navy officers that this was indeed a suspicion in the U.S. intelligence community but not an established fact. Fact or fiction, everyone looked down lustfully at the white ships whenever any of us flew over them.

One pilot who had several sky encounters with the Soviet Bears was a tall, handsome, sensitive man of VF-11, the Red Rippers, Lieutenant Brad Goetsch. He came by my room one day to talk about life on the carrier. We got to talking about the Bear hunts. As he talked, my long-held view that there is no such thing as "the military mind" but instead different kinds of minds in the military was reinforced. His remarks added depth to the storybook portrait of fighter pilots and humanized the Bear vs. Carrier, Carrier vs. Bear contests waged six miles high in the sky out of sight of everyone but the combatants.

On one hunt, Brad recalled, he flew his F-14 so close to the Bear that he and his backseater could feel the tremble of the bomber's four engines. The intercept started hundreds of miles from the carrier. The F-14 and Bear flew alongside each other for ninety minutes, an unusually long time for such intercept missions.

"We flew beside them so long that we had plenty of time to get close and take pictures and study the airplane. We could see what the guys were doing inside. One guy had just a T-shirt on and his little leather helmet. He was the guy in the back window which stretches across the aft end of the bomber, right under the tail fin. We could see him move from side to side, from one window to the other, to look at us. After we were on him for about an hour, we had our masks off and were just taking it easy. They signaled us to sweep our wings so they could take a picture. They were holding up cameras. So what the heck, we swept our wings, and they took pictures.

"Then I saw the guy in the little bubble window behind the cockpit. I could see he was eating a sandwich and had a little cup in his hand. My backseater pulled out his little water bottle that we keep and he held it up like a toast. And the guy in the bomber broke into a great big smile and held up his cup. And then my backseater and the Russian drank.

"You could see the pilot craning his neck to look at us. We were on him so long that we had time to think about what we were doing. It kind of made me think of the book *Stranger to the Ground*. I was thinking about what the life of the guy in the bomber was like. What was he told about us versus what we were really like? What was he thinking right then about our aggressiveness? He probably knew about riots in our cities. Does he think our country is screwed up?

"I'm looking at him and thinking there are people starving and held ransom while he is over here flying. I wrote to my folks and an aunt and uncle I lived with in Colorado for a while —they're strong Episcopalians who've been behind the Iron Curtain on missionary things—how silly it was for each side to know so little about each other and to hate each other for reasons we don't even know why.

"I said it would be so neat if these guys could just come and land somewhere. The way they acted when they were in the airplane I feel I could walk up to a table and drink a beer with them and just sit and talk. I just said it would be so nice if we could do that. We could tell them what our family was like, what our home was like. They could tell us what theirs was like. We could be just like regular people. Then we could take off in our airplanes and do our jobs again."

I asked Brad as we talked on into the twilight whether he would dare talk so philosophically about the enemy, the Commies, in the ready room of the Red Rippers, one of the most macho squadrons on the carrier.

"I say it, and I catch a lot of crap for it. I'm also an environmentalist, still. So when they talk about strafing the

whales or dolphins, which people have done in the past—not in
this squadron—I say if I'm flying and I see them doing that, I'd
shoot them down. I think I'm serious. I don't know if I am or
not. So I catch a lot of crap.''

Not that Brad Goetsch would not be a warrior in a war. He
said he would do his damnedest to shoot down any Soviet plane
in his range. But the prospect of having to do something like
that in wartime did not stop him and a few other pilots with
whom I talked on the *Kennedy* from seeing the men inside the
Bears as human beings looking for a little light and laughter
with their fellow fliers.

The aviators told me that relationships with Soviet fliers were
not always cordial, however. The current state of affairs between
Washington and Moscow influenced what happened during
Bear intercepts. In times of tension, they said, instead of
toasting each other through the windows of their planes the
Americans and Russians gave each other the finger. I was told
that Navy aviators in the past had painstakingly made big signs
in Russian to be held against the cockpit plastic during an
intercept. They said favorite signs were: "Your mother sleeps
with a MiG pilot. MiG pilots eat shit."

On 1 September 1983, shortly before the *Kennedy* left
Norfolk, the Soviet air force shot down Korean Air Lines Flight
007, killing all the passengers on the civilian airliner which had
strayed into Soviet air space. Knowledgeable officers on the
Kennedy had no doubt the Soviets knew what they were
shooting down if for no other reason than that the passenger
plane was "squawking," sending out steady and internationally
known radio signals identifying itself. In light of that
shootdown, nobody I talked to on board expected the Bear
intercepts between Norfolk and Rio de Janeiro to be cordial
encounters. As we passed Cuba on our way south, I was half
listening for the order to start a Bear hunt. It came close to
midnight when I was in my room reading in my bunk.

"Launch the alert aircraft! That is, launch the alert aircraft!"

I got up and learned what little I could from the CAG office
and operations center about the launch. It was a Bear hunt. I
watched the launch and talked to the F-14 fliers after the hunt.

When the launch order resonated through the carrier, Lieutenants Dave "Tag" Price and Dan "Traps" Cloyd of VF-31
were on call to intercept any passing Bears. They were supposed
to be sitting in the ready room dressed for flight so they could be

shot off the bow within fifteen minutes. They quickly zipped up their heavy flight survival vest, which raised the weight of their flight gear to 40 pounds, yanked on their helmets and hurried toward "the roof," the flight deck.

Price was the pilot; Traps was the radar intercept officer, or RIO, in the backseat. The moon was high and bright as their steel-toed flight boots clomped across the catwalk. The boots were laced up high and tight so they would not scrape off if they got caught on the cockpit counter during ejection. The aviators did not have to snap on their flashlights. The moon lit the steel catwalk which hung over the starboard side of the ship above the hissing, black sea. They climbed the ladder leading up from the catwalk to the more reassuring, wide expanse of the darkened flight deck.

Pilot Tag Price was grateful for the moon, the naval aviator's best friend at night. With moonlight, he could see the horizon and know when it came time to land whether he was upside down or right side up as he hurtled down at 150 miles an hour toward the tiny flight deck pitching up and down on the dark, forbidding, unforgiving ocean. A full, bright moon was called a "commander's moon," one which would help the older pilots of commander rank and weakening eyesight land safely on the deck at night.

Tag had flown off and on carriers at night many times. But no landing was ever easy. He confided to me that night landings pushed him to the edge of terror. And the night landings never seemed to get any easier. He often longed to be off the carrier and back home in Mississippi shooting the rapids in a canoe, backpacking, and fishing. He owed the Navy another year of service for sending him to the U.S. Naval Academy and to flight school. He planned to gut it out. But he told me that his loss of enthusiasm for flying off the boat worried him. He worried about dulling his edge to the point he might do something wrong and kill himself and his radar intercept officer. But the moonlight took a lot of the worry out of the upcoming Bear hunt.

Tag and Traps reached their Tomcat, gave the outside a quick once-over, along with the Brown Shirt, a young sailor who, as plane captain, had checked over the plane earlier. Tag and Traps were looking for the obvious things that could kill them, like a wrench left in the intake or a leaking hydraulic line. Everything looked all right as best they could determine in the moonlight.

They climbed up the fold-in ladder on the left side of the plane and strapped themselves into the cockpit, Tag in the front and Traps in the back.

Tag went through the checklist of gauges to read and dials to set, with each step written out on a long piece of cardboard he had stuck on his right knee. Traps was going over the gadgetry in the back seat the same way, setting up the navigation system, punching the airborne equivalent of word processors and clicking the radio dials to the right channels. Tag started the engines, first the left and then the right. He set the twin gray-white throttles by his left hand at idle and waited for the deck crew to break down the plane, the expression for unhooking the parking chains and removing the chocks around the wheels. He followed the signals of the Yellow Shirts, young sailors who comprise one of the many specialty teams on the flight deck, to the catapult's launching spot. The Yellow Shirts waved pale yellow flashlights, called wands, to direct Tag across the deck. The Blue Shirts stabbed the dark with blue wands as they looked over the flaps and other control surfaces of the plane on the verge of being shot off the bow. The red lights of the Red Shirts joined the probing. They were the ordnance men, the ordies, who removed the safety wires on the Sparrow radar-guided missiles and Sidewinder heat-seeking missiles so that they could be fired. The noses of those Sidewinders were so sensitive to heat that they would send a hum into the pilot's earphones when they felt enough heat from another plane's exhaust to home in on it. The ordies tested the nose at this moment by passing their flashlights past it. This set off the hum that said death could be dealt out if the pilot squeezed the trigger on the control stick.

A Green Shirt standing on the deck to the left of the F-14 held up a lighted board with the number 66,000 on it. This confirmed to Tag and Traps that their takeoff weight was 66,000 pounds. The shot of steam which would hit the cylinder yanking the catapult hook down the deck would have to be strong enough to get a 66,000 pound plane from standstill to 170 miles an hour in two seconds. Traps acknowledged the weight as 66,000 pounds by waving his flashlight in a circular motion.

A hookup man went under the plane in a duck walk and hooked the launching bar on the nose gear into the shuttle. The catapult hook protruded from a long slot running the length of the takeoff path on the flight deck. Out of sight beneath the flight deck was a track and an eight-wheeled trolley. The hook was attached to the trolley which raced along at launch, pulling hook and airplane behind it.

The Green Shirt, seeing the launch bar in the plane's nose was firmly attached to the catapult hook, checked the holdback bar of the F-14. This bar led from the rear of the nose gear to a slot behind it in the catapult track. A thick bolt, shaped like a dumb bell, linked the hold-back bar on the plane to the steel deck of the ship. The bolt was supposed to hold the plane back until the instant the catapult hook exerted a precise and pre-set amount of pull. The pull would break the bolt, sending the plane racing down the deck and into the air—if everything worked right.

The catapult officer, carrying a green flashlight wand in his right hand and a red one in his left, waved the green light horizontally. This told Tag to push the throttles to full power, called military, but not up to the final notch which touched off the afterburners. The heavy fighter strained to break the grip of the holdback bolt. Tag tested the stubby, black control stick between his knees: left, right, forward, backward—or Father, Son, Holy Ghost, as some pilots repeated to remember the sequence. He tried the left and right rudder pedals to make the amen, the pilot's final blessing signifying that the plane's controls were working.

The catapult officer moved his green wand up and down this time rather than horizontally. Tag pushed the throttles the rest of the way in. Giant plumes of flame leaped out from the rear of two engines, lighting up the jet blast deflector wall behind them. The Tomcat struggled even harder against the bolt. It held.

The hookup man crawled under the straining plane for a last check. Everything looked hooked in solid. The hookup man gave a thumbs up in the semidark under the plane and scrambled out from under it.

Tag pulled on the red and green navigation lights, making his Tomcat look like a Christmas tree lying on its side. The lights told the launch crew on the deck, the captain on the bridge, and the Air Boss in the tower that the Tomcat was all set to be flung off the bow and into the night to chase the Russian Bear. Tag and Traps bent their heads slightly forward and tensed their neck muscles to take the shock of the catapult shot.

The catapult officer knelt down, facing the bow, and touched the deck with his green light. The Green Shirt standing on the catwalk on the dark edge of the deck saw the go signal, pushed the red, rectangular "fire" button on his instrument panel, which looked like a home fuse box, complete with hinged cover. His touch opened the gate for the tremendous burst of steam to smack the cylinder pulling the shuttle with the airplane attached down the catapult track. Tag and Traps felt the familiar smack in the back as the steam yank pushed them deep into their seats. The sudden speed compressed everything for an instant, including their eyeballs. There were two seconds of trolley rattle and then nothing but black as the Tomcat sailed into the night sky in front of the carrier.

"Good shot," Traps said to Tag over his microphone. This meant the catapult had given them enough momentum to allow the Tomcat's engines to keep the plane airborne. They might have had to eject and risk being run over by the ship if the cat shot had been too weak to keep them airborne for the precious seconds the engines needed to assert themselves. The flight deck crew which had done the launching stood in the cloud of steam rising up from the catapult track and watched the Tomcat rise high in the night sky, its afterburners glowing like twin planets in a race.

Commander Curly Paradis was in the eerie green semidark of the combat information center watching the hunt unfold on the radar scopes. The controllers sitting at their consoles studying the green dots reported three blips off in the direction of the Bears. The Soviets appeared to have sent three Bears out of Cuba, possibly to locate and fly over the *Kennedy*. The *Kennedy* launched two more Tomcats into the night.

Tag and Traps could see on their own radar screens that there were three Bears out in front of them. Traps, figuring the Soviet bombers were about 100 miles away, punched the keyboard buttons above his radar screen and worked a control stick between his knees. The stick focused the plane's radar beams on different portions of the sky. Traps relayed over the intercockpit communications system the best course for Tag to fly to intercept the lead Bear in the three-bomber formation. They heard over their radios that two other Toms had been launched to join the hunt. The *Kennedy* combat information center was not sure how many Russian planes were aloft when Tag and Traps were launched. Seconds mean miles of sky for supersonic aircraft. Command did not want to waste any time in getting the first fighter off the bow, so it did not wait until radar could tell them for sure how many Bears were up. Standing orders were to intercept enemy planes while they were hundreds of miles from the carrier.

Tag decided to intercept the lead Bear. The Tomcats coming up behind him could take on the other two. Tag pushed the throttle ahead a bit, thrusting the jet to a speed of about 575 miles an hour, 115 miles an hour faster than the Bears were going. He could have pushed the throttles all the way forward to light the afterburners for more speed, but this would have caused the engines to gulp fuel and a KA-6D tanker would have to be launched to refuel the Tomcat in midair. This would have added one more complication to the first hunt of the deployment.

Tag suddenly saw the distinctive pattern of the lead Bear's red anticollision lights and its red and green navigation lights. The Bear was winging northward up the American coast, making no apparent effort to search for the *Kennedy* farther out to sea. The Soviet bomber was maintaining a homeward course at a steady 460 miles an hour. Tag wheeled his Tomcat around and slid it into a spot about a quarter mile off the Bear's right wing. This would keep him between the Bear and the carrier. Tag and other F-14 pilots were instructed to steer clear of the Bear's tail, where guns were mounted. The Soviets shot something else from the tail this night: a blinding beam of light. Tag and Traps were startled. But they concluded the Bear crew was not trying to blind them because the light moved along the fuselage and wings of the Bear and then on the Tomcat, as if the Soviets did not want to risk any case of mistaken identity. The Soviets' downing of the Korean airliner was still fresh in everyone's mind. The Tomcat had the weapons to down a Russian bomber. The Bear crew might have figured they were going to be blown out of the sky under the same rationale their own leaders in Moscow had used: a Russian spy plane had intruded into American air space and was shot down. The Soviets, in wake of the downing of Flight 007, claimed they were going after a U.S. Air Force spy plane. The Air Force admitted that one of its reconnaissance planes had flown out of Alaska on a routine reconnaissance mission that same night, but was not in Soviet air space and had returned to its base before the Korean Air Lines 747 strayed into Soviet air space.

Frenchie Jancarski and Ollie Wright—who were to crash a month hence—were teamed up for the hunt. Frenchie roared into the formation and picked up the second bomber, keeping several yards of air space between them. Frenchie arched his Tomcat over the Bear, flying over the right wing and then the left. They got the same spotlight treatment as Tag and Traps as they looked over the second Bear in the formation. Lieutenant Commander Chuck "Mumbles" Scott and Lieutenant Commander Jack W. "Jocko" Lahren, his RIO, flew along the third Bear, keeping away from its lethal tail. Mumbles noticed that the bright light stayed focused on his plane. He concluded the Russians inside the Bear were photographing the Tomcat in great detail for their technical experts who would analyze the aerodynamic features of the advanced American fighters and enlarge the photographs to see what they could learn from them. It was all part of the cat-and-mouse game between the two superpowers.

The three Soviet bombers did not veer off toward the carrier to their east. They kept flying north, as if they were simply heading home to the Soviet Union after completing their rotation to Cuba. The *Kennedy* launched another plane to keep track of the Bears and the three Tomcats pursuing them. This fourth plane to join the hunt was the Grumman E-2C Hawkeye, an ungainly looking aircraft because of the huge pancake it carried on its back. The pancake housed a rotating radar unit which could see up, down, and all around. Three men sat in the back of the Hawkeye to work its sophisticated gear. The pilot and copilot up front just flew the plane. The Hawkeye positioned itself about halfway between the Bears and the carrier. This way the Hawkeye could serve as a radio relay station between the carrier and the Tomcats. The Hawkeye would relay instructions to the fighters in code. Even if a hostile aircraft homed in on the signals, it would be led back to the Hawkeye, not to the ship. The three men studying their radar scopes in back of the Hawkeye could see nothing unusual as they studied the blips of the hunted and the hunters on their scopes. No one in the combat information center in the ship, also watching on radar, saw anything to be worried about either. It looked as if the Russians were simply flying home after completing their temporary duty in Cuba. The Hawkeye orbited at 30,000 feet in the starlit sky, listening for instructions from the ship. Commander Robert L. "Bunky" Johnson Jr. was sitting in the middle of the three seats in the back of the Hawkeye. He was commander of the aircraft with the radio call sign of "Closeout." He received from the ship the message he had been anticipating and relayed it to the three Tomcats.

"Bandwagon. This is Closeout. RTB."

RTB stood for "return to base." The fighters were called home. Another U.S.–Soviet confrontation in that twilight zone between all out war and all out peace had ended peacefully. The point men for the two superpowers had brushed up against each other and then gone their separate ways.

There were several more Bear hunts as the *Kennedy* boiled south to the equator. The electronic wizards in the later hunts practiced their dark art with considerable success. Living or dying in any future war may well depend on who detects the other first in contests as far apart as 1,000 feet under the sea and six miles up in the sky. The United States and Soviet Union try to build each new submarine quieter than the last one, for example, to make it harder to detect. Both superpowers have put the keenest ears they can design into their attack submarines in hopes of hearing the other's first while sliding quietly through the depths. The same is true of aircraft. The keenest ears in the *Kennedy*'s air wing were in the EA-6B Prowler, S-3A Viking, and E-2C Hawkeye. All three were launched in some of the hunts conducted during the run south to Rio. Whenever all three picked up radar or other emissions from the Bear, they would trade information to make the points of a triangle. The triangulation would pinpoint exactly where the Bear was in the sky.

Happily for the United States, the Soviet Union was as noisy in the sky in 1983 as it was under the sea. This made their planes easy to detect. U.S. electronic eavesdropping planes, particularly the EA-6B, and Electronic Sensing Measures —called ESM—on the *Kennedy* would hear the Russian bombers when they were still hundreds of miles from the carrier. These "cuts" on a bomber's position enabled the E-2C Hawkeye to hang and direct the F-14 Tomcat fighters to the Bear. The Soviets knew the general hunting abilities of U.S. carrier aircraft from years of such confrontations, but kept trying to learn more about them to develop countermeasures.

By the time we approached the equator, the Soviets stayed out of hunting distance. This relief from alerts enabled the whole ship to concentrate on the ceremony to mark the crossing of the equator. I was among the majority, a low-life wog who had not crossed the equator before. Those who had crossed were shellbacks. I vainly tried to convince Fred Major, a shellback, that my flying over the equator on the way to Vietnam qualified me for his fraternity. He served me a summons to appear before the royal court of King Neptune on the morning of 8 October 1983. The end of my long summons stated:

"Whereas: You are specifically charged with the heinous crimes of impersonating an aviator on the Fathom Show and stating that your job was to write a book, thereby admitting you do not work for a living!"

On the appointed morning, I reported to my master who put a rope around my neck and ordered me to stay on my knees and crawl with thousands of other wogs down to the hangar bay for breakfast. We crawled like the cattle we were to a trough of spoiled food and had our heads pushed deep into it several times. We were whacked with short lengths of fire hose all the way to the plane elevator, taken to the flight deck, and driven through a shower of water—which felt good and cleansing. Then we were herded into a pig sty, a tank of green water, and an appearance before King Neptune. I was locked in the stocks several times and ordered to roll in the garbage-filled sty repeatedly until deemed eligible to crawl down to the finish line on the flight deck. Once across, I was embraced as a shellback and invited to throw my foul clothes into the Atlantic Ocean. A Russian trawler stood about two miles off our stern watching. I wondered as I tossed my torn khakis toward him what he thought of the crazy Americans circled in his binoculars.

"Hey George!" Sammy said to me a few mornings after going through the shellback initiation. "Why don't you leave these black shoe pukes and come up and live with us? We've got a room for you. You've spent enough time down here with these black-shoe pukes. Come on up, I'll help you move."

I thought about the order for a few seconds. The idea of a carrier was to launch airplanes. And I had been spending more and more of my time with squadrons. So, sure, why not get deeper into the main action on the carrier? I accepted Sammy's offer with no offense intended to my roommate, Rick Titi, or anyone else in the ship's company. We grabbed my gear and stowed it in another two-man room. My new roommate was Lieutenant Tom Duntemann, an affable flight surgeon who loved to fly in the backseat of the F-14 when hops were available to him. Our room was one of four along a short passageway of four two-man rooms, each occupied by officers from the CAG staff. We came to call our complex The Condo and would celebrate our fellowship often and loud in the next six months of the cruise.

Sammy gave me a second invitation: "Why don't you join our admin in Rio?"

He explained that an admin resembled a fraternity house party. The members of the admin chip in to rent a suite of rooms, make one the party room and bar, and sleep in the other two with far more people than the hotel management suspects or charges for. I said sure, kicked in my share, and looked forward to celebrating the first liberty of the cruise with my colorful shipmates who had overlooked my affiliation with the press—at least until they saw whether I would be a player or not in Rio.

7   Rio—First Liberty

"HEY! Understand you're going hog hunting in Rio," one sailor said to his buddy in the tower while they were waiting for planes to start landing.

"Yeah. You coming?"

"Naw."

"Why not? Them girls is really hot."

"Don't want the clap."

"So who's going to get the clap?"

"You are."

"Shee-it!"

"See you in the clap line."

I laughed over my shoulder as I left the sailors in the tower for the chaplain's office deep in the ship. When I arrived, Chief Chaplain Jim Doffin was rereading the teletype message which confirmed that the Navy sticks the chaplains with many of the tedious duties of a port call, like leading schoolchildren on a tour of the ship or meeting with local citizen groups. The message presaged that Doffin and his fellow men of the cloth would be school painting while many of the sailors would be "hog hunting," looking for easy women to bed down with during liberty.

GARY, started the message from a naval attaché in the U.S. Embassy in Rio,

IF JFK IS INTERESTED IN A HUMANITARIAN PROJECT WHILE IN RIO, I HAVE A GOOD ONE FOR YOU. DISCUSSION WITH LOCAL SCHOOL OFFICIALS AND LOCAL AMERICAN WOMAN'S GROUP IN RIO REVEALS THAT THERE IS A BRAZILIAN PUBLIC SCHOOL NAMED ESCOLA PRESIDENTE JOHN KENNEDY. IT IS A SMALL SCHOOL OF APPROXIMATELY 400 STUDENTS LOCATED IN ONE OF THE POOR SECTIONS OF RIO. THE SCHOOL IS VERY MUCH IN NEED OF PAINTING. IN RIO, LABOR IS VERY INEXPENSIVE. PAINT AND PAINT BRUSHES ARE VERY EXPENSIVE. TWO HUNDRED GALLONS OF WHITE PAINT WOULD PAINT THE SCHOOL. IDEALLY, THE SHIP WOULD PROVIDE THE PAINT AND PAINT BRUSHES AND A GROUP OF SAILORS, PARENTS, AND TEACHERS WOULD PAINT THE SCHOOL. AGAIN, IT IS THE MATERIALS WHICH ARE BEYOND THE MEANS OF THE SCHOOL. THIS PROJECT IS WORTHWHILE AND WOULD RECEIVE POSITIVE REACTION FROM THE PRESS.

The cable had pulsed the *Kennedy* management. Wheatley had scrawled a note across the top of it to Executive Officer Pieno: "XO—let's do it." The next note said: "Chaplain Doffin for action." The buck had stopped with the chaplains. Now they had to scare up the paint from the first lieutenant and find twenty sailors who would volunteer to paint a school during their liberty rather than go hog hunting. The U.S. Embassy would provide a bus for this carrot part of the *Kennedy*'s gunboat diplomacy. The Air Wing would stage an air show later to reveal the stick.

Commander John J. Mazach, the commander of Air Wing Three who was called CAG by everyone on the ship from the days when planes on a carrier were called an air group and its commander CAG for commander of the air group, would have to perform some special duty, too, before he could cut loose in Rio. Captain Wheatley had informed him he would be anchoring the ship in the harbor. Senior aviators were given practice anchoring a ship against the day they might be selected to command a carrier. Aviators like Mazach were far more comfortable in an airplane's cockpit than on a ship's bridge. But orders were orders. Mazach would try his hand at dropping a huge anchor on a designated patch of bottom once the *Kennedy* reached the inner part of the harbor of Rio de Janeiro.

"Here's the whole shiteroo," Mazach told me in his one-man cabin as he handed me the thick packet of instructions for anchoring the *Kennedy*. The paper documented the obvious by stating early on that anchoring can be dangerous for the ship and the men on it if not performed correctly. The Navy seems to write papers for everything. Whole forests must go down to make all this paper.

"Because *John F. Kennedy* has no underwater protrusions at the bow, such as a sonar dome," the paper stated, "the starboard anchor may be dropped with weigh on without fear of damaging the chain or underwater hull structures. Too much weigh on could, of course, overstress the chain; therefore, except in emergency situations, the starboard anchor is not lowered to the bottom at more than two knots or trailed in the water at speeds above eight knots."

Anchoring day dawned foggy but calm. Mazach would not have to fight wind and waves in trying to get the *Kennedy* over the X on the chart on the bridge. I shuttled between the bridge and the forecastle where the dirty work of lowering the anchor would be done.

Mazach stood in the center of the bridge looking through the eyecup of a precision navigation instrument called an alidade. Captain Wheatley sat on the port side of the bridge in his leather chair pretending he had no qualms at all about this new hand on the rudder of his ship. The ship's navigator, Captain Gary Witzenburg, called Gator, stood on Mazach's right also trying to look unconcerned. Mazach was trying to drop the anchor on that imaginary spot where his bearing intersected the two landmarks on shore to the left and right of the bow. He dared not wait until he reached the intersection to tell the gang in the forecastle to start lowering the anchor. He had to allow time for the anchor and its huge chain to reach the bottom and bite into the mud deep enough to hold the 83,000-ton carrier.

"All engines ahead two thirds," Mazach commanded. He felt he was bearing down upon the auto bridge dead ahead of the carrier uncomfortably fast. Could he stop this big mother if he had to? The X was still 5,000 yards ahead. An arched auto bridge was beyond the X—something he would not like to hit.

"All engines ahead one third," Mazach ordered to slow the carrier's forward speed. He felt the ship ease back. He gave the next command from the anchoring instruction book.

"Commence walking anchor out to the water's edge."

The walking command sent into action the crew in the forecastle, the narrow compartment in the bow of ship where the anchors and chain are stored. I went there to watch the art of anchoring a carrier close up. The anchor chain was lying across the blue and silver deck of the forecastle like a menacing boa constrictor. Every deck hand in the forecastle was respectful of the anchors and their chain. Each link weighed 360 pounds. The starboard anchor which was to be dropped this morning weighed 30 tons. A man could get killed if he got in the way of the chain as the anchor pulled it out of the ship and down to the harbor bottom. Joel Geister, who loved to get his own hands dirty, and a chief were supervising the kids, as had been the case in Brinson's boiler room. The deck apes, boatswain's mates, and the pit snipes, boiler technicians, had a lot in common. They were rough to each other on the surface but fraternal underneath. They all did heavy lifting.

Geister ordered his men to release just enough chain to hang the anchor a few feet above the water but not in it. A boatswain's mate picked up a sledge hammer and slammed off the stop keeping the anchor chain inside the ship. The chain raced across the deck, rattling and smoking with dust as it followed the anchor down toward the water. Brakes! The chain was braked to a stop, leaving the 30-ton anchor hanging over the greasy water of Rio's harbor. The water was 66 feet deep where we were now. The *Kennedy* drew 36 feet, 9 inches. The harbor tide was about two feet. No way the *Kennedy* could go aground at low tide in this spot.

"All engines stop," CAG Mazach commanded.

"All engines back one-third."

The *Kennedy*'s four propellers reversed to break the forward momentum of the carrier. She was only 420 yards from the imaginary X on the harbor's slightly ruffled face. The ship seemed to come to a full stop, but it was hard to tell whether she was drifting forward, backward, sideways, or standing still because there was no reference point on the water. The *Kennedy* would have to make its own reference points on the surface of the harbor, and quickly. The carpenter shop had anticipated the need.

Captain Wheatley left his chair on the port side of the bridge, strode over to a plastic bag on the starboard edge and drew out a block of mahogany with his left hand. He wound up his body like a baseball pitcher and hurled the block of wood out the open window of the auxiliary conning station.

"Nobody can throw a chip farther than the captain," Wheatley exclaimed challengingly.

His chip from the bagful sent up by the ship's carpenter arced down from the bridge and splashed out of hearing on the water hundreds of feet below the bridge. Other officers hurled chips, each trying to outdistance the captain. Soon a fleet of mahogany chips bobbed together like toy boats abeam of the bridge. They did not look as if they were moving forward or backward. Mazach decided the *Kennedy* had come to a dead stop. I wondered if the skippers of sailing ships used the same primitive method for determining when their ships were dead in the water. Nobody seemed to know, but the officers said twentieth-century technology has yet to come up with anything more foolproof than the chips.

"Let go the starboard anchor," Mazach commanded.

Geister's crew in the forecastle let the anchor ride down to the bottom of the harbor. Mazach ordered the ship to back away from the anchor when it hit the mud. This stretched 462 feet of heavy chain straight across the bottom. The chain was braked so no more of it would pay out. The *Kennedy* kept backing down, pulling the anchor chain taut so the huge flukes of the anchor dug themselves deep into the mud.

"Pass stoppers," Mazach commanded. The boatswain's mate picked up his sledge hammer again and pounded home the stop to lock the anchor chain in place. Geister radioed to the bridge that the 83,000-carrier was safely anchored in Rio's harbor mud. He wrote the time down in his green book: 0830 13 October 1983. The *Kennedy* was solidly anchored. The liberty exodus could begin.

I left the forecastle for my room to get ready for liberty. On the way I walked through the sleeping compartment of sailors. They were gleefully pulling on Adidas, blue jeans and colorful shirts in between running to the head for one last look at themselves in the mirror. Civilian clothes, not uniforms, was the designated dress for sailors on liberty. The Navy was sensitive to the possibility that citizens in foreign ports might resent an invasion of American military men. Civilian clothes would make the Navy's presence in Rio less visible and strident. The sailors shouted to each other the names of places to meet once they got off the boat. Somebody shouted that the Cowboy Club in the Gut—the string of tawdry bars closest to the landing—was supposed to have everything: hot women, cold beer, and loud music. The sailors could not go ashore all at once. They would be going to town in shifts on the liberty ferries which were now heading out toward the carrier to fulfill their Navy contracts.

In the midst of getting ready for liberty myself, I stopped in Sammy Bonanno's room, just around the passageway from the new one I shared with Tom Duntemann. Sammy was a fun-loving F-14 pilot until he got out on the platform at the edge of the flight deck to help pilots down as the landing signal officer. Then he was deadly serious—and damn good, according to the pilots. Sammy was angling a broad-brimmed hat on his head when I entered his room. Commander Robyn "Potsie" Weber, the thirty-six-year-old chief of staff for Air Wing Three, saw the hat and recoiled in horror. Potsie was so fastidious, particularly with his hair, that aviators had nick-named him after the character in the *Happy Days* television program.

"You're not going to wear that hat in Rio, are you?" Potsie asked incredulously.

"This is a great hat," Sammy answered. "Sure, I'm going to wear it."

Sammy sure as hell was going to look like a money-pockets American tourist on this beach. Below the straw hat were a loud sport shirt, dark slacks, and moccasins. He took one look at me in my sport coat and open-necked shirt and shouted:

"George! Where the hell are you going? This is liberty, Boy!"

I was overdressed for Navy liberty. But I kept the coat on, not so much for formality, but because I needed the pockets for my passport, notebooks, tape recorder, camera, and other para-phernalia of the peripatetic chronicler. I walked with Sammy and Potsie toward the hangar bay where another member of our admin was standing guard over parachute bags containing key ingredients for the liberty in Rio: bottles of all kinds of booze. The Navy forbids keeping or drinking liquor in rooms aboard ship but it can be purchased and stored in the hold for parties on shore.

"I think we got it all," said Lieutenant Commander Ronald "Hawk" Hoppock, thirty-two, an imposing looking A-7 pilot

—six-foot-four, bushy eyebrows and mustache, and piercing brown eyes. He earned his nickname by spotting airplanes before anyone else could see them during aerial dogfighting. Hawk was standing above two olive drab parachute bags with thick cloth handles. Sammy and Hawk carried one of the heavy bags; Potsie and I hefted the second one. We walked down a steep ladder to the float set up to enable officers to walk onto the ferries and liberty launches. We finally wrestled ourselves and heavy bags aboard a liberty boat and scanned the shore for our first look at Rio de Janeiro. It was still too foggy to make out the mountaintop statue of Christ looking down on the harbor. Even so, the aviators were already calling the statue "Paddles" because its outstretched arms reminded them of the landing signal officers of an earlier day who waved paddles to help get planes safely down on the deck.

Sammy, Potsie, Hawk, and I stood under a tree at Fleet Landing trying to get out of the drizzle. We finally snagged two cabs and headed out of downtown Rio for the Royal Othon Hotel out on Copacabana Beach, Rio's Miami Beach. As the cab snaked through the city, I was struck by Rio's drabness and joylessness. I had read how this Paris of South America had been laid low by galloping inflation and harsh military rule, but I did not expect this joylessness to be so obvious on the faces of the ordinary people.

"I got the gouge," (navalese for hot information), enthused one of the pilots from the air wing as we got out of our cab in front of the Royal Othon. His eyes were shining. He urged us to move off the driveway, quickly change American money into Brazilian, check into the hotel, and then rush with him to the hot spot he had heard about.

"A foreign service officer told me about it. It's the Oasis. The girls are government-inspected. They give you blow jobs and cold beer. Come on. The word will spread like wildfire. We've got to get over there before it gets crowded. Go get some money."

His breathless commercial drew raucous laughter but few takers. Aviators are pretty systematic people—perhaps from having to push all those switches and buttons in the cockpit in a certain order. Most of them wanted to change money, check into their hotels and admins, and only then decide where to go and with whom. They discovered that the bank with the best exchange rate was the white Ford parked alongside the hotel. It soon became known as the Banque de Ford.

"Welcome," laughed Lieutenant Commander Don "Rookie" Williams, the CAG staff intelligence officer, as I entered the admin on the 26th floor of the Royal Othon. "Have a drink," Rookie said, sweeping his hand over the desk loaded with bottles of gin, vodka, bourbon, scotch, rum, and Coca-Cola. We had taken sixteen days to make Rio. The departure blues had dissipated. There was no way to know the rest of the deployment would bear no resemblance to the schedule and that the *Kennedy* would stay at sea for a hundred days without going into another port. We were ashore at the moment. Rookie and everyone else piling into the admin seemed to be in the mood to celebrate.

I set down my bag, took a drink of bourbon and water and soaked up the scene. This fraternity party of grown men was just starting its roll down the runway. Some of the CAG staff officers had not yet arrived, including my roommate, "Doc" Duntemann. His fellow flight surgeon and constant rival, Lieutenant Joe "Fighter Doc" Piorkowski, had beat him to the admin, stowing his guitar in the corner of the suite's living room. The playing and singing would not start until after the officers went to the "must attend" cocktail party hosted by the Brazilian Navy. The U.S. Navy and Brazilian Navy officers were kindred spirits even though their governments were on opposite sides during the war over the Falkland Islands. Brazilian officers told some of the *Kennedy* officers that they were embarrassed by the poor showing Argentina had made and were glad to see a carrier back in Rio.

I left the admin to explore the rest of the hotel. Some officers were already feeling mellow at the cocktail lounge on the roof by the pool.

"You should be proud of me, George," shouted one, a former hotshot pilot, who had needled me about being a newspaperman. "The first thing I did when I got here was buy a newspaper. Only after that did I buy a blow job."

I laughed and gave him a thumbs up. The officer was famous for both telling and living tall tales. I did not know which was the case this first day of liberty.

After the must-attend formal reception hosted by the Brazilian Navy, the *Kennedy* officers returned to their hotel admins, hung up their choker whites, slid into plaid shirts, and proceeded to party. Our admin rocked into the pre-dawn hours, thanks to an indefatigable Joe on the guitar and an endless stream of songs led by Potsie.

I walked through the lobby a few times and joined friends for drinks in the bars outside the admin. I noticed the most sedate officers were those who had sent for their wives. I learned that with the high officer pay of the 1980s, together with the salary of working wives, the camp followers for aircraft carriers were often well tailored suburban housewives or careerists who flew in during the cruise to rekindle the marriage and break the loneliness of separation. I saw only three Navy wives this first night in Rio. I was told that most of the women were waiting until later in the cruise to join their husbands, they hoped in a European port. Most wives and girlfriends were back home in Navy towns signing up for charter flights and planning tours together after the carrier took their men back out to sea after a few days liberty somewhere on the other side of the world.

At first light the morning of 14 October 1983—the second day of liberty—everyone from the CAG admin was, to use navalese, tits up. Dead in their beds, including me. Chaplain Jim Doffin, by contrast, was bustling around the ship like Santa Claus packing his sack. He and his two fellow chaplains, George Byrum and Mike Walsh, were frantically assembling their volunteer work party of twenty-two sailors and checking out the paint and brushes. They were trying to get off the carrier before 8:00 A.M. so they could get an early start painting the John F. Kennedy School. The bus would be waiting for them at Fleet Landing if the embassy had come through as promised. I interviewed the chaplains afterward to find out how their unusual day of good works and public relations had gone for them.

Carrying 200 gallons of paint, dozens of brushes, and 27 box lunches, the *Kennedy* work party climbed into the liberty ferry. Chaplain Doffin had gathered himself for the Rio liberty in the quiet of the finally still ship. No sailor presented himself at his door to discuss a heart-wrenching problem. No frantic calls from the XO jangled the phones in the chaplain's office and stateroom. Doffin was glad to have something to do in Rio. He looked from the liberty boat and decided the rain coming down on him would last all day. His work party could not paint the outside of the John F. Kennedy School this day. It would have to paint the inside.

A crowd of curious teachers, wide-eyed Portuguese students, and a few American officials watched the free-swinging American sailors climb down from their big bus. Stiff greetings gave way to laughter as the brushes and rollers started to spread glistening white paint all over the school walls. The students from grades one through eight showed off their dancing and soccer ball kicking as these crazy Americans cheered and worked. Then the big Americans suddenly went away in their big bus at 4:00 P.M. They had painted seven classrooms, two offices, the stair well, and portico. And now they were rushing off someplace else in the rain.

"Hey, Chaplain!" shouted one of the sailors as the bus snaked along Copacabana Beach. "You can baptize us right out there in the ocean."

Doffin, Byrum, and Walsh conferred. They told the driver to stop the bus. The sailor was right. They could baptize the four sailors who had been requesting the rites, here and now. The painting party left the bus. Four sailors stood on the edge of the surf in paint-blotched work shorts or their skivvies. Chaplain Byrum rolled up his khakis. The party of five waded out into the surf as a soft rain coated their bobbing heads.

Byrum took the first man. They stood face to face in the surf. Byrum held the man at the waist with his left hand and raised his right one over the head of the sailor for the baptismal pronouncement:

"Upon your profession of faith, I baptize you in the name of the Father, of the Son and of The Holy Ghost."

He pushed the sailor backward until the sea covered him totally. Byrum after a few seconds pulled the sailor up from the back of the neck. The sailor felt born again as he shook the Atlantic Ocean out of his ears.

Byrum performed the baptismal ceremony three more times as Doffin, Walsh, and the rest of the work party sailors stood on the beach like disciples at the Sea of Galilee. The sailors walked out of the surf to the cheers of their buddies on the beach. The newly baptized men were Petty Officers, First Class George Adee, Third Class Larry Darvin, Third Class Mark Escamillia, and Second Class Mark Patterson. Chaplin Doffin saw the four baptisms in the sea as cause for celebration. He told the bus driver to leave the work party off near Fleet Landing for a celebration dinner—at the Rio McDonald's. An aircraft carrier is a city full of different people who do all kinds of different things with their lives at home, at sea, and on liberty.

8 Mishaps Continued

"PLANE in the water! Plane in the water!"

I heard the call boom out of the loudspeakers shortly before noon on 11 November 1983. We were orbiting off Lebanon after an uneventful crossing of the Atlantic. I rushed up to the bridge from the 03 level of the carrier. I took two of the steel steps at a time, entered the captain's sanctum of the inner bridge, and immediately felt the gloom of a funeral parlor. The officers and sailors standing on the bridge were talking in whispers. The *Kennedy* had lost Bam Bam and Belly just three days earlier when their plane crashed into the Mediterranean and disappeared with no final sound of distress. All of a sudden this lucky carrier, this great ship which had won so many awards seemed cursed. Had we just lost two more fliers to the Med for no apparent reason?

"What did you see?" I asked the sailor who had been the lookout on the outside balcony in front of the captain's bridge.

"The end was toward the water, and the nose was up in the air, and then it hit," replied Seaman Recruit Nathan B. Amos.

That was all anyone had seen four miles out in front of the ship as Frenchie Jancarski and Ollie Wright left the safety of the sky and plunged into the sea. No one on the carrier knew that Frenchie was near death as he bobbed unconscious on the Med while Ollie was frantically waving at the searching helicopters he could see so easily. But the helicopter crews could not see him because it takes only a small wave to hide a human head in the folds of the Mediterranean.

Up in the back of helicopter Number 610, Petty Officer Third Class John Curran suddenly saw something red on the sea. Lieutenant Commander Tom Withers, the pilot, headed toward it. It was the red of a helmet. Withers radioed to Airman Daniel Rockel, twenty, of Dixon, California, to get ready to jump out of the hovering chopper. His first job would be to determine if there were a body under the floating helmet. His second would be to attach a rescue harness to the body, if there was one.

Curran tapped Rockel on the shoulder three times. This was the jump signal.

Rockel coiled his body slightly for the jump into the sea fifteen feet below. He told himself to keep his legs at a slight angle so they would prevent his body from going too deep into the water. A deep dive would cost seconds which might mean the difference between the man below him living or dying. Holding his right hand over his face mask, Rockel jumped. Withers pulled the helicopter higher into the sky to reduce the spray being kicked up by the downwash of the whirling blades.

Rockel swam over to the red-and-black helmet. A head was inside it and a body was still attached to it. "Thank God," Rockel thought as he put his mouth close to the ear of the helmet.

"Hey Buddy!" he shouted above the noise of the helicopter. "Can you hear me? Are you OK?"

No response. Rockel removed the torn oxygen mask. He saw Frenchie's face. It had the sickly white, blank look of a dead man. Frenchie's open eyes stared unblinking. Rockel thought Frenchie was dead. Then he noticed Frenchie was breathing. Rockel paddled himself down into the water to search around Frenchie's body for injuries and entangled parachute shrouds. He touched Frenchie's left ankle and felt it swivel as if it were on a thread. Rockel gave the hand signals to the helicopter to lower the horse collar. The collar descended from the hoist on a steel cable and rested on the water. Rockel pulled the collar over to Frenchie. The rescue swimmer snapped himself and Frenchie into it and gave the hoist signal. Curran twisted the collar around so Frenchie could be laid on his back on the helicopter floor. Frenchie's lips had turned blue. Rockel and Curran read Frenchie's name tag on his flight suit and identified him to the pilot and copilot who, in turn, radioed the news to the anxious ship. Pilot Withers raced for the flight deck about five miles away.

The second helicopter kept searching in a systematic pattern for the second aviator now known on the ship to be Ollie. Ollie heard the helicopters but failed in repeated attempts to attract their attention. He remembered his survival training and tried to follow it as he bobbed in the water. He pulled out from his survival vest a day/night flare. The day end for emitting smoke would not light. He lit the red flare at the other end designed for nighttime. The red flame would attract rescuers at night but would not show up as well as smoke in bright sunlight. If the day end did not work, Navy instructors had told Ollie to douse the night flame in water and then hold the smoking night flare above the waves. Ollie tried to go by the Navy book but the red flare would not go out and start smoking. So he decided to hold up the flaming red night torch. Theory be damned. Somebody in the helicopter spotted it. The rescue bird flew to Ollie and perched itself in the sky over his head.

Airman Mark Phillips, twenty, of Charleston, South Carolina, the swimmer in the helicopter, stood in the open doorway above Ollie. First Crewman Mike Mellema, twenty-two, of Cadillac, Michigan, tapped Phillips on the shoulder three times. Phillips jumped, holding his legs in the bent position for the same kind of shallow dive Rockel had executed. He swam over to Ollie as the helicopter pilot, Lieutenant Rich Strickland, thirty-five, of Worland, Wyoming, took the helicopter up to 40 feet to reduce the wind the blades were sending down on Ollie and Phillips.

"Where's your D ring?" Phillips shouted into Ollie's helmeted ear.

Ollie held up that ring anchored to his survival vest. Phillips signaled to the helicopter to lower the rescue cable. Mellema sent down the hook. Phillips let it hit the water to draw off any buildup of static electricity before grabbing it. He snapped the cable into the D ring on Ollie's vest and snapped himself to Ollie as well. He raised his hand for the hoist signal.

"OK," Phillips shouted into Ollie's ear. "We're going up."

With some difficulty, Mellema and Phillips twisted the bulky

Ollie so his back was to the side door. Then they worked him onto the floor of the helicopter on his back. His feet were still sticking out over the Mediterranean when Mellema ripped the Velcro-secured name tag off Ollie's flight suit. The crew up front radioed the ship that Ollie was safely in hand. After feeling him over for broken bones, Phillips and Mellema helped Ollie to a seat on the nylon bench running along the inside of the rear helicopter compartment. His life preserver was still inflated. It bloated his body so much that he had to use the female end from one seat belt and the male end from another to strap himself into the chopper.

"After surviving the ejection," Ollie told me later, "I didn't want to fall out the damn door."

Mellema asked Ollie: "Are you the only one?"

"No. There were two of us."

"Two airplanes?" Mellema pressed.

"No," Ollie replied. "Just one airplane. An F-14. Two guys."

A few minutes later Mellema returned to Ollie and said, "We picked up the other guy. He's got a compound fracture of his leg, but he's still alive."

Ollie felt a little relieved. He still wondered how Frenchie was doing. He looked out the side door and caught a glimpse of home, the carrier. The door slid shut. He felt the helicopter settle down on what he assumed was the carrier. The side door slid open again. He saw the black, nonskid surface of the flight deck beckoning. He unsnapped his double length seat belt, walked toward the open door, and jumped out onto the deck. He hit hard. The drop was farther than he thought. Flight Surgeon Tom Duntemann rushed up to him.

"Are you hurt?" Duntemann asked.

"No. I'm fine."

Ollie walked toward the battle dressing station inside the carrier island on the starboard side of the ship. He dropped sea water as he walked. He took off his helmet and the scull cap under it as soon as he got inside the station. He turned to the medical team that had been escorting him.

"Well, that's a shitty way to end a hop."

Frenchie was landed on the flight deck a few minutes after Ollie. He was still unconscious, near death. The medical team gasped inwardly when they first saw him as they leaned into the helicopter. His face was ashen, his lips blue. Corpsmen lifted him as gently as they could onto a stretcher and carried him to the elevator on the flight deck. The doctors surrounded Frenchie as they walked hurriedly to the sick bay two decks below. Dr. Howard H. Kaminsky, assistant chief of surgery at the Naval Medical Center in Bethesda, got his first look at Frenchie there. He feared he would die. Kaminsky was on temporary duty on the *Kennedy* while its regular senior surgeon, Lieutenant Commander William Hamilton, was back in the United States taking board examinations.

The medical resources of the ship were mobilized. Kaminsky and Duntemann ministered to the patient directly while Commander Myron Almond, the ship's senior medical officer, brought in the dental surgeon to help with the blood work. Frenchie was out of his head, yelling obscenities. This was good. It showed life.

"Get your fucking hands off of me," Frenchie shouted.

Kaminsky went after the most obvious problem first. He and Duntemann stanched the bleeding from the broken left leg. They cut away the irreparable tissue and splinted the broken bone. Frenchie was in shock. His pulse was extremely weak. He was clearly in grave trouble. Intravenous tubules were inserted in both arms to feed liquids into his body. X-rays were taken to see where else he might be injured. He needed blood. The ship put out a call for O-negative over the loudspeakers. This type would mix with whatever type Frenchie had. The response to the call was immediate and heartfelt. Sailors lined the passageway outside the hospital ward to offer their blood. They wanted to save him even though they did not know him. They were all shipmates now. A second call went out for A-positive blood, Frenchie's type. More sailors responded.

Warm whole blood soon was flowing into the dying aviator. But the transfusions brought an unexpected and unwelcome result. Frenchie's blood pressure went down rather than up. The whole blood had brought Frenchie out of shock. The phenomenal human body shuts down the blood vessels leading to any but the most vital areas, like the brain, when it goes into shock. The transfusions had fooled the body into letting go of its grip on these less vital vessels. Frenchie's pressure dropped because he had a bad leak in one of these vessels and the blood was pouring out of it. This would kill him if the leak were not patched.

Frenchie's abdomen was swollen, perhaps from the leaking blood. Kaminsky pierced it with a straw-like tube to find out. The tube filled up with blood. The leak was inside the abdomen. Kaminsky felt he had to subject Frenchie to the strain and risk of an abdominal operation to stop the internal bleeding.

Frenchie was put under by Lieutenant Commander William Noble, an anesthesiologist, who carefully hand-squeezed the bulbs sending the anesthetic into Frenchie. Lieutenant Greg Lescavage, the ship's dental surgeon, stood beside Frenchie overseeing the transfusions. It would have been nice to have a blood-gas machine during this operation. The *Kennedy*'s was sitting on the dock in Norfolk waiting to be shipped. Hospital Corpsmen Third Class Gary Green, Victor Marsh, Walter Dixon, and Patrick Hopkins shuttled in and out of the operating room.

Kaminsky sliced open Frenchie's abdomen. Blood gushed out the opening and flowed onto the floor all around Kaminsky's feet.

"Get some sheets!" he commanded. They were thrown on the floor so Kaminsky could keep standing over Frenchie without slipping on blood.

Kaminsky deftly clamped his hand over the aorta while he examined Frenchie's spleen. The spleen was ruptured beyond repair. It was leaking blood. It would have to come out. Kaminsky told Duntemann to put his hand on the aorta so Kaminsky could cut out the ruined spleen. Kaminsky tied shut the blood vessels that had led in and out of the spleen. Frenchie's blood pressure started rising; the leak was fixed. Kaminsky sewed up the incision. Frenchie's blood pressure stabilized. Lady Luck, and the medical team, pulled him back from death's door. He could live, even fly, without a spleen; though he would have to take drugs to substitute for the immunity the spleen provides against some diseases.

Frenchie had other medical problems. His calcium count was low. This might mean his pancreas, which produces digestive juices, had been torn. Juices leaking from the pancreas could eat body tissue. Frenchie was also incoherent after his blood pressure stabilized. His brain could have been gravely injured as he smacked into wreckage on the surface of the sea. He needed to be diagnosed by specialists and by equipment which the *Kennedy* did not have. The medical team decided to have

Frenchie flown off the carrier to the Army hospital in Landstuhl, West Germany, the next morning.

Commander John Burch, skipper of VF-31, came down to see the corpsmen carry Frenchie out of the sick bay as I stood to the side. Burch's face as he looked down on Frenchie was the picture of devastation. Frenchie's mustache looked limp on his still ashen face. He made no sign of life as the corpsman carried him past.

The Navy is infuriatingly brief when it comes to telling families about airplane crashes at sea. The bureaucracy steps in between the skeletal notification of a "mishap under investigation" and the flesh of the accident. Navy women know this, tolerate it, but use the unofficial network to find out what really happened to their men 7,000 miles away out on some damn ocean somewhere. Ollie tried to relieve the anxiety he knew his wife, Sue, would feel once she heard whatever few words the Navy put out officially about the crash. Ollie sent her a wire from the ship saying he was all right. Navy rules restricted what he could put in the wire. The details would have to go into a letter which Sue might not get for two months.

Every wife of a naval aviator lives in dread of seeing a Navy officer from the squadron come walking up the front walk in full uniform. This is the way the Navy tells the fresh widow that her husband is lying on the bottom of the ocean somewhere and will stay there forever. The messenger of death cannot tell her how or why it happened. Usually because, as in the case of Bam Bam and Belly, nobody knows. Sometimes it is because the pilot made a dumb mistake that the men try to keep quiet. But this usually becomes known in the special club that is squadron wives. The quiet knowing of the women becomes part of the weave of the squadron. The men talk to each other about "the dumb shit who got too low." The women utter to each other only the code words and change the subject. The men have blind faith in their flying machines. The women do not. They know better. They know machines break—every machine. A washing machine. An airplane. They know also men make mistakes —every man. Their husband. Everybody's husband.

Often the women hear about a Navy airplane crashing, but not who was in it, from newspapers or television stations before the Navy bureaucracy gets the few lines of notification written, approved, and released. Navy wives and girl friends take to the telephone to figure out who could have been killed. They narrow it down from the sketchy details on where and when it happened. Aviators in position to communicate send the word a hundred unofficial ways back over the oceans to let the women know it was not them this time, just as Ollie did. The women who learn it was not their man, thank God, just as Ollie's wife Sue did. It is not shameful within the sorority of aviator wives to feel glad Death picked out somebody else, although the letter Sue wrote to Ollie at 7:00 A.M. the morning after the accident which killed Bam Bam and Belly illustrates an aviator's wife's uneasiness about these and other feelings which well up after death comes so close:

11/9/83 7:00 A.M.

Dearest,

Just a short note to say I love you and while I'm very sorry about Cole and John I'm just very grateful that it's not you. I love you.

For a change we got the news before the news did. Roy Cash is now at FITWING (Fighter Wing) and he told Kathy Burch. Sue Snead was told as she did the calling to tell those wives whose husbands were all right that there'd been an accident. This was about 12:30 P.M. They wouldn't tell us who until the parents were notified. I guess I can understand that but it sure is hard waiting. I knew it wasn't you, Jim Snead, Gerry Slain—and I figured the Skipper was OK or Kathy wouldn't be doing the calling.

I called my parents but I couldn't get your Dad because it was a nice day and he was outside all day. I finally took a chance and called your Mom at work and got her. I didn't have Bill or Becky's work numbers at work but your Mom said she'd call them. I called Raymond. I tried to call anyone who might hear it on the radio and worry about you—C. R. and Marla, the Lawlers, Mary. I even called Midge Dwyer. She was really appreciative. Bonnie Slain called really early, about 6:00 P.M. with the names. I didn't know O'Neal at all but John Fowler did. He said he was one of the better pilots coming out of the RAG (Replacement Air Group). Obviously, John Scull was experienced. We are all waiting to see what caused the accident.

Sue Snead said that the French ship reported it said no chutes were seen. As soon as you can I sure would like to know what happened. It strikes too close to home. You're an experienced RIO too.

I was at the office till 7:00 P.M. making calls. I thought to get in touch with Cath Cross but nobody had her number. I finally found an address and called info. As it turned out, Bill had gotten a message at work. They were close to the Sculls and will be coming down in a day or two. Mary Paul wants a memorial service here at Oceana.

10:00 P.M.

I just got back from a wives mtg. The memorial service is Fri. at 11:00 A.M. VF-11 and VA-75 wives are taking care of all the food and arrangements afterwards. Mary Paul wanted it to be at her house because she didn't want to go back to an empty house. We're all arranging to take food to her over the next three weeks as that was the one thing she said she needed.

I still feel somewhat detached from all of it because I still don't feel completely part of the squadron yet. All of the wives have been doing their own thing together for a year and I'm still out of it. It's harder this time than the last time we came back—maybe because I'm older and don't relate to the younger ones as well. I'm working on it but I still feel strange . . .

To change the subject again, I sent all your change of address forms. I also paid to renew your *Combat Handguns* and *The Economist*—at $67—that ought to be your Christmas present. It will take about 6–8 weeks to take effect however.

I'm going to bed now. I may write more in the morning before I seal this and go to work.

One more thing. Gary called me from Naples today. He'd heard about the accident and that it was VF-31's plane but couldn't get the names. I didn't think to call him because I figured he'd know before we did. He was worried about you. He figured I'd call if it was you but he just wanted to make sure you were all right. Said he sent a Class Easy message. Write to him when you can.

Life goes on and I know it does. It makes you stop and think and I'm very grateful that I have you. Becky called me last night just to say, "I love you." Sometimes we forget to say that to each other enough and then it's too late. I love you.

Now I am going to bed. Take care and let me hear from you. Please write your Dad even if you have to pass up a letter to me. He's fussing because he's writing and you're not. I tried to explain but he doesn't listen. He did the same thing one other cruise. I guess we each have fathers with their strange ways. Take care.

Love & kisses,
XXXXOOOO
Sue

November 14, 1983

Dearest,

It's now Monday and I've had time since Friday and all that counts is that you're all right. Kathy Burch called me Fri. about 9:00 A.M. while I was getting ready to go to John Scull's memorial service. I must be terrible or something because it didn't upset me because she said you weren't hurt. And the rest didn't matter. I couldn't see any point about worrying at that stage as everything was over and you were all right. I am sorry Dave was hurt. I will be glad to get details and I do thank you for the telegram. I called everybody Fri. again. Again I couldn't reach your parents. This time I called Bill. Becky wasn't even available. He promised to call everyone and then I called your folks again in the evening after I got back from the get together after the service. It was a moving service. I just hope I never have to go through another one.

I want you to know I got the giggles after finding out about your accident. I remembered your story about the new guy you were going to the boat with and him worrying about scaring you and you told him if he showed you something you'd never seen before you'd talk about it in the raft. I guess you saw something you'd never seen before.

The word we're getting now is that Dave stalled the plane. Is he not an experienced pilot? I hope he heals OK. I understand his foot is bad. How come he got hurt and you didn't? Not that I wish you had. I'm tickled pink. I guess your pride is only a little damp (ha!) and it will dry. How was the Med for swimming? Was departing the plane for real anything like the practice? I love you.

I'm sending a picture for you so you don't forget what I look like. Dot Sparrow came Sat. and went to the art auction at the club with me.

Sat. on NBC news they interviewed Weinberger. I didn't see it but Phil did. He called to tell me the news that the Syrians had shot you down and you had to ditch the plane because you couldn't make it back to the boat. I told him I didn't think that was true because that's not what we were getting from the Navy. He said the Navy lies to you all the time and that even you wouldn't tell me the truth if the Navy said not to. He then said it was better to be shot down because then you'd be a hero and get a medal than just ditching the plane if there was a malfunction. I told him it didn't matter as long as you were all right and he said, ''Yes, yes, but it's better to be a hero.'' He's strange.

I've got to finish getting dressed. I'm going to Mathews, Va., again today. I'll write more tonight.

Love & kisses,
XXXXOOOO

I am very glad you are not hurt . . .

Love Sue

P.S. You also made the newspaper. I'll send a copy as soon as I photostat one.

Skipper John Burch of VF-31 had a crisis of confidence on his hands. The same squadron, his, had lost two F-14s in three days. Two men were dead. A third might still die. Was the squadron jinxed? Was there something wrong with the maintenance of the squadron's aircraft? Was he doing something wrong? If he could not lead the squadron out of its gloom, he might well get fired as its skipper. Burch, a graduate of the U.S. Naval Academy who had always felt things breaking his way in the Navy, was up against a cliff. Could he scale it? Would the squadron follow him if he did? He had to gain the aviators' confidence. He had to convince them that despite two accidents in three days, their squadron could regain the form which had made them the best in the Atlantic Fleet. They just had to go out and fly the hell out of those Tomcats like they always had; that they had to believe they had just hit a stretch of bad luck.

I sat down with Burch, who looked young enough to be a college graduate student even though he was forty, and asked him how he intended to put his squadron back together again. He talked openly, not defensively, and even managed to find places in our long conversations to smile.

"I've got a very young squadron. Most of my guys are on their very first cruise. The question that has been on my mind is how is this going to affect morale?

"We're going to try to find out first why we lost the airplane and try to explain it to them. We have to address how we can prevent something like this from happening again. After we explain to them to the best of our ability what happened, then we have got to explain why we must put it behind us. In the Navy we call it compartmentalization. The wife problem, the dog problem, the car problem—whatever—they all have to go away when you strap on an airplane. Belly and Bam Bam are going to have to go away, too. We've got to concentrate on the job at hand. We are as close to combat as we can get without actually being in it. Everybody acknowledges the risk when they sign up for naval aviation. It's a voluntary program.''

Right after the second accident, Burch and his executive officer, Commander Wigs Ludwig, spent a lot of time talking one-on-one with junior officers, asking them how they felt, telling them the two accidents coming so close together was a fluke. Burch also assembled the whole squadron of 350 officers and enlisted men in the hangar bay to try to reassure them that VF-31 would be great again if everyone put the accidents out of his mind and went back to working hard. He praised the round-the-clock effort of the squadron which kept the planes flying off Lebanon day in and day out. He stressed that there was no indication that faulty maintenance caused the crashes. He admitted he did not know why the crashes had happened but said the squadron could not afford to let up because of them during this crucial commitment of the *Kennedy*. "I have nothing to offer you but more hard work," he said.

He called the aviators together for a second, separate meeting in their living room on the ship, the VF-31 ready room. He stood at the podium in front of the rectangular room and said if there was anyone who, because of the accidents, felt he could not give full concentration to flying or feared it, "Come see me." He spoke softly, almost pleadingly. There was no Great Santini macho talk, like, "Anyone who can't stand a little blood ought to get the hell out of my fighter squadron." Burch was instead acting as the healer and gracefully inviting anyone who had lost his nerve because of the accidents to hand in his wings and do something else before he killed himself, the RIO in the back seat, and lost another airplane.

It is a radical act for a Navy pilot to hand in his wings of gold. He is scorned for the rest of his life by the aviators he used to fly with. He, in their view, quit in the middle of the game because he was afraid of getting hurt. He said their way of life was not worth dying for. He said there are more important things for a man to do than stay a boy zooming around the sky in airplanes.

The fraternity cannot judge him brave and rational for handing in his wings. Otherwise the other aviators who keep flying until they are killed, or gray and grounded, are stupid or cowardly; they are afraid to try to do something else with their lives; they keep letting themselves be catapulted off the end of a boat to see if they can land back on it two hours later. But Burch's words pulled one aviator in the squadron across the Great Divide between those who fly and those who don't. He decided to hand in his wings. He would be scorned. But he would be doing the right thing by his lights—and he would be alive to go back home to Mississippi to do the fishing, white water canoeing, and backpacking he loved far more than trying to land a 28-ton Tomcat on a gray wedge on the ocean in the middle of the night.

His name is David Price. His call-sign nickname, Tag. He is lean, tall—6 feet 3 inches—and quiet. I can see him in the rear seat of a canoe or expertly tossing plugs from Mississippi river banks at large mouth bass. He was twenty-seven years old at the time of the two accidents. He's a 1978 graduate of "The Boat School," the U.S. Naval Academy, and proud of it. His quiet but competent manner would make him great company on the backpacking trail. I could see that just from being around Tag in the VF-31 ready room. But I could not see him enjoying the highly competitive life of the fighter squadron where almost everyone is looking for the chink in the other guy's armor and poking at it.

The reason Tag opted for flying after graduating from the academy in the upper quarter of his class was the expectation that he would feel joyous doing it. He looked for the sense of release and joy he felt on dewy mornings on a thin trail winding through hemlocks laced with fast brooks. And flying did feel that way at first. He loved it and did well, graduating first in his class in primary and second in advanced training. This won him a highly prized seat in an F-14 fighter. Tag was delighted at putting that baby through its paces—"the ultimate toy" he called it before things turned sour for him on the boat.

The Navy's management system of teaming inexperience with experience did not work for Dave Price. He said his first RIO was such a worry wart that he took the joy out of flying the F-14. The RIO, who only had a short time to go on flying status, kept telling Tag all the things that could go wrong with the F-14 if he were not extra careful up there in the front seat of what can be one of the world's truly fun machines.

"Instead of going out and having fun," Tag told me in a long talk about his decision to do the unthinkable for fighter pilots, "we went out and worried about something happening. I think that kind of got the ball rolling—started to take away some of the fun of flying. Now it wasn't fun; now it's a job; now it's a task. Later it developed into my dreading having to do it.

"I was never real good at landing on the boat, but never really had any problems. In fact, my landing grades were continually improving. I was developing properly. I was real scared at night landings. Your heart rate triples and quadruples. I assumed this would go away with experience.

"Bam Bam's accident made it easier for me to address the problem and ask myself, 'Hey, you're not having fun doing this. Should you be doing this?' Even before his accident I had started saying to myself, 'I wish there was a way I could get out of this gracefully.'

"After the second accident, I said: 'Wait a minute! If I'm in a scenario where I'm not having fun and my edge is gone, maybe there will be short breaks in concentration which could be generated by not having fun and not being pumped up. This could end up with somebody getting killed.'

"The night after Frenchie's accident the skipper called an air crew meeting and stood up in front of everybody and asked each and every one of us to evaluate ourselves as to whether we wanted to be doing this. Obviously the squadron couldn't continue having accidents. That made me say, 'Maybe I need to address this problem with somebody else rather than just myself.' I wanted to get some feelings from others I trusted about it. I started talking to the operations officer about it—Lieutenant Commander Tim Higgins. We talked about it and he said he completely understood how I felt, having been around this a long time. He said, 'Well you know you need to talk to the skipper about it.'

"I agreed and went to see the skipper. He reflected on how he felt about what the effects of the decision could be. At no point did he try to influence my decision. He came up with some interesting comments that helped put it all in perspective. He said he really didn't know whether he wanted his son out here doing this thing. He's very much a people person.

"I thought about it for a day and a half. I didn't do anything else. Then I talked to several other guys around the squadron. I decided probably the best thing for me and the squadron was to get out. When I decided that, it was like something had lifted a big weight off my shoulders and set it over to the side. I feel happier overall. I don't see I have much of a career opportunity left. I still owe sixteen months.

"When I get out of the Navy, I'll go back to Meridian and probably lead a very quiet, normal type life—like my wife and I were both raised. If I could just get something simple. I never have been out to make a lot of money. If I thought I could buy a small farm and make a living doing that—well, that's the dream over here. Then you come back to reality. I'll probably end up with a technical job with the power company or the phone company or something like that.

"Most of the guys in the squadron have been real super about it. People who haven't discussed it with me treat me just like they have before. There's been no difference with 95 percent of the guys. There's a couple of people I get a little negative feeling from. They don't talk to me as much as they did before. It's like I have the plague or something.

"Sometimes I get the feeling that maybe the fighter community is a little bit much for me. The fighter community is a lot more high strung; a lot faster paced. Competition among people is a lot higher. I feel also that maybe this fighter-type life—I just wasn't getting along with it. The shipboard environment. The fighter-type environment. I personally have a quite different view of a lot of things. Right now I don't drink. It's my Southern Baptist type bringing up. I never strayed from my roots on that. I wouldn't have any trouble playing war, but I was never the best at ACM (aerial combat maneuvers). I always kept plugging away at it.

"I like the guys in the squadron. The skipper offered to have me out of here in two or three days so I didn't have to face everybody. Or I could stay as the photo reconnaissance coordinator. I'm going to stay as long as there is another job for me. My wife, Etta, we grew up in Meridian together, is probably the happiest person of all about this."

I saluted Tag inwardly. He had done the harder thing, I thought, and perhaps saved another's life.

The news of Price's decision to turn in his wings—an expression he could not bring himself to use in our long conversation—seeped through the ship. Reaction ranged from "a guts-ball decision" to "why didn't he think of that before he came out here?" Tag not flying at all meant that other pilots had to fly even more during the around the clock flight operations off Lebanon. Resentment against Tag deepened. Burch's magnanimous gesture to let him stay in the squadron aboard the ship looked increasingly troublesome for Burch, for Tag, and for the squadron. Plans were mapped to fly Tag off the ship and let him finish his obligated Navy time ashore—out of sight and out of mind of the resentful members of his squadron.

Two F-14 crashes in three days impelled not only VF-31 to go through an agonizing reappraisal but its sister squadron as well, VF-11, the Red Rippers. The Rippers a few years ago had the reputation, deserved according to its own aviators, of being the worst F-14 squadron in the Atlantic Fleet. They could not keep their planes ready for launch. They were sloppy in the air, and drunk in the bars. A fiercely competitive former high school teacher vowed to change all that when he ascended to command of VF-11. Commander John Combs told me that the reason he quit teaching and joined the Navy air corps was that the high school administration forbade him from continuing his practice of whacking miscreants on the rump with a paddle and then ordering them to shake his hand "for making them a better man."

Combs and carrier aviation were a perfect fit. He loved flying, the aerial combat he did in Vietnam, the drinking and hell raising in the bars, the closeness of the squadron fraternity, the competitiveness, and the chance to visibly excel in ceaseless competition with macho men like himself. He did not pretend to have Burch's intellect or way with words. But he knew how to relate to the common man—the sailors and chiefs—and motivate them to give their all for the Red Rippers. One officer in the air wing called him "the pure warrior." At forty-three with steel gray hair, Commander John Combs was the gray eagle of the squadron skippers. Command had come to him later than he had wanted. But he sure was going to make the most of his eighteen month command tour, which encompassed our cruise. He was determined to win the Navy E for excellence to remove the stains from the Red Rippers' reputation. He knew he would lose that chance if his aviators crashed into the sea. He called them together right after the crashes in VF-31 to dissect them; to try to learn from them; to warn against complacency and lapses in concentration in the cockpit. Combs himself had bailed out of a flaming McDonnell-Douglas F-4 Phantom as he was returning to the carrier from a mission over Vietnam. He had seen many of his friends die in airplanes. I wondered whether a middle-aged pilot like Combs did not feel the percentages were bound to catch up with him if he kept flying. I asked him about this while we discussed the two F-14 crashes in a long conversation in his one-man stateroom accorded squadron skippers.

"Any accident makes me a little more cautious. When I come into the break, I think I'll be more alert and thinking about the possibility. I'll be making sure I have my power (enough engine power to keep up the plane's air speed). I do understand it could happen to me."

A few officers were blaming "supervisory error" for the crashes, contending the air crews were being ordered to fly too much. Others rejected this idea, declaring the *Kennedy* had only been on station a few days when the accidents occurred.

I asked Combs—the Iron Man, the closest resemblance of the Great Santini among the squadron skippers—whether he thought flying air crews around the clock over-stressed them.

"It hasn't been more than you would stand in a wartime environment. I'm forty-three years old, and I don't have any problem. I don't see why these youngsters in their twenties and early thirties should have that kind of problem with it. I think they could do more. I think we could stress them to the point that you could go and fly; come back and sleep two or three hours and go again. But I think you really have to discipline yourself to do that."

"How about the distraction and depression from seeing two aviators at breakfast and learning at supper that both are dead in a crash nobody can explain?" I asked Combs.

"When you strap that aircraft on you really have to put everything else behind you. Whether your roommate was killed yesterday, or your wife wrote you a letter and said she doesn't love you anymore and wants a divorce, you've really got to put that behind you."

The compartmentalization aviators force on themselves to keep ahead of the deadly airplanes they fly often takes hold on their personality, on their emotions, and on their feelings. They hold themselves back from total commitment to anybody or anything. This can make them maddenly self-centered and cold to the women trying to draw out full love. Many marriages break against this invisible wall of compartmentalization. The wall hardens into a permanent one for many aviators. They find they cannot take it down when they get off the carrier and sit by the fireside with their families.

"Many times my wife, Tanya, has accused me of loving the squadron more than her," Combs told me. "She feels she is a little bit in second place sometimes. It's true to a certain degree that we hold back emotion. We never get so reliant on our best friend because, I think, we realize our best friend could be gone tomorrow. We just don't totally wrap ourselves around anything, except an airplane when we're flying."

Skipper Burch of VF-31 was confronted with a cruel dilemma. He and Wigs Ludwig, the executive officer, had been counseling their aviators to put the two crashes out of their minds and go back to aggressive flying of the F-14. But Burch felt he owed the families of Bam Bam and Belly a memorial service on the ship. He could not just let them lie on the bottom of the Eastern Mediterranean where the *Kennedy* was still stationed without noting their passing. Yet the service might resurrect all the fears that he and Wigs had been trying to still ever since the crashes. Aviators hate memorial services. Many refuse to attend. It is too hard on their compartmentalization and it cannot do anybody any good anyhow. They would rather honor their dead by laughing in a bar at all the crazy things the dumb bastard did when he was alive. Let civilians go reverent and pretend the dead guy is bigger than he actually was. We will laugh and scratch about the guy who bought it because that is the way he would like us to mark his mort. It is not uncommon for aviators to tell their wives in their wills to take $100 or more down to the O-Club bar after he morts and let everybody have a drink on him. Ollie Wright told me his will reads like that.

I was prepared for a spartan memorial service as I entered the blue and silver forecastle in the forwardmost part of the ship on the evening of 13 November 1983. The harsh look from the anchor chain and windlasses in the forecastle was softened by the table holding a cross and candles and the upholstered chairs set up in front of it for the top officers on the *Kennedy*. Metal bridge chairs for VF-31 officers formed a separate rectangle in front of the makeshift altar.

The aviators filtered into the room wearing work khakis and baseball caps with the number of their squadrons emblazoned on them. The officers from VF-31 sat. The rest stood, as did the sailors wearing dungarees and the sweat shirts colored to designate their jobs: green for maintenance, yellow for flight deck, purple for fuel. Commander Dan Roper, executive officer of VAQ-137, the Rooks, sat at the portable organ to the side of the altar playing mournful tunes.

Chaplain Jim Doffin, also wearing work khakis and the dark blue baseball cap with the ship's name on it, opened the service with a call to remembrance. He followed with The Lord's Prayer, a hymn, bible readings, and another prayer, then stepped aside for the eulogy to be delivered by Skipper Burch.

John Burch stood behind the podium looking from a distance like a student council president under heavy strain. He had worked hard on the eulogy, determined to keep it from being flowery, but hopeful of capturing the essence of Bam Bam and Belly as living people. He spoke clearly, feelingly. Somehow he managed to keep from breaking down.

"We are gathered here today to pay homage to our two fallen shipmates, Commander Scull and Lieutenant j.g. Cole O'Neil who died in the service of their country on 8 November 1983. Over fourteen years ago, when eulogizing his brother, Robert, Ted Kennedy told a stunned nation that it should not make Robert in death more than he was in life. Likewise, tonight I do not intend to create images of death that were not true in life.

"Both these officers were simply solid, down-to-earth people, committed to their families, their Navy, and their country.

"They collectively represented the old, the new, and the future in the challenging business we term tactical carrier aviation.

"John Scull, Belly to all of us who served with him, first started crossing the ramp in 1971. His career was steeped in all the traditional tapestry associated with carrier aviation. Tours of duty with VX-4 and as an F-14 instructor with VF-101, coupled with two previous tours of duty with VF-32 molded Belly into one of the finest radar intercept officers in the fighter community.

"The USS *John F. Kennedy* played an important part in Belly's career. He had accumulated over 700 arrested landings aboard Big John. His technical expertise was unequaled. I just recently had the pleasure to strongly endorse John's official request to the chief of Navy military personnel for John's entrance into the NASA (National Aeronautics and Space Administration) space shuttle program.

"Belly's exemplary professional naval career did not stop

him from being an outstanding leader in the civic organizations in Virginia Beach. His work with the local police force and other social organizations were instrumental in fostering good relations between the military and civilian communities within the Tidewater area.

"Because of John Scull's extensive fleet experience, I specifically chose him to fly with our younger pilots. Lieutenant j.g. Cole O'Neil was Belly's latest charge. Cole reported aboard VF-31 in July of this year, just prior to an ORE (operational readiness evaluation).

"It was hard not to admire the way Cole handled the immense challenge of being a nugget and stepping into the fast pace of an ORE scenario.

"Cole was right out of the pages of a book: honest and innocent would be good words to describe him. He neither drank, smoked, nor cursed. He called everyone sir and could not complete a sentence without saying thank you. The world really never got a chance to corrupt Cole O'Neil. His moral virtues were pure and intact until the day he died.

"His physical prowess will be a source of stories for years to come amongst his squadron mates. Cole was a gymnast in college and had lost little of his physical prowess. While standing only five feet seven inches tall, Cole was undoubtedly the strongest member of the command.

"As a fighter pilot, Cole was the emerging star of the future. Those of us who flew with him could see his talents grow almost on a daily basis. Our executive officer, Commander Wigs Ludwig, took Bam Bam under his tutelage as section leader and was personally grooming his tactical repertoire. Everyone knew that Bam Bam was destined for greatness. He was simply too dedicated, and too nice a guy, to miss.

"The families of these two men are left now with nothing but lasting memories. Mary Paul Scull and John Woodward can be proud of their husband and father. He died serving his country. His legacy will live on. The people he touched in life are better because of his association.

"Likewise Dana O'Neil can draw strength knowing her husband is giving the ultimate sacrifice in the service of his country. None of us who served with him will ever forget his innocence and the remarkable character of Cole O'Neil.

"Ted Kennedy said of his brother, Robert, 'Some men see things the way they are and ask why. Others see things that never were and ask why not.' Certainly these two gentlemen had similar views concerning their future in the United States Navy. They were both action people who did not let the world pass them by. The quotation by Theodore Roosevelt which is prominently displayed in our ready room is a fitting conclusion for our final respects to Belly and Bam Bam:

" 'It is not the critic who counts nor the man who points out how the strong men stumbled, or where the doer of deeds could have done them better. The credit belongs to the man who is actually in the arena; whose face is marred by dust and sweat and blood; who strives valiantly; who errs and comes short again and again; who knows the great enthusiasms, the great devotions and spends himself in a worthy cause; who, at the best, knows in the end the triumph of high achievement; and who, at the worst, if he fails, at least fails while daring greatly so that his place shall never be with those cold and timid souls who know neither victory nor defeat.'

"John Scull and Cole O'Neil. We salute you, and may God bless your souls."

The men filed out of the forecastle. "I've been to too many of these," a Navy captain told me softly as we left.

With two airplanes on the bottom of the Mediterranean, two men dead inside one of them and Frenchie still struggling to live after having ejected from the second, I thought the *Kennedy*'s streak of bad luck was bound to end. But the night before Thanksgiving more bad news sifted through the ship. Petty Officer Third Class Fernando "Mex" Pena, only twenty-five years old, had been killed in a midair collision while flying in the *Kennedy*'s utility plane as a crewman. The pilot was not a member of our crew. He was ferrying the plane from Rota, Spain, to the carrier. I sought out his friends on Thanksgiving Day on the hangar bay. They told me Pena had been in the Navy for almost seven years; was on his way up because of his good work; was full of hope about the life he would resume in Troy, New York, after the Mediterranean deployment with his wife, Kathleen, and daughter, Nicole, four, and son, Richard, two. And then suddenly this Thanksgiving Day he was gone. I felt bad. I had never even known his name. Another example of how big our town could be.

9 Terrorism

THE mishaps of 8 and 11 November 1983 came as the *Kennedy* was struggling to fit into a new role for an American aircraft carrier—performing as an antiterrorist weapon. The *Kennedy* in this role was supposed to help defend other U.S. ships off Lebanon against sudden terrorist attacks. Those ships, in turn, were to do what they could to defend the *Kennedy* and the other carrier which she joined off Lebanon in November, the USS *Eisenhower*. The *Kennedy* was also on call to protect the U.S. Marines at the Beirut International Airport and to avenge the 23 October 1983 attack upon them.

President Reagan contended that the presence of American warships offshore, together with the marines on land, would help stiffen the backbone of Amin Gemayel, the new president of Lebanon. The President also felt, or was persuaded, that this show of force would make Syria and the Soviet Union think twice before making any rash moves in Lebanon. Some Reagan administration officials believed this updated gunboat diplomacy would push Syria into removing the troops it had sent into Lebanon in 1976, at Lebanon's request, thus advancing the President's Middle East peace plan which called for removing all foreign troops from Lebanon. When the *Kennedy* arrived off Lebanon, there were Syrian and Israeli troops as well as an international peacekeeping force of American, British, French, and Italian forces in the hemorrhaging country.

Embracing the challengeable calculus that firepower equals

usable military and diplomatic power, President Reagan had deployed an American armada off Lebanon, a country about the size of Connecticut. For the first time, there were two carriers off Lebanon, the *Eisenhower* and the *Kennedy*, together with the battleship *New Jersey* and the high tech Aegis cruiser *Ticonderoga*, plus an assortment of escorting destroyers, frigates, amphibious vessels, and oilers. The USS *Independence*, detoured to Grenada for the invasion there, was now steaming toward the eastern Mediterranean to relieve the *Eisenhower* around mid-November so that two carriers would remain on station. Each carrier packed more explosive power in its ammunition rooms than the entire U.S. Navy carried in the prenuclear days of World War II.

The on-scene wielder of all this might was an admiral who called himself SLUF, an acronym for short little ugly fucker. He was known officially as Rear Admiral Jerry O. Tuttle, commander of Battle Force Sixth Fleet and Commander Carrier Group Two, or CTF 60 for short, commander of Combined Task Force 60. Tuttle was five-foot-nine, 160 pounds; maybe ugly, although his wire-rimmed glasses, pipe, and furrowed brow made him look more professorial than ugly; and he indeed could be a fucker. A fully certified workaholic, SLUF could be brash, demanding, impossible, dangerous. He could also be brilliant, warm, inspiring, futuristic—the kind of a son-of-a-bitch you would want to go to war with if you had to go at all.

"I didn't get as good an education as you younger fellows, so I've got to read to catch up," Tuttle would say in explaining why he slept only about three hours a night. His humor was strictly wire brush, especially on the people he liked the most. "Who invited him here?" Tuttle once asked his aides when CAG John J. Mazach, whom he deeply liked, entered the admiral's cabin for an urgent meeting. "I only want people here who know what they're talking about." Tuttle on a visit to the *Kennedy* greeted me with: "I'm going to learn from you, George. I'm going to use you. We've got to understand your business better." And to a Navy chief who hung back during a ceremony where he was to receive a medal, Tuttle kidded: "Hey Chief, you're as ugly as I am. Stand up here and get your picture taken with me."

Tuttle seemed completely at home on a ship, especially on the *Kennedy* which he formerly commanded. He would walk around any ship he was on at all hours of the day and night, seeing nothing wrong at all with barging into ready rooms and offices to ask questions, to kick ass, to philosophize. The only thing he seemed to love more than the Navy was the naval air part of the Navy. A former A-7 attack pilot, Tuttle thought carrier air wings could do almost anything if they were pushed hard enough and creatively led. His critics said he pushed too hard, wearing out whole ships and leaving almost nothing for the next commander. His champions said he made you realize you could do much more than you realized if you only tried. As CTF 60, his command over the ships in the battle group was horizontal rather than vertical. That is, he told the skippers of the ships where to go and what to do once they arrived in the eastern Mediterranean. It was up to the skippers to command vertically within their own ships to carry out Tuttle's orders. Tuttle was riding on the *Eisenhower* as a royal tenant when the *Kennedy* arrived off Lebanon. Rear Admiral Roger E. Box was Tuttle's deputy and rode on the *Kennedy* in equal splendor. Each admiral had his own staff, cabin, dining room, and bridge on whatever carrier was driving him around the Mediterranean.

Despite all the fire power at his command, Tuttle often found himself a Gulliver pinned down by Lilliputians. This became painfully obvious on the *Kennedy* as its air wing was sent out on one false alarm after another to head off terrorist attacks—none of which materialized. No one knew who the threatening terrorists were, where they were located, or what they would do next. The U.S. intelligence community tried to find out but could not. With no reliable information in hand, intelligence officers in Washington were like assayers who could not tell real gold from fool's gold. They seemed to buy everything put down before them, and then passed on what they had purchased to Tuttle and other commanders in the battle group off Lebanon. Warning after warning of imminent terrorist attack flooded the in-baskets in officer country. Tuttle and his commanders had no way to assay what they were getting. They did not dare ignore the warnings, ridiculous sounding or not, given the bizarre attack the lone terrorist had made on the marines on 23 October. The dark art called "terrorism" was impelling everyone from intelligence officers in Washington to admirals and captains 7,000 miles away to play the old game of CYA—cover your ass.

"The terrorists are coming, the terrorists are coming," became the new battle cry of the intelligence bureaucracy. Ships in the battle group, according to the alarms being sounded in Tuttle's ear, were in imminent danger of being attacked by high speed boat, by slow rubber boat, by small plane, by old propeller-driven military transport, and by hang gliders launched by anti-American zealots from the coastal hills of Lebanon. *Kennedy* pilots came to believe only the intelligence boys saw the ghosts.

Because it would be difficult to hit a terrorist speed boat at night with iron bombs, the *Kennedy* loaded its bombers with APAMs which bomb by the acre. The APAM is a bomb-shaped canister filled with tennis ball size bomblets which exploded over several acres, killing people and destroying anything soft in their path, including the sides of speedboats. The red-shirted ordnance men, the ordies, had to remove these APAMs from the A-6E bombers every morning and load iron bombs in their place. The iron bombs were for bombing by daylight when pinpoint accuracy was achievable, even against small boats.

As a last ditch defense against terrorists boats or planes that the carrier air wing might miss, the *Kennedy* rigged 50-caliber machine guns on the catwalks below the flight deck and had them manned by marines and sailors all night long. Helicopter crews and marines were also trained in antiboat night operations just in case. Ships closest to the beach were armed with Stinger heat-seeking antiaircraft missiles to combat kamikaze attacks by light planes or transports rumored to be in the making. The addition of Stingers meant that planes from the *Kennedy* and *Eisenhower* had to remember to stay above the proscribed buffer zone of 3,000 feet or risk being shot down by their own ships.

Whenever an F-14 fighter or A-6 bomber was launched to combat some feared terrorist attack, other planes had to be put in the air to support them. A KA-6D aerial tanker full of fuel had to be airborne in case the warplanes were low on gas. A helicopter had to be orbiting off the stern to rescue fliers who crashed into the water. Often an E-2C Hawkeye warning and control plane had to hang in the sky to guide fighters and bombers to their quarries.

Just by telephoning threats to embassies around the world or making speeches or issuing press releases, a lone terrorist could impel the United States to launch planes from the carriers off Lebanon and put the other ships in the battle group on alert around the clock. The mightiest armada ever assembled was in danger of being worn out by phantoms because the United States was never sure what was going on in the shadowy world of the terrorists. The pilots, radar intercept officers, bombardier-navigators, bomb loaders, mechanics, shooters, hook runners—almost everyone on the *Kennedy*—worked harder and longer to combat threats they could not see. Frustration, fatigue and anger climbed as November wore on toward Christmas. The officers grappling with the phantoms reminded me of battalion and company commanders I had known in Vietnam who went out after the Vietcong day after day, night after night without seeing Charlie. The sailors bitched like the grunts of Nam about working their asses off for no good reason. Terrorists, both real and imagined, contorted the battle group into unnatural and uncomfortable defensive postures. Terrorist threats were pushing Tuttle toward violating the military maxim that he who tries to be strong everywhere ends up being weak everywhere.

Besides contending with the threat of sneak terrorist attack on his ships, Tuttle had to have his battle group ready to protect the marines from a human wave invasion at the Beirut International Airport. He also was ordered to be ready to knock out a unit as small as a mortar squad hiding in the fold of a hill or in the backyard of a house outside the airport or, failing that, to bomb a target afterward associated with the tribe that fired the mortars. Knowing which tribe is firing what at whom has been a sticker in Lebanon for centuries. But Tuttle had to prepare retaliatory targets ahead of time anyway for carrier bombers to strike on short notice. The targets eventually became so numerous and widely scattered that air crews carried the maps and photographs out on patrol with them in case they were suddenly ordered to strike one. The bombardiers folded the target papers into narrow sections so they could flip through them while resting them on their right knee, like subway riders reading folded newspapers.

Then there were the more conventional, and comfortable, threats for Tuttle and his deputies to worry about. Syria, the Soviet Union, and Libya had to be reckoned with. Tuttle had to prepare for a thrust into Lebanon by the Syrian air force. He had to keep track of every Soviet warship sailing in and out of the Lebanon area. Libyan leader Muammar Qaddafi had a couple of old Soviet submarines that could sneak up on a U.S. ship to try to torpedo it. Tuttle had to worry whenever a Libyan sub was in his area or whose whereabouts were unknown to the intelligence community.

To combat the air force of Syria—the Lebanese government in 1976 had invited the Syrians in as a peacekeeping force —Tuttle divided the skies off Lebanon into five ambush stations which were manned intermittently by F-14s from the two carriers. Stations One and Five were the main ones. Station One was just west of Beirut to intercept any unknown planes flying out of Lebanon toward the ships at sea. Station Five was off the southern end of Cyprus to cover planes coming from the north and northwest. The pilots were supposed to orbit about 12,000 to 20,000 feet high in a racetrack pattern with straightaways 15 miles long. Their F-14s were armed with four AIM-7F radar-guided Sparrow missiles, four AIM-9L Sidewinder missiles and a 20mm cannon with rotating barrels like a Gatling gun.

The F-14 pilots usually orbited two hours and then returned to the carrier. Some radar intercept operators eased the boredom of guard duty aloft by drawing cartoons with grease pencils on the inside of the plastic canopy—erasing their art before landing. The Red Rippers wired their helmets so they could hear tapes of Merle Haggard and other favorites on Sony Walkmen. The fliers referred to the morale boosting hookup as TISS for Tomcat Integrated Stereo System.

Life could also be boring for the A-6 bomber pilots as they stood guard against attacks on the marines or on the ships in the battle group. They were eager to practice their arts of low level evasion, bombing, and shooting. The crews in the other specialized squadrons on the *Kennedy*—the VS-22 Vidars antisubmarine, the VAQ-126 Seahawks warning and control, the VAQ-137 Rooks electronic warfare, and the HS-7 Dusty Dogs antisubmarine helicopter—were happier because they were getting plenty of air time to hone what they would do in wartime. Everybody in the air wing and its supporting cast of thousands, meaningful work or not, was getting worn out by the furious pace of air operations off Lebanon.

Only a few people on the *Kennedy* knew in early November that a top secret mission was in the works. Higher Authority —presumably all the way up to President Reagan—had decided to let carrier bombers strike a target in Lebanon to retaliate for the attack on the marines. The nation's leaders needed only the right plan and the right moment to send the battle group into action.

As soon as the *Kennedy* arrived on station off Lebanon, Tuttle ordered Mazach to come see him on the *Eisenhower*. "Bring a strike planner with you," Tuttle added. Strike meant A-6 bombers. Mazach wanted someone experienced in flying the bomber, in planning bombing strikes, and who would keep his cool under the pounding Tuttle would give him in the coming hours. He chose Commander Paul Bernard, executive officer of VA-85, the A-6 squadron called the Buckeyes. Bernard had 2,200 hours in the bomber and was rock steady under pressure. Bernard also would work around the clock to help the Navy which he felt had done so much to help him.

"I owe everything to the Navy," Bernard told me fervently in a long chat we had one day. He had enlisted in 1959 as a confused eighteen-year-old from Kelso, Washington, with no prospects for a bright future. He gravitated to electronics and submarines and won the backing of the officers in the nuclear submarine fraternity. They pushed him into the college education program for exceptional sailors. He took wing, earning a bachelor's degree in metallurgical engineering at the University of Washington, a master's degree in aeronautical engineering and, in 1970, his pilot wings.

"I'm a Navy success story who gets better with age," quipped the forty-two-year-old Bernard who was receiving landing grades higher than his juniors when Mazach tapped him to go with him to the *Eisenhower* for the secret meeting with Tuttle.

As the gray-and-white SH-3H Sea King helicopter of HS-7 whumped-whumped its way from the *Kennedy* to the *Eisenhower*, Mazach wondered what kind of strike the fiery little admiral was cooking up. He told me later that he figured it would be a bombing strike against Lebanon. But then again the battleship *New Jersey* could do that from close in shore without risking getting American pilots shot down over Lebanon. You just never knew with Tuttle or his bosses on up the chain of command in these twilight zones of military presence but not military action.

I sensed, but was not told, that the ship was getting ready to go into combat for the first time. Intensity burned through the fatigue on the faces of the officers on the carrier who would plan and execute the bombing raid. I saw the chopper leave for the *Eisenhower* and was told much later about how the meeting went. The officers from the *Kennedy* strode into the room called Civic which carriers use for secret meetings and briefings. Civic comes from the acronym for the room, CVIC, with CV standing for carrier and IC for intelligence center.

Mazach brightened into the characteristic, open-mouthed smile which seemed to light up his whole face when he spotted Commander Joe Prueher, an old high school buddy from Nashville who flew A-6s and was now the *Eisenhower*'s CAG, sitting at the conference table with Tuttle and another officer. The other officer was a captain with the sharply pressed khakis that shout "staff." The top secret papers in his briefcase were to be the subject of the meeting.

The papers were a description of targets in Lebanon which Higher Authority had decided would be appropriate for the United States to bomb to retaliate for the terrorist attack on the marines at the Beirut airport. It would be the first time the United States bombed an Arab country. The raid, if it were launched, would be put under a critical microscope not only by the U.S. Congress but by every government in the world.

"We want complete professionalism," Tuttle told his CAGs. "We want precision. And we don't want to lose any airplanes. We can't afford to fuck this one up."

Military theory holds that the best results are achieved by leaving it up to the commander on the scene to decide how to take the hill, sink the enemy ship, or bomb the chosen target. But this theory has seldom been put into practice by the United States since World War II. One reason is that there have been no all-out wars since then. Korea was termed a police action; the Bay of Pigs invasion included an attempt to hide the U.S. military's participation; the Cuban missile crisis was seen as such a high stakes confrontation between the United States and the Soviet Union that former Defense Secretary Robert S. McNamara stood over the Chief of Naval Operations in the Pentagon war room as American ships imposed the quarantine; Vietnam was a half-war in which civilians in Washington dictated what the commanders on the scene could and could not do. Military screwups and outright failures further eroded the tradition of letting the on-scene commander have his head. The rescue of the *Mayaguez* and its crew in 1968 ended up killing 41 marines and Air Force personnel to rescue the crew of 40. The Joint Chiefs of Staff planned the rescue of the American hostages at the U.S. Embassy in Tehran in 1980 only to have it called off after helicopters broke down on the Iranian desert. And, most applicable to the situation confronting Tuttle and his battle group in 1983, since World War II a succession of

American Presidents had tried to fine-tune the military by bringing just enough of its power to bear on a diplomatic problem to resolve it without war or dangerous confrontation of the superpowers. Both the civilian and military bureaucracies of the post–World War II era felt compelled to hold reins on the on-scene commanders to keep them from applying too much military power.

"They expect too much of us," a frustrated Army battalion commander told me that in Vietnam in 1968 as he tried to kill Vietcong while negotiating with the South Vietnamese province and village chiefs on what firepower he could use where and when. "Civilians should treat us like a watch dog. Let us off the chain and we'll eat up the burglar. Then put us back on the chain. Don't send me out here to be a killer one minute and a diplomat the next."

From my Vietnam experience, I felt sure that Tuttle, Mazach, Prueher, Bernard, and other officers out on the point would feel Higher Authority's reins tugging on them as they read the top secret descriptions of the targets compiled by unnamed and untitled U.S. civilian and military officials. Higher Authority did not dictate by a written order what target they were to bomb. It did not have to. The one they wanted bombed looked like a red headline on the menu of choices. Its identity has been mentioned publicly but never officially confirmed by the Navy.

Target X was a military complex in the Bekaa Valley near the Syrian border. Iran's Red Guard revolutionaries suspected of planning the bombing of the marines at the airport were inside the complex in the fall of 1983 when Tuttle was sifting over the list of retaliatory targets. Hitting Target X would fulfill President Reagan's demand that any retaliatory bombing kill those directly linked to the terrorist act without killing civilians in the area. The military euphemism for not killing innocents was "no collateral damage."

Tuttle's planners figured just eight A-6 bombers, each carrying twelve 1,000-pound bombs, could level Target X at night in fifteen minutes without killing civilians outside it or losing any airplanes to ground fire. Syria had minimal night antiaircraft defenses in that part of Lebanon. One reason the strike planners felt the strike would be successful stemmed from the prominent ruins on the ground near the target. The ruins would make it easy for the bombardiers in the A-6s to check their exact position before punching off their bombs. The forward-looking infrared and other gadgetry on the bomber would do the rest to get the bombs right inside the pickle barrel. Tuttle, the veteran warrior who knew something could always go wrong at the last minute, decided to increase the strike force to twelve A-6Es, eight from the *Kennedy* and four from the *Eisenhower*. Each would still carry twelve 1,000-pound bombs.

Tuttle's CAGs and other planners turned their eyes into the other end of the telescope—they could see what would happen if things went right on the raid but what would happen if something went wrong? What if the Syrians detected the incoming bombers and shot off some of the long range missiles they had in the Bekaa Valley? What if there were short range antiaircraft missiles and/or antiaircraft artillery close to the barracks, which U.S. intelligence had not detected? What if an A-6 got shot down and the pilot and bombardier-navigator ejected? Where should the fliers be told to go in the middle of the night in a possibly hostile town on the edge of Syria? What if Syria broke precedent and scrambled its fighters at night to intercept the bombers? What if fliers had to eject over the Mediterranean at night? What if Higher Authority suddenly ordered the raid launched and the twelve 1,000-pound bombs were not loaded on all the bombers? What if the A-6s armed for the strike could not get off the deck because of mechanical or electronic failures? What if Tuttle wanted to call back the bombers at the last second? What if one of the pilots strayed into Syria? What if a pilot was wounded and could not land his plane back on the carrier or tried so many times he ran out of gas over the Mediterranean Sea?

CAGs Mazach of the *Kennedy* and Prueher of the *Eisenhower* could answer most of those "what ifs" right off the tops of their heads because they dealt with most of them every time a single plane went off a carrier to do anything and had to be taken back aboard. This was carrier aviation, living with the "what ifs." The starting point was the fundamental tenet of the American military: everything possible must be done to save the life of one soldier. Cost effectiveness would not apply. At the same time, it would be a given as the bombing plan was refined that any military operation is dangerous and men might die trying to execute it. The idea was to minimize the risks.

Like a football coach huddling with his assistants before a big game and analyzing the opponent man by man, Mazach and a couple other *Kennedy* officers looked at the "what ifs" one by one and came up with these answers:

- Commander Bud Holloway of VAQ-137, the Rooks electronic warfare squadron, would be cut in on the top secret plan and told to assess the Syrian antiaircraft defenses and recommend counter-measures. Holloway, a thirty-seven-year-old son of a Navy chief who wanted nothing more in the world than for his son to become an officer, was the resident electronic warfare whiz on board.

- Navy intelligence leaders would be queried about what fliers should do if shot down over the target where hostile Syrians, Shiites, or Iranians might capture them. Only those few aviators to fly on the raid would be briefed for fear word of the strike would leak out even though the carrier could be sealed by such measures as holding mail and restricting departures.

- F-14 fighters from the *Kennedy* would be sent up to orbit off Lebanon the night of the raid and would be directed against any Syrian fighters which scrambled to attack the A-6 bombers. This was standard procedure. The prospect of shooting down an enemy plane and winning a medal after so many weeks of tedious flying would rejuvenate the air crews.

- Rescue helicopters from the USS *Guam* with marine crews expert in plucking fliers out of the sea at night would be kept on alert without disclosing the target. Other helicopters on ships along the fliers' homeward route would be alerted as well to form a rescue chain all the way back to the *Kennedy*. This was not too far from standard procedure for carrier operations where there were no "bingo" fields on land for fliers to use in an emergency.

- At least six A-6s would be kept loaded with ordnance for Target X in case they were suddenly ordered to strike. The bombs would be changed every three days to check wiring and other equipment subject to corrosion from salt air and spray. Only four of the six bombers would be launched. The other two would be on standby to take the place of a bomber that might experience mechanical failure either before take off or while in the air.

- Tuttle could call back the strike or order any other action once the bombers were on their way by radioing directions to the air controllers flying inside the E-2C Hawkeyes. Two Hawkeyes would be up the night of the strike, one from Tuttle's flagship and the second from the *Kennedy*. The E-2C crews would watch the bombers every foot of the way on their sophisticated radar scopes and warn any flier if he strayed off course. The E-2C's had been doing this kind of watching and warning ever since the carrier planes began flying in the tight, dangerous skies over the Middle East.

• If a pilot got wounded and could not make it through the night sky to a safe landing on the carrier, he would be told to eject at a point where helicopters could reach him quickly. There are no dual controls in the A-6. The bombardier-navigator in the right seat could not bring home the plane even if he knew how to fly. He would have to eject along with the wounded pilot. Again, the pilots would kid, "Who ever told you carrier aviation was safe, Boy? Fun maybe. Exciting maybe. But Safe?"

Bud Holloway did not think there was much for the bomber boys to worry about when they went over Target X. He knew from intense study and thousands of hours of flying in an EA-6B not only what almost every Soviet antiaircraft missile and gun could do but what it sounded like when it was on the hunt. Every radar gives off a different sound as its radio waves search the sky. The searching radars make one sound; the close range radars for directing the guns or missiles to their targets make another. The night of the raid, the EA-6B would hang up in the sky with Holloway in the back listening to the Soviet-made radars used by the Syrians to warn of approaching aircraft and to guide antiaircraft missiles to them. If a radar signal sounded menacing to the attacking bombers, Holloway would direct a jolt of jamming radio waves into it. This jamming action would be like a block for a halfback dashing down field with the ball. It would give the A-6 the instant or two it needed to evade the enemy fire. The Syrian gunners on the ground would be confused by a sudden snow of false targets and other radar images on their scopes. Jamming is more like a block or a stiff arm than a tackle. Given time, the gunners can overcome the interference and figure out where their quarry is—at least until better jammers come along. Electronic warfare is a constant, grim cat and mouse game between the United States and the Soviet Union—"the silent war" some call it.

The Soviets had sent Syria these antiaircraft missiles at the time the *Kennedy* was off Lebanon:

* SA-5 Gammon. Akin to the U.S. Army's Nike Zeus, the SA-5 was an old, long-ranged missile—180 mile slant range and about 18 miles straight up—which sent out radar waves as it flew along to find and lock on to the target airplane.
* SA-6 Gainful. This missile acquitted itself well in the 1967 Arab-Israeli war. It can be aimed with eye pieces and guided by radio commands or be hooked up to a variety of Soviet radars and ride their beams to the target. The SA-6 can be carried around on large tracked vehicles. This required Tuttle's battle group to employ reconnaissance aircraft to keep tabs of where the SA-6s were located in Lebanon on any given day. The missile's reach straight up is about ten miles.
* SA-7 Grail. The big surprise. This weapon can be fired by one soldier as he rests it on his shoulder. The heat-seeking missile flies into the hottest part of plane or helicopter if it can catch the aircraft. Syria seemed to have SA-7s deployed all over Lebanon in unexpectedly high numbers during the *Kennedy*'s deployment. Syrian gunners learned to fire them in barrages. The SA-7s' straight up reach was about 8,000 feet. Its slant range was greater. Reconnaissance F-14s flew low over Lebanon at high speed, about 600 miles an hour, too fast for the SA-7 to track and catch.
* SA-8 Gecko. A low-altitude missile guided from the ground out to a slant range of about seven miles.
* SA-9 Gaskin. This heat-seeking missile with a slant range of five miles and a straight up reach of about 12,000 feet, almost three miles, was the Tuttle battle group because it could be trucked around the country and set up to fire in a hurry from almost anywhere. One truck could carry a battery of eight missiles.

The airplane tactics for foiling SAMs were developed in Vietnam. The four general counters to SAMs were to stay out of their reach; jam their search and guidance radars; twist and turn the plane so sharply that the missile could not stay with it, called jinking; drop flares or other decoys to draw the missiles to them and away from the airplane.

Holloway, after studying the strike plan, told CAG Mazach that the A-6s would have the mountains to shield them from the long range missiles Syria had deployed in its part of the Bekaa Valley and that Syria did not seem to have any significant antiaircraft missile deployment around Target X. He added that he would be in an EA-6B the night of the attack ready to jam any radars which threatened the attacking bombers swooping in on the barracks complex.

Mazach told the squadron skippers in the *Kennedy* air wing about the planned strike on Target X but ordered them to keep it secret. I did not know about the plan at the time it was sensitive but reconstructed the events after the target was "cold." Mazach and the skippers selected what they thought would be the best combination of fliers to fly in the A-6 bombers, protecting F-14 fighters, E-2C Hawkeye command plane, EA-6B Prowler jammer, and SH-3H helicopters. Mazach would lead the eight bombers from the *Kennedy* and Prueher the four from the *Eisenhower*. Everything was set. I sensed the tension all around the carrier and saw the loading up of the A-6 bombers, as did the Soviet trawlers and warships which shadowed the carrier the whole time it was in the Med. They often hung back only a mile, once in a while even closer, but usually three miles away. Several times crews were awakened from a sound sleep, ordered to dress in their flight and survival gear, briefed on the strike and ordered to the roof to man up the airplanes.

"We're going to fly over there, drop our bombs on the target, and come back," he said at one night briefing just before the anticipated launch. "It's going to be a piece of cake."

Lieutenant William "Catfish" Davis was thirteen-years-old during the 1968 Tet offensive in Vietnam. He was to get his first taste of combat on the Bekaa Valley raid by flying as bombardier-navigator in an A-6 piloted by one of his roommates, Lieutenant Tim Williamson. Davis put his faith in Mazach, the veteran: "CAG knows. He flew in Vietnam. I'd follow him anywhere," Catfish told me in one of our chats in the VA-85 ready room.

The alerts for the strike and the accompanying tension climbed night after night. Higher Authority each time called off the raid at the last minute. The *Eisenhower* headed home. The USS *Independence* on 17 November took her place off Bagel Station, including the responsibility to strike Target X at a moment's notice. Tuttle transferred to the *Independence*, making that carrier the flagship for the battle group.

On 20 November I saw Xerox copies of the 18 November 1983 Paris *International Herald Tribune* being slapped down on desks all over the air wing. The lead story revealed that French bombers had struck Baalbek in the Bekaa Valley near the Syrian border. The strike made Camp X a cold target for the *Kennedy*. The elaborate bombing plan had to be put back in the locked files of the battle group's flagship. Both intelligence agencies and newspaper accounts issued a few days after the strike said that little damage was done. "They woke up the gardener," said one despairing officer of the French strike. *Kennedy* fliers were confident they would have leveled their target in the night raid. Not getting the chance deepened their frustration. They were wearing themselves out chasing shadows in the twilight zone of half war and half peace. Invisible terrorists continued to torment the mightiest armada ever assembled off Lebanon. It seemed shackled. One reconnaissance flight would unshackle it.

10   Bombing Raid

"I DIDN'T know I was going to start a war out here," Market (because he played the stock market) Burch would tell me later. I watched as he and Lieutenant John "Fozzie" Miller prepared their fighter plane for the mission that would trigger a chain of events which would kill one of our most popular fliers, lead to the capture of another, and spotlight incompetence in the high command of the American military.

I was standing behind the Air Boss in his glassed-in tower, musing to myself how characteristically different Burch and Miller looked even from my high perch as they walked around the F-14 searching for a forgotten wrench in an engine intake, dripping hydraulic fluid, cracks in the wings, or breaks in the tires. Burch walked quickly with the choppy steps of a young business executive. Burch was six feet tall, compact looking. Fozzie was over six feet and lanky. Fozzie walked around the plane in his usual thorough, Mr. Easy-Does-It style. His squadronmates agreed Fozzie was bound to make admiral because he never left anything undone.

I knew the mission Burch and Miller were supposed to fly this sunny morning of 3 December 1983. They were to fly fast and low past the Beirut International Airport on the coast and over prospective targets inland. The camera slung under the belly of their F-14 would take hundreds of closeup pictures of everything on the ground in their swatch as they raced along through the Lebanese sky. U.S. Marines were still staked to that vulnerable low ground of the airport. They were forced to act like turkeys ducking behind a log at a turkey shoot to survive the potshots of invisible riflemen and mortar squads firing from outside the wire. U.S. military leaders had pictures from satellites staring down on Beirut from space. But these shots were not as detailed or current as the ones Higher Authority hoped Burch and Miller would get with the tactical aerial reconnaissance pod system, or TARPS, encased in the long cylinder under their plane. The TARPS pictures would warn of any buildup of hostile forces near the marines.

The *Kennedy* had just returned to Bagel Station, that familiar patch of water some 70 miles off Lebanon. We had been in Haifa on a rare liberty for four days. We had been told that we would go from there through the Suez Canal and on into the Indian Ocean to show the flag. While the crew was buttoning up the ship for the transit through the Canal, where the skipper worried about terrorists sinking boats in front of and behind the carrier to embarrass the United States, Higher Authority got nervous. It worried about not having enough bombers available in the Mediterranean to protect the marines from a human wave assault or to support the beleaguered government of Lebanese leader Amin Gemayel. Higher Authority changed *Kennedy*'s sailing orders again and sent her back to Bagel Station. We were still on 24-hour alert, meaning it would take that long to go into battle rather than the four-hour alert we had maintained before going into Haifa. The difference in alert status would prove tragic.

Assured by their walk around the plane that nothing obvious would imperil them in flight, Burch and Miller climbed into the fighter. Once their F-14 had been snapped into the catapult, I saw Burch and Miller tense their heads forward. I knew from having been catapulted off the deck more than a dozen times myself at this point in the cruise why they were doing this. The catapult would yank the plane from standstill to 150 miles an hour in two seconds. The slingshot action would snap back their heads if they did not brace them. They could push their heads back into the headrest of the seat, but this would tilt their faces upward, making it harder to focus on the instruments during the dash down the deck. Reading a warning light in time might save their lives by providing the instant needed to eject from the fighter before plunging into the sea off the bow where the onrushing carrier would plow through the plane and anybody strapped inside it.

Whooom!

I saw and heard Burch's F-14 roar off the bow on twin plumes of afterburner flame. It was soon an arrowhead racing through the sky toward Lebanon 70 miles to our east. Burch intended to race over Lebanon at about 600 miles an hour at an altitude of 3,500 feet. This would hopefully make the plane too fast to hit by the Syrian gunners manning Soviet antiaircraft guns and missiles. With luck, Burch and Miller would be "feet dry," meaning over land, for no more than two minutes. Lieutenant Greg "Road" Streit, a nugget pilot, and Lieutenant Jim "Mac" McAloon, his radar intercept officer, were flying on Burch's wing to shoot down any fighter which rose out of Syria to stop the reconnaissance mission.

"Are you sure we're on the right course for Beirut?" Burch asked Miller in the back seat as he saw the dark shadow of Lebanon on the horizon dead ahead.

"I'm sure," Miller said into his lip mike. "Press on."

As soon as they crossed over the coast, they looked down at the brown hills and cream buildings racing under their speeding jet. They saw the bright winks of antiaircraft guns shooting up at them. This did not alarm them. They had been shot at before with those guns on earlier TARPS runs. Suddenly they saw a sequence of smoke corkscrews rising from the ground. This sight did alarm them. The corkscrews were the signatures of SA-7 heat-seeking missiles. These missiles, which can achieve a height of 8,000 feet, could easily reach the two F-14s streaking through the December sky at 3,500 feet. Burch radioed back to the *Kennedy* to inform Rear Admiral Roger E. Box that the reconnaissance planes were being fired on by missiles. Box was the deputy to Rear Admiral Tuttle.

The two F-14s flashed in and out of Lebanon without getting hit, but the sight of the corkscrews of smoke had loosed surges of adrenaline inside the fliers of both planes. The pilots were promptly debriefed about the missile firings when they returned to the *Kennedy*. Their accounts formed the basis of a report Tuttle sent on up the chain of command toward President Reagan in the White House 7,000 miles away. Washington might regard the missile firings as an escalation by Syria and choose to retaliate. Tuttle's secret message zinged through the air in the form of coded radio waves which made teletypes chatter at each stop in this long chain of command:

(1) From Tuttle on the *Independence* in the Mediterranean to Vice Admiral Edward H. Martin, commander of the Sixth Fleet, on his flagship in Gaeta, Italy; (2) from Martin to Vice Admiral M. Staser Holcomb, deputy commander of U.S. Naval Forces Europe, with headquarters in London; (3) from Holcomb to Air Force General Richard L. Lawson, deputy commander at the U.S. European Command in Stuttgart, West Germany; (4) from Lawson to Army General Bernard W. Rogers, supreme allied commander and commander of U.S. forces in Europe with headquarters in Mons, Belgium; (5) from Rogers to Defense Secretary Caspar W. Weinberger at the Pentagon in Washington via the Joint Chiefs of Staff there; (6) from Weinberger or his deputy to President Reagan in the White House.

The big question which formed in the minds of military officers reading the top secret teletype messages about the missile firings was whether President Reagan this time would order retaliatory action. The Joint Chiefs of Staff met at the Pentagon in Washington to discuss whether to recommend a military response, and, if so, what kind. They agreed to recommend that planes on the *Kennedy* and *Independence* be sent into Lebanon to bomb antiaircraft sites manned by Syrians. This would be a tit-for-tat response—the kind civilian leaders forced on the military during the Vietnam War. Your guns hit our planes; our planes will hit your guns. Neat. Tit for tat. Not a big escalation by Reagan who had said he was trying to bring peace to Lebanon. The battleship USS *New Jersey* was floating off Lebanon. Her 16-inch guns could retaliate for the firing on the reconnaissance planes. This would avoid risking fliers' lives. Admiral James D. Watkins, chief of Naval Operations at the time, explained to me later why he and fellow chiefs opted for Navy bombers rather than the battleship's guns.

"Those reconnaissance planes were shot at," Watkins said. "There was a feeling at the time that a response in kind was a legitimate thing. In other words, if you're shot at, you shoot back. A tit-for-tat kind of thing."

As far as using the battleship, he continued, "there is always concern that without the forward spotter you cannot be sure of achieving pinpoint accuracy. Here in Lebanon we had a very complex environment, a peacetime environment where collateral damage is a very big concern to us." (Collateral damage is a military euphemism for killing innocent men, women, and children in the target area, as well as destroying buildings beyond those aimed at.) "By peacetime I mean less than full wartime operations. So collateral damage is always of concern.

"And we have pinpoint accuracy in modern weapon systems that are airborne. Without the kind of full support you would have ashore for a normal fire mission, which includes all the kind of forward spotters and communication links and everything just the way you would do it if you were on a practice range, you worry about collateral damage. So my feeling is that it was the right decision to recommend using airplanes from the carriers *Kennedy* and *Independence* rather than employing the 16-inch guns on the *New Jersey*."

Because Washington was seven hours behind Beirut on the clock, it was still morning in Washington when Deputy Secretary of Defense Paul Thayer (Weinberger was out of town) and General John W. Vessey, chairman of the Joint Chiefs of Staff, brought their recommendation to Reagan. The President, according to White House officials, at first asked why the 16-inch guns of the *New Jersey* should not be used. He heard an explanation similar to the one Watkins gave me, and then approved the chief's recommendation for a bombing strike.

Out of the Mediterranean, Tuttle was drafting a concept of operations, or ConOps, the written blueprint for how he would bomb targets in Lebanon if the President asked him to do so. As the afternoon of 3 December wore on, Tuttle was receiving messages from up the chain indicating a bombing strike would really go this time. He called his planners to a room in his flagship to make detailed preparations for a strike. The planners included Commander John J. Mazach, commander of the *Kennedy* air wing, and Commander Ed "Honiak" Andrews, commander of the *Independence* air wing.

After high level negotiations between Tuttle and his superiors, the targets selected for bombing were in three previously prepared folders named RS (for Ready Strike) 7, 8, and 16. The pictures, maps and teletype information from the folders were spread out on the table. The air wing commanders immediately saw they had a problem with the targets in folders RS 7 and RS 8. The targets were so small that they would not reflect radar beams or radiate heat sufficiently to activate the precision bombing gear in the A-6E bombers. The fliers would have to find with their naked eyes the tiny antiaircraft guns and missiles hidden in the folds of the brown hills of Lebanon, no easy job while roaring along at 400 miles an hour. Folder RS 16, in contrast, contained an ideal target for bombers. It showed a big white building housing Syria's electronic junction for the links connecting the network of antiaircraft guns and missiles in Lebanon.

Mazach and Andrews worked into the night of 3 December updating the information in the target folders and blocking out routes for the bombers. Tuttle, Mazach, and Andrews concluded that there were so many antiaircraft missiles dotted around Lebanon that there was no risk-free entryway for their bombers to take into the targets. So they decided to send the bombers in above 10,000 feet to keep them above the 8,000 foot reach of the SA-7 heat-seeking missiles which had been fired at the TARPS reconnaissance planes. Tuttle planned to launch the bombers from the carriers about 11:00 A.M. the next morning. This would give the ordnance men time to break out the cluster bombs. These bombs would be best for destroying the antiaircraft guns and missile emplacements scattered on the hills on the westward and southward sloping ridges east of Beirut because they exploded over a wide area. The late morning launch would also have the advantage of having the sun high in the sky. If the pilots were launched at first light, they would have the sun in their eyes as they flew east toward the targets. But with a high sun there would be a minimum of shadows to hide the targets.

Tuttle, Mazach, and Martin all would tell me independently later that they did not know as they worked through the night of 3 December and into the predawn hours that Washington wanted them to strike the targets at first light and that Higher Authority would insist on it. This would foul up everything. At midnight, Mazach, believing that his bombers would be launched at 11:00 A.M. if Higher Authority issued an execute order for the raid, telephoned from the *Independence* to the *Kennedy* to tell Commander Robyn "Potsie" Weber, his chief of staff of Air Wing Three, to order the squadron skippers to select crews for the bombing raid. The air crews would have to be awakened in time to attend strike briefings at 5:00 A.M., Mazach said. This would give the bomber crews time to study their targets and work out the check points to be cranked into their navigation computer system. Weber woke up squadron skippers all around the ship. They, in turn, telephoned the officers responsible for matching up the crews with those bombers which were mechanically fit for flight.

Most of the fliers who would soon be risking their lives to deliver a political message to Syria were allowed to sleep on into the early hours of 4 December 1983. I was asleep, too. I knew the eight bomber pilots and navigators who lived together in an eight-man around the passageway from me. They soon would hear wakeup calls. These young lieutenants acted like fraternity brothers in their eight-man and around the ship. They always tried their damnedest to squeeze some fun out of the unnatural situation they found themselves in on a boat 7,000 miles away from wives, children, girl friends, parents, and other loved ones. They were Mainstream, USA; Mr. Everyman. Their families were neither very rich nor very poor. The fliers themselves were neither brilliant nor stupid; neither physical klutzes nor super jocks but in between. They were Middle America the way they waved the flag, distrusted politicians, and saw the world in black and white, good and evil. The eight fliers only looked like warriors to me when they were suited up for flight. In a few hours six of the eight fliers would be called upon to act like warriors and dive down low on targets so small that on the photos they looked like little metal washers lying in the dust. One of the eight would die, a second would be captured. None of the other six young men in the room would ever be the same afterward, whether they admitted it to each other or not. A Who's Who of the six lieutenants to fly the *Kennedy*'s first bombing strike read like this:

- Gil "Beaver" Bever, thirty, pilot; grew up in Glendora, California, where father ran a restaurant; graduated from California Polytechnical Institute; tried selling building materials, considered going to law school but this seemed like a boring career; joined Navy in 1979 in search of excitement; brought his guitar along on cruise.
- Tom "Percy" Corey, twenty-eight, pilot; son of a Navy chief who said "only thing I want you to do is to go to college"; graduated from Atlantic Christian College, Wilson, North Carolina; joined Navy 1979.
- Bill "Catfish" Davis, twenty-seven, bombardier-navigator; grew up in Orlando, Florida; graduated from University of

Florida; father a doctor; saw Navy as more exciting than engineering or other options he had considered.

* Bobby "Benny" Goodman, twenty-seven, bombardier-navigator; only black in room; son of a retired Air Force lieutenant colonel who gave him "lucky socks" to wear on missions; graduated from U.S. Naval Academy in 1978 where he played intramural sports; quiet but confident New Hampshire man.

* Mark "Doppler" Lange, twenty-six, pilot; born in Detroit, grew up in Fraser, Mich.; graduated from U.S. Naval Academy where he sang in glee club and chorus; separated, one child. Raised daughter, Jamie, on his own while home; parents cared for her while he was at sea.

* Mark "Mork" McNally, thirty, pilot; one of nine children; father retired astronomer; graduated from University of Missouri where he majored in physics; on his third deployment aboard the *Kennedy*.

Bever was called Beaver not only because his name sounded like beaver but he looked like one too when he smiled—which was often. He helped lighten the grayness of shipboard living by playing the guitar and harmonica at the same time. He was teaching Lange how to play the guitar.

Corey, a quick-witted, scrawny southerner, was called Percy to put down his macho pretensions. The nickname did not seem to faze him. Corey was the most frequent leader of alpha strikes in the eight-man bunk room. An alpha strike consisted of several fliers suddenly diving through the closed curtain of a roommate's bunk, breaking his solitude and yanking off the head phones feeding him soothing stereophonic sounds.

Davis was called Catfish because he definitely looked like one and, some said, chewed like one. He was seldom without a plug of tobacco in his mouth and a spit cup in his hand. His green eyes twinkled mischievously as he needled his roommates or participated in some prank.

Goodman was Benny some of the time but really starred as Stevie Wonder in the skits the squadrons intermittently put on for the air wing. Goodman would wear the dark glasses of the blind Stevie Wonder and the white jacket of a landing signal officer or the yellow shirt of a plane director. Pilots often regarded LSO's who graded their landings as blind. Plane directors sometimes caused planes to collide on the deck as they directed them to parking spaces there. Goodman's act was sure-fire.

Lange was called Doppler after the navigation system of that name to kid him about being spacey about some things. He often protested the cigar smoke generated in the eight-man, inspiring his roommates to pass out cigars when he was in his upper bunk and blow smoke his way. He also objected to putting a weightlifting bench in the eight-man on grounds the room would end up smelling like a gymnasium. His objections made it more fun for his roommates to lift weights—the chief form of exercise on the crowded carrier.

In early November, Lange discovered that he was not among the few to be briefed secretly on the plan to bomb Target X. CAG Mazach and the skipper of VA-85 were trying to put together the best blend of experience and knowledge in the left and right seats of the A-6s to go on the raid. Lange did not make this first cut, presumably because he and Bobby Goodman did not have as much experience and expertise as other crews selected. His roommates who had been chosen could not resist needling Doppler when they got back from their secret briefings:

"Ha, ha, you didn't get your ice cream," was the taunt.

Lange, like most aviators, was highly competitive. He did not want to be left out of anything. He went to his squadron skipper, Commander Kirby Hughes, to complain. If there was something big going on, he told Hughes, he wanted in on it, despite his special obligations at home.

He and his stunning blonde wife, Cheryl, were separated. He met her while she was an enlisted woman in the Navy and married her after she left the service. They had a lovely one-year-old daughter, Jamie, whom Lange adored. Cheryl said she was not ready to settle down to rearing a family. Under the separation agreement, Lange had custody of Jamie. He took care of her while home and his parents in Fraser, Michigan, kept Jamie while he was at sea. Mark confided to his shipmates that he was considering quitting the Navy, even though he loved it, so he could be home full time rearing Jamie. He was planning to ask for a shore billet before giving up on continuing his Navy career.

"A very traditional person," Ensign Brian Ahern, the intelligence officer of VA-85, said of his best friend, Mark Lange. "He believed in one wife, scratch a nest, have children.

That's the way he grew up. He was a very devoted father, a very devoted husband. Liked to take his wife out, dance, enjoy the night. Go to the Lutheran Church on Sunday. That was the way he wanted his life to be.''

McNally was called Mork after the television character of that name. He was the senior lieutenant in the eight-man. His juniors in the room wanted to remind him that he was still spacey. McNally's salty background of three cruises before the current one made him wiser than most about the need to spice up Navy chow by bringing a larder of goodies onto the ship: fancy cheeses, meat, crackers, and pickles. Every so often McNally would unlock the larder for a party in the eight-man's living room. This was the rectangle of free carpet in front of the four tiers of double bunks pushed to the rear. The weightlifting bench took up the left hand corner of this living room. The eight desks along the front and sides ate up the rest of the free space in front of the bunks.

At 3:45 A.M. on 4 December Catfish went from bunk to bunk to shake six of seven roommates awake. Catfish had been told by his squadron that they were going on a bombing raid. He had heard this so many times before he did not take it seriously. His roommates reflected his own incredulity as he wakened them one after another. "Another fucking Chinese fire drill!" Catfish decided to let Lieutenant Mark "Sonny" Beach, son of a Navy pilot, sleep. He had only been on the *Kennedy* for four days. He would not be sent on the raid if it did go. But as the seven men awoke, they reverted to their needling style, shook Sonny awake, and chanted: "Ha, ha, you didn't get your ice cream." Like Lange before him, Sonny Beach was being served notice, aviator style, that he was being left out of something really big.

The seven aviators clomped into Civic for the briefing on this latest drill. CAG Mazach looked rumpled, tired, and deadly serious. He obviously had been up a long time.

"You've only got a few minutes to go over this stuff," he warned, "because your target time for launch is 7:20."

"Sure, sure," McNally said to himself as he looked at his watch which showed 5:00 A.M. He knew that if the bombing raid were really going to go, they would have provided more time to brief. He had stayed up whole nights getting briefed and refining routes and checkpoints in preparation for hitting Target X in the Bekaa Valley. Then again, McNally thought to himself,

"This one is so screwed up it will probably go."

Commander Jim Kidd, a tall, dedicated former A-7 bomber pilot in charge of Strike Operations for Air Wing Three, had been told at 4:05 A.M. to make sure his mix of bombs were loaded on the bombers in time to make an 11 A.M. launch. He told me afterward that his reaction was that this would be tight but doable.

With the help of a computer in his office, Kidd figured how many of what type of bomb stored deep inside the *Kennedy* should be hung on each of the attacking bombers to destroy its assigned target. He immediately determined that the widely scattered antiaircraft sites in the hills of Lebanon would be most vulnerable to bombs which send out showers of shrapnel over acres of ground when they exploded. He planned to put ten Rockeye cluster bombs on each A-6 bomber. This would be a lethal load but not so heavy that the pilots would find their planes too heavy to jink—zig and zag—to dodge missiles.

Kidd received a second call at 5:40 A.M. "Your birds have to be loaded up in time to launch at 0630 so they can be over the beach by 0730," the caller said.

"No way!" Kidd exploded. "Not only no way, but no fucking way. It cannot be fucking done."

From that moment on, Kidd felt he was engaged in a half-assed bombing mission in which men would be sent off without either the right number or right type of bombs for the targets they were risking their lives to destroy. He grieved about it, telling me in a voice heavy with fatigue and sadness: "Someone somewhere doesn't understand the problem. This is the worst I've ever seen. The guy who is going in harm's way should have the right to decide how we should do it."

The seven fliers from the eight-man and the others who had been summoned for the quick, initial briefing were handed folders containing maps and pictures of their targets and were ordered back to their ready rooms to study them. Each A-6 crew, a pilot and bombardier, got together to study the material and mark checkpoints for themselves along the assigned route to the target. McNally was to fly with Commander Kirby "Skip" Hughes, skipper of VA-85, a bombardier-navigator. They had been assigned an airplane. Other crews in the VA-85 and VA-75 A-6 squadrons had not. The ordies, who had thought launch was going to be at 11 A.M., not 7:20 A.M., had not had time to break out the ordered mix of bombs from their packing cases and get them attached to the bombers. Planes were being assigned to crews as they got loaded, snarling the usually ordered assignment process. To save time in case they really were ordered to launch at 7:20, McNally, the pilot, went up to the flight deck to check over his assigned plane while Hughes went to the armory to draw out a pistol. He might get shot down over Lebanon, if the raid went this time.

"Check one out for me, too, OK?" McNally called after Hughes as they split in the passageway.

McNally, Hughes, and the other aviators assigned to the strike reassembled at Civic for Mazach's final prelaunch briefing. Mazach had on his survival gear, signaling that he was going to lead them into Lebanon rather than stay back on the carrier and coordinate the mission by radio. This reassured Catfish. He knew Mazach had flown through a lot of fire in Vietnam in his A-7 bomber and would know how to get them in and out of Lebanon alive.

"OK," Mazach began. "I want to talk about this for 10 minutes, so get your shit together. We need to man up in 10 or 15 minutes so we can make our target time for launch of 0720 so we can be over the beach at 0805."

He outlined the one-two punch of the *Independence* and *Kennedy* bombers flying straight in eastward from the beach, and told them to maintain radio silence to avoid tipping off the gunners that planes were on the way. Corey was bold enough to ask why it would not be better to sneak around from the north. Mazach told him that this and other ideas had been considered. The raid was going as now planned. End debate.

Corey and Catfish walked up to the flight deck to find their assigned bomber, triple nickel, or number 555—a lucky number so far. They were the envy of their squadron mates still pacing the ready room waiting to be assigned a bomber. The loading was way behind schedule, holding up assignments of planes.

"Damn, don't call it off here," Catfish said to himself as he checked out number 555 with Corey. They both looked at each other aghast. There were no bombs on their plane. Yet they were supposed to launch in a few minutes. The ordies could not get enough Rockeyes, the assigned cluster bombs, broken out and loaded to get them on the bombers waiting to go. Everything was in a mad flail of ball-busting effort on the flight deck because of the earlier than anticipated launch time.

"Throw some bombs on there," Corey ordered one of the ordies from his squadron. Corey had seen some iron bombs stacked up on the flight deck near the plane. The hell with waiting for the Rockeyes. Going with something was better than missing the launch altogether or going to Lebanon completely naked of bombs.

The young ordie, already stressed from trying to meet an impossibly early loading deadline, blinked back at Corey uncertainly. His chief had not yet told him what to do with the bombs Corey wanted.

"Go ahead," Corey insisted. "I'll take the responsibility."

The ordies rushed into action. They knew everything was running late. They wheeled two Mark-83 1,000-pound bombs under the A-6 and clamped them on the fittings. Catfish and Corey climbed quickly up the ladders to the cockpit, strapped themselves in, and fired up the engines.

"Hey Tom," Catfish said with a whoop. "This is as far as we've ever got." The aviators' adrenaline pump was pushing them into a high of excitement as the engines roared to life.

McNally preflighted his A-6 and climbed in. He saw his skipper, the six-foot-four Kirby Hughes, who would be his bombardier-navigator in the right seat, hurrying across the flight deck. He looked like Ichabod Crane on speed. Hughes snaked up the ladder and snapped himself in. Usually both crew members check over the plane before taking off.

"I didn't preflight," Hughes told McNally. "I hope you did."

"Yeah. We're all set. Did you get my gun?"

"No. I forgot."

"Can I have yours?"

"Fuck you!"

McNally and Hughes laughed, started the engines, and waited for the Green Shirts to break them down—unchain the airplane from its pad eye fastenings recessed into the flight deck. The Yellow Shirts were busy directing other planes to the catapult. McNally and Hughes waited anxiously. There had been no time to change the bomb load under their A-6E. They would have to go with the light load which had been put on yesterday in case the bombers had to be launched at night to destroy an attacking speedboat or give quick help to the marines in Beirut. They would fly into Lebanon with what was called a recoverable load. A recoverable load is light enough to be flown aloft and then to be landed back on carrier. A heavily loaded bomber might break or unloose its bombs when it slammed down on the deck and caught the wire. McNally and Hughes had to settle for the four APAMs already on their plane, though it could carry 12 APAMs with ease.

Lange and Goodman grew impatient as they sat in the VA-85 ready room waiting for a plane. Lange went up to the roof to help preflight other planes while Goodman waited in the ready room for their plane assignment to come through. Lt. Mike "Skimmer" Dulke saw what his roommates were up to and rushed for the same door to beat them to a plane. Lange squeezed past Dulke and headed for the last available plane, the one that would be shot down, killing Lange. Dulke lost the race for the door—and lived.

Goodman joined Lange on the flight deck, hunted around, and spotted A-6 number 556, one of the bombers belonging to VA-85. He asked his roommate, McNally, what munitions were loaded on it. McNally told him the bomber was the only which had been fully loaded. It held six Mark-83 1,000-pound bombs.

"Our target is for 83s," Goodman said. "We'll take it."

Bever and Lieutenant Keith Goeke scouted around the deck looking for a ready-to-go A-6. The only one they could find had a nothing load on it—only two APAMs. There was no more time. They either had to launch or stay home. The *Indy*'s bombers were already in the air. Bever and Goeke climbed into the A-6 and fired it up. They would do what they could with what they were given. They were like two soldiers who had been issued only two bullets but would risk their lives trying to make them count.

Three other crews out of the ten awakened for the raid found bombers with at least a couple of APAMs or iron bombs on them. CAG Mazach and Lieutenant Commander John Jones, his bombardier-navigator, climbed into one of them. Commander Paul Bernard, executive officer of VA-85, and Commander Steve Day, his bombardier-navigator, found another. So did Commander Dave Burlin, pilot, and Lieutenant Commander Jim Linquist, BN. This made seven crews from VA-85 strapped in or already launched out of the ten *Kennedy* bombers which would go on the raid. The other three came from the second A-6 squadron, VA-75.

Commander Jim Glover, skipper of VA-75, and Lieutenant Commander John Tindle, his BN, also had figured when they had been awakened out of a sound sleep, that they were suiting up for one more drill. All the aviators from VA-75 would tell me that they figured nobody would order them to conduct a raid so soon after celebrating their brief escape from the ship in Haifa.

Besides Glover and Tindle, VA-75 woke up pilot-bombardier-navigator teams of Lieutenants Bob Solik and Pete Frano, Rick "Blue Ribbon" Pabst, and Ian "Jabbo" Jablonski. Frano was so sure it was just another drill that he did not bother to lace up his boots tightly. He worried the whole time he was over Lebanon about what would happen if he ejected in those loose flight boots.

Glover, Tindle, Solik, Frano, Pabst, and Jablonski all joined the parade tramping down to Civic for the strike briefings. They stayed there until 6:30. Glover broke off to return to the VA-75 ready room to go over the thousand details of the raid with the two air crews who would fly beside him into hostile fire.

The three VA-75 bomber crews tramped up to the roof still believing they were just going through the motions. They changed their mind only when they saw how fast bombers were being hurled off the front of the boat by the shooters—the launching teams. The *Kennedy*'s E-2C Hawkeye was already in the air. It was ready to coordinate the raid by radio as it orbited off Lebanon. Its call sign was Close Out. The EA-6Bs were being launched ahead of the bombers. Their job would be to jam Syrian fire-control radars for a few crucial seconds —jarring the aim of the gunners on the ground in Lebanon. The Yellow Shirt directed Glover's A-6 into the slot. He was shot off the bow, the first *Kennedy* bomber to hit the sky the dawn of 4 December 1983.

CAG Mazach taxied across the deck to the catapult shuttle. He noticed as he went into tension that the Soviet eavesdropping trawler was hanging in close—it looked to be only a half-mile off the port side of the ship. The Russians were watching, listening, and presumably radioing "the Americans are coming" to Syrian command posts in Lebanon so they could alert the gunners scattered all through the country.

"I wonder what that guy is thinking," CAG quipped over the lip microphone to Jones, his BN, as he pointed to the Soviet Tattletale.

The shooters hurled Mazach's bomber into the sky. He circled over the ship at 12,000 feet waiting for the rest of his boys. Soon they looked like gray-and-white guppies circling in a limitless fish globe of gray sky.

As hard as everybody had tried to make the early launch time, the *Kennedy* bombers were up later than the bombing plan stipulated. Mazach worried if the delay in getting airborne would ruin the timing of the one-two *Indy-Kennedy* punch. He hoped Tuttle had held the *Indy* bombers back until the *Kennedy*'s could assemble in the sky. He saw nine other of his A-6 bombers were circling with him. He pushed for the IP—the initial point—the spot in the sky where the bombers would start their run to the targets. Mazach had to know whether his part of the raid was still go. Tuttle might have decided to send in the *Indy* bombers already. The *Kennedy*'s might not be sent in at all. Mazach did not want to make it any easier for the Soviet eavesdroppers to find out what was going on. He went on the radio to check the status of the raid with Navy lingo the Soviets hopefully would not understand.

"Steel Jaw," Mazach began to catch the attention of the *Indy* E-2 which was coordinating the raid. "State the status of Broad Sword."

Steel Jaw was the E-2 commander and Broad Sword was CAG Andrews of the *Independence*.

"Green Lead. This is Steel Jaw. Broad Sword is rendezvousing."

"Well, shit," CAG said to himself. "That means they haven't pushed yet. I've got time."

The *Indy*'s five A-6s and thirteen A-7s were circling to gather everybody together just like the *Kennedy*'s ten bombers had been doing before CAG called Steel Jaw.

Mazach pushed off to his IP. His bombers followed in waves of two and three in a wide spread to make it harder for gunners to track and hit them. The sun was up. The bombers were flying right into it, exactly what you do not want to do to survive antiaircraft fire and pick out small targets on the ground.

Mazach and Jones clicked onto the radio frequency specified for the bomber crews to use when assembling overhead for the strike. Mazach heard the two flights of bombers from the *Independence,* called Red Flight and Blue Flight, check in. Then he heard the familiar voice of CAG Andrews of the *Independence* calling him across the sky separating the two carriers.

"Green Flight. This is Red Flight. Are you up?"

"Red Flight. Green Flight is up."

"Green Flight. This is Alpha Bravo," Tuttle rasped through his transmitter on the *Indy*. "You're a go."

Mazach and his bombers were on their way to the first bombing strike ever launched from the *Kennedy*. He was proud of his young aviators for maintaining radio silence as they knifed toward the Lebanese coast. Then to his horror he heard a stray bomber from the *Indy* ask for vectors so he could catch up to the strike group. This radioed query and answer might have been intercepted by the Soviet ships eavesdropping. If it was intercepted, the Syrian gunners would know where the incoming bombers were in the sky and what course they were flying. Aviators call such breaches in radio security "poor discipline." Mazach could only hope nobody exploited the radio message as he continued to lead the *Kennedy* bombers eastward at a speed calculated to take them over the beach seven minutes after the *Indy*'s bombers had become "feet dry."

A few seconds after the *Indy* bombers had become feet dry, the *Kennedy* bombers trailing after them heard through their earphones the excited reactions of young aviators being shot at for the first time in their lives:

"SAMS! SAMS! SAMS . . ."

"SAM 7!"

"Left! Keep it coming. Keep it coming."

"I'm hit . . . I'm hit . . ."

"Looks like CAG is hit at 6 o'clock . . ."

"CAG, where you at?"

"May Day! May Day! This is three zero five. I'm proceeding out over the water now. I want you to join up with me. I got 250 knots."

"I'm looking for you."

"I'm back behind you."

"Right."

"They're shooting at us."

"How you doing back there?"

"I'm fine. Almost clear right now."

"We're looking for you right now."

"Honiak out of here." (Andrews' message that he had ejected from his burning A-7 light bomber.)

"Good chute. Good chute," Andrews' wing man called out. Then he started talking to the two rescue helicopters, called Primo and Dancer, which had already taken off from the *Guam* in search of Andrews.

"Did you get a good tally on him?"

"Searching for him in the harbor area," Primo replied.

"Steel Jaw," the wingman called out to *Indy*'s E-2 Hawkeye warning and control plane orbiting off the beach. "Red Two is down. On scene commander is active three zero four. Primo is inbound."

A Christian fisherman and his son pulled Andrews into their boat. A speedboat carrying French newsmen took Andrews from the fishermen. A Zodiak rubber boat manned by the French military took him from the newsmen to shore. A Lebanese helicopter then flew the still dripping-wet Andrews to a soccer stadium in Beirut where a U.S. Marine helicopter landed and took the *Indy* CAG back to his carrier.

I was asleep when I heard the first planes rattling down the deck directly above our bunks. It was not unusual to launch a few planes in the predawn dark. But as I heard one after another pounding down and off the deck above my head, I knew something big was up. I hurriedly dressed and went to the CAG office and then to the Operations Center and then to the Tower. But jet bombing attacks happen so quickly that the planes were headed back before I had gathered all the details of the strike. I interviewed everyone who had gone on the raid afterward and listened to the tapes of the radio talk to fill in the many blanks in my account of exactly what happened.

Catfish told me that as his bomber approached the Lebanese coast, the radio chatter about SAMs wiped out his remaining doubts about this mission being another false alarm. This was for real. People will be shooting at me, he thought as Corey pressed on toward their target. The first sign of war Catfish saw was the flashes of the *Indy*'s bombs going off on the ground.

"Hey, this is real!" Catfish said into his microphone to Corey.

CAG Mazach looked into his cockpit mirror when he heard the *Indy*'s missile calls. He wanted to make sure his boys were jinking. He need not have worried. Every pilot was jinking left and right, up and down, in hopes of missing whatever was exploding in the sky ahead of them. Mazach had been shot at before when he was flying A-7 light bombers in Vietnam. John Jones, sitting on his right, had not. CAG told Jones to keep looking for the launch smoke of SAMs so he could dodge them. He was crossing the coast at 12,000 feet.

"Fireball! Fireball!" Mazach and Jones heard through their helmets.

It was too late to be from the crash of CAG Andrews' A-7.

"Green Lead. This is Ace Lead. I think five zero two is down in the target area."

Green Lead was CAG Mazach. Ace Lead was Jim Glover, skipper of VA-75 Sunday Punchers also called the Flying Aces. Flying in 502 were Lieutenants Pabst and Jablonski.

"Steel Jaw," Mazach called to the E-2 Hawkeye orbiting off the coast. "This is Green Lead. I've got five zero two down about 15 miles east of Beirut."

"Roger that Green Lead."

Pabst heard the call that he had crashed while he was safely in the air behind Mazach. He could hear over his radios but not transmit because of a breakdown. So he pushed in the throttles, caught up to Mazach and flew alongside him to catch his attention. Mazach saw 502 was alive and well at the same time Paul Bernard called to report that the missing bomber was Number 556. He had noticed a blank in the sky off his wing where Lange and Goodman were supposed to be flying.

"Steel Jaw. This is Green Lead. Forget about five zero two. It's five five six. Got five zero two here and have seen an airplane go down."

"Green Lead. This is Steel Jaw. Roger that."

Corey slid his A-6 closer to Bernard's right wing. Bernard pulled up to fire a strike antiradar missile. Catfish looked down and saw the corkscrew smoke from a missile that had just been fired his way. Then he saw seven more corkscrews down on the ground and the white clouds of bursting ack-ack about 2,000 feet below his bomber. He lost sight of Lange and Goodman off Bernard's other wing. Corey and Davis were concentrating on the missiles so they could dodge them if they reached their altitude. An SA-7 came up right between Bernard and Corey but did not have enough strength left to veer off to hit either of them. The shoulder fired SA-7 is only effective up to 8,000 feet, usually less.

One of the SA-7s in the barrage or a longer-range missile apparently smashed into number 556—Lange and Goodman's A-6. Solik and Frano were feeling lucky as they looked down and saw that the guns and missiles were exploding far below their 12,000 feet altitude, probably because the Syrians were expecting the American planes to come in at the same altitude as the F-14 TARPs flew—between 3,000 and 6,000 feet. They saw the plane carrying Lange and Goodman tumbling in a waving scarf of flames. It smashed into the side of a ridge and then tumbled down it. The two stunned aviators could see hunks of flaming wreckage cartwheeling down the ridge ahead of the main part of the plane. They did not see any parachutes. They looked ahead and saw the skipper rolling in on his target. They had to forget about the downed plane for the moment and set up for dive bombing their own target. It was a tank and artillery dug into the side of a hill. Their A-6 was loaded only with three APAMs and a Shrike instead of the ten Rockeye cluster bombs they were supposed to carry on this raid.

Lange was less nimble in the air than the others. He was carrying the only heavy load of bombs. Perhaps he could not jink as well, dove down lower than the other bombers to gain the speed he needed to catch up to Bernard, or was just the victim of a lucky hit. He struggled to control the flaming bomber but could not. Its tumbling made Solik and Frano think it had lost big chunks of its control surfaces—like the ailerons, the panels hinged to the trailing edge of the wing; or the elevators in the tail. If Lange got too close to the ground before he ejected, his parachute would not have time to open. Lange and Goodman independently pulled the yellow-and-black loops under their seats to eject themselves. The rockets under the seats went off, shooting them up and through the canopy, which disintegrated in a shower of plastic bits—the way it is supposed to do. The high backed seats, not the fliers' helmeted heads, smashed the roof off the cockpit. In the F-14, the canopy flies off before the fliers are rocketed out of the cockpit.

Lange was hurled out of the cockpit and through the air at 200 to 300 miles an hour. His parachute opened at almost the last second needed to break his fall to the ground. He glided down to earth and hit the ground hard. Something, perhaps his metal seat pan, severed his left leg on impact. *Kennedy* doctors who examined Lange's body afterward theorized that Lange bled to death for want of a tourniquet. The Syrian gunners might have saved his life if they had applied one quickly.

Goodman landed hard, broke some ribs, separated his left shoulder, and tore up his left knee. He was immediately captured by Syrian gunners, who roughed him up but did not seriously hurt him. They summoned news photographers in Beirut to the crash site to take Goodman's picture, along with wreckage of the plane, to show the world what the United States had done. The six 1,000-pounds on Lange's plane were in the wreckage. The only heavily loaded bomber never reached its target. Goodman was taken to Damascus along with Lange's body.

Bernard and Corey did not realize Lange and Goodman had been shot out of their three plane V-formation. They continued flying inland, looking for their designated patch of Lebanon some 15 miles in from the beach and slightly north of Beirut. They headed toward a high ridge which formed the outer wall of the Bekaa Valley curving through Lebanon. They stayed on the coastal side of this ridge to keep out of range of the heavy Syrian antiaircraft defenses, which included medium range SA-9 missiles on the valley floor. Bernard and Corey were searching for their targets: antiaircraft sites. They saw the big white building, called the white house, which Lange and Goodman were supposed to hit. They had been told in the briefings to hit anything they found in the designated area once they got there. All the antiaircraft gun and missile sites would fit Higher Authority's tit-for-tat rationale for the raid. Corey started to dive on the white house. Davis had already punched the instructions into the computer so it would release their two 1,000-pound Mark 83 bombs at the right instant. Corey's dive was too steep for the white house so he went after two buildings near it. The bombs released and he pulled up out of his dive to the left so he could see the bombs he had dropped go off behind the plane.

"Shit, look at all that Triple A they're firing at us," Corey remarked to Davis as they looked down at the hilly ground they had just bombed. Then they realized as they turned around to head back toward the beach that the flashes were APAMs exploding. They had been dropped by other A-6s they could see pulling out of dives over the same general target area.

"Pull hard right! Hard right," Davis snapped as he saw an SA-7 missile coming toward them.

Corey, who already was jinking the plane violently, pulled left instead of right, making Davis fear they would put themselves right in the path of the upward rushing missile.

"I said right! Right! Try your other right!"

Corey snapped the lightened bomber to the right. Davis lost sight of the missile. As he looked around for it he saw another A-6 off the right wing. He assumed it was Lange and Goodman.

It was Bernard and Day. Corey skidded down the ridge and stayed low all the way out to Juniyah on the coast and on out over the water. He stayed 100 feet over the sunlit Mediterranean for 25 miles. Then Tom "Percy" Corey and Bill "Catfish" Davis realized that they had survived their first combat. Tension drained out and jubilation poured in.

"Now you know what a dove feels like on opening day of hunting season," Corey quipped. They both laughed. They did not yet know that their roommates had not been as lucky.

THE SHIP | The USS *John F. Kennedy* (CV-67) was christened on 27 May 1967 at Newport News, Virginia, by President Kennedy's daughter, Caroline, and soon became the star of the U.S. Atlantic fleet, winning many awards. U.S. Navy

The *Kennedy* (bottom), seen here from above with the USS *Ticonderoga* (top) and the USS *Detroit,* measures 1,051 feet long, 270 feet wide, 229 feet high, with a flight deck that is 4.56 acres. U.S. Navy

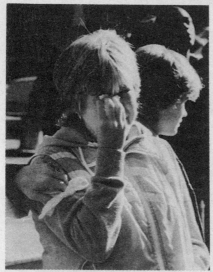

DEPARTURE/The hardest thing about the Navy are the goodbyes. Tearful farewells mark the *Kennedy*'s departure from Norfolk's Pier 12 for a seven-month deployment on the other side of the world.
U.S. Navy

SHIPMATES / Kids right out of high school run the most sophisticated, dangerous, and powerful war machine ever built—an aircraft carrier.

Hook runner Michael Goulette has one of the most dangerous jobs "on the roof," the flight deck, where he risks being maimed by the arresting wire as he runs toward it as each aircraft lands.

Thomas Brinson (right) also works in a risky job—the boiler room. Here he shows Steve Benoit and the author (middle) how to light off a boiler without causing an explosion.

Boatswain Mate Robert "Marty" Martell, twenty-five, typifies the young men who found a home in the Navy. He felt important for the first time in his life as he launched planes off the *Kennedy*.

Air Boss Mike Boston (right) looks in on Tom "Zippy" Larson in arresting gear compartment where he sets the tension wires that catch planes as they land.

Aircraft have become so sophisticated that civilian technical experts must sail along on carrier deployments to keep planes flying. Here a representative from Pratt & Whitney, Leo Piwniczka, instructs sailors on aircraft engine-tuning.

The catapult crew, seen here taking a break between launches.

Hoist that flag!

KENNEDY *INCORPORATED*/Command is lonely. *Kennedy* skipper Gary F. Wheatley was responsible for everyone and everything—twenty-four hours a day—whether he was on the bridge, as here, or sound asleep in his cabin.

EXECUTIVE OFFICER/John A. Pieno.

John J. Mazach ran the *Kennedy* air wing in between flying A-6 bombers and F-14 fighters. He led the bombing raid over Lebanon.

Chaplain Jim Doffin was in charge of Trouble Central and tried to ease the plight of his isolated flock.

Command Master Chief Stanley G. Crowley was Mr. In-Between for the captain and his crew.

BEAR HUNT/Navy F-14 fighters raced aloft whenever a Soviet bomber like this Bear came near the *Kennedy*. The idea was to demonstrate in peacetime that a Soviet bomber could never get within killing range of a carrier in wartime. U.S. Navy

American pilots like Lieutenant Brad Goetsch stared across the narrow space of sky at Russian counterparts and wondered what they were like.

WOG DAY/Wogs were initiated into the Order of the Shellbacks as the *Kennedy* crossed the equator on way to Rio de Janeiro. Sailors, transformed into "beauty queens" for Wog Day, graced King Neptune's court on flight deck.

U.S. Navy

U.S. Navy

U.S. Navy

LIBERTY IN RIO!/After days of being locked inside the steel walls of the carrier, officers and sailors looked for action whenever they pulled into port.

Chaplain Doffin spent his Rio liberty doing good deeds, here painting a school named after President Kennedy. U.S. Navy

F-14 pilot Sammy Bonanno does some high flying in Rio.

CAG staff whooping it up.

BOMBING RAID/ Kennedy bombers struck Lebanon on 4 December 1983, before they were even completely loaded up and ready. Rear Admiral Jerry O. Tuttle (right), battle group commander, was ordered to strike "at first light" in communications breakdown.

Ordnance men rushing bombs across hangar bay toward elevators leading up to flight deck where planes are loaded.

The A-6E Intruder bombers shown here were the *Kennedy*'s big stick.

Survivors: Frenchie Jancarski (left) and Dan Rockel, who rescued Jancarski from the Mediterranean.

Death strikes with numbing suddenness on an aircraft carrier. The shipmate you joked with at lunch can be dead by suppertime without anyone knowing how or why, as was the case in the "mishaps" during the *Kennedy* deployment when three planes crashed into the Mediterranean, a fourth collided in midair, and a fifth was shot down over Lebanon. The toll: four dead, one seriously injured, one captured.

Lieutenant Commander Ollie Wright (right) and Airman Mark Phillips, who dived from a helicopter into the Mediterranean to rescue Wright.

Those who died:

Lieutenant (jg) Cole "Bam Bam" O'Neil. U.S. Navy

Petty Officer Third Class Fernando "Mex" Pena. U.S. Navy

Commander John "Belly" Scull. U.S. Navy

AFTERMATH / Mark Lange U.S. Navy photo on left and Bobby Goodman (shown with his wife, Terry Lynn) were shot down over Lebanon in their A-6E. Lange bled to death on the ground. Goodman was captured and eventually released by the Syrians. Photo by James M. Thresher, courtesy of The Washington Post

Marines waiting for Mark Lange's casket on flight deck of the *Kennedy*. U.S. Navy

OFF-DUTY/Bob Hope and Brooke Shields briefly lifted the spirits of the *Kennedy* men at Christmas, a sad occasion for those at sea while their families were at home.

Sailors with tailor-made jackets try to make the most of Naples liberty.

Dear Daddy,
Right now I'm at home with blisters all over my body called CHICKENPOX I've had them sence Tues. very boring tha 3d I went to Christine's Birthday She had a Slumber Party it was fun! I Love you abt

P.S. The groundhog saw his Shadow

Riley

Happy Valentines

A sample of kids' letters to their dads: Riley Weber's Valentine card to dad, Commander Ronald Weber, and Mikey Williams's card to dad, Lieutenant Commander Don Williams.

Daddy
I wont be able to talk to him. I love to go on the sidewalk and beach with Daddy. I want to splash Daddy and going swimming with Daddy. I love you
Mikey

Kennedy returns to Norfolk after steaming 55,000 miles. Families press against the restraining ropes at the pier. The women broke through the rope and embraced their men with tears, laughter, and shouts of "You're home!"

11 Aftermath

I FELT as if I were at a wake rather than a celebration as I made the rounds of the ship right after the last plane had returned from the raid over Lebanon. I found rage, bitterness, sadness, rationalization, and protest. I heard no more talk about bombing Lebanon back to the Stone Age. It had become painfully obvious in less than one half hour on 4 December 1983 that Navy fliers got killed that way—even in peacetime.

"What a fucked-up mission," shouted a hotshot fighter pilot as I sat with him and other aviators in the Air Wing office rehashing the raid. "I don't see how you can't retaliate when they fire on your planes. But we lost two airplanes. That's a big victory for them."

The pilot was an outspoken Republican who had sung Reagan's praises long and loud around the ship. So it was radical for him when he said in summing up his protest: "I'm going to vote Democratic because of the way they micromanaged this raid."

Another officer called me into his office, closed the door, and raged and grieved about the raid, declaring at one point: "If the American people ever find out that we sent ten airplanes over there from this carrier to do what one plane could do, they'll never forgive us. I'm embarrassed. Vietnam taught us how to do it without losses. You go in with the A-6 in one or twos at night with standoff maneuvers and weapons. I wonder if we learned anything at all from Vietnam."

Of the ten A-6 bombers which had taken off from the *Kennedy*, only Lange's had carried a respectable load of bombs, and his plane was shot down. CAG Mazach's bombs had become hung up and did not drop. The eight remaining bombers dropped in total such a light load of munitions that one A-6 could have carried it all: four Mark 83 1,000-pound bombs and fourteen APAMs.

A veteran aviator from Vietnam, who flew on the raid, said: "One lesson from all of this is that the Navy has been worrying too much about defending the carrier and not enough about getting bombs on the target."

"A foul tip, an abortion," said one high-ranking planner who had done his best to make what he considered a "tactically unsound" plan work. "You just don't use an air wing against guns. Don't give me a 400 acre field to find a gun in. Hardly anybody saw his targets because they were so small and so hard to pick out. We couldn't go in low because we did not have enough time or target information to do the preplanning required for that.

"If Higher Authority insisted on using 28 carrier airplanes against guns packed into the same small space, I would start off with three airplanes max from the *Kennedy;* 37 minutes later two airplanes from the *Indy* would show up from another direction; 15 minutes after that two would go in from a third direction from the *Kennedy.* Over a six hour period I could get 28 airplanes in and out of there with no problem. There would be a lot more freedom of movement. The guys on the ground wouldn't know where the planes would be coming from next. It's just common sense militarily. It reeks politically because it takes such a long time to accomplish."

A veteran bombardier-navigator who had narrowly escaped death in the raid spoke with me softly but feelingly as we sat together in the back of his ready room. He had been sitting all alone back there since coming in from the flight deck. He had been trying to figure out how, after all the fastidious planning of the raids which did not go, his Navy could launch the real one with almost no planning or briefings or bombs. We talked right after the raid and several times subsequently. "We need to surprise the enemy more and ourselves less. It was ridiculous the way we did it. We need time to plan our targets and ordnance so a strike is executed the way it is planned. We had been planning for almost a month before this strike to go to————. We had been single-minded about it. We briefed every other night—when we were the go carrier for hitting ————. We loaded the ordnance for it. Hitting————was our whole focus.

"Then we get up in the morning and find out that something entirely new had been designed. That strike was completely foreign to us. We had to shift gears.

"If we had had the time, we would have done a much better job. Mark's death could have been prevented if we had had the proper time to plan and execute. We just weren't allowed that option. I feel really depressed.

"I would go in much higher to get away from the Triple A and the SAMs. We could roll in from a higher altitude and still get accurate delivery, if you had good photos.

"The marines told us they were standing there at the airport watching us go in. They said they saw a tremendous number of SAMs, Triple A, and flak. They couldn't imagine how any of us could survive. They said it was amazing how much stuff was in the air. They saw all of us roll in and one guy hit from their vantage point at the airport. That shows you how close in the targets were. They should have been hit by naval gunfire. I feel fortunate to have survived all that stuff. Very fortunate."

Going in from the north, other aviators told me, would risk having the bombs skip down the north to south slope of the ridge where many of the targets were located.

A bombardier-navigator in another squadron told me this: "The targets weren't suitable for our ordnance load. I was wondering when I got back why we went after those small, individual targets without the load we planned on. I was sitting around the ready room with the guys who were getting ready to be the second wave when we found out we had lost two airplanes. Wow! That set us back a little bit. We were wondering, 'What the hell is going on? Why are we doing this?' They really didn't explain it very well."

A pilot who had managed to pick out his target—a Triple A site—in the folds of the hills northeast of Lebanon and drop his three APAMs on it shared with me his evolution of emotions: "First, I was happy we got there, we did it, and we got back. It wasn't till well later that I wasn't really pleased that we couldn't have had the time to put on the ordnance we should have had. It had to be a political thing—show our resolve. Had to be. Because we didn't hit them with anything much. I wouldn't do the same thing again. We should go around the Triple A.''

''I'm as far right as you can get,'' said an F-14 flier who was briefed on what to do if he were shot down over Lebanon. ''But when that guy talked to us about him sneaking into Lebanon at night and getting a phone book and ripping out a phone because our embassy didn't have any funds for that shit, and he wanted to teach us how to use the phone in Lebanon in case we got shot down; when he talked about getting the right coins for the phone and how this tribe will kill you and this one won't, providing they're the older guys, and that we've decided the Syrians are the best captors, I figured: 'What the hell, once I'm down, I surrender.' The plane was my protection. I'm for the first time wondering what the hell are we doing here. I'm for getting the hell out.''

''They've got no oil, no nothing,'' said a young pilot-father in taking a new look at the Lebanon which had killed one of his shipmates and captured another. ''I don't want my son to be fatherless for Lebanon. This cruise sucks.''

''There'll be people licking their balls for a long time after this one,'' said one of the staff officers who had vainly pleaded for more time to get the *Kennedy* air wing ready before the raid was launched. ''I wrote my wife that I hang my head in shame for the part I played in this strike.''

What kept the fliers on their feet spiritually as the negatives about the raid piled up all around them was the conviction that they had done the best they could to execute a flawed strike plan handed to them at the last minute:

''If it hadn't been for our training, we would have lost more guys,'' said a bombardier-navigator who escaped heavy fire during the raid. ''Our training proved valid. I think we did a pretty good job considering what we were up against.''

The fliers' anger was not personalized against any one person because they could not find out who ordered the raid and who refused the *Kennedy*'s request to launch at 11:00 A.M. instead of 7:30 so the sun would not be in their eyes as they flew. More important, the later launch would have given the ordies the time they needed to load the bombs on the planes. Tuttle, even though he was the on-scene commander, was not condemned by the fliers he sent over Lebanon with so little preparation. The men who flew the mission assumed, but did not know, that Higher Authority had tied Tuttle's hands. They had heard this is what had happened during the Vietnam War when most of them were in junior high school. One declared:

"Everything I've ever been taught in the Navy is to go in low just as fast as you can, put the bombs on target and get out of there the same way. This strike was briefed against those principles. And I didn't like that. I, as a JO (junior officer), said to myself as I flew in toward the beach, 'This is crazy. I'm up here high. I'm a sitting duck.'

"Now I realize if I had been down there, I'd be gone. I counted five SAMs trying to reach me. Admiral Tuttle once again knew exactly what he was doing. He was the expert. He was right. The low fliers who got away with it did so because they had the advantage of surprise."

I did find one happy place on the *Kennedy*—the vertical world of the red-shirted ordies. This world consisted of the storage rooms just above the carrier's keel, and the elevators leading from there to the hangar bay and the flight deck.

The ordies for months had been taking bombs out of a big store room deep in the hold, loading them onto special carts, pushing and pulling the carts onto the elevator going up to the hangar bay, wheeling the bombs from there onto the elevator going up to the flight deck, pushing and pulling the wagons of bombs to the bombers dispersed on the flight deck and wrenching the bombs onto their fittings. This had been going on day and night in all kinds of weather, including squalls which spit raindrops across the deck like bullets. The ordies hated to see *Kennedy* Bombers bring their bombs back to the ship. This meant they had to go through the bomb handling process in reverse. The Red Shirts wanted their bombs to kill some bad guys or blow up something. Then they would feel as if they were personally punching the enemy—inspiring them to work another seven-day week of 12-hour days.

"The *Kennedy* lost her cherry," exulted Aviation Ordnance Man Third Class John Colage, twenty-one, of Uniontown, Pennsylvania, as he and fellow red-shirted ordies struggled with a fresh load of bombs that they hoped would follow the others which they assumed had blown up the bad guys in Lebanon. "This a good day for bombing," added Colage. "It's the Feast of Santa Barbara, patron saint of ordnancemen."

Colage and fellow ordies Billy Martin, twenty-one, of Dallas and Dale Houston, twenty-three, of Calera, Oklahoma, stopped struggling with the bombs in the hangar bay to pose proudly in front of them.

"They don't mind loading up," said Lieutenant Don Howard as he watched the ordies congratulate themselves for bombing Lebanon, "but they do mind loading down."

From the hangar deck where the ordies were gleefully pushing more bombs up to the flight deck I went to the Chaplain's Office two decks below to talk to a sailor who did not share the ordies' enthusiasm for the strike. He wanted me to understand why he was not going to eat or do any more work on the *Kennedy* until the Navy let him off the ship which, in his view, had gone from defender to killer that morning of 4 December.

Leaning forward in one of the three chairs in the chaplain's office, Yeoman Third Class Nicholas Eugene Patrick twisted his hands and stared at me intently as he began his explanation.

"When I joined the Navy, I anticipated I'd be staying in some shorelike thing. I answered the question on whether you were a conscientious objector. I was, but I put no because I felt if I put yes, they wouldn't let me in. I wanted something to tide me over until I was ready to go back to the seminary.

"Then, after I entered and realized what I had got myself into, I told everybody that if the day should come that our squadron should go into combat, drop bombs or something, I would cease doing anything to support the military because I'm a man of peace. I am against war. I am against violence of any kind. I am against killing of any kind. I will not kill for anyone. I'll die for you. I'll die for anybody. I won't kill for you. I won't kill for this country. I'll die for this country. But I won't kill for it. I will not kill at all.

"Now that we have already bombed today and everything, I'm now ready to put my words into action. Everyone in the squadron is well aware of how I felt. There are even jokes made about it. This past week I was telling Chaplain Doffin that the only reason we're staying here (off Lebanon) is so that they can make a retaliatory strike. Some of them (in the squadron) were saying, 'Yeah, we'll enjoy dropping them and we'll make sure (as squadron yeoman) you put it in green in our books.' I didn't joke about that. I said, 'It won't come to that.' It did.

"I just came down from talking to them upstairs. My schedules officer (Lieutenant William 'Catfish' Davis from the eight-man) was the one that talked to me. He wrote the report chit (equivalent to a civilian summons citing a violation of the law) and everything. He said he was against my point of view

violently, but he said he admires me for my convictions.
Although with his two buddies shot down and everything, he
couldn't possibly accept my position. But I felt at least, though,
there wasn't a hatred toward me. That kind of support I
welcome.''

Captain Wheatley sentenced Patrick to the brig for refusing to
obey orders to work. The Navy eventually granted Patrick a
discharge as a conscientious objector. He told me as he left the
ship that he would resume his training for the priesthood.

The men in VA-85 owed Lange a final tribute, a memorial
service aboard ship. Then they would have to force him out of
their minds so they would not make fatal mistakes in flying.
Naval aviators prefer brief services—something Chaplain
Doffin knew all too well from arranging more of them than he
cared to remember during his five deployments on carriers.
Skipper Hughes made the mistake of telling Doffin he did not
want a drawn out service. The chaplain replied acidly that he
had been around long enough to know what was appropriate.

On the evening of 9 December 1983 officers and sailors from
the air wing filed quietly into the blue and silver forecastle for
Lange's memorial service. The officers wore khakis and the
colored baseball caps of their squadrons while the enlisted men
wore the colored sweat shirts designating their jobs. Officers of
VA-85 gathered closest to the altar in a tight square. The service
opened with a hymn played mournfully on the organ by
Commander Almond. Then Gil Bever delivered the eulogy for
his roommate.

"We called him The Doppler," Bever began, "for he once
rode up to the O Club with no lieutenant bars. Another time as a
boat officer he forgot to wear his wings. Each humanizing
element in Mark's behavior in no way diminished his professional desire to excel as a naval officer. He provided us with
many happy memories as an experienced junior officer who
gave of himself wholly and unselfishly.

"He was dedicated to his family and to the men who served
for him. He was known to be a compassionate man. He had
time for everybody. He was proud to serve his country. His
regret was his daughter growing up without him. He loved this
country and the ideals it stood for. And he fully exploited his
second love, flying.

"His first love, his daughter Jamie, who was being raised by his parents, bolstered support for the point of those ideals for which Mark died. A man who gave his life to serve his country. Mark Lange along with those gathered here today are men who are still willing to sacrifice in order to safeguard the ideals still held dear by our country.

"Pericles some 2,500 years ago, when reflecting on the greatness of Athens, said: 'What made her great was men with the spirit of adventure. Men who knew their duty. Men who were ashamed to fall below a certain standard. They gave to her their lives, to all of us for their own selves. They won prizes that never grow old.'"

Bever left the lectern without breaking down. He had tried to distill, in a few minutes and a few words, the life of a man he had come to love. Many of the aviators sitting and standing in the forecastle knew what he was going through. They, too, had given eulogies for friends who were suddenly gone.

"Would you please rise for our closing hymn and remain standing for the benediction and Taps?" asked another of Lange's shipmates.

The aviators had the words of the Navy hymn printed on VA-85's black and white memorial program. But only a few of the men sang the pleas about protecting aviators in the hymn. Nothing could help Mark Adam Lange now.

Marine Lance Corporal R.L. Fisher played a shaky "Taps." The congregation left the forecastle wordlessly.

After talking extensively with everyone on the *Kennedy* who flew on the 4 December raid as well as most of those who planned it, I concluded that the fundamental error was not giving those involved the time they needed to prepare the mission for minimum risk and maximum effectiveness. The targets were not going anywhere. They could have been bombed the next day or the next week. President Reagan wanted to deliver a political message, not win a battle or start a war. So there was no compelling reason for launching the bombers at first light before their crews or their planes were ready to go. The fact that men were ordered to risk their lives to carry out such a flawed plan said to me that the American military command structure is broken and must be fixed. If it is not fixed, the United States is in real danger of losing any next war.

After leaving the *Kennedy* at the end of her deployment, I interviewed most of the top people involved with planning the raid of 4 December. Nothing I learned changed my mind that admirals and generals who were not on the scene let their men down. I tried through interviews and correspondence to pinpoint which link in the chain of command failed. But the testimony was so contradictory that only a Congressional committee, which could put everyone involved in the same room at the same time for questioning, and could demand the relevant secret documents, could ferret out the whole truth. The contradictions underscored the need to weed out the military bureaucracy; to streamline the chain of command; to fix responsibility for a military mission at the outset; and to give that commander the credit or blame afterward. The bombing mission was steered by the Joint Chiefs of Staff in Washington, but they distanced themselves from it afterward. Either the chiefs should be all the way in or all the way out for such military operations. If they are going to tell the on-scene commander what to do and when, then the chiefs should be placed in the chain of command to take responsibility for their decisions. If the chiefs are not going to see a mission through to the end, then they should leave it to the commander on the scene to make the tactical decisions, such as the best time to launch bombers.

These were the representations made to me by top officials involved with the bombing raid on 4 December 1983, and their jobs at the time:

• Rear Admiral Jerry O. Tuttle, battle group commander. He said he assumed as the commander on the scene that he would be given the authority to pick the times for launching the planes and putting them over the target. He said Higher Authority ordered him to strike the targets in folders RS-7, RS-8, and RS-16; that it was not his idea to try to bomb so many targets at once. Higher Authority gave him so many targets to hit that he had no choice but to employ the bombers on both carriers, as well as send for those which had been flown to Sigonella, Italy, for maintenance work. He said he worked through the night of 3 December and into the predawn of 4 December on the strike plan, going to bed shortly after 4 A.M. His plans called for launching the planes at 11 A.M. and putting them over the target at 11:30 A.M. He said at about 5:30 A.M. he was awakened by a telephone call informing him that his bombers had to be launched by 6:30

A.M. "You've got to be shitting me," he said he replied. He asked for more time, he said, and was denied it. This triggered the flail to get crews briefed, and the bombers loaded and launched. He said hitting the targets with the 16-inch guns of the battleship *New Jersey* was not a viable option because it was carrying only 110 sixteen-inch shells which could not have been put on the assigned targets accurately.

- Vice Admiral Edward H. Martin, commander of the Sixth Fleet. He said, "it was no sooner than 2 A.M. and more like 5 A.M." when he first learned that the bombing strike was to be launched at 6:30 A.M. He said he asked his superiors repeatedly for more time on behalf of Tuttle but was not given any more than an hour extension. He said he assumed he had informed his superiors that the *Kennedy* had reduced its readiness from a four hour to a 24 hour alert. The Navy could not document that such notice was given. Martin said superiors on up the chain of command should have known the *Kennedy* was not in a quick alert because "she was buttoning up to go through the Canal" when she suddenly was ordered to detour to Bagel Station. He said he had told Tuttle not to ignore the possibility of using the *New Jersey* for the retaliatory strike.

- Vice Admiral M. Staser Holcomb, deputy commander of U.S. Naval Forces in Europe, with headquarters in London. He said that after he arrived at his London command post on 3 December, he got on a three-way radio hookup with Martin and Tuttle. He said that all three admirals knew on the evening of 3 December that Washington had chosen three folders of targets to be hit at "first light." He said Tuttle and others on up the chain weeks earlier had mapped out plans for hitting one set of targets with one carrier but not several sets at once. "The plan for targeting A, B, and D came from Washington," Holcomb said, presumably from the staff of the Joint Chiefs of Staff. He said he studied the targets in the RS-7, RS-8 and RS-16 folders on file at his London headquarters and concluded only a white building outside Beirut housing the Syrian radar net (RS-16) was worth striking. And that could be destroyed by 16-inch shells fired by the battleship *New Jersey* then standing off Lebanon. He said he telephoned his immediate superior in the chain, Air Force General Richard L. Lawson, deputy commander of the

U.S. European Command in Stuttgart, West Germany, to suggest using the battleship instead of Navy bombers. He said Lawson replied: "It's too late for that." Holcomb said he telephoned late in the evening of 3 December to ask for a later launch. "I conveyed to him that the guys in the fleet said they needed more time. Lawson answered: 'I got us an extra hour and that's all I can get.' I remember that clearly." Holcomb said he thought he had made that call around 10 P.M. London time. In another two-way telephone conversation (which Lawson said was about 2 A.M. Beirut time), Lawson asked Holcomb if Tuttle's bombers could make the 6:30 A.M. launch and whether the bombing strike would be successful. Holcomb said he checked with Tuttle and replied to Lawson in the affirmative.

- Lawson in Stuttgart. He sent me a memo in response to my questions and draft chapter which included these statements: "The chain of command was not advised of any change in the alert status of the *John F. Kennedy*. To the best of anyone's knowledge at either Naval Forces Europe (in London) or the European Command (in Stuttgart), the alleged change of status from three hour alert (actually four, but I had written three in the draft chapter) to 24 hour alert was never communicated . . . The actual operational planning for this mission was never performed any higher than Rear Admiral Tuttle's staff . . . All levels from the Joint Chiefs of Staff down understood that TOT (time over target) would be selected at the time of the decision to go. When the orders to proceed with the mission finally came from the Joint Chiefs of Staff in Washington, they suggested 'an early morning strike' to retaliate within 24 hours of the attack on the TARPS mission." (The Joint Chiefs' orders to proceed, called an execute order, were not issued by Stuttgart to London until 5:33 A.M. Beirut time, according to Lawson, which was about when Tuttle said he was awakened to learn for the first time that his bombers were supposed to be over the target by 6:30 A.M. This allows for the possibility that Tuttle's superiors knew through earlier communications than the execute order that the launch was to be at 6:30 A.M. but neglected to inform Tuttle.)

"It was Rear Admiral Tuttle's decision to employ aircraft from both carriers in the strike mission. That required a reworking of the plans at the last minute. Rear Admiral Tuttle decided to greatly increase the size of the attack force (38 aircraft versus 29) over that contained in the previously approved plans. That decision proved to cause severe ordnance loading problems.''

(Lawson's memo leaves hanging whether the Joint Chiefs or Tuttle decided to hit three folders of targets at once. If it was the chiefs, as Holcomb asserted to me, then Tuttle had to employ the bombers from two carriers to cover all the targets.)

Lawson said he called Holcomb ''for assurances from the Navy that (a) the mission was understood and (b) that it could be completed successfully with the time over target of 6:30 A.M. Beirut time.'' Holcomb called Lawson back at 2 A.M. Beirut time who ''then passed those assurances back to (General Bernard W.) Rogers, who passed them to General (John W.) Vessey in Washington.''

Lawson told me during an interview in his Stuttgart headquarters that ''if I had known this thing was as twisted as Hogan's goat, I wouldn't have gone ahead with it.'' He said he could not recall Holcomb's telephonic plea for more time.

• General Bernard W. Rogers, supreme allied commander and commander of U.S. forces in Europe. He told me it was he who asked for the assurances from the Navy, not Vessey, but otherwise added few details to the chronology when queried.

• Admiral James D. Watkins, Chief of Naval Operations, told me he did not know who was responsible for not giving the *Kennedy* adequate time to prepare for strike. ''If you find out,'' he told me, ''you'll be the first. There are too many doors.''

• Gen. John W. Vessey Jr., chairman of the Joint Chiefs of Staff, told me he wanted a strike reasonably close to the firing on the reconnaissance mission but would have yielded more time if he had known of the difficulties the early launch imposed on the *Kennedy*. ''I left those details to the theater commander, Rogers,'' Vessey told me. ''Most of all we wanted the mission to be successful. There were communications problems—both ways.''

My conclusions: the targets were not worth bombing, except for the white house with the radar hub inside; loss of two modern jet bombers to primitive shoulder-fired antiaircraft missiles demands a Congressional reassessment of Air Force and Navy bomber construction plans; Admiral Martin or his staff failed to inform the chain of the *Kennedy*'s change in readiness; the Joint Chiefs of Staff failed the men out on the point by ordering them to strike at first light of 4 December 1983 when the targets should have been hit no sooner than 11:30 A.M. or even the next day since the objective of this raid was to send a political message, not score a military victory; Admirals Martin, Holcomb, and Tuttle failed to protest vigorously enough about the strain the early launch was putting on the carriers; Lawson and others in his headquarters should have questioned the wisdom of bombers flying into the sun and granted more time if indeed Holcomb requested it, as he says he did.

The chain of command did not work. Was it the system or the people? If it was the system, the system should be repaired beyond the changes Congress already has made. If it was the people, they should be held accountable. If a Navy skipper loses his ship, the Navy conducts a court of inquiry to find out why. The Navy did not do this after the 4 December raid. The bone left in the nation's throat should be removed through a Congressional inquiry. I seek no victims. I do feel, however, that the nation must learn from mistakes made on military operations. Don't we owe at least that much to Mark Lange?

12   Christmas

THE grim events of early December—the fouled-up bombing raid which killed Mark Lange and the relentless pace of flight operations since then—made it difficult to generate the Christmas spirit inside our walled city.

The *Kennedy* management tried. Captain Wheatley, XO Pieno, and Master Chief Crowley told the crew every way they could think of—over the ship's TV, over the loudspeakers and face to face—how important their work was to the folks back home. They also ballyhooed the upcoming Christmas shows of Wayne Newton and Bob Hope on the *Kennedy*. Managers farther down the line encouraged Christmas decorations in the normally austere working spaces of the carrier. And the chaplains planned special Christmas services.

These efforts by the management received assists from the outside world in the form of Christmas presents mailed to the ship. But even here the terrorist threat intruded and distorted. Sergeants-at-arms ruined the surprise of every Christmas present by opening it in front of the recipient to make sure no explosives were inside.

As Christmas Day drew closer, I noticed more hang-dog looks on the men. I read "what the hell am I doing here?" on the faces of the officers and sailors I passed in the passageways of the ship. Skipper Jim Eckart of the Rooks said I looked as if I were asking myself the same question.

Mean One of the Red Rippers refused to be brought down by

the Christmas blues—at least outwardly. He stiff-armed them by bringing an at-home kind of Christmas to his home on the ship. He lived with four other fliers and an intelligence officer from the Red Rippers F-14 squadron in a large compartment off the Dirty Shirt wardroom. It was called a six-man. One night Mean One and his roommates decided to have a party in the six-man to light the Christmas lights and to usher in the holiday season ceremoniously. He asked me to join this sea-going Christmas party to brighten the world of gray around us all.

When I was admitted through the locked, red door of the six-man, Mean One—also known as Mean Jim, The Ripperman, and Lieutenant Jim Greene—was standing on a chair stringing tiny Christmas lights around the pipes and wires which snaked across the steel ceiling of the square room. He seemed jolly enough as he went about his task to play Santa Claus for the whole ship.

Mean One's roommates, Santa's helpers this night, were Bad Bob, Bo Bo, Spanker, Turps, and Precious. They were earnestly cutting tiny Christmas hats out of sheets of red cardboard and taping them to the heads of the *Playboy* magazine centerfold bunnies decorating the walls. Precious—Lieutenant (junior grade) Peter Davis, a lawyer—served as the formal greeter. He walked over to me, extended his hand in welcome and asked:

"What would you like to drink?"

Drinking alcoholic beverages is forbidden on Navy ships. I figured Precious, in the spirit of Santa Claus, was pretending that the six-man had bottles of Christmas cheer to go along with the lights, hats, music, and cookies infusing the room with holiday spirit. I decided to go along with the gag.

"What do you have?" I asked.

"We've got scotch, bourbon, gin, rum, vodka, wine, and, I think, a couple of cans of beer in the fridge."

"Great! I'll have some scotch and water."

Precious went to a cupboard full of what looked like genuine liquor bottles and poured amber fluid into a glass filled with ice.

"Merry Christmas!" Precious exulted, handing me the glass and raising his own to toast the holiday season on the USS *John F. Kennedy*.

"Merry Christmas," I replied feelingly. The scotch and water tasted like real scotch and water. But of course it could not be because of Navy regulations. But it was a great imitation.

We kept up the game hour after hour, going to the cupboard

repeatedly—pouring, toasting, laughing, singing, and telling stories. Mean One, Bad Bob (Lieutenant Bob Brauer—U.S. Naval Academy, 1978; pilot), Bo Bo (Lieutenant Bob Clager —U.S. Naval Academy, 1976; pilot), Turps (Lieutenant Chuck Turpen—U.S. Naval Academy, 1976; pilot), and Spanker (Lieutenant Scott Francis, Salem State College, 1975; radar intercept officer), and Precious, together with people from the neighborhood who stopped in to sample what had to be ersatz Christmas cheer, kept the party swinging well into the morning.

After the party, I had trouble negotiating the steel ladder down to my room one flight below the six-man. The imitation booze had kicked me just like the real stuff. Perhaps it was the one foot chop of the Mediterranean which made us all feel tipsy on the night we lit up the six-man for Christmas not far from the place where Christ had lit up the whole world almost 2,000 years earlier.

Two sailors were struggling with plywood and pipe on the hangar bay the morning of 16 December. They were assembling the stage for Wayne Newton who was to give two shows later that day, one in midafternoon and the other at night.

"We're treating this asshole as if he were head of state or something," complained one sailor as he hefted a long piece of heavy pipe.

"He makes more money than a head of state," his buddy replied.

Wayne Newton did not just appear on their stage a few hours later, he exploded on it. His band blasted out its music, often with Newton playing solos on several different instruments one after the other, so every sailor standing or sitting on the deck or perched on one of its beams felt it wash over him warmingly. Newton played, sang, danced, and talked with such verve and penetration that the depressed sailors were yanked out of their funk. He filled them up with joy for the moment, took them off the carrier, took them home. They applauded thunderously.

"I don't believe you." Newton shouted into the microphone as the sailors whistled, screamed, clapped, laughed, and cried after hearing songs that touched their souls and transported them into the arms of loved ones.

Only Newton's tired jokes fell flat. The guys longed for soothing music and singing. They had heard every joke Las Vegas could think of several times over, including this one Newton told about the first man being Polish.

"God gave him an apple and a woman and he ate the apple."

Newton hit a more responsive chord when he talked about his recent visit to the battleship *New Jersey:*

"Watching those boys fire on the coast is really kind of fun."

"Yeah! Yeah!" the *Kennedy* men shouted back in an expression of frustration over not being able to attack the enemy who was keeping them at sea over Christmas.

"Kicking ass and taking names!" Newton added. Then he mined the geographic lode spread out before him in the cavernous hangar bay.

"I believe it's possible we've got some rednecks out there."

"Yeah!" roared back at him.

"Oklahoma."

A few yeahs.

"Indiana."

Fewer yeahs.

"New York."

Lots of yeahs but not the roar the rednecks made.

"New Yorkers hate Indians because when we owned New York we showed a profit."

"How about San Francisco?"

Almost no response.

"I know why, too. I may dress funny, but I don't go in for that nonsense. I just can't figure out for a group that can't reproduce why there's so many of them."

Newton did best with the love ballads which, he explained to the audience, he had shied away from at first for fear of making the sailors even more melancholy about being away from home at Christmas.

Newton crooned to the hangar bay jammed with young fathers the ballad pleading with daddy not to walk so fast.

"I almost lost it on that one," Lieutenant Commander Monty Willis, sitting next to me, confided after Newton finished the wrenching song. Monty was nuts about his little daughter, Katie; missed her terribly; envisioned her walking beside him; trying to keep up.

Most sailors found ways to attend both of Newton's shows. So did I. Newton and his band belted out ballads, patriotic numbers, and country tunes, including what he called "my all-time favorite: 'Please Release Me.' " I wondered how all the officers and sailors who had received "Dear John" letters felt as Newton sang so soulfully.

His voice raspy from an exhaustive city to city tour in the States he had just completed, Newton broke off his singing and playing to give two heart-to-heart speeches in both shows.

"The feedback that you guys get from the States is usually by the news, either the written word or the television station," he said. "Let me tell you that the American perception of what you're doing is not what you're getting back from the news. That's been slanted for a long time. The American people are with you and always will be and appreciate the sacrifices you are making."

In the first show, he said the people who purvey the news "are a bunch of asses, most of them."

I went to the XO's reception in the wardroom for Newton in between the afternoon and evening shows. I congratulated Newton on his show and introduced myself as "one of those asses from the press."

He recoiled in mock horror. We both laughed.

"I heard you were on here," Newton said warmly. "You're one of the good guys. I'll fix it up in the next show."

In the next show he said of the media: "They should all have their asses kicked." Newton had gone from *most* to *all* since our talk. So much for the good I had done the press.

"There's a sadness," Newton said in bidding his audiences on the hangar deck farewell, "because we've made a lot of friends here. And I guess you never should be sad about making friends, but when you have to leave them—as you guys know—it's like leaving a part of your family. It doesn't really matter how it all ends for me. Only thing that matters for any of us is the hearts and the souls that you touch along the way. You guys have touched a lot of hearts and you certainly touched our heart and soul, and, for that, I thank you."

His band struck up a medley of patriotic songs, ending with "America the Beautiful." The thousands of sailors and officers reluctantly left the momentary magic and went back to work. The old familiar sounds of fans, pumps, and engines took over and filled up the hangar bay which Newton had turned into Camelot for one brief, shining moment.

"Hey, George," Skipper Eckart of the Rooks urged as I entered their ready room on Christmas Eve afternoon, "try some of that salmon and fudge up there." On the table was a smorgasbord of

Christmas goodies—canned salmon from their home area of Washington State, fudge, cookies, cake, a long meat roll, and cheese. "Be supportive of the Navy's weight gain program," commanded the sign above the table.

Eckart and his Rooks, maybe because they were from the informal, friendly Far West—Whidbey Island, Washington —were open, warm, interested, and helpful whenever I visited their ready room, which was often. This Christmas Eve Day they were watching on the squadron's television set the Merry Christmas tape which the wives, children, and girl friends of the Rooks had spent months making to bridge the distance between their homes on Whidbey Island and the *Kennedy* at sea.

The color movie opened with the wives and children sitting in front of banners saying: "Merry Christmas. We Love You." The children, dressed in their Sunday best, waved to their fathers at sea as the camera panned over them. The wives put on brave smiles, many of them holding up babies to show Dad how much they had grown in the three months the *Kennedy* had been gone.

The men in the Rooks' ready room searched the crowd of smiling faces for their own wives and children. Their throats must have clutched the instant they spotted their loved ones. Mine did just watching them studying the screen and suddenly blooming into smiles; I had not seen smiles on their faces for weeks.

The all-amateur production moved on to local scenes around Whidbey Island—the center of the town, a wife playing fetch with a dog in a vast field of soothing green, a country grave yard, a kid's tire hanging from the branch of a gnarled tree, rabbits playing in the grass, ducks swimming along free in the sunshine, Trader's Wharf, and Camp Casey.

"Merry Christmas, Darling" played in the background. Everyone in the Rooks' ready room went dead quiet. I knew without looking that eyes were filling and throats were closing. It was an excruciating moment. But nobody broke down. The strain of holding back was nearly unbearable.

The wives went upbeat in the next segment of the film, putting on a fashion show with a costume for each month of the year—fur coat for January, Valentine get up for February, wedding dress for March, an Easter bunny for April and so on through the year. The wife posing as the Easter bunny surprised her husband with this announcement when she turned around to show her tail: "I got a job." Giggles rippled through the room every time a wife was recognized. The husband-flier seldom said anything. He just smiled and occasionally averted his eyes from the TV screen to the ready room floor.

In another scene, wives needled their men about the need to send them the monthly allotments of money on time. A wife sat before a telephone taking calls from one bill collector after another, telling each one: "My allotment didn't come in. I'll get the payment to you just as soon as I can . . . This is a Navy town. Surely you've heard this before."

Then the wives made cameo appearances, often holding babies or standing with sons and daughters, under the banner: "Navy wife. It's the toughest job in the Navy."

"Hi," said one lanky son to his father. "How's it going? Basketball is going pretty good. So far we're 3 and 1. We have another game tonight. Hope you feel OK." Then a long silence.

The wife took over from the obviously embarrassed son, saying firmly but sweetly: "Everything is fine. The truck is fine. Don't worry about it. No scratches or dents. Write and take care. Love you. Your son's grown another foot. Merry Christmas. Love you and miss you."

One wife read her husband the 27th Psalm and said, "I really think that says it all, Hon. That we don't have to worry about anything. That you're safe and you're in the Lord's hands."

Many wives tried to express their love through the cold eye of the camera but obviously felt inhibited. Several urged their tots to sing or do little tricks that had been rehearsed for Dad. Most froze from stage fright when the camera focused on them and could not perform.

Belva Mazzeo, wife of Lieutenant Dan Mazzeo, a pilot, packed the most emotional punch for me. She stared steadily into the camera with their three-year-old son, Gennaro, in her lap and told Dan without choking up:

"Although we have an empty feeling in our lives and in my bed when we go to sleep at night, our lives have been running rather smoothly. We try to fill our days as best we can and keep ourselves busy with household chores and keeping the vehicles running and just each other, right?" she asked turning to her son.

"Not a day goes by we don't think of you. And our special

time to think about you is at night. We have our special times together. We sing two songs together.''

Mrs. Mazzeo leaned into her little boy's head and asked him to sing with her, just like he did at bed time. He tried to squirm away from the camera. Belva Mazzeo sang alone, without a quiver, these lyrics to the tune of *When Johnny Comes Marching Home:*

> When Daddy comes flying home again, hurrah, hurrah.
> Mommy will cry and Gennaro will shout
> We'll be so happy we'll jump about.
> And we'll be so glad when Daddy comes flying home.

Gennaro could not bring himself to sing. But he did look into the camera as his mother said in closing her brief appearance on the squadron film:

"I'm very proud you participate in the purpose that unfortunately keeps us apart—that of safeguarding our country and keeping ours the land of the free and, surely for the job you do, the home of the brave. May God keep you safe and bring you home to us soon.

"Throw Daddy a big kiss, Gennaro.''

He did, with a little help from Mom.

"We have our good times and our bad times,'' said another wife in a succinct but emotional Christmas greeting. "Love you—and come home.''

Rear Admiral Roger E. Box obviously was as moved as I when he saw a similar film. He sent this message to all hands which was printed in the Plan of the Day of 24 December:

"Recently I viewed a Christmas greeting TV tape from families on one of the battle group ships. In that tape were the women who patiently await our return after this deployment is complete. Beside them and in their arms were the children with their eyes full of that special magic that comes from Christmas time in a free country. I want each of you to know that free people, and especially Americans, throughout the world are grateful to you for that gift of freedom your service preserves. You should be proud that your personal dedication and sacrifice is a special gift to mankind. Merry Christmas and God bless.''

XO Pieno, striving to lift morale during the low point of Christmas, kept reminding the men in the Plans of the Day that there soon would be "lots of eyeball liberty" on the ship when Bob Hope and his beauteous entertainers arrived.

I thought there would be something symbolic about flying over the Holy Land on Christmas Eve. The Rooks would be patrolling along the Lebanese coast in their four passenger EA-6B to see if there were any unpleasant surprises for the marines at Beirut. I asked Skipper Eckart if I could fly in the empty fourth seat during this Christmas hop.

"Sure, glad to have you," he replied in his typical generous manner. Our mission would be to patrol close to the Lebanese coast to look for and photograph any new ships, with Soviet warships of special interest, and listen for radar signals in hopes of determining if the Syrians had put any new antiaircraft defenses in Lebanon. Intelligence officers had told the Rooks that a MiG-23 fighter was in the area. We were to listen and look for the plane. Rooks were the inveterate eavesdroppers of the *Kennedy* air wing.

"I plan to stay at 5,000 feet," Eckart said at the crew briefing which preceded every flight. This is a relatively low altitude for a jet, but it would make the job of identifying the ships off Lebanon easier.

The plane would have its IFF squawking. IFF stands for Identification of Friend or Foe. The IFF gear sends out distinctive radio signals from the plane so that other planes in the sky and ships on the sea can intercept and identify the originator of the signals. We were told to listen for Soviet Band Stand and Peer Pear radars as we flew along.

"We're scheduled for a 2:30 launch and a 4:30 recovery. It will be a pinky recovery," meaning the day would fade to the faint pink light of twilight by the time the two-engine jet came back to land on the carrier.

We went over emergency procedures. Eckart made sure I understood where the ejection alarm light was located and what to do if it went on during the flight.

"I'll eject you," he said. The pilot of an EA-6B can rig the ejection system so he can eject everyone in the crew by pulling his own ejection loop. The EA-6B ejection rocket under the seat shoots you through the plastic canopy of the plane. The high back of the seat punches the hole in the canopy. It is a dicey evolution, no matter how thoroughly the ejection procedure is briefed.

"I'll slow down to 250 knots (285 miles an hour) for a controlled ejection," Eckart said in the way of reassurance. "Lean back so we can break through the canopy clean. At 1345 we need to be on the roof," Eckart continued. This would allow 45 minutes to check out the airplane on the flight deck, strap ourselves inside, and steer it carefully into the catapult slot for launch.

Skipper Eckart, would fly the plane from the left front seat. Lieutenant Dennis "Sluggo" (because his butch hair cut made him look like the cartoon character of that name) Watson would sit in the right front seat as electronic counter measures officer and navigator, while Lieutenant Commander Bob McNamara would wield most of the eavesdropping equipment in the right rear seat as the second electronic countermeasures officer. I would sit in the rear left seat where other electronic equipment had been removed. All I would have to do this Christmas Eve afternoon was watch and listen.

I pulled on the 40 pounds of flight gear with the help of Parachute Rigger Second Class Don Creamer. We four then trooped up to the roof to find where EA-6B number 606 was parked. Once at planeside, we walked slowly around it looking for a wrench or hunks of metal in the air intakes leading into the turbine blades of the two jet engines; leaks of fuel or oil; torn metal; looseness or breaks in the all important flaps and other flight control surfaces; bruises in the tires which would have to withstand the jolt of the heavy airplane smashing down onto the steel deck at 130 miles an hour.

The brown-shirted plane captain looked on with a combination of pride and anxiety as we made our way around the plane. He had readied it for flight. It was standard practice for the crew who would fly the plane to recheck it. The Brown Shirt hoped none of the aviators would find anything wrong.

"How about this leak?" Eckart asked when he spotted hydraulic fluid leaking out of a connection on the left side of 606. The plane captain and his maintenance crew scurried around and fixed it.

We climbed up the ladders leading up to our seats in the large cockpit. I pulled the pins—thin bolts inserted in various places to prevent such accidents as seats ejecting accidentally—and settled in my seat. I reached for the rear and lap safety harness connections, buckled them together with some difficulty—I never did get nimble at strapping on a Navy jet—twisted the oxygen hose into its socket and snapped the short leg restraints into their fittings. The leg restraints hook in above the ankle and are anchored to fittings just off the floor of the cockpit. The restraints keep your legs from flailing out in front of you on ejection where they can be amputated by the edge of the cockpit as the rocket shoots your body up and out of the airplane. I clumsily adjusted the lip microphone attached to my helmet. I figured I would swallow the damn thing if I ever had to talk fast because it pressed right against my mouth.

My three fellow crew members were old hands at strapping on jets. They settled into their seats with the ease of people settling into the family sedan for a Sunday drive. Eckart started the engines, the Green Shirts broke us down, the Yellow Shirts directed us into the catapult slot where a long list of last minute checks of the airplane were made. Eckart saluted the launching officer to signal he was ready to be shot off the end of the boat.

"Here we go," Eckart said over the intercom.

I pushed my head tight against the back headrest to keep it from being snapped back by the catapult. I could see men with cameras standing on the balcony known as vultures row peering down on us. I tensed my body for the big kick of the catapult.

Wham! Hiss. Rattle-rattle. Zoom! Quiet. Slowdown.

Those sensations galloped through my mind during the two seconds it took to hurl us from a standing start to a speed of 150 miles an hour in 200 feet. I tried to see through eyeballs flattened by the yank of the catapult. I could make out only pieces of gray deck and slices of water as the plane, in the grip of the catapult, hurtled toward the end of the flight deck. The catapult's energy weakened and the two engines of the EA-6B took over, pushing the plane along with less acceleration.

We were on our own, airborne and climbing. I relaxed, and took off my oxygen mask. Down below me danced waves of the Mediterranean in the golden sunlight of Christmas Eve afternoon. Above were puffs of soft white clouds. We were free. Free from the routine of the ship. Free from its grayness and sameness. Free from its confinement. Free from its grating noises. Free from packed humanity. All around us was God's handiwork of blue sky, clouds, and sea. Off in the distance to the east I could make out the brown shadow that was the coast of Lebanon. Flying, for men confined on a ship or in an office on the ground, has the restorative effect of a walk in the woods spiced by the knowledge that danger and instant death always lurk in the shadows.

"Closeout. Rook six zero six checking in."

That was Eckart checking in with the E-2C Hawkeye command and control plane orbiting above the *Kennedy* to watch planes on its radars and keep track of every one minute by minute.

"Six zero six. Closeout. You're clear for coastal patrol."

"That's good," Eckart told us over the intercom which does not go beyond the confines of the plane. "We'll get to see something."

We were off the Lebanese coast in a few minutes. Warships from the United States, Soviet Union, and France were spread out before us, dominated by the fearsome looking lines of the battleship *New Jersey*. The ships did not bob from our vantage point high in the Mediterranean sky above them. They looked like toy warships pasted on a blue mirror. The crew recognized the warships and recorded the names and positions of each one for the intelligence officers back on the *Kennedy*. Now and then we saw a cargo ship on the move. We flew down low, figuring they had no antiaircraft weapons even if they were hostile, and circled the ships to photograph them with hand held cameras. We wrote down their names.

As we ran close to the coast, I focused on the city of Beirut. I tried to identify the places I had walked in the city in 1970. I picked out the point where the St. George's luxury hotel, a famous oasis for wealthy Arabs, had been located. I saw the green open spaces of the university. I was looking at a city which had been invaded most recently by Israeli troops, although Beirut had known other invaders through the centuries. The city at Christmas was chopping itself to pieces in tribal warfare. Despite all that wounding, Beirut from my perch up in the EA-6B seemed amazingly intact and hauntingly beautiful this Christmas Eve afternoon. The city seemed to be saying she was greater and stronger than the men who built her and would outlast the men who were now wounding her.

"Six zero six. Closeout," radioed our mother hen in the sky. "Turn north now. You're at the end of your clearance.

"Six zero six," resumed Closeout after he saw on his scopes our turn. "You're back to 340. Left 15."

This was radio shorthand for you are now flying on a course

of 340 degrees and I want you to turn left and stay on a course of 325 degrees.

"Closeout. Six zero six. Heading 325."

"Six zero six. Closeout. Request you turn coastal 080."

We swung back eastward to the Lebanese coast to inspect a ship some other plane had spotted. The ship was a new addition to the international fleet that the *Kennedy* and the *Independence* kept track of through almost daily patrols like this one and by other means. We flew over the ship and photographed it. It looked like a harmless merchantman sailing purposefully westward, not hanging around with a hold full of explosives to detonate when it got near an American warship. Closeout cleared us to RTB—return to base.

"See, George, how boring this is?" Eckart asked me over the intercom. "How would you like to do this twice a day?"

"Yeah, but it's great to get off the ship," I replied.

"That's true. I love to get off it and see something different."

"Six zero six. Closeout. Vector 33. You're at the southern end of your clearance."

We swung back toward the *Kennedy* for the second time in the hop. Eckart radioed the controllers in the ship, called "Strike," to let them know he was coming in for a landing with 9,800 pounds of fuel from an altitude of seven thousand feet—angels seven.

"Strike. Rook six zero six. Nine point eight. Angels seven."

We settled back for the return flight. The sun was setting, firing the low, white clouds all around us.

"Going to chase any clouds, Skipper?" Sluggo asked expectantly. Eckart and other pilots often did sharp maneuvers around clouds just for the fun of it, pretending they were enemy airplanes. "There's some communist clouds over there."

Eckart did not take the bait this time. He was hurrying to make his scheduled 4:30 trap. Light was fading. Pilots hate night landings. We left the clouds alone and glided past their fluffy edges in the near twilight of the Mediterranean winter afternoon.

Bob McNamara tapped me on the shoulder and signaled me to turn on to the same HF channel he was on. Christmas music from the British Broadcasting Corp. was pouring into our ears and filling us with a glow. I imagined the big cloud on my left looked like Santa's sleigh. I wondered what all the Frenchmen down below us on the aircraft carrier *Clemenceau* were doing this Christmas Eve. I mused at the irony of studying warships, listening to Soviet radar signals, and hearing Christmas music all at once while racing along in a military jet a few miles from the land where Christ was born, preached and was crucified. The words "peace on earth, good will toward men" came through my earphones from the BBC broadcast while we still had bleeding Lebanon in sight.

Eckart flew the EA-6B over the starboard side of the *Kennedy,* snapped the plane into a sharp 90 degree turn at the break point in front of the ship, headed downwind parallel to the port side of the carrier, turned left across the greenish-white wake and then turned left again to line up with the canted flight deck.

"Prowler six zero six. Seven point eight. Ball."

This brief radio call from Eckart told the Air Boss in the tower, the controllers in Catsie inside the ship, and the landing signal officer on the platform on the port side of the carrier that EA-6B number 606 was coming in for a landing with 7,800 pounds of fuel in the tanks, enough to go around several times if Eckart missed the wire on this first pass, and that he had spotted the round yellow light in the Fresnel lens known as the ball. Eckart's job was to keep that ball next to the green arms on either side of it by flying down a precise glide path onto the deck.

Along with the rest of the crew, I snapped on my oxygen mask in case we crashed into the sea or on the deck. I also reached down beside my seat to work the lever that locked my shoulder harness into the no-give position. This was so my body would not fly forward when the plane's tail hook grabbed the steel cable stretched across the carrier deck. I tried to spot the yellow ball but could not. It was twilight and the forward part of the plane obscured my vision. The carrier looked small as we fell down through the sky toward it—too small, I thought for this big heavy plane full of fuel. I felt and heard the 25-ton plane—3,000 pounds lighter than when we took off because of the fuel we had burned—slam onto the deck. We went into what felt like a controlled skid at high speed. The squealing, screaming, and grinding noises made me think something was bound to give or catch fire. I felt as if I were hanging from my shoulders because the grab of the arresting wire had thrown my body forward into the shoulder harness. Everything held. The plane stopped. We were safely down. Eckart followed the

Yellow Shirts waving long lemon flashlights to the parking spot on the flight deck.

"Wonder if they'll credit us with a night trap," Sluggo asked over the intercom as he looked out the cockpit to the gathering darkness.

I wriggled out of my flight gear, left it with Don Creamer in the Rooks' rigging room, and went in and out of the other ready rooms along the passageway to say Merry Christmas. I left Officer Country on the 03 level and went to the preserve of the sailors, the big square room under the aft mess decks called The Crew's Lounge. I figured once they saw my khakis bore no insignia the sailors would relax knowing I was neither chief nor officer and thus could cause them no grief this lonely Christmas Eve.

"Ready for Christmas?" I asked with a smile as I walked through the lounge door and stopped before the card table where five sailors were smoking and playing the game, Richthofen's War, The Air War 1916-18. A painting of the *John F. Kennedy* on the cork wall looked down on the players and kibbitzers.

They all looked at me quizzically, scanning my khakis. Then one replied:

"Just another day."

I knew that was close to the truth. Most of the sailors would be working at least 12 hours tomorrow, Christmas, as usual. I decided to leave them to their game and remove any anxiety my khakis might be provoking in this enlisted man's preserve of dungarees.

"Hey, Mr. Wilson," hailed Petty Officer Third Class Mark Granito, twenty-four, of Pittsburgh, as I passed him and some friends sitting together in a quiet side corner of the chow hall. "Come join us for a cup of coffee. I've got something special."

I settled into the bench under their table. Granito, dark eyes shining, opened his attaché case with the careful moves of an international jewel thief. He extracted his jewel and showed it to me—a red tin of Cafe Amaretto. I noticed some of the other prized possessions in his case, a Pace textbook on English grammar and a Navy commendation for recruiting fifteen men into the Navy. He fixed me a cup of Amaretto, returned to the table and took a leading roll in the discussion that washed back and forth over the tape recorder on the table. I warmed them up by asking why they joined the Navy and how they coped with that special pain of feeling alone in the crowd on an aircraft carrier.

Granito led off by saying he came from Midland, Pennsylvania, a gritty steel town outside of Pittsburgh where he did not think he had much chance of getting ahead. He saw the Navy as a step up, had been on the *Kennedy* for three years, was now a cook and hoped to open a restaurant when he got out of uniform.

"Each man on the ship comes in because inside of him there is this feeling that he wants to make it in life. Sometimes I get down and out, and I want to give up all hope. But there's just always that little thing in there that says you've got to make it in life; that you can't fail. To succeed you know there are sacrifices. One of them is leaving your family.

"To get over my loneliness, I get with guys like my friends here. We sing. We play musical instruments. I never knew how to play a piano until I came to this ship. The other guys taught me. I build on what other guys on the ship teach me. You know, just picking up pieces here and there. I compose my own music now.

"I use my music and use God to strengthen me. Being a devout Catholic, I go to church a lot to pray for God's help and for all my shipmates."

Unlike Granito, Dave Voytak of Latrobe, Pennsylvania, did not like the idea of being on chow hall duty Christmas or any other time. He joined the Navy in 1981 to learn electronics and felt he was really picking it up as a beginning technician with VAQ-126, which flew the E-2C Hawkeye. But because he was so junior, Voytak said he kept being assigned to temporary duty at the mess decks. Each unit on the *Kennedy* had to loan men to the chow halls temporarily—called TAD for temporary assigned duty.

"I really can't stand TAD. I like electronics. I'm a little pissed about being down here. Couple of days ago I'm working on radar, and all of a sudden I'm pushing milk.

"The loneliness—you've got to keep it out of your head. You're lonely, but you're not lonely alone. If once you let loneliness get into your head, it's going to eat at you until finally you're going to have an anxiety attack. You got to keep it out. Once you let it in, it's in, and you ain't going to get it out until you pull in.

"The letters help. Everyone on this boat lives for mail call.

When they make that call on the flight deck for C-2 (the plane that usually delivers the mail to a carrier) recovery, I'm the first one out of the shop wanting to see how much mail they're going to bring on.

"This is the first time I'm going to be away for Christmas. Got me a lot of mail, and that helps a lot. I can at least be home in thought. But I'm still here. I'm still going to have to work my 12 hours tomorrow—Christmas. I don't want to be here, but I've got a commitment."

Bernard Terrell, twenty, of Chicago, worked up on the flight deck launching planes from the waist catapults in the heart of the action and danger. He joined the Navy in 1982 to see something else of the world and find excitement.

"It's done me a lot of good," he said of the Navy. "That first strike we launched against Syria, I launched it. So I'll remember that for a long time. I worked 27 hours that day. Longest I've worked is 43 hours straight without seeing the rack. Hours are just too long up there on the flight deck. Right now they're twenty hours on and nine hours off because of the state of readiness we're in.

"If I was home, I'd be having fun. Everybody comes over to my grandmother's house. They go all out. They have everything. Next year at Christmas I'll be celebrating with my new wife. I'm getting married July 16th next year, so I'll be celebrating with her.

"This Christmas won't seem like Christmas. Just another day. I'll take it as another day."

Radames Alonso, twenty-two, of New York City, agreed that was the way to get through tomorrow. He was on TAD from his job as an E-3 clerk in disbursing. He missed his five-year-old son, Mark, at home in Virginia Beach.

"Just try not to think of home—that's the first thing," he told his friends at the table in advising them how to get through Christmas at sea. "Just see it as, 'This is what I'm out here to do.' Doing the job for the Navy. Each man has his own job.

"I try to maintain some kind of Christmas spirit without thinking of home so much. That's what makes people miss home so much—thinking about it. Try not to get your mind away from your job. Do your job. Accomplish what the Navy wants you to do first. Concentrate on it enough to make it through the situation we're in out here and just pray for the best."

Larry Conley, nineteen, of Abilene, Texas, an airman who took aerial photographs, said he would try to do that. "It's kind of rough. I never realized how nice it would be to be home with the family and all. This is my first Christmas away from home. Just kind of do it as best I can. Try not to think about it too much. I'll be right out here cleaning the bays."

Samuel E. Tyce of Charleston, South Carolina, an airman whose ebullient manner gave him the nickname "Tiz Nice," said he would try to dance through Christmas Day on the *Kennedy*, just like he danced through every other day he was on the ship.

"The main thing I do around here is dancing—the kind you saw in *Flashdance*. I dance all around the ship on an everyday basis. I don't think there's too many of the 5,000 men on the ship I don't know. I make a tour around the ship every night."

"And our ship is the *John F. Kennedy*," Granito chimed in. "He was a good President. I was only three years old when he was killed but I heard about him."

Joe Smith, twenty-seven, of Baltimore, Maryland, said "right now if I were home I'd be looking for Christmas presents because I'm a last-minute job." He said Christmas would not be too tough a day for him because he would be leaving the ship in ten days for shore duty in Bethesda, Maryland.

I left my sailor friends at the chow hall table and climbed the ladders leading to the 03 level and my rack. I slid into bed and tried to remember their advice and not think too much this Christmas Eve about my wife, Joan, my daughter, Kathy, and my son, Jim, at home. "You're lonely, but you're not lonely alone," Voytak had said. He was right.

Christmas morning found Chaplain Doffin bouncy and optimistic as he opened the 9:30 Protestant service in the crew's lounge.

"Nineteen-eighty-four is going to be a good year," Doffin assured the audience of about fifty sailors, six officers and a few chiefs attending this first of several Christmas services. He smiled and then gave the reason for his optimism: "Because we're going home sometime that year."

Later in my room, the phone rang. "Hey, George," the always considerate "Potsie" Weber began. "We're all going to meet in my room to open our Christmas presents. Why don't you join us?"

We were like overgrown children celebrating Christmas in the living room. We sat on the bunks, in chairs, and on the floor with our presents—most of which had the battered look from being inspected by the sergeants-at-arms ever wary of bombs or other illegal items coming through the mail to the carrier. Christmas goodies were spread out on the desks. Guffaws erupted whenever one of our number held up a loud shirt or a flashy bathrobe. Hawk Hoppock, at home a compulsive do-it-yourselfer, got what he wanted from his wife, Chris: a tiny tool kit for fixing things on the ship. Rookie Williams ended up with three copies of James Michener's book *Space*. CAG Mazach's wife only managed to get a juggling set sent to him in time for Christmas. He had been scheduled to be home for the Big Day, but the Navy had extended his tour in case President Reagan ordered another bombing raid. Pat Mazach back in Orange Park, Florida, had to put away for his late return the pillow she had bought him for Christmas, embroidered: "We interrupt this marriage for football season."

As night fell over the ship at the end of Christmas Day, I moved around the working and sleeping compartments of the enlisted men, saying hello here and there and listening when the sailors wanted to talk. I spotted my old friend Marty Martell and asked him how he was going to end this special day.

"Take a shower. Read a book. Just another day."

"Are you down, Marty?"

"A little bit."

Bob Hope strode off the marine flying banana helicopter swinging his golf club and made his way across the flight deck midmorning of 26 December 1983. Trailing behind him were the first glamorous American women the 5,000 men on the *Kennedy* had seen since leaving Norfolk 90 days ago: Cathy Lee Crosby, Ann Jillian, Brooke Shields, and Julie Hayek, Miss USA. They lit up the ship the moment they came aboard. They were whisked into the admiral's cabin and other guest quarters to prepare for the fervently anticipated Christmas show in the hangar bay.

The *Kennedy* sailors, and more than a few officers, were taking no chances on missing this fabled comedian who had been dancing, singing and joking before most of the men on the *Kennedy* were born. They started to pour into the hangar bay at 10:50 A.M. for the afternoon show. Hope himself was resting in the captain's sea cabin one flight of stairs below the bridge. An elevator whisked him up there. Various shops on the ship had strung up posters of welcome, like a partisan crowd at a football game. "VAST—WELCOME TO BOB HOPE" read one sign. "SEASONS GREETINGS FROM EMO BRANCH" read another.

Two workmen with the Hope troupe hauled in a giant box of cardboard cue cards with the jokes painted in thick black lettering which would be easy for the comedian to read from the stage. A technician got on the microphone and made the first of several announcements that served notice that the sailors and the *Kennedy* were backdrops for the Bob Hope Christmas Show to be televised back home. They would be entertained, too, of course, but making a good tape for commercial television was obviously the main concern of the technicians. The first announcement was designed to keep the sailors from taking flash pictures of the show because "flashbulbs affect the quality of the tape." Another announcement from the stage warned that it was illegal for anyone in the audience to make videocassettes of the show.

This turned me and some officers off. "I feel like a prop," one officer told me. "I hope you write in your book what an asshole this guy is." But the sailors did not seem to mind anything as they waited for the living legend to show them his magic on this instant stage erected where planes squatted and dripped oil, grease, fuel, and hydraulic fluid.

Brooke Shields was guarded almost in lockstep by her mother as the beauty moved around the ship. The first hint that something was fouled up came in several pleas from technicians on the stage for sailors to help them find a box marked "Wardrobe." The Hope troupe had left the box, with costumes for the show, on another ship in the Med they had visited during their Christmas swing.

"The whole ship smells different," said one sailor sitting near me in the hangar bay waiting for the Bob Hope Christmas Show to begin. The sailor said he could smell perfume. All I smelled was the same old jet fuel.

Two officers sitting in front of me marveled about the great lengths and expense the Defense Department had gone to to get the Hope troupe out to our carrier off Lebanon.

"Well," said Commander "Supo" Smith, "he's a national asset."

Master Chief Crowley took to the stage. He suggested the crew shout, "Thanks for the memories," at the conclusion of the Hope show. Crowley gave it a trial run. The sailors shouted back lustily.

Shortly after noontime, XO Pieno dressed in a flight jacket, strode up to the mike and shouted that it was his pleasure and privilege to present to the men of *John F. Kennedy* "a great patriot, a great American—Bob Hope."

Hope bounced onto the stage with a golf club in his right hand and *Kennedy* ballcap on his head. Wearing an open shirt and blue sweater, Hope tried to swing into his machine gun delivery of wisecracks, but his monologue misfired and jammed repeatedly.

"It's easy to tell this ship is atomic powered," Hope said reading the cue card. "I shook hands with the captain and my nose lit up."

Someone forgot to tell him the *Kennedy* was oil fired rather than nuclear powered. His lines and the applause got better as he read deeper into the cue cards standing on a big easel out of camera range.

"If this is peacekeeping, wouldn't you hate to be in war."

Now that the sailors had seen Bob Hope in the flesh and heard jokes which had little relevance to their generation or situation, they grew audibly and visibly restless for the appearance of the beautiful young women the comedian had brought with him. When the women finally marched onto the stage, one after the other, the sex-starved sailors cheered, whistled, and stamped their feet. I thought to myself that they would have set off the same pandemonium if Little Orphan Annie had gone on stage—as long as she wore a dress.

The loss of Hope troupe costumes turned out to be a lucky break for the sailors. Brooke Shields looked absolutely luscious with her long legs poking out of an officer's khaki shirt; Cathy Lee Crosby looked ready for bed in her white, silky night dress; Julie Hayek, Miss USA, a tall buxom girl, was adjudged a wonderful armful by the sailors sitting around me; Ann Jillian managed to project that she really was glad to be here. She looked and acted like the caring sister trying her damnedest to say, "Thanks, fellows, for everything you're doing for me." From what I heard from the men afterward, Ann Jillian won the popularity and talent awards hands down.

Hope, national asset or not, came over as old and cranky as

he complained about muffed scenes and snapped at the cast, and ordered retakes of the taped skits designed for the audience back home, not the men on the ship. Wayne Newton had electrified the men much more by beaming everything he did to the sailors spread out before him. For Hope, we were just a backdrop.

Hope's troupe also included singer Vic Damone and comic George Kirby. I showed my age by being able to tell inquiring sailors who Damone was. They knew Kirby, who drew some laughs. But the sailors wanted to see more of the girls. They did not care that Cathy Lee could not sing. She was standing right there next to them in her bare feet and sexy nightgown, wasn't she? Ann Jillian, her voice told them, not only looked good —not as sexy as Brooke or Cathy, though—but could sing and dance better than anybody on the stage.

After the show, the Hope women dutifully toured much of the ship, including the ready rooms, and ended up in Admiral Box's cabin to receive farewell gifts and say goodbye. Box and Wheatley tried to outdo each other in repeatedly kissing the girls farewell. Box also showed them how he could dance—but only on one foot. Hope was breathing hard on the couch. The elevator which ordinarily would have taken him from the hangar bay to the admiral's cabin became overloaded and did not operate. So Hope had to walk up the steep stairs. He watched all the kissing of his girls by Box and Captain Wheatley and finally quipped from the couch:

"All right, Captain. Don't make a lunch of it."

The troupe left the cabin, pulled on their survival gear, and walked across the flight deck to the calls of the grateful, homesick sailors. Then they disappeared inside their helicopter and were soon a dot in the winter sky—taking with them the magic which had lit up the lives of the men on the *Kennedy* when they needed it most.

13   The Box

THE *Kennedy* settled back into the old routine of work and fly, fly and work, after Christmas. Her men hardly noticed that 1983 had given way to 1984. The *Kennedy*'s mission, like that of the marines at the Beirut International Airport, became harder and harder to understand as time wore on. The marines were supposedly providing ''a presence.'' They were not allowed to be combat troops. The *Kennedy,* too, was providing a presence. Its warplanes, except for the fouled up 4 December raid, were not allowed to go into combat, either. The carrier reminded me of a giant milling in place.

The giant was becoming so physically and spiritually exhausted that I believed only the prod of constant danger kept everyone going after Christmas and into January. Knowing that if you got careless on an aircraft carrier, you got maimed or killed was the one remaining stimulant that offset the deepening fatigue. This was especially true on the flight deck. Death was always coiled like a snake up there, ready to strike without warning. Two of the aviators from the VA-85 A-6 bomber squadron I had come to know learned this anew in the dark of the predawn of 11 January 1984.

Lieutenant (junior grade) Mark ''Sonny'' Beach and Lieutenant William ''Catfish'' Davis (he had been on the 4 December bombing raid) believed they were launching off on another routine mission when they climbed into their A-6E bomber. They already had walked all around bomber number 556, a replacement for the one with the same side number shot down over Lebanon, and found nothing amiss. The flight deck crew unchained 556 from the flight deck. Beach steered the bomber toward the starboard catapult for the launch. It was still so dark that there was just the suggestion of the horizon to tell him where sea and sky met—an invaluable reference point for pilots.

Beach was a twenty-four-year-old beginning pilot on his first cruise. At the end of the two and a half hour mission, he would make his 24th trap on the boat if all went well. It would be light by then. He hated landing in the dark on the pitching rectangle. Despite such fears, Beach had never thought of doing anything else but joining the Navy. His father had 5,000 hours of flying Navy planes, including combat time over Vietnam.

"Being a Navy brat is the only thing I can remember," Beach told me once. "All I've ever wanted to do is fly in the Navy. My brother, too."

Beach in these first weeks at sea discovered that he liked the free flying he could do around the boat. There was not always some ground controller banging your ear over the water as there was back on land. He told me he underestimated, though, how much he would miss his fiancée, Lynn Nabours of Galveston, Texas, who was well on her way to becoming a medical doctor. All he wanted to do now was perform well on the boat, then go home and marry Lynne. "It's the only thing I really look forward to," he told me.

Beach eased the bomber into the slot of the catapult. The deck crew checked the launching bar and found it solidly attached to the hook of the catapult trolley. Pilot Beach and Bombardier Davis scanned the instruments once again. Everything looked green for go.

"You ready?" Beach asked Davis.

"Roger. Let's go."

Beach turned on the plane's red and green exterior lights, the signal to the catapult officer that he was all set to be shot off the bow of the carrier and into dark pit of air beyond it. They felt the sudden yank of the cat shooting them forward down the deck. Then they felt a softness, a slowing up, in their roll.

"Something's not right," Beach said into the lip mike.

"Brake it! Stop it!" Davis snapped.

"I can't! I can't. It won't stop," Beach answered. He already was standing on the brakes.

Commander John Sulfaro, a veteran A-7 pilot sitting in the tower as Mini Boss of flight operations, saw to his horror that Number 556 was not going fast enough down the deck to become airborne when it ran out of deck.

"Put on your emergency brakes!" Sulfaro commanded. But the 25-ton A-6E kept rolling toward the edge of the cliff.

Beach had already pulled on the emergency brake and pulled back the throttles to cut the power. Still the plane rolled down toward the end of the flight deck, too fast to stop, too slow to fly when it dropped into the empty air dead ahead.

Beach and Davis were in what aviators call "The Box." They were confronted with desperate choices with time running out on them. If Davis and Beach ejected too soon, they might end up in one of the engine intakes of planes warming up behind them. If they waited to eject until their plane was falling off the cliff, the rockets under their seats might blast them against the steel side of the ship or into the water, killing them. If they stayed inside the plane, they would probably die—either from the explosion of the plane when it hit the water or from being run over by the carrier plowing along at 28 miles an hour.

Catfish Davis looked outside the cockpit and saw the end of the flight deck just ahead. He figured he was out of time. The plane was not going to stop.

"Hey, I'm getting out!" he shouted over the lip microphone to Beach.

Catfish pulled the yellow-and-black ejection loop under his seat. The rocket fired, shooting him through the roof of the A-6E's canopy. Plastic shrapnel flew all over the dark deck. Aircraft engines might suck up the pieces and stall, endangering another crew.

Beach feared Catfish saw something he did not. Beach pulled his own ejection loop. The rocket fired, hurtling him in his seat straight up into the air ahead of Catfish. The carrier was racing toward them, still going into the wind.

Catfish looked down as soon as he cleared the cockpit and the flying bits of plastic. He saw the fireball of Beach's ejection rocket. Then he tasted the rocket smoke. He breathed in so much of the smoke as he hurtled through the black sky like a man shot from a cannon that it choked him for a second or so. He tilted his head back and saw to his relief the opening blossom of the parachute canopy. Then came the "gotcha" yank everybody who ejects prays for. His descent slowed. But he could not breathe. His emergency oxygen was not working. He unscrewed its hose and ripped off his face mask. He was falling slowly downward. He had time to look around him. He searched for Beach in the dark sky. He spotted him floating down from what looked like a good chute. He was ahead of Catfish and drifting slowly left. Thank God Mark's chute opened, Catfish said to himself. Now Catfish worried where he was going to land. He looked down. Dark water was rushing up toward him.

"Oh shit!" Catfish said to himself. "I'm going in. This is not what I want to do."

Catfish, remembering the horror stories about parachutes drowning fliers, started fiddling with his Koch fittings as he saw the water rush up toward him. He did not pull the beads above his belt to inflate his life preserver. With luck, it would inflate automatically when it sensed salt water, as Frenchie's had done. He was focusing all his desperate effort on getting rid of the chute before he hit the water. He could swim away from the carrier if he got rid of the chute, perhaps escaping the suction that would pull him through the propellers. He could inflate the life preserver if he got clear. Then he saw the carrier had replaced the dark water under his feet. He was going to smack down on the fucking boat!

Wham!

Catfish slammed down on the steel flight deck, feet first, with his chute still attached. He felt the sting from his feet hitting the deck stab his brain. Ouch! Then he felt another stab of pain as his legs crumpled and his butt slammed down hard on the steel. Luckily he was still wearing his metal seat pan. It cushioned the blow, perhaps saving him from breaking his back.

The parachute canopy filled with the wind and pulled Catfish across the non-skid surface of the flight deck. Catfish still could be pulled into an engine intake. Sailors who had been frozen stock still by the sight of a man falling out of the dark sky recovered their wits. Several of them jumped on top of Catfish to stop his slide across the deck. Others gathered in the parachute. The chute had pulled him some 100 feet, rubbing through his flight suit and undershirt. The skin of his left shoulder had been scraped, forming an ugly abrasion. But the sailors had stopped his skidding before the wound went danger-ously deep. Catfish dared to think he might have been lucky one more time. He was on the flight deck, not in the water. That was one lucky thing, for sure. He felt all over his body for breaks. The still startled sailors stood over him. Nothing felt broken. He could move all his limbs. Hot damn! He looked up into the face of one of the sailors and asked:

"Where's Mark?"

Nobody but Catfish had seen Mark Beach's chute open. Everyone else on the ship feared the young pilot had either gone off the cliff, still strapped in the plane, and was already drowned, or had landed out there in the black water somewhere in his chute. The plane guard helicopter was already looking for Mark Beach. Its searchlight stroked slowly back and forth across the wave. Power skiffs were readied for launch to join the search.

Beach, like Catfish, worried about getting rid of his parachute before he hit the water. He forgot to pull the beads above his belt to inflate his life preserver. He, too, was worried about getting run over by the carrier or getting sucked through its screws. He had his hands on his Koch fittings when he felt a jolting yank through his harness. He was flung against the port side of the ship. The impact knocked the wind out of him, bruised his right arm and cut his right knee. The canopy of his parachute had snagged on the tail of A-6E number 504—from that second on his lucky number. The plane was parked on the port side of the carrier. Its tail stuck out over the water. Beach was dangling by his parachute shrouds from the tail like a hooked fish waiting to be reeled up to a high bridge.

"Oh shit!" Beach said to himself as he looked down at the black water and sized up his predicament. "I'm hanging on something."

He realized his parachute could pull loose from the tail of the parked plane any second. He belatedly pulled the beaded loops to inflate the left and right sides of his life preserver. He was hanging below the catwalk in the dark where nobody on the flight deck could see him. They could not hear him, either, for the roar of airplane engines. If his chute gave way, he would hit the water right next to the ship and almost certainly be sucked into the propellers.

A sailor, sauntering around the flight deck, looked over its edge for no particular reason. He spotted a man hanging from the tail of an airplane. He jumped up on the parked A-6, saw he could not pull in Beach by himself. "Hold on! We'll get you," the sailor assured the dangling pilot.

The sailor collected buddies and led them down the ladder to the catwalk running under the outer edge of the flight deck. The sailors heaved and pulled on the collapsed parachute and hauled Beach up.

"Are you all right?" a sailor shouted.

"Yes," Beach tried to answer, then realized he still had his oxygen mask snapped against his face. He pulled it aside. "Yes," he repeated.

"Are you hurt?" asked a sailor.

"Just my right arm," Beach replied.

A boatswain's mate suddenly punched Beach in the chest, figuring this was what it took to free the parachute. He was out of date. Nothing gave. Another boatswain's mate drew a big knife and sawed through Beach's parachute harness. Beach wiggled out of his harness; he stood up on the catwalk.

"How's Catfish?" Beach asked the thickening crowd on the catwalk.

"Mr. Davis is OK," a chief answered.

Beach began walking toward the interior of the ship. The medical staff intercepted him.

"Lie down! Lie down!"

Beach spotted Catfish. Catfish gave him a thumbs up. Beach lay down on the deck and quietly thanked God for saving them.

XO Pieno came up, leaned down over the now horizontal Beach and smiled devilishly. "Good morning!"

The two fliers were carried to sick bay in stretchers. Catfish was X-rayed and released. Beach was ordered into bed in sick bay.

I caught up to Catfish in the wardroom. He was Mr. Cool, eating eggs and smiling. He saw his scraped arm as a lucky wound. Fellow aviator Lieutenant Mike "Zone" Jones came up to Catfish.

"Hey, Buddy," Zone boomed. "I'm glad you're with us. Holy shit!"

"Cold Cat, that's what it was," Catfish replied with that big smile. "Landed in style, too. Right down the center line."

XO Pieno, himself an A-6 bombardier-navigator, congratulated Catfish.

"Great job. You saved his life. You did the right thing. Another second, and it would have been too late."

When the crowd of congratulators thinned out, I talked with Catfish for a long time over several coffees in the ward-room.

He was on a high—having just cheated death. We went through the morning's narrow escape and then got into the appeal of ever present danger, of living closer to the edge than most people.

"I never felt I had to make all this money that they told me was so important when I was going to Georgia Tech in 1974," Catfish told me. "I figured if I had enough money to buy a couple of six packs, play a couple rounds of golf and go fishing—long as I had enough money to buy bait—I'd be all right."

Catfish took two years of premed after switching from the pressure cooker of Georgia Tech to the University of Florida. His idea was to go into practice with his father, a medical doctor in Orlando, Florida.

"But I'm not the memorizing type. There's a lot of memorization in premed. I wasn't willing to put in the time that you have to to be good at it. I got back into engineering where I was happy as a lark. I loved the University of Florida, the Gators. I got a bachelor's degree in aerospace engineering in 1980.

"I got three job offers after graduation, including Lockheed and General Dynamics. Lockheed would have paid me $23,000 a year to start. But I had always wanted to fly off a carrier. I told myself, 'No, you can always get a job.' I wanted to fly while I could. To me, the pilots who land on this thing are the best pilots in the world. You can't persuade me any different. Those Air Force pilots have 12,000 feet of runway."

Catfish cut his long hair, joined the Navy to be a pilot and found because of a slight weakness in one eye he would have to settle for being in back or side seat as radar intercept officer or as bombardier-navigator. He wanted to fly in the A-6. The only way to be sure of doing it was to be first in your class in flight school. Catfish was. He joined VA-85 in April 1982 and went off on the USS *Forrestal* for his first cruise. He had never ejected before. "Has it spooked you?" I asked.

"Naw. Everyone out here lives with the fact that we're in a dangerous profession. I think Mark Lange would tell you the same thing if he were here today. He died a happy man because he was doing something he believed in. I couldn't think of a better way to go than the way Mark went.

"I think all of us out here are a little bit looney to do what we do and keep coming back for more. I never wanted to do something that was safe, something that was completely ordinary.

"I go home and I see friends of mine as insurance agents, accountants, and all that stuff. I'm glad they like it and are making money. I'm happy for them. But to me that's just boring. I feel like I'm cheating death every time I go flying. To me, it's fun. If I had to get out of this, I'd probably take up hang gliding or something. This is adventure if you do it smart.

"Seems as though nobody is ever serious out here. Everybody is bullshitting or grabbing ass or doing something to keep it from getting heavy. We say the Buckeyes' motto is, 'Pipper to People.' You always have your guard up, and you're always ready to have verbal battle with anybody.

"As long as we stay busy, I don't miss the beer on shore. I can handle the separation most of the time. I'm not married. I've got a girl friend in Virginia Beach and one I see in Orlando, and my folks and stuff. I think the worst part of being out here is not being able to do what you want to do when you want to do it. If I wanted to go out and have a beer and pizza right now, I couldn't do it. I miss just the little things. I miss mowing the lawn and even taking out the garbage. Nobody can relate to this who hasn't done it. I don't care what anybody says, nothing is like being out here.

"I can't remember what I did the last 72 hours because I kept doing the same thing over and over again. All of us complain, all of us bitch. But all of us know right in here it has got to be done. It makes it a lot easier knowing that people back home support us. I've gotten packages from a couple of different people who wouldn't ordinarily send me packages. I've gotten cards saying, 'Hey, we support you.' I haven't got one negative thing yet. That's why it pisses me off that some of the press coverage is so negative."

Zeroing in on the newspaper stories and magazines pieces he had read about the 4 December raid, Catfish railed at the comments that the crews had no battle experience and that their A-6E bombers were old and slow planes.

"Their comments about no battle experience is bullshit. We haven't been in a war for 12 years. How the hell are we supposed to come up with guys with all that combat experience? The public is going to read those comments and say, 'What's wrong with our Navy?'

"Cutting down the A-6! The A-6 is the world's best all-weather attack airplane. What airplane does the United States not export to anybody? The only one is the A-6. We export the F-18, the F-14, the F-15, the F-16, the A-7—all of them. As far as them writing about our not being able to go supersonic, you can't deliver bombs supersonic."

Catfish had been wanting to register those complaints to a real live reporter for some time. He obviously felt better about getting it off his chest. We both chuckled after his outburst and returned to his morning brush with death—and the ever presence of death on a carrier. He wanted to talk about the young kids on the flight deck who had helped save him not only this morning but many other mornings.

"I'm really impressed with these young kids. They're only 18-, 19-, or 20-years old and not making that much bucks. You see these kids reacting out there on the flight deck, risking their lives, and then you read about a football strike where guys are complaining about not making more than $200,000 for playing a goddamn game—a goddamn game. I wrote a letter to the editor back home about that. These kids aren't risking their knees or their shoulders. They're risking their lives. Up on the flight deck an arresting cable can snap and cut you in half. This has happened. Nobody ever sees that.

"The way I handle death of somebody close, like Mark Lange, is justify it and then put it out of your mind. I know Mark was happy because he was doing the one thing he loved—flying. Unlike the F-14 we lost, we know how he went. He died in a gallant effort. I think all of us become a little bit callous toward death because we live with it. You have to keep going.

"Last year I was up on the flight deck when we lost a guy off the front end. The ship ran over the pilot. We launched five minutes later. I came back down and reflected on that; asked myself, 'How can we do that?' Everybody keeps right on going. If we had gone off the front end this morning and not gotten out, there is no way they would have canceled the flight schedule —not in our business."

I left Catfish in the wardroom and walked down to see Mark Beach in sick bay. I wanted to see how he was and ask him if he felt like talking. He was all alone in the ward lying in a cot. His right knee was bandaged and his right arm was in a sling. He welcomed the company. He was interested in what Catfish had said about his ejection. We started talking about the problems of being on a first cruise and then got around to the big question: Did he want to go back into the cat after what happened this morning?

"There was no doubt in my mind that I was going to get out of the airplane before we went over the side. I didn't think we were as far down the deck as we were. I still felt I was moving straight down the deck. I wasn't going to stay with it a whole lot longer. I remember saying, 'This isn't right.' I remember Catfish saying, 'Get ready.' I had this fear he saw something I didn't see because he's looking out the window as well as at the instruments. In the night shots I'm looking inside the airplane because there's nothing outside that's going to tell you anything. After Catfish got out, I had no choice but to follow. Catfish has a lot more experience than I have. I told myself 'I'm going to pull the emergency brake and if that thing doesn't stop, I'm gone.' I didn't feel it stop. Whoomf. Catfish was gone. I was gone."

How about the next time you go into tension on the cat?

"I'll probably have some qualms about the first cat shot. But if it's during the day the first time, that won't be so bad. The systems worked this morning. The seat worked good. The chute worked good. People aboard the ship did a good job of pulling me up once they saw me. Oh yeah, I want to keep flying. I'd like to be able to call my fiancée in Galveston. She'll be worried sick when she hears about this. My Dad has 4,000 or 5,000 hours. He'll understand. So will my Mom.

"I'm alive. That's the upside of this morning. The investigation will determine what happened."

The investigation threatened to polarize the air department and the air wing. The air department ran the flight deck and controlled the air space for five miles around the ship. Carrier Air Wing Three owned, maintained, and flew the *Kennedy*'s planes. Who was responsible for the near tragic launch of Λ-6 number 556? Did the sailors who hooked up the plane to the catapult fail to make a solid connection? Should the catapult officer, also part of the air department, have detected the faulty hookup before he touched the deck—the signal that sends a plane hurtling down the deck? Did the crew feeding steam into the piston which drove the catapult hook do something wrong? Did the air wing—specifically VA-85 squadron—fail to notice something was broken in the launching mechanism of the plane?

Relations were tense as the investigation focused on these questions. The film, which is made of every launch, seemed to take the air department off the hook at first look. It seemed to show the launch bar flying apart after the plane was headed down the deck. The hookup man—a young sailor—would be in the clear if the fault lay in the launch bar itself. Perhaps it was cracked or fatigued. The squadron studied the records. The bar had not exceeded the number of launches it was supposed to be able to take. Bloodless, unaccountable machinery apparently was the culprit.

"Stand by to rig the barricade!"

The call booming out of the loudspeakers signaled a plane in the night sky above the carrier was in trouble. The barricade is a nylon net stretched across the flight deck to catch a plane in trouble.

I rushed down to operations and learned Lieutenant Robert "Bo Bo" Clager and Lieutenant Scott "Spanker" Francis were in the box. They were so low on fuel that they had three choices: eject near the boat and let their F-14 Tomcat crash into the sea; take the risk—which always included fire—of smacking into the barricade on a final landing attempt, find the tanker in the night sky and take enough fuel from it to make several more passes.

Bo Bo and Spank did not like the idea of ejecting at night. No aviator does. Each knew the odds of being found as they bobbed on the dark Mediterranean were slim. Both had wives they wanted to see again. Spanker had two children.

Until now, the Navy had been so good to Bo Bo and Spank. Bo Bo, a native of Lake Worth, Florida, was easygoing, almost listless. He loved the camaraderie of his squadron, the Red Rippers, and usually had a clever quip. Spank felt the Navy had given him a new, more exciting career than the one he left in Salem, Massachusetts. He had graduated from Salem State College prepared to teach school only to find there was no need for his teaching services. He had managed his father-in-law's grocery store and, when the store closed, saw the Navy as a chance to do something different.

Bo Bo and Spank searched the night sky for the tanker. The controller said it would be at their 10 o'clock about five miles away. They raced for the rendezvous with Texaco. They spotted the tanker and lined up behind it. The tanker's long hose with the female connection marked by a circle of lights danced in the sky ahead of them. Bo Bo maneuvered the plane as precisely as he could and drove the Tomcat's probe toward the lighted basket. It failed to make a solid connection. The planes separated for another try. Red lights warning of low fuel glowed in the Tomcat's cockpit.

Skipper John Combs of VF-11 stood at the microphone in the air operations center on the carrier trying to calm his pilot. "You've got plenty of time," Combs lied. "Take it easy."

Bo Bo tried a second plunge and missed. He was getting down on himself. He did not want to go swimming. He told himself this would be a stupid way to lose an airplane—running out of gas right over the ship. He saw himself as the Charlie Brown of the Navy—missing the basket like Charlie missed the football.

"Let's climb out of here and get up where the air isn't so rough," Spank said from the back seat, trying to sound calm. Bo Bo could not see that Spank was clearing away everything so he could eject cleanly from the cockpit when the engines quit from lack of fuel.

"Let's just be professional," Spank said, as Bo Bo lined up for the third try at the higher altitude. Bo Bo knew Spank meant well. But his chatter from the back seat was pissing him off. Bo Bo went for it. Clunk! The probe snapped into the basket. Life-saving fuel started flowing into the Tomcat. They took on 4,000 pounds, enough for several passes. There was elation all around the sky; all around the ship. A relieved Skipper Combs came back on the radio.

"Now we'll do anything you want. The ship is at your disposal. You're cleared to fly straight in or you can fly around a while to calm down."

"No sir," Bo Bo replied. "I'm going to come back right now."

His flight suit was soaked with sweat. He bit down hard on himself and lined up for the landing. The plane slammed down in the usual shower of sparks. Bo Bo and Spank waited to feel the tug from the hook catching the wire. They were thrown forward. The hook had caught. They were down. Bo Bo tried to get out of the Tomcat, but his legs caught. He had forgotten in the rush to leave the plane to unhook the leg restraints.

I was in the operations center where Combs and CAG Mazach had been trying to help talk Bo Bo and Spank down to the deck.

"Skipper," CAG kidded, "do you think Spank lost any weight?" Spank had been grounded for a while because he was overweight.

"He has now," Combs replied.

Bo Bo and Spank poked their heads into the six-man where they lived. "We're home," they announced.

Rippers had been watching the passes on the television screen and keeping up with the radio talk back and forth across the night sky. Their tenseness gave way to the usual kidding by the time Bo Bo and Spank clomped into the ready room with the light of triumph on their faces.

"It was water, water, water, steel," Bo Bo said of his last landing. "I built the box and couldn't get out of it."

Lieutenant Commander "Arlo" Guthrie smiled across the room at Bo Bo and offered some advice on how to plug into a tanker basket dancing up and down in the night sky:

"Just imagine hair around it."

14 Secretary Lehman

THE *Kennedy* drew distinguished visitors from the world, including members of Congress, admirals, and generals. Usually these visits were bothersome but not worrisome for the officers on the carrier who had to prepare briefings, find suitable living quarters on the crowded ship and plan dinners and tours for the VIPs. But the upcoming visit of Navy Secretary John F. Lehman, Jr. was, in contrast, indeed worrisome. He was bound to ask right after he arrived on 11 January 1984 how the hell the bombing raid of 4 December got so screwed up.

The secretaries of the Army, Navy, and Air Force were not consulted in advance about the advisability of bombing Lebanon on 4 December. They do not get into such operational matters. They are outside the chain of command which goes from the President to the Secretary of Defense and out to the theater commanders. A President usually appoints secretaries of the Army, Navy, and Air Force from the band of party faithful who helped elect him. The secretaries seldom come to their jobs with any military expertise. Their charter is not to help plan military operations but to implement and oversee the policies of the Secretary of Defense down through their services. They are in the corporate sense vice presidents of the various departments under the chief executive officer of the Pentagon, the Secretary of Defense. They are not supposed to champion the causes of the admirals and generals. Admirals and generals sometimes suffocate their civilian secretaries with paper work and ceremonial duties to keep them from speaking out on the big military decisions. Lehman from day one in the job of Navy secretary showed he was not going to be suffocated by the admirals but would jump into the middle of the biggest decisions, ranging from where aircraft carriers should fight in wartime to which admirals should be promoted and where they should serve. Shortly before the *Kennedy* went to sea, Lehman had been in a verbal slugfest with Deputy Defense Secretary Paul Thayer on how much of the Pentagon's total budget the Navy should be allowed to spend on ships to protect carriers in the future. Thayer contended that the Navy had earmarked too much money for ships to protect carriers, given the future needs of the other armed services, particularly the Army.

By January 1984, when Lehman was winging toward the *Kennedy,* the Navy Secretary had won his fight with Thayer.

Fan or critic of Lehman, the word around the carrier was that this particular Navy Secretary could not be charmed into administrative impotence by giving him a fancy cabin, flying him around in the carrier planes and telling him sea stories. He would want answers. "Answer his questions but don't volunteer anything," became the unofficial guidance from the top of the admirals' club, perhaps the world's most effective protective society.

Lehman—an energetic, chunky man, five-foot-nine, with a pugnacious approach—galloped through a tight schedule right after landing. He talked to sailors on the mess decks; was interviewed over the ship's television; went from one ready room to another seeking information and answering questions. He donned his orange flight suit and flew in the right seat of the A-6 and the back seat of the F-14 as a reserve naval flight officer. He was an A-6 enthusiast. He came aboard the *Kennedy* convinced it was not used correctly in December.

I told Lehman his views on the bombing raid would be uniquely enlightening. They would combine his Washington perspective, Navy flight experience, and distillation of the information gathered during his swing through the battle group. I received permission to fly from there back to the United States with Lehman in a dressed-up version of the propeller-driven P-3 antisubmarine plane. I figured I would not miss any action on the *Kennedy* because she had just received orders to break off from Bagel Station and steam to Naples for liberty. Several *Kennedy* men were taking leave to fly home at the same time. They would hitch a military plane from the States back to Naples to rejoin the ship. Other officers were busy cabling their wives to fly to Naples for a midcruise honeymoon. I decided a short leave would not be giving myself special treatment as long as I went back aboard the *Kennedy* with my shipmates before she left Naples. I could fly back on a commercial airliner.

My conscience thus salved, I hitched a helicopter ride to Cyprus where I joined Lehman for the long flight back to Washington. I had a long list of questions I hoped he would answer during the flight. He was ready for them. My first question was what he thought had gone wrong with the raid.

"We have got to do something about the bloated, bureaucratic chain-of-command here in Europe," Lehman said, zeroing in on what he believed had been the root cause of the problems. "It has made the most inefficient use of an air wing I have ever seen."

He was visibly angry as he elaborated on why he believed the bureaucracy had kept the men on the scene from doing the job they knew how to do best.

"Our hands were really tied," Lehman continued as the P-3 lumbered northwestward through the winter sky. "The targets were not allowed to be picked by the task force commander.

"It's the unified staff system," the Navy secretary lamented, that took the choice of targets away from the commander on the scene, Admiral Tuttle. "We've reformed and consolidated to the point that the targets are not allowed to be picked by the task force commander. They're picked by the bureaucrats. They're picked by the consolidated Defense Intelligence Agency in Washington and the consolidated Joint Staff in Stuttgart.

"The raid in the parameters that were given to it was a success. It hit the targets; it did a lot of damage but it took eight percent attrition (two bombers lost out of 28 on the strike) which should have been predictable for that raid.

"The overall exercise of the raid as an exercise of national power was a success because it was intended to send a message that we will go into any defenses any time and hit them and do damage.

"The battleship *New Jersey* could have been used on those targets. If they were able to put 28 airplanes over the target, they certainly could have put one over the target to direct the fire from the battleship to the bullseye." (Spotter planes that do this are called FACs for forward air controllers. The FAC pilot under Lehman's alternative scenario would have flown above the range of SA-7 heat-seeking antiaircraft missiles and told the gunners after each round how to adjust their sights.)

"To sum up the raid it was a success in that it put the bombs over the target. It was a clear message to the Syrians. But we lost two airplanes. That was not a success."

Given the loss of the subsonic A-6 to fairly primitive Soviet antiaircraft missiles, should the Navy take this as a warning against building new versions of the same bomber which would have to fly against even better defenses in the future?

"To go do any daylight bombing today, you better have a benign environment. It's no criticism of the A-6. No other airplane could have done it better. It's just dumb to use a $20 million airplane as if it was an A-4 (Skyhawk, a small Navy bomber). And that's what was done."

Several of the senior pilots on the *Kennedy* had told me that they thought Lehman was making a mistake by pushing the Navy into buying updated A-6s, called A-6Fs, instead of putting those billions into the all new F/A-18, a combination fighter and bomber. They argued that the F/A-18 is smaller than the A-6, advantageous for evasion in the air and parking on the crowded carrier deck. It also is faster. "Speed is life," said one flier in quoting Captain Sam Flynn, a legendary naval aviator. "Fixing up this old dog is not the way to go," said a senior pilot in discussing the A-6 vs. F/A-18 choice.

Lehman disputed this: "The F/A-18 going into that attack would have gotten shot just as dead," Lehman said. "To get the speed or energy advantage for the sustained G (gravitational force), you've got to go into burner (turning on the after burners on the aircraft engines, which burns an enormous amount of fuel). And when you go into burner you negate the use of flares (which are dropped during a bombing run to draw heat seeking missiles to them rather than the bombers. The fires of the afterburners would draw the missiles into the tails of the bombers).

"You're talking between an 8 mil and a 6 mil system in comparing the bombing systems of the A-6 and F/A-18. So in daylight bombing from 4,000 feet, with the F/A-18 you'll get four times six, a 24 foot error, while with the A-6 you'll get four times eight, or a 32 foot error. So they're both damn good systems.

"The pilots of the A-7s like to say, 'Oh we can always beat the A-6s' because the A-7 has a tighter, better system for daylight bombing. The F/A-18 bombing system is better, more flexible than the ones in either the A-6E or the A-7. We want to put it in the A-6F for daylight bombing." (The F/A-18 bombing system constantly shows the pilot where the target is even during violent maneuvers to avoid missiles. The A-6 bombardier-navigator has to put the pipper on the target himself while flying along.)

"To say buy more F/A-18s vs. A-6s says you need that yanking and banking over the target because we're still going to do the classic light attack alpha strikes (featuring the kind of dive bombing that brought losses in Vietnam and on 4 December). If you buy more airplanes to do that, you're going to do just that. To take a $20 million F/A-18 to lose it to an SA-7 (Soviet heat-seeking missile) while you're trying to bomb a $10,000 57mm site is plain stupid. It's a way to lose the war.

"The SA-9 (long range Soviet antiaircraft missile) goes about Mach one point six. It pulls something like 40 Gs. So if you've got 30 more knots like an (Air Force) F-16 (fighter bomber) or F-18 and you've got two more sustained Gs, it doesn't make a damn bit of difference because you're still so much within the missile's envelope that you don't buy anything from it. Bobby Goodman (who was shot down in his A-6 over Lebanon) looked at the air speed indicator just before he was hit. He was doing 470 knots. Well, you can't bomb much faster than 470 with an F/A-18 or F-16. Speed is not the answer. You just can't go into unattrited defenses without countermeasures."

How is it, that the Israeli air force manages to bomb targets in Lebanon week after week without suffering the kind of loss the United States experienced?

"When they do go into that kind of target, as they very rarely do, they take the same losses. On the Israeli's raid that went in the two weeks before 4 December, they sent in six F-16s and they lost one to SA-7s. There are also other losses that we don't hear about. We know that through other intelligence. But when there's not an Associated Press writer around, nobody finds out about it. They never publicize it the way we do. We don't know what the Israeli losses are. But they will not accept eight percent losses by any means. Their loss rate is much lower because they plan. They don't do things on the spur of the moment. They have preplanning. It's a lot easier for them because they only have one set of contingencies and one little piece of geography on which to do their targeting. And they know every rock, every aim point and they use deception. And they use imagination. They're damn good. But they have a lot of advantages. Our air wings have to plan and have the capability to respond to an infinite set of contingencies.

"If we kept *Kennedy* on her present station for two years with the same air wing, our crews would know the terrain well, too. But we won't let them fly over the terrain even when they are on station so they can get to know it. The Israelis never do a raid without the pilots who are going to carry it out actually flying over the area. They call these 'take a peek' flights and always do them. Sometimes they'll go in—run the whole raid and turn away short as if they're practicing. They'll do that twice. The third time they'll do it exactly the same way except they'll keep going and hit them."

How about pilot for pilot, and—in the case of the Navy F-4s which the Israelis have in their inventory —backseater for backseater, are the U.S. Navy's as good as Israel's?

"To generalize, yes. They're as well trained. But to make any fair comparison you have to understand that our air crews have to be able to do many more things than the Israelis in areas all over the world, not just the Middle East. If our crews have been doing a lot of air-to-ground work, then they're as good as Israeli's air-to-ground pilots. But if you're asking me if the *Kennedy* air wing is as good in air-to-ground work as the Israeli pilots are now I will have to say no because they haven't been practicing it.

"The A-6 in my judgment is the most capable attack airplane in the world without any question. It's better than the F-111. But you got to do it. It's like playing tennis; like playing the violin. If you don't do it, you lose it."

Lehman added that the crew of the battleship *New Jersey* needed realistic training, too, to learn how to get the most out of its array of guns.

"One of the reasons the battleship was not used is that it's a brand new weapon system and it just hasn't been in the thinking or the strike planning of the battle group. They don't have the procedures down. They don't even have a hard data base. There's still confusion over the accuracy of the system. We're wringing that out; getting the data; getting the planning into the system; and now we've got to go develop how to use it. We've got to redevelop a fast FAC (forward air controller) capability as part of the air wing."

Pilots on the *Kennedy* familiar with both FAC missions and the small targets in Lebanon had told me that spotting from the air for the *New Jersey*'s guns or other bombers had proved extremely difficult. Picking out from 10,000 or even 5,000 feet an empty lot in Beirut or a fold in a hill from which a mortar team had fired on the marines was virtually impossible, they said, even when scanning through special binoculars. Syrian antiaircraft sites were not much easier to find because they were usually dug into the side of a mountain with no easy-to-see complex of buildings nearby. Flying lower to see better increased the risk of being downed by the SA-7. Armed with this information, I asked the Secretary of the Navy why it would not make sense to turn to low level, unmanned drones for both photography and spotting for Navy guns offshore.

"We ought to try it. It certainly makes sense to go drones for the TARPS mission in some circumstances."

Lehman was less certain about using drones as aerial spotters for the battleships. His first priority in this area was to train Navy or Marine airplane crews to perform the spotting mission.

"It's not the safest of missions, but it's safer than sending an Alpha strike in. If you go in at 500 knots at 20,000 feet with stabilized binoculars and spot from that height, at least you're out of most of it."

I ran through the way the multitude of terrorist threats passed on to the commanders in the battle group had triggered all kinds of exhausting alerts: fighters stayed ready to shoot down light, bomb laden planes that did not materialize; sailors and marines manned machine guns on the *Kennedy* all night to combat terrorist speedboats said to be in the area; A-6 bombers searched the waters below them for hostile craft. This in my view distorted and undercut the mission and effectiveness of the carrier battle group. I asked Lehman if he agreed.

"The terrorist threat is a new complication to the mission. First of all, whenever a large task force becomes immobile and goes and sits off the beach, it becomes much more vulnerable. The security of it is much more difficult, not just from the terrorist threat but from surprise attack because the whole idea of a battle group is built around its mobility. The battle group's tactics and its survivability are built around movement. When you suddenly have to become a police force standing at one place, then you take on new vulnerabilities, particularly against the guy who is willing to shoot first.

"So it's not terrorism per se, it's surprise attack, whether by terrorists or by the Soviets. And the most realistic threat here is either a retaliatory threat from the Syrians or the Libyans or something like that. There is a second order of threats from any one of a number of crazy groups. But to mount a serious threat against one of our ships, you would have to have the support of a major power like the Libyans or the Syrians.

"The targets that worry us the most are not the carrier. The carrier is not particularly vulnerable to a terrorist attack because it has its own defenses. Neither is it the combatants. It is the amphibs—the amphibious ships. They generally are not very well armed at all. That has concerned us. We have changed the operating rules. We keep them moving.

"The difficulty for the carrier—you used the right word, distorting. What the terrorist threat is doing is distorting the readiness. It is not reducing the readiness; it is distorting it. The fighter guys are getting 40, 50, 60 hours a month, and they're getting fairly good training. They're running intercepts. They're doing air-to-air on every hop. (There was of course no way for Lehman to have known this, but the F-14 pilots and radar intercept officers complained constantly about being confined to fly in boring circles off Lebanon at the speed and altitude to conserve fuel. They usually returned directly to the carrier without doing any mock aerial combat. But the *Kennedy* was in an unusually demanding situation for such fighter patrolling.)

"The E-2C (Hawkeyes warning and control planes) are getting good training.

"The A-6 air crews bitch about the SUCAP (surface combat air patrol—circling over the waters off Lebanon in case a hostile boat or ship makes a run on a ship in the battle group or the marines call for instant fire support from the air). SUCAP is not really just against the terrorist threat. That's a part of it.

"It is also to have the alert response to give direct support to the marines. And that's the thing that really ties them there (to patrolling back and forth over the Mediterranean). SUCAP against the terrorists is a temporary burden that's being put on them until we get our act together on how we're going to handle this terrorist speedboat threat. Until we get ourselves organized and get the weapons we need out on the ships. We've got a crash program. We're putting now the CIWS (close in weapons system which fills the air close to the ship with lead from the rapid firing of a gun with rotating barrels like the old Gatling gun) on all the ships that are coming out here to the Med. We're getting Stinger (antiaircraft missiles effective against low flying planes) out here. It's very effective against the cheap shot.

"We've sent over two new, fast patrol boats with 40mm. We've got two of them in the area to protect against surface threats. Using A-6s for this is not the way to go. The assets are being misused right now. We're trying to pool our tactics and get the right assets together to do it right. We've got two alert Cobras on the *Trenton* (an amphibious ship) and their primary mission is the terrorist threat. That's an appropriate way to do it. We need the terminal defenses on the ships so a cigarette boat going 70 knots could, with the proper rules of engagement, get shot. It's the night time environment that is the problem.

"We need to get more of a patrol capability than we have because there are situations like this where a patrol boat can do good things. But you have to be careful not to overdo responding to the current situation. There's a danger that once you get the bureaucracy in motion, you'll plan for the last war—in this case the last peacekeeping. It may be 20 years before we have another peacekeeping mission.

"The terrorist threat is a complicating threat. It's more a burden on a routine day-to-day training because the battle group, the strike planning is still oriented first toward the Soviet threat. The ships of the battle group would swing right away to a different posture if we went to an alert status. It is a pain in the butt for the normal peacetime routine to keep up readiness."

What I saw on the *Kennedy* documented for me that the U.S. intelligence community sent all kinds of warnings out to the ships in the battle group about imminent terrorist attacks or other threatening activity. The warnings did not seem to be graded by degree of authenticity or probability. Whether they were or not, the usual reaction of the top officers in the battle groups was to order more intensive and exhausting alerts—just in case. These alerts exhausted the air crews and sailors, usually for no good reason. I came away with the strong conviction that the U.S. intelligence community needed nothing as much as a good manure separator so they would not fill up the in-baskets with bogus warnings. Lehman did not agree with me here.

"You can be overwhelmed if you want to be overwhelmed by the intelligence coming in. Both raw data is available and then the evaluated filtered data which says, 'Hey you guys, taking everything into consideration, here is what we think is happening.' And that comes out from NIS (Naval Intelligence Service) and from DIA (Defense Intelligence Agency). But you still get the raw intelligence. If you want to say, 'I'm a better evaluator than NIS evaluators,' then you're perfectly free to say, 'I think that Bonanza sitting on the field is going to hit me tomorrow.' I don't think unfiltered information is a problem. The battle group commander is responsible for making the judgment on intelligence.

"We've gotten in the habit of treating the intelligence gathering and dissemination and other broad endeavors as a big automatic machine—all you have to do put oil on it and tinker with it; tighten a bolt—the mechanistic view. The whole Dave

Jones (retired Air Force General David C. Jones, former chairman of the Joint Chiefs of Staff, who recommended an overhaul of the Joint Chiefs organizational structure) debate. Aw, if we'd only fix the organization we wouldn't have bad rescue missions. That's baloney. You've got human beings and you ought to hold them accountable. If you've got a mediocre battle group commander, with the best intelligence filter, he's going to foul up. If you've got a good one, if you give him the raw data he'll put it together in the right way. We've got to get back to more of that individual accountability. These guys are human beings. Same with air crews. It's the individual performance."

Does the fact that a Third World country tied down two of the Navy's giant carriers at once strengthen the argument by Senator Gary Hart and others that the nation would get more bang for its buck by building smaller and less expensive carriers so the Navy could afford more of them?

"The experience out here illustrates exactly why only the large carriers can do the job. Look at what is happening right now. One carrier is sitting out there keeping 24 hour fighter CAP (combat air patrol). There also is an E-2C in the air around the clock. At the same time the carrier is working the zones where submarines might be hiding. It is keeping the S-3s and SH-3s (antisubmarine planes and helicopters) working. You can't do all that from a small carrier.

"If you put a small carrier out there, you still would have to give it ASW (antisubmarine warfare) protection. You have got to keep the barriers against subs. There are no land-based P-3s out there to provide the ASW barrier 24 hours a day. And the subs are there. If it weren't for the barriers, they could get in for the cheap shot. But you can't get one of those big carriers we have had out there with a Libyan submarine or by buying a German submarine because they can't get in for that cheap shot. We knew where the Libyan sub was all the time it was out there. Maybe they didn't know on the carrier, but the battle group commander knew where it was. The submariners knew where it was, and it would have been shot before it got within firing range. You can't do that with a little carrier.

"To perform all the missions we have to do out here with a single carrier operation requires depth of people. The *Kennedy* has kept above 80 percent mission capability (meaning eight out of ten aircraft and their crews are ready to go) while they're running at this operational tempo. That's fantastic! You know what would happen on a smaller carrier? You would have fewer people to carry the load; you would have a smaller supply of spare parts to draw on and fewer planes available for fighter CAP, SUCAP, and E-2 CAP. A small carrier couldn't do what the *Kennedy* is doing.''

I was struck during my months on board how the threat to carriers had been turned upside down. I had heard admirals tell Congress repeatedly that submarines were the biggest threat to carriers. Then at sea I witnessed how the threat of terrorists attacking the carriers or other ships in the battle group with light planes loaded with explosives or with speedboats at night tied everybody in knots. Did not this experience dramatize the carrier's vulnerability to comparatively primitive threats as well as sophisticated ones, I asked Lehman. I hit a nerve. He slammed his fist down on the desk between us as he began his reply.

''George! This is a perfect illustration of what I've been saying for years about the way the whole issue of the carrier *is* turned upside down. The target is not the carrier off Beirut. The target is the task force, especially the amphibs. If you're a Syrian and you want to hit something, you're not going to hit the carrier. You're not going to go after the battleship. You're going to go after something that might sink. Something that's not well defended that gets you the headline.

''So a Cigarette boat comes out to try to get the carrier. What chance does he think he's got to get to it with the destroyer and a frigate and a CIWS (close in weapons system) aboard the carrier itself? And so if he hits the carrier, so what? So he punctures through one of seven baffling hull layers. That makes a hole. He kills nobody. Even the size of the bomb that went off in Beirut would not have been a particularly big deal on the carrier. It would not have gotten through the hull.

''The carrier is there worrying about the protection of the task force. It itself is not a particular target. When it worries about that Libyan submarine, it's worrying about it sneaking in to one of the small ships and knocking off the *Trenton* or knocking off the LST (landing ship which can carry tanks but has virtually no defense of its own). The terrorist would go after something that has got no protection and a single hull. If he puts a hole in it, it is going to go right to the bottom. That's the worry of the cruise missiles. We're not worried about the cruise missile being shot at the carrier. The whole carrier is built to take that kind of hit. But the small ships (like the amphibious vessels and small destroyers which were standing off Beirut) are not. You get an Exocet hitting the *Trenton,* and the *Trenton* could end up on the bottom. That's what worries us, not an attack on the carrier.

"The submarine threat is there in the waters off Beirut simultaneously with the surface threat and the air threat. It's a classic in miniature of why you have to have the carrier there to combat those threats to protect the rest of the battle group. The task force is not there to protect the carrier, it's vice versa.

"The carrier always exists to help protect a task force, even though the debate has been built around the contention that you have to buy this big task force to protect the carrier. It has never been that way. The carrier doesn't exist to be a target that has to be protected. You have to buy a carrier because you have to be in places like Beirut or the Falklands. Or you have Army soldiers in merchant vessels going from point A to point B who have to be protected. So you buy a carrier to protect them. The destroyer is in the task force to kill submarines trying to sink the carrier, the heart of the task force and its main striking power. But to say that therefore the task force is there to protect the carrier—whether it was 20 years ago, or 10 years ago or today—is just nonsense.

"The Beirut deployment very well illustrates the inherent flexibility that is in naval task forces. Because you may be sent to high threat areas, you always have to be ready to operate in four dimensions. You've got a lot of assets. You turn an unpredictable task like Beirut over to a fleet commander, and he has in his quiver many different kinds of arrows in the various capabilities in each of the ships in his task force. He can mold and tailor his force and deal with the threat, the geography, the environment. The only extraordinary thing we've done off Beirut is deploy the battleship. This also will be a routine action when the four battleships are returned to the fleet.

"The versatility is demonstrated by the fact that you have on scene an A-6 carrier that was put together for a very different task. The idea was to maximize its deep strike, long range strike, deep interdiction, and long range war at sea capabilities. Yet today you're putting the carrier in a close air support mode where the A-6s are in SUCAP (surface combat air patrol). That is a distortion but a temporary distortion forced on us by the terrorists.

"The idea of kamikazes has sort of been absent from our operations since the end of World War II. Now it's back again. But what we're doing now to protect our amphibs from kamikazes is not that different from what my father had to do at Okinawa after the invasion. His job as skipper of a gunship was to protect the destroyers and the amphibs from suicide speedboats coming out of Karama Retto, a Japanese island 14 miles from Okinawa; and the suicide planes. This is back 40 years ago. Any time some guy is willing to commit suicide to kill you, you've got a problem.

"I can't think of any changes we have to make in our shipbuilding and conversion plan to combat this new terrorist, kamikaze threat. If this should go on in other areas, we might want to think about bringing out the Salem class 8-inch automatics. That would provide us with firepower between the 16-inch and the 5-inch guns. Our experience off Lebanon certainly has reaffirmed our belief in the wisdom of naval gunfire and the mistake of phasing it out during the 1960s and 1970s. What we've got to do is rebuild expertise in using gunships. It's not there.

"We've got two battle groups out there. Each one has a totally different set of statistics about what the battleship can do in its strike plan. Both of those are different from the one the battleship has. There is no agreement on how to use the *New Jersey*'s 16-inch guns, what their accuracy, range, and weapon effects are. It's a brand new weapons system and we didn't have time to work it up because this is the shakedown. Everybody is still writing the book.

"The *New Jersey*'s 16-inch guns have made a quantum leap in the firepower we now have available. But if you want to get a particular bunker or radar site, then you need to have a spotter so you can correct your aim between rounds. Nobody really knows what happens when you shoot a 16-inch shell up to 30,000 feet and it goes through a 90 knot wind that nobody knew was there. But with a spotter, you can crank in the correction and the second or third round will be on target."

Is it time to deploy V/STOL—for vertical or short takeoff landing—planes which could take off by themselves from a small stretch of carrier deck, thus increasing the number of planes which a ship could carry and removing the vulnerability of the launching gear on today's carriers?

"I was very disappointed that we lost the money for the STOL demonstrator for the A-6. We could make the A-6 free of the catapult and arresting gear. We know we can do it. But they killed it in Congress. So STOL is attractive, but it's expensive. It's a useful way to go because the catapults and arresting gear are the most vulnerable parts of the carrier. It would be nice to keep launching no matter what's happening. With four cats, it takes a lot of hits to put them all out of commission. Nevertheless, that's a vulnerability.

"The big drawback in taking off vertically or in a short distance is the extra fuel you have to burn to get airborne. The amount of gas left for the mission is greatly reduced. Taking off with a roll, STOL, makes a lot more sense than trying to go vertical. STOL capability can be achieved with less loss of fuel, and with a variable camber wing you make a STOL fighter without the penalty imposed by V/STOL."

From flying with the Rooks of VAQ-137, the electronic warfare squadron with four EA-6Bs, I learned about the big debates within their community. One was over whether it made sense to keep improving the EA-6B which would stand away from the target and try to jam the defenders while bombers attacked. One school said this was the way to go. The other said it made much more sense to build the electronic jamming capabilities within the attacking bombers themselves rather than send an unarmed and highly vulnerable EA-6B aloft to do the job. The second debate was over whether the EA-6B should be armed with air-to-ground missiles rather than just be a harmless platform for electronic gear. The missiles at issue were the antiship Harpoon and the Harm which rode down the radar beams of the defending radars and blew them up. One school said becoming offensive would interfere with the primary electronic warfare mission of the four-place EA-6. The other school argued the potential of the plane for offensive operations should be exploited. **There was also the continual debate of how much should be spent to keep ahead of the Russians by buying the latest in black boxes for electronic warfare. I doubted Lehman would have gotten into the complexities of the electronic warfare argument but decided to ask him anyhow. The depth of his knowledge here surprised me.**

"Whether to keep redoing the EA-6B or build its capability into the bombers is one of those unresolvable debates. We're putting huge amounts of bucks into ECM. It's an expensive game. The ASPJ, the self-protection jammer, costs a million bucks to build into an airplane.

"But you see what the Russians and Syrians have done in response to the Israeli raids. They're going much more to IR (infrared missiles). They're bringing in the SA-9s (long range antiaircraft missiles). They're netting their assets. It's like everything in warfare. Challenge, response. New offense brings out a new defense. The debate over how much to invest in soft kill vs. hard kill. We may even be going too far into the soft kill, the electronic warfare. We found in the exercises that you just kind of challenge and excite a defense when you start throwing electrons in there. It gets to be an Atari game. 'Oh they're getting us on band X. With frequency agility we'll switch to this.' Whereas, if something goes boom—a preparatory stand-off weapon—everybody gets under the table. The boom weapons make the defenders on the ground nervous when they're twiddling their knobs. That's the difference between hard kill and soft kill. I think you need a specialized airplane like the EA-6B up there as well as built in ECM (electronic countermeasures) into the planes carrying out the attack."

Satellites soon will be able to find carriers, and cruise missiles already are accurate enough to hit them. Given such threats, does it make sense to keep building carriers costing $4 billion plus each?

"I don't see how you can get around the fact that you're going to need real estate that you can move around. You're not going to have land bases for most of the world. So you've got to have a base that you can drive around and put somewhere. You've been out there and seen the tempo of ops and what it takes to support a war fighting capability. For the range of contingencies, the carrier has got to be big. You need that volume. So I cannot envision any circumstance where we would not want to keep a large number of very large aircraft carriers. The bottom line is that ships are real estate that you can move around. It's the weapons system that you put on them that are going to keep changing.

"With the new air wing to go on the big carriers, we'll have eighteen F-14s, sixteen F-18s, and eighteen A-6Es. The development of the JVX (a STOL transport under development in 1984) might enable us to move antisubmarine warfare operations onto smaller ships. But to do serious business—to do strikes, to provide fighter CAP and electronic warfare capability, you have to have a big carrier. You can't do it with small carriers unless you do it in pairs. There's the *Kennedy* sitting out there by itself keeping 24 hour a day fighter CAP. Try to do that with the smaller Oriskany carriers. Impossible.

"I think fifteen is a good number for big carriers, as long as the allies keep up their cooperation and the Air Force doesn't lose ground and can carry its load. We need Air Force aircraft for the Aleutians and for Iceland and for Japan and the Southern flank in NATO. Fifteen is a good number."

After landing in Paris to refuel, the P-3 labored off the runway at Orly where Charles Lindbergh had landed 57 years earlier after crossing the Atlantic—opening the eyes of the world to the endless possibilities of aviation. After more than three months at sea, I was bound for a short liberty at home. My friends on the ship had been making bets on whether I would ever return to the *Kennedy* for the rest of the cruise.

15 "Smart" Bombing

WITH difficulty, I wrenched myself away from home after a short visit and flew back to Naples to rejoin my shipmates on the *Kennedy*. I soon was standing on her signal bridge watching the colorful harbor fade into a soft outline of haze. We were headed back to Bagel Station to do more of the same off Beirut. The bombers and fighters would resume around the clock flight operations in case the marines at the airport called for emergency help or the Syrian air force did the unexpected and rose to take on the Americans in the skies off Lebanon. Nobody was expecting, in light of the foul-up on the 4 December bombing raid, to be sent out on another strike. But Higher Authority had other ideas. The *Kennedy* was going to be ordered to try a different kind of bombing this time. The weapons would be "smart" ones—a test by fire of the latest in American bomb technology.

I marveled at the recuperative powers of the American Navy men. Everyone before the liberty had a gray, joyless look. Now the old smiles were back along with the zesty needling and bitching. Naples had been a form of artificial respiration for the men who had been drowning in toil, sameness, and aloneness. I wondered if the bad luck was over or whether the *Kennedy* would lose more planes in this second half of the seven month cruise. Two F-14 Tomcats, one with Bam Bam and Belly inside, and an A-6E bomber were lying on the bottom of the Mediterranean at Bagel Station. Veterans of carrier cruises told me that aircraft accidents seemed to run in streaks. But they said you never know. There is a first time for everything.

We reached Bagel Station on 3 February 1984 and quickly settled into the old routine of serving as a floating firehouse for the marines at the Beirut International Airport. If the marines sounded the alarm, the *Kennedy* was ready to respond with A-6 bombers loaded with everything from flares to laser guided bombs. The red-shirted ordies were back to their old day-and-night labors of manhandling one set of bombs for night operations and another set for day bombing. I wondered as I watched them struggle with their loads of bombs whether I could keep doing such back-breaking work for 12 hours, seven days a week for months on end with only a crowded sleeping compartment to repair to when the shift was over. The key, I decided, was to be young like these sailors, most of them under twenty-five and many of them still in their teens.

The *Kennedy* fliers, too, were back to fatiguing duty. They were standing alerts around the clock. The three most common alerts were alert thirty, alert fifteen, and alert five. If you were on alert thirty, you could almost live the normal seagoing life as long as you remained ready to rush into action. If the squadron duty officer rang the telephone in your room when you were sound asleep and told you to man up the alert thirty airplane, you would have to dress; rush to the ready room for last minute briefings on your mission and the weather; pull on your flight gear; trot to the airplane; walk around it to make sure everything was ready for flight; climb into the cockpit and go through the long check lists; snap on switches, turn knobs and punch keys to get the electronic gear warmed up and operational; check the status of weapons hung on the plane; start the engines; taxi toward the catapult; unfold the wings; case into the catapult slot; go through more checks; recheck everything and then brace for the catapult shot. Fifteen minutes was not enough time to do all this. So you stayed awake and dressed in your flight gear while on alert fifteen. On alert five, you sat in the cockpit of the plane hour after hour waiting for the order to be launched. Five minute alerts could be excruciatingly boring. On warm sunny days the fliers sat there in the cockpit with the canopy open reading paperback novels or writing letters home. At night, they would half sleep and try to pick up some music on the plane's radio or bring their Walkman tape players into the cockpit with them.

The six-man continued to be a social center, although everyone was getting sick of each other, mostly as a result of the unremitting and unvarying standing of alerts and boring holes in the same pieces of sky day after day, night after night. Often I would see a pilot who had come in to socialize to break his routine fall asleep in the chair from near exhaustion. A big break in the routine came on 6 February.

On that night, Commander Greg Brown and Commander John Ertlschweiger of VA-75 were sitting on alert five in the cockpit of A-6E number 502. They had two smart bombs and two pods of Zuni rockets slung under the broad belly of their fat plane. The smart bombs were called smart because they could follow a laser beam to their target. The bomb's laser guidance system, which featured a protruding glass eye, was hooked into an old-fashioned iron bomb. This night there were two Mark 83 1,000-pound iron bombs made smart by the laser guidance systems in their nose. The Zuni rockets were fired off the airplane the old-fashioned way: aim the airplane and pull the trigger. Each pod carried four rockets with high fragmentation heads. The two Mark 83s strapped under the A-6E this night could level a building while the Zunis could spread shrapnel over a wide area to wipe out a squad of infantry or drive antiaircraft or field artillery gunners away from their guns. Brown and Ertlschweiger figured they were sitting in the dark on five minute alert in response to one more false alarm. Their feeling was confirmed when they heard the Air Boss blare out over the loudspeaker system:

"Secure the alert five."

Brown, the pilot, unsnapped the lap belt and Koch fittings on the shoulder harness, unhooked his oxygen tube and radio wire, snaked himself out of the left pilot seat of the A-6. His profile as he stood on the ladder leading down the side of the plane to the flight deck lived up to his nickname, "Zipper." He had told me that his wife, Alice, at a party long ago had said to her lanky husband with the Abraham Lincoln long face:

"Turn sideways, Sweetheart. Now stick out your tongue. There, doesn't he look just like a zipper." He did. The name Zipper stuck.

Ertlschweiger, nicknamed "Turtle," was chunky and

compact—like a college scat back. He swung himself out of his bombardier-navigator right seat with relative ease. He caught up with Brown and walked gingerly across the darkened flight deck. The Mutt and Jeff team had known each other for years and shared deep religious beliefs. They talked unashamedly of God and church—something of a rarity in the ribald ready rooms on aircraft carriers. They decided to swing into the Dirty Shirt wardroom on the 03 level and treat themselves to soft ice cream from the vending machine. They were back down to alert fifteen—meaning they could eat ice cream or do anything else as long as they remained dressed for flight and could be back inside the cockpit within 15 minutes.

Kennedy men ate tons of soft ice cream made from a powder mix. Getting a glass, dish, or cone of this ice cream and bringing it back to a table in the sailors' mess or in the officers' wardroom was a bit of luxury, the closest you could come on the ship to stopping in for a beer at a neighborhood bar. The ice cream was usually vanilla or chocolate. What made it special was the topping: usually chocolate, often strawberries, and once in a while pineapple. Brown and Ertlschweiger each went to the machine and filled a water glass full of vanilla ice cream. It was so late that all the toppings were gone. They sat at the wardroom table spooning soft ice cream into their mouths. They looked more like two oversized kids than two of the most highly motivated and finely trained attack aviators in the United States Navy with 1,800 hours each in the A-6.

Brown, thirty-eight, was the only son of a blue-collar father and Catholic schoolteacher mother. He grew up in Lincoln Park, New Jersey. He joined the Navy as an enlisted man right after high school because there was not enough money for college. He went into submarines and did so well that the Navy selected him to attend its Naval Academy Preparatory School in Bainbridge, Maryland. He did well there and went on to the Academy in Annapolis. He was wondering which branch of the Navy to join when a sudden event decided him. He told me he was standing in luncheon formation at the Academy one day when two F-4 Phantom jets roared over, kicked in their afterburners and zoomed up into the sun.

"Fuck it!" Brown exclaimed out loud in the no-speaking-aloud formation, "I'm going air."

He was restricted to the Academy grounds for the next three

weekends for the outburst. But he went Navy air instead of returning to submarines. He opted for the A-6. The Navy chose him to do advanced work with the A-6 at its flight test center at Patuxent, Maryland.

"I am totally dedicated to making the A-6 as efficient as it can be," Brown told me, "and to making VA-75 the best attack squadron in the world." He was executive officer of VA-75 when we talked in February 1984. He was slated to take over the squadron as commanding officer in the following year. "The upside of the Navy for me is being given a complicated task to do and doing it right and recognizing what you're doing is paying off for the country. The downside is having to leave your wife and two kids at home to come out here. I know it's even harder for those who sit home and wait. Patriotism keeps me in here."

Ertlschweiger, thirty-seven, was the son of an Army colonel. The young Ertlschweiger told his father that he could not see plodding along the ground as a soldier when he could fly over it as an aviator. He thought about joining the Air Force and then decided that flying on and off carriers in the middle of the ocean would be the most exciting kind of flying of all. He was graduated from the University of Virginia in 1969 and joined the Navy with the idea of becoming a carrier pilot. This did not work out. He happily settled for being a bombardier-navigator. He figured he would still be flying and it was the bombardier-navigator of the A-6 who harnessed its electronic wizardry to put bombs right in the old pickle barrel. He told me that bombing challenged his mind and landing on a carrier fired up his spirit.

"Flying over the beach and having people shoot at you does absolutely nothing for my pulse rate, perspiration or anything else. But coming back aboard the ship at night gets my old heart going. If I can keep doing that, I know I'm alive. The downs are being away from my family. I will have been in the Navy for 15 years come this June. I've been away from home five years and three months out of those 15 years. One of the things that keeps me going is my faith; knowing there is a God."

Brown, a Catholic, and Ertlschweiger, a Baptist, were sympatico in the air as well as on the ship. They had settled into chairs in the VA-75 ready room, waiting for their time on alert fifteen to pass so they could hit the sack. Suddenly the loudspeaker boomed a command:

"Launch the alert fifteen! Launch the alert fifteen!"

Ertlschweiger was studying the radio frequencies and other data kept on cards pinned to his knee board. He jumped up, looked around for Brown and saw him sitting in the back of the ready room.

"XO," Ertlschweiger shouted excitedly, "we gotta go."

Brown and Ertlschweiger pulled on their helmets and trotted down the passageways and out onto the darkened flight deck which they had left less than 30 minutes earlier. Somebody ran up to Brown and told him the marines at the airport were taking heavy fire. The A-6 was to fly over there and bomb the hostile positions at the edge of the Beirut airport. A marine on the ground would designate with his hand held laser gun where the smart bombs were to hit.

"Launch five zero two," the Air Boss commanded impatiently.

That was their plane but Brown and Ertlschweiger were not yet inside it. They were still trotting across the flight deck toward it. They climbed inside without repeating the external preflight checks they had done before manning up for the five minute alert. A Yellow Shirt ran up beside Brown's side of the cockpit and gave the hand rotation signal for starting the bomber's two engines. The external electric power needed for starting was already plugged into Number 502. The engines were turning within three minutes. Brown and Ertlschweiger raced through their checklists, reading dials, gauges, snapping on switches and punching keys to warm up the electronic gadgetry and computers, including the FLIR (forward looking infrared), the inertial guidance navigation system, and laser ranging gear. The bombs slung underneath them had to be checked out to make sure their laser guidance was in order. All this took ten minutes. More checks would have to be done in the air while they raced toward the marines at the Beirut airport. They were broken down—meaning the chains anchoring them to the deck were removed. A Yellow Shirt directed them into the slot of catapult two. The Air Boss radioed up to all the other *Kennedy* planes circling around the ship waiting to land to hold everything. He wanted to hurl 502 off the front end first. The marines needed help now.

Scream, rattle, whoosh. A-6 Echo Number 502 was off the boat and flying on its own power through the black night. Brown headed straight for the beach at a course of 090—dead east. He and Ertlschweiger still had to punch keys, flip switches, twist knobs, and adjust lighting to bring their airplane, bombs, and rockets fully to life. They did not have much time to do all this. They were going 575 miles an hour. They would be over the beach in a few minutes.

Ertlschweiger switched from button 14—the radio channel connected to the Air Boss who controlled the air space for ten miles around the carrier—to the channel that the strike controllers inside the *Kennedy* were using. The strike controllers would be watching the green blip of 502 on their radar scopes and talking to the plane all through the bombing mission.

"Five Zero Two. This is Strike. Check in with Hot Shot. (I have changed the code names at the Navy's request.)

This was a code for the controllers sitting at radar consoles inside the USS *Guam*, an amphibious ship close to the Lebanese coast. One of them would take hold of 502 and direct it.

"Hot Shot, Hot Shot," Ertlschweiger radioed down to the *Guam*. "This is Ace Five Zero Two checking in." The A-6 bombers in VA-75 were called Flying Aces or Aces in radio talk, not their formal name of Sunday Punchers.

"Roger Ace Five Zero Two. Hold at Pearl for Tea Time One Four. You work with Tea Time One Four on Scarlet."

Pearl was the code word for a specific spot in the sky off Beirut. Tea Time One Four was the code name for the marine captain who would be standing in a bunker at the Beirut airport to serve as the forward air controller, or FAC, for the bomber. Scarlet was the code word for the radio frequency which the A-6 and Tea Time One Four would talk to each other on during the bombing strike. Code names were used so hostile gunners could not switch to the same frequency to eavesdrop on the communications and anticipate the plane's movements. Tea Time One Four was a former A-6 bombardier-navigator himself. He knew what the bomber could and could not do. His own wonder weapon was a laser pistol he pointed out of the bunker window at the place he wanted bombed. The laser beam generated from the device called a mule was supposed to bounce back from the target and display what compass heading and distance it was from the marine's position. When the A-6 the marine was controlling got near, he was supposed to shoot the laser beam at the target. The beam, if all went well, would reflect up into the air. The smart bomb was supposed to fall through the sky and enter the reflected cone of laser beams. The smart bomb's guidance system would ride the reflected laser beam down to the object it was reflecting off of—the target. The marine FAC also had electronic gear with him in his bunker for talking to the A-6 bomber. He would punch in the latitude and longitude of his own position and where the target was in reference to him. The FAC's black box would transmit the information to other black boxes in the A-6. With help from the bombardier, black boxes in the cockpit would display the marine's position as a bright dot on the radar scope. The bearing of the target from his position would also be written on consoles in the A-6. It was high tech bombing.

As Brown circled at Pearl, Ertlschweiger studied the radar scope for the information he needed to set up for the bomb run. It flashed on quickly. The marine at the southern end of the airport gave his own position and said the target was 158 degrees magnetic from him at 2,240 feet above sea level. Ertlschweiger typed this and other information into the computer which, in turn, did the arithmetic and displayed for the aviators where their plane was in reference to the target and what course they would have to fly to get right over it. Brown and Ertlschweiger figured if they went out 20 miles from the coast and headed in again on a course of 100 degrees they would be on the right path for dropping their smart bombs into the laser cone. They flicked a lot more switches to make their bombs hot. Ertlschweiger punched more keys on the computer board so the navigation and aiming system would release the bombs at exactly the right instant to fall down into the cone of light reflecting off the target.

"Tea Time One Four. Five Zero Two is inbound at 20 miles hot," Ertlschweiger radioed down to the marine FAC.

"Five Zero Two. Tea Time One Four. Continue."

"Tea Time One Four. Five Zero Two. Are we cleared to drop?"

"Roger. Cleared to drop."

Brown and Ertlschweiger were hurtling from out over the ocean toward the beach at 575 miles an hour at an altitude of 2,500 feet. They saw the black water of the Mediterranean one second and nothing but mist the next as they went in and out of the clouds piled up near the Lebanese coast. All of a sudden they broke through the last cloud and saw a city gone mad with fireworks: bright globes of flares, flashes of exploding artillery shells; winks of light from rifles; fiery arcs of rockets. Everybody seemed to be shooting at each other.

Brown told me later that as he looked down at Beirut he said to himself, "That city down there looks like a Christmas tree full of sparklers lying on its side."

The A-6E bomber, like most modern warplanes, has radar detectors which light up when radar beams hit the plane. If the plane is "painted" with a radar beam, the crew is warned by a red light going on in the cockpit. Brown and Ertlschweiger saw to their horror that every such warning light was lit. The radar beams painting the bomber streaking through the night were from Soviet radars on the Russian guided missile destroyers lying off Beirut; from the antiaircraft guns spotted around Beirut; from SA-2 Guideline missile sites of Lebanon. There was no place for Brown to fly to escape the radar trained on Five Zero Two. "Fuck it," he said to himself, and just flew on toward the target.

Ertlschweiger—perhaps mercifully—had his face pressed into the tunnel of the radar scope in the cockpit. He was watching intently for the blip that would mark where the marine with the laser gun was located within the compound at the Beirut airport.

Three miles from the drop point Brown saw the road map of lighted lines on his five-by-eight inch video tube known as a vertical display indicator, or VDI. Brown could tell whether he was flying on course in the critical last seconds before dropping the bombs by studying the map which told him if he had to twist left or right. A black bar flashed on the right side of the map. This told Brown he was in the zone where the computer could release the bomb and be sure it would fall into the laser cone. Brown squeezed the trigger, setting the computerized bombardier into action. The computer told Brown to pull four Gs while flying straight ahead. He did as he was told, pulling up the A-6's nose at about a 20 degree angle to exert the 4 Gs of gravitational pull on the plane and its bombs. Brown and Ertlschweiger felt a shudder. An amber light on the bomb control panel confirmed that the shudder had come from one of their two bombs being released by command of the computer. The bomb arced ahead of the plane and then fell down toward a spot of unknown ground in Beirut. The marine FAC never told Brown and Ertlschweiger what he was asking them to hit. It was all detached computing. Bloodless for the men in the plane. A flaming holocaust for anybody under the 1,000-pound bomb when it went off. Hopefully it would kill whomever was firing at the marines—not unsuspecting Lebanese civilians. Nobody knew for sure as it sailed through the sky.

Brown flew over the southern end of the airport to reach the safer sky over the sea. He glanced down at the airport and saw flares so thick they looked like a pack of fireflies bursting into light on a summer night. He noticed the marines' Foxtrot Company was pouring fire at a position outside their wire. A flashing gun was shooting up at the plane. Then there were clouds and blackness as 502 reached feet wet.

"Bombs away," Ertlschweiger radioed down to the marine FAC. Ertlschweiger knew the bomb from the plane's sudden pullup would arc out in front of the release point before heading down. It would take some seconds to reach the ground. He wanted the marine FAC to train his laser on the target when the bomb was at the top of its arc. This would be several seconds after release. Ertlschweiger punched the clock on the instrument panel of the A-6 and waited for its thin hand to sweep off the right number of seconds.

"Basket," Ertlschweiger radioed to the FAC at the eighth second. This told the FAC to turn his laser gun back on so the bomb could home in on the beams of light reflecting up from the target.

Brown and Ertlschweiger studied the ground below. They saw a mushroom shaped cloud rise up from the dirt. It looked like a small nuke.

"Did you have a release?" the marine FAC asked.

"Roger," Brown radioed back. "We observed the impact."

"I didn't see it," said Tea Time One Four.

"We've got one more weapon."

"Come back in and make the same run."

Brown duplicated his first bombing run and squeezed the trigger to start the drop sequence from the same spot in the sky. The second 1,000-pound laser-guided bomb was flung from the plane. The marine FAC peering out of his fortified bunker where bomb fragments could not reach him saw the bomb hit this time.

"Looks like it's 2,000 meters to the south," the FAC said.

The two smart bombs had landed in the same place but missed the target on the map by 2,000 meters, hitting instead the one pinpointed by the marine on the ground. Brown and Ertlschweiger felt they had followed the FAC's instructions flawlessly. They checked and rechecked the plane's bombing and navigation system. Everything seemed to be in perfect order. The FAC, they concluded, had given them the wrong offset—the compass heading of the target from his own position in the bunker at the edge of the airport. Perhaps his laser gun was flawed. Everybody was an expert in what he did the night of 6 February 1984, and every gadget was the highest tech the Navy had in its inventory. Still, the smart bombs had missed their target and exploded on something else. Reports coming into the ship after the night strike said it appeared as if the two bombs had hit an apartment building, setting it afire. There was no mention of whether anyone was in the apartment building at the time 2,000 pounds of explosive ripped it apart.

Brown headed back over the dark water to the *Kennedy*. He ran into a driving rain storm. He tried to set up for his night landing. A radio voice told him to call the ball when he was three-quarters of a mile from the carrier. They got to that point and could not even see the ship, far less the ball, for the rain. Brown flew on down toward the ship anyhow. He saw the ball during the last few seconds of approach, adjusted slightly, and felt his plane slam down on the deck and stop. He had caught the wire on his first pass.

"My heart rate was probably ten times higher on that landing than it was when we were over Beirut," a smiling Brown told me in the ready room after he had trapped.

I congratulated him on his airmanship. "We had a hook extended," he said modestly. Pilots kid about needing an extended tail hook to catch one of the four arresting wires on the deck, especially on the kind of night Brown had had to contend with.

Brown, Ertlschweiger, and I discussed in the ready room what might have made the bombs miss.

"There's no doubt in our mind that where he told us to go is where we went," Brown said.

Ertlschweiger in recalculating everything back in the ready room and studying the charts figured the bearing the FAC had given them for the target in relation to his position on the ground had been about 40 degrees off the heading needed to hit the x on the map, perhaps due to a flaw in the laser gun which had given the FAC the readout.

"That kind of error put the bombs outside the basket (the cone of laser beams reflecting from the target at the time of drop)," Ertlschweiger said. "Therefore it missed."

Another A-6 loaded with smart bombs was in the sky over Lebanon along with 502. Its air crew could not correlate their data with that of the marine FAC on the ground and thus held onto their bombs. The air crew from VA-85 also had trouble with the bomb release mechanism. The uncertainty about the target information plus the mechanical problem impelled the fliers to return to the ship without trying to drop their smart bombs.

The U.S. Army, Air Force, and Marine Corps all are counting heavily on their smart weapons to overcome the Soviet quantitative edge if war ever comes. Pentagon civilian leaders, with former research director William Perry a leading example, have urged the services to adjust their tactics to the potential of smart weapons. Perry, who headed Pentagon research in the Carter administration, predicted smart artillery shells which could break up an armored assault with a comparatively few shots would revolutionize warfare if the Army would build tactics around them. Military leaders have been burned in all past wars by wonder weapons which did not work when the crucial moment came. So some have been reluctant to bank on smart weapons, like the laser guided bombs tried the night of 6 February 1984. This reluctance seems justified in light of the actual experience. Yet U.S. war strategy remains based on the assumption that the quality of its weapons will offset Soviet quantity in a war. The smart weapons will just have to be made smarter, barring a reversal in national strategy.

The 6 February 1984 bombing was the case of two of the Navy's most skillful fliers flying the Navy's smartest bomber loaded with its smartest bombs against a stationary target without any interference from fighters or antiaircraft guns or missiles. Yet the two bombs missed their target by more than a mile. The actual fell far short of the theoretical. I left the VA-75 ready room more convinced than ever that the Navy, Army, Air Force, and Marine Corps all have to do more testing of their "smart" weapons before they entrust lives and the nation's security to them. The men did their jobs the night of 6 February 1984. It was their tools that failed.

16   Antisubmarine Warfare

FEBRUARY'S smart bombing of Beirut turned out to be the first and last for the *Kennedy* battle group. It was becoming obvious to everyone, even us out on the end of the spear, that President Reagan was having no success in translating American military power into political power for himself or for President Amin Gemayel of Lebanon. He had sent in 1,200 marines, ordered a big daylight bombing strike, a small night one, and shelled from the Lebanese coast with the mighty 16-inch guns of the battleship *New Jersey*. Still the government of Amin Gemayel continued to unravel. Reagan's peace plan for the Mideast was in tatters. Tribal warfare continued in Lebanon apace. Even the hawks on the *Kennedy* began to concede by mid-February that they were shoveling against the tide in trying to use the battle group's power to bring peace to Lebanon. The fighters and bombers continued to go aloft prepared to do battle—if they could decide who the enemy was and where he was located, and if Higher Authority passed the go order through its tortuous chain of command. But nothing happened. Almost everyone on the ship sensed that President Reagan's experiment with military "presence" had brought no positive results. We were beginning to make bets on when the marines would be pulled out of Beirut. The crazy war we had been in was over. Most of the squadrons were just marking time until the marines left and the *Kennedy* could leave Bagel Station. There was nothing for the F-14s to shoot at or the A-6s to bomb.

But there was one squadron on the ship which fought the same kind of war no matter what was happening in Beirut. This was VS-22, the Checkmates. Their enemy was invisible under the waves: the hostile submarine, the ever worrisome shark which could attack an American ship without warning. The Checkmates flew the Lockheed S-3A Viking, a handsome, high-winged jet nicknamed the Hoover because it sounds like a vacuum cleaner when its throttles were jockeyed, especially on landing. The Hoovers flew back and forth over the ocean day after day, night after night looking for the steel sharks lying quietly in the depths of the Mediterranean. Neither human nor mechanical eyes can see down through 400 to 1,200 feet of sea water where the subs prowl. It is the human and mechanical *ears* that decide who wins in this grim and endless contest between the hunters and the hunted in the depths. The United States and Soviet Union have spent billions of dollars on antisubmarine warfare, called ASW. They have been obsessed with trying to improve their hearing under the sea. A counter obsession has been to make their submarines quieter and thus more difficult to hear.

In peacetime, U.S. and Soviet submarines constantly try to sneak up on each other. In wartime, the submarine which hears the other first will live. His quarry will die a horrible death as tons of sea water pour in the torpedo hole and drown the crew of over one hundred men who are too deep to escape to the surface without perishing on the way up.

The United States hunts Soviet, Libyan, and other potentially hostile submarines from under the sea with killer subs, from land through mechanical ears sown on the ocean bottom off the American coast, from the surface of the sea with destroyers and other ASW ships, and from above the sea with land-based planes like the Navy Lockheed P-3 Orion and carrier-based aircraft like the S-3A Viking and the Sikorsky SH-3H Sea King helicopter.

Of all these ASW detection systems, Sosus is the most elaborate and far-hearing. Sosus is the network of underwater microphones strung along the Atlantic coast of the United States. The underwater eavesdroppers hear whales mating, shrimp feeding, and Soviet missile and attack submarines sliding along under the waves. The undersea noises are sent to shore over lines on the bottom. The noises are recorded on big spools of tape. Computers play the tapes for themselves and sift out the significant sounds. It is high-tech panning for gold; the gold being a potentially hostile submarine. Every submarine makes a slightly different noise as it moves through the water. The United States records the distinctive noise of every submarine prowling the depths and keeps it on file like the FBI keeps a fingerprint. When any part of the nation's ASW network picks up the noise of a submarine, it can find out which one it is by digging into the computerized file of signatures.

The trouble with Sosus is that it is stationary—the Maginot Line of submarine defense. The United States does not own the shoreline so it cannot build a Sosus along the Mediterranean. The battle groups which sail into that hotly contested, noisy sea must bring their ASW systems along with them. No battle group commander is ever comfortable in the tight quarters of the Med. There is always a chance his ASW forces missed a submarine which is lying quietly underwater, ready to bushwhack a ship. Rear Admiral Tuttle was no exception. He kept pressing his ASW forces to find Libyan and Soviet subs that American intelligence said were in his operating area. His battle group lost track of a Libyan submarine for a while, causing a full-court press on the ocean until it was located.

Detecting, locating, isolating, and "prosecuting" a sub in the Med or any other sea is what the Navy calls an "all hands evolution." No one ASW system can do the whole job. Intelligence officers collect and analyze data from their vast worldwide net as high as satellites and as low as submerged U.S. subs. Intelligence officers tell the fleet commanders when Soviet and Libyan subs leave port for the open sea. This often gives time for U.S. hunter subs to set up a picket line of quiet listening or to follow the quarry at a silent distance. Other information about subs threatening a battle group come from destroyers trolling for submarine noises with a long line of underwater microphones, each tilted at a slightly different angle to pick up sea sounds from every direction. The destroyer skipper alerts the task force commander whenever his five-mile-long fishing line strung out from the fantail hooks submarine noise. The destroyer skipper tells the task force commander where the noise is coming from—a bearing of 90 degrees from his ship, for example—but can not tell how far away it is in that direction. This is when S-3 Viking aircraft are sent along the bearing to find where the submarine is hiding.

The S-3 Viking's ASW weapons include 60 sonobuoys packed under its fuselage like eggs in an egg crate with an open bottom. Sonobuoys are dropped like little bombs in the patch of ocean where the submarine is believed to be hiding. The sonobuoys can be active or passive. The active ones send out sound waves, called sonar, which bounce back to the sonobuoy if they hit big objects like submarines or schools of fish. The passive ones float on the surface and release a listening device down deep into the water, like a fishing hook dangling from a bobber. The sonobuoys radio what they hear up to the S-3 in the sky overhead. The plane's sensor operator in the back seat of the S-3, called the Senso, plays his gadgetry like an organist so the computerized detection system has the best chance of picking up the sound of a submarine. He listens to the sounds as does the computer. When the computer recognizes signatures that have been programmed into its mechanical brain to find, the Senso sees the word flash on his screen; there is a shark down there. In wartime, the next step would be to kill it or, as the ASW boys say, "prosecute the target." The S-3 tactical coordinator, called the Tacco, would instruct the computer to drop an antisubmarine torpedo on spot X in the ocean. The torpedo could hunt down the submarine by homing in on its sounds. Or the torpedo could be set to send out its own sound waves to find the hiding submarine. If the waves bounced back from the sub to the torpedo, the torpedo would follow them to its quarry like a fish chasing a trail of blood in the water.

If a submarine slipped through a carrier battle group's outer defenses of killer subs, destroyers, and S-3 Vikings, then ASW helicopters like the six SH-3H Sea Kings would provide a last ditch, close-in defense. An SH-3H helicopter hunts subs by stop-and-go flying over the water, making it look like a hummingbird going from flower to flower. Each time the helicopter stops to hover low over the water, it dips a cylinder into the water by unwinding a long line from inside the cargo bay. The cylinder is a transducer which generates sound waves. The idea is to lower the transducer under the first layer of water which often obstructs or bends sound waves going down into the sea or up from its depths. The transducer's sound waves bounce back to it when they hit something big. The helicopter crew is wired into the transducer and its men can tell when the pinging under the water has revealed a target. The antisubmarine helicopter also carries sonobuoys and torpedoes when intruders are believed close to the battle group. Task force commanders strive to find subs before they have to rely on the last ditch defense of the short-ranged helicopters.

In Washington, Navy leaders seeking additional billions for ASW constantly warn Congress that enemy submarines pose the biggest single threat to carriers and other surface ships. It would seem to follow that those who combat this dark threat would be regarded as among the heroes in the carrier air wing because they are protecting everybody from the hidden menace below. Not so in real life at sea. ASW officers and enlisted men are more often treated like the Rodney Dangerfields of the air wing. They get no respect—at least not conversationally in the constant give and take of shipboard life.

"I can't believe you're going out with those pukes after flying in a Tom," chided Sammy Bonanno when I told him I was going up in an S-3 to watch the VS-22 antisubmariners in action. "You'll fall asleep and come back with a numb ass," he warned of the ASW mission, which usually takes about five hours—twice the time fighters and bombers stay up.

"They always call us aviation weights," said Tim Fox, twenty-three, in relating how the other sailors deprecated enlisted men of his rate, AW for antisubmarine warfare. A weight is like a "no load," navalese for someone who does not carry his share of the work load on the ship. AWs are the elite among the enlisted people on a carrier because they fly as virtual equals to officers in the S-3 on sub hunting missions. Technology can be a great leveler, even in the Navy. The person who can make the computers and black boxes dance is considered royalty in this age of high tech, regardless of his Navy rank.

"We have to remember we're enlisted and they're officers," said AW Third Class Fox in talking about his life in the air in an S-3 and in the ready room of the VS-22. "They accept us because we all fly in one airplane together. If it crashes, we all go down together."

The AWs stick together, increasing their mutual bond but intensifying the resentment of many of the workaday sailors. Fox as a flying third class petty officer was receiving $700 a month in take-home pay during the *Kennedy*'s 1983-84 cruise,

$84 of it flight pay. He and the twelve other AW's from VS-22 ate together on the mess decks and slept in the same section of the main berthing space. They felt and acted special.

"My AW schooling lasted almost two years," said Fox. "A lot of their rates," he said of fellow sailors, "are done in two to six months." Fox said he joined the Navy and applied for ASW because there was nothing exciting to do around home after high school. He wanted a break from studying; to see something different; to save money for college while serving a hitch chasing subs with electronic gadgetry.

"The best part is tracking a sub," Fox said. The Tacco lays out a buoy pattern, which is an attempt to predict the evasive course of the sub being hunted. "Then you wonder, 'Is he going to get away?' It really is a chess game. I refer to it as a multimillion-dollar video game."

Besides, continued Fox, "this is a steady job. A lot of my friends back home have been laid off even though they have graduated from college." The young sub hunter said his plan was to finish his enlisted tour, go to college as a civilian with the money he saved as a sailor, reenter the Navy as an officer and become a Tacco who commands the movements of an ASW airplane when it is hunting down a sub.

Sammy's knock against "the S-3 pukes" failed to dampen my enthusiasm for the night submarine hunt I was scheduled to make with them in the S-3. The plane itself is handsome from the outside and an electronic marvel from the inside. Its huge, high wing is filled with 13,000 pounds of fuel, and with two optional wing mounted drop tanks of 1,800 pounds each, the S-3 can stay up for six and a half hours without refueling in midair. Its turbo fan engines burn about 2,000 pounds an hour, or about one-sixth the consumption of the F-14 Tomcat. The broad wing, besides forming a giant gas tank, helps keep the plane rock steady for the landings on pitching carrier decks.

It was already dark on the flight deck when I joined my three companions for an antisubmarine patrol in the S-3. Lieutenant Commander Glenn "Porky" Pittman was the pilot. He would sit in the left front seat of the four place, high-winged plane. Lieutenant Commander Jim Hilt, "Big Jim," who swung an ax and sledge in his off-duty job of lumberjack but had a delicate touch with ASW gadgetry and was considered one of the best submarine hunters in the Navy, would take the co-pilot's right seat. He would operate the nonacoustic sensors and serve as navigator and tactical communicator while I took his regular left seat in the back. Senior Chief Bill Moore would take the right rear seat as tactical coordinator. He was one of the few enlisted antisubmarine specialists who have advanced to Tacco, a job usually performed by officers. I was instructed to climb out the roof hatches if we crashed in trying to land back aboard the carrier after the mission. The impact would crush the front doors shut. The S-3 crew can also eject themselves, either all together by one man pulling the loop, set on command, or individually. I could tell as I strapped myself in that this launch would be much different than my previous ones. The cockpits in the EA-6B, KA-6D and F-14 jets I had flown in were picture windows compared to the view from the back of the S-3. Only a plastic porthole in the back of the plane gave you a view of the outside world. The ASW people who laid down the specs for the S-3 obviously wanted the backseaters to do their submarine hunting by listening and looking from an isolation booth.

Despite the difference in the view, I experienced the same sense of tense anticipation as I felt the S-3 go into the slot of the catapult. Suddenly came the rapid fire yank, whoof, rattle, quiet, slowup. Then we were flying on our own power through the moonlit night some 80 miles off Beirut. Our ASW arsenal included the sonobuoys; FLIR—the forward looking infrared radar—which can see a submarine on the surface of the sea in the dark by feeling its heat and etching a picture of it on scopes in the cockpit and on film to be developed back on the carrier; radar so sensitive that it would detect something as small as a bag of garbage as it combed back and forth across the waves; magnetic gear which, at close range, would detect the disturbance in the magnetic field made by the sub; electronic eavesdropping equipment which would pick up radio and data transmissions from a sub, called ESM for electronic surveillance measures.

We hunted for subs hour after hour. Big Jim Hilts and Senior Chief Moore set up their electronic chess boards like old masters. The eerie green boards showed where everything we knew to be on the ocean and suspected to be under it was located in relation to our S-3. If the tactical coordinator wanted the plane to fly to spot X and drop buoys when it got there, he only had to punch some "fly to" instructions into the S-3's computer system. The computer would show the pilot where he was going in relation to the "fly to" drop point. Once he reached that spot of ocean, the computer would release the number and types of sonobuoys its human masters had requested. We swept back and forth over our assigned area of ocean with the care of a farmer plowing his field furrow by furrow. The intelligence officers told us before we took off that they did not expect us to find any submarines in our hunting area. Our part of the sea proved barren.

This lack of contacts did not dull the mission for me. I thoroughly enjoyed the ride. Pittman invited me to take the right seat up front and fly the S-3 for a while. Moving from the front to the back was like going from a closet onto a balcony in the sky. I looked out from the copilot's seat at moonlight silvering the tops of puffy cumulus clouds. I could see moonlight on the Mediterranean by looking down through the holes in the clouds. It was hard to believe we were floating above all that beauty to find something dark and menacing under the sea.

The S-3 was the only jet on the carrier which had dual controls. I have flown light planes but none with a broad wing like the S-3. It responded smoothly. High speed Navy jets, unlike comparatively slow light planes, require almost no pushing of the rudder pedals with your feet. The thick stick seems to do it all.

I returned to my seat in the back for the landing. A night landing on a carrier always causes your body and mind to tense. There is nothing you can do to keep a plane from crashing when you are sitting in the back out of reach of the flight controls. The suspense of waiting for the crash or landing is deeper in the back of the S-3 because in its closed rear compartments you cannot look out. In other jets, I could see the carrier flying up into my face. In the S-3 I could only listen for the slamdown onto deck or water. I felt us sink, heard the slam, and felt the yank on my shoulder harness. The "gotcha" yank told me the wire had caught our plane and stopped its 110-mile-an-hour roll.

The flying part of the ASW mission was over. The second part was about to begin. Jim Hilts took the big reel of taped sea sounds and the FLIR film out of the plane. Technicians in the ASW module inside the *Kennedy* would direct the computers to study the thin lines, thick lines, and squiggles the sounds make when transformed into a readout. This would be the second opinion on whether the S-3, through its mechanical ears, had heard something significant while prospecting for submarines over a dark ocean. Other specialists in the intelligence center would develop the FLIR film and tell us what our plane had seen.

Sammy had been right about one thing. Flying back and forth over the ocean for five hours does give you a numb tail. And yet I did not have to go up again in a few hours like my companions. They would fly out over the Med again and again hunting for submarines with the help of 17 different high tech ASW systems. It was tedious, exacting work. The men who went submarine hunting reminded me more of white coated lab technicians trying to isolate a virus than white-scarfed pilots looking for a MiG to shoot out of the sky. And these sea-based technicians did not have the consolation of drinking a martini or kissing their wife at day's end. It was eat, sleep, and get ready to do the same thing tomorrow and the tomorrow after that. I asked several senior submarine hunters, whose skills private industry would pay high salaries to acquire, what kept them willing to stay imprisoned on ship far away from the people and things they loved most.

Several admitted the duty in the back of the S-3 is dull when there are no submarines to hunt; when they are just flying over the water hour after hour identifying surface ships.

Committed submarine hunters who love flying the S-3 are like incurable fishermen who believe they will hook a big one the next time out. And if the submariners do get their special kind of fish on the line, they become as ecstatic as any fishermen. Two of the S-3 enthusiasts on the *Kennedy*, even after flying more than 2,000 hours in the plane, were Commanders Tim Winters and Jim Jones. Winters was skipper of VS-22 when we left Norfolk in September. He was succeeded by Jones in February when I flew on a night mission in the S-3.

"It's a mission you do for real every day," Winters told me when I asked why ASW kept him interested. "You're out there going against a submarine, and that's what you're going to do in war. You don't go out there like the attack guys and bomb smoke. You're doing your thing for real every time you fly. They say ASW is hours upon hours of sheer boredom spattered with moments of sheer panic. It's a searching game. Once you find the guy, you've got to attack, get on him, get him before he gets away. You're working in an environment—a very dynamic environment of acoustics where so many things affect how you detect a submarine. If you hesitate one second, that guy is gone. He gets deep, he puts on speed, he makes turns and before you know it he's out of your pattern and you've lost him. You've got to make instantaneous decisions like the fighters do, except we're doing it for real every time. I really enjoy it.''

Winters left the *Kennedy* midway in its cruise to train to be her navigator, a step up for his Navy career but several steps away from the arts of ASW. Jones made the whole cruise, first as executive officer of VS-22 and later as commanding officer.

Jones, forty-two, looked like the farmer he had been back home in Tennessee: rangy, red-haired, open-faced, rough hewn. He ambled rather than strode down the ship's passageways and across the flight deck, as if he were walking to the barn at milking time. He talked down-country with a southern accent muffled by a pinch of Copenhagen between his gum and cheek. He recounted for me in how he came to leap from farming in Sante Fe, Tennessee, to chasing submarines in the Mediterranean Sea.

"I grew up in a home built in 1881 by my grandfather. It was part of a land grant given to Captain Willis Jones after the War of 1812. We have about 400 acres. Raise tobacco, soy beans, corn, livestock. My Dad is a farmer but he always did more than farm. He helped establish and was on the board of the local bank. A wise investor.

"I had always planned to be a country doctor back home, like my uncle who was the first Navy doctor to fly Navy aircraft in 1914 and who later was a state senator. I went to the University of Tennessee in 1960 to take premed. I wasn't disciplined enough or studious enough and dropped out after two quarters." He joined the Navy, becoming a Naval Flight Officer rather than a pilot because his vision was slightly below that required. If he had to be an NFO, he wanted to do something more challenging than sitting in the back seat and pulling G's while the pilot fought mock duels in the sky. He requested duty in the E-2 Hawkeye, the plane which hangs in the air orchestrating the movements of dozens of planes at once—directing them to targets on the ground, on the sea, or in the air.

"I wanted a mission that had the overall picture," he recalled. "I requested a squadron that was going to Vietnam. I wanted to be where the action was."

Jones made commander in 1980. Everything was looking up for the accidental Navy careerist. Then came an even bigger setback than being denied the chance to go to medical school. The Navy decided he was not ready to command a squadron.

He went to sea again. The Navy in its second look at Jones decided he was ready to command. He was sent to VS-22 as executive officer, the preliminary step to becoming skipper.

"My whole world changed in the fall of 1981," Jones said with a smile. "It seemed that at last all my sea duty and dedication were recognized." He was on the way to what many Navy fliers consider the best job in the world, squadron commander. He could exploit his technical background in running the submarine hunts while out over the sea in the S-3 and back on the boat could try his art of motivating men to pursue excellence for their sake, not his.

Jones told me that pitting himself, his crew, and the S-3 weaponry against a Russian sub playing hide and seek always generated adrenaline.

"It's like nothing else," he said.

17   Marine Pullout

CONSTERNATION washed through the *Kennedy* on 26 February 1984. The marines were pulling out of Lebanon. President Amin Gemayel of Lebanon could not hold his government together. His cabinet ministers were resigning. There was no longer any pro-American government in Beirut for American troops to provide a presence for. Lebanon was back to ancient tribal warfare with modern weapons. The Phoenicians, Egyptians, Greeks, Turks, Syrians, French, British, Israelis, and now the Americans all had tried to get a firm grip on Lebanon and failed. Conflicts between tribes, between Christians and Moslems dating back to biblical times kept breaking out like a congenital rash.

Lieutenant Scott "Stewie" Stewart was one of the radar intercept officers who had looked down on Lebanon many times from the backseat of his F-14 Tomcat. A Boston born, blunt speaking son of a truck driver who had felt unconnected to the establishment when he went through the U.S. Naval Academy, called the shots as he saw them. He sat in the Dirty Shirt wardroom the morning the marine pullout became official and bellowed the lesson of the whole U.S. misadventure in Lebanon:

"That ought to teach Reagan to fuck with the Bible."

After we all finished laughing, I concluded Stewie was right. Reagan and his deputies had ignored both ancient and recent history by sending marines into Lebanon the second time with no clear cut objective. I had felt from the start of the marines' commitment to defensive positions at the Beirut International Airport that Reagan's decision repeated most of the mistakes of Vietnam. As in Vietnam, the United States had sent troops to help a foreign country which did not have a stable government. As in Vietnam, U.S. troops had no clear military objective; were hobbled by complicated and ever changing rules of engagement; found themselves in a civil war which they did not understand; had to contend with open borders while hunkered down on the low ground where they were subject to lethal sniper and mortar attacks by unseen forces. The marines in Beirut in 1983 and 1984 reminded me of the marines I had seen in Khesanh, South Vietnam, in 1968. The big difference between Lebanon and Vietnam was that the American President withdrew his troops after he realized his military venture was a loser. Reagan cut his losses. Presidents Kennedy, Johnson, and Nixon tried to be half-pregnant. They kept American forces on the untenable ground of Vietnam year after year without giving them any plan for winning whatever it was the nation was trying to win.

As the first marines were sent by Reagan into Lebanon, a four star Marine general I had come to know and admire said: "I know how to get them in there. But I don't know how to get them out."

My shipmates, even those who never thought Lebanon worth a single American life far less the 241 lives lost at the Beirut International Airport, and the four from the *Kennedy*, found it hard to confront the reality that two aircraft carriers and a battleship had not been enough to influence events in Lebanon.

I asked a number of officers how they felt about the withdrawal.

"If you sent me in now, who am I supposed to get?" replied one senior bomber pilot.

"Might as well get them out of there," said a captain about the marines. "If you go in to help a government and the government isn't there, why stay?"

On 12 March 1984 our battle group commander, Admiral "SLUF" Tuttle, bade a memorable farewell to all the frustrations he had suffered off Lebanon. He had never been authorized to execute what he had considered to be the flawless plan for bombing the terrorist complex at Target X. Well, by God, he would execute the plan right off the *Kennedy*, as a training mission using up some of his bomb allowances. A grid of ocean was marked on the pilots' maps as The Camp. Twelve A-6E bombers were loaded with 12 bombs each as would have been the case in the raid. They flew in the planned formation and dropped their live bombs in the heart of the target replicated on the surface of the Mediterranean. I stood on the signal bridge in disbelief as one bomb after another exploded in a giant plume of water off the port side of the *Kennedy*. Such an ending to the Lebanon adventure.

The most sophisticated warship in the world dropping 72 tons of live bombs on the unsuspecting fish of the Mediterranean. Then SLUF and his battle group staff departed the USS *John F. Kennedy* for other duties ashore.

Poor dead marines. Poor dead fish. To what end?

18   Riding the Tomcat

AFTER the marines had withdrawn from Beirut, life on the *Kennedy* eased up a bit. Its air wing at last could carve out time on its schedule for orientation flights in the supersonic F-14 Tomcat for those who had passed survival training and knew how to work the gear in the back seat of the fighter. Although I had qualified in cockpit ejection, high-altitude pressure chamber responses, and water survival before leaving Norfolk, I needed to learn how to work the electronic gear before being hurled off the end of the boat in the high performance, supersonic fighter. I went down to the hangar bay to confront the gadgetry in the back seat of the Tomcat in hopes of mastering the essentials.

The collection of keys, dials, gauges, scopes, handles, sticks, knobs, buttons, pedals, circuit breakers, hose connections, and warning signs was indeed intimidating.

"No way I can work all this stuff, especially if we're flying upside down," said a voice in my head as I went over the procedures outlined by a helpful RIO and printed in detail in the Navy manual. But I was sure as hell going to give it a try.

The manual told me that beside my left knee there were buttons, switches, and knobs which controlled, among other things, the flow of oxygen, navigation gear, liquid cooling of the computer, and radio transmissions. Staring into my left eye were all the doo-dads which gave the Tomcat killing power—the armament panel. I would not have to run it during my flight but I wanted to know what they did just the same. There were other things to work and watch on the center panel, center console, left vertical console, left knee panel, right instrument panel, right vertical console, and right knee panel. On my right were three more groupings of switches and knobs. On the floor there were two foot rests, each with a button like the one in a car for dimming headlights. Push down the left button with your foot and you talk to the pilot up front. Push down the right button and you are talking to the whole world outside the airplane. Dominating everything was a thick stick in the middle of the cockpit which the radar intercept operator manipulated to focus the radar antenna in the Tomcat's nose on various quadrants of the sky. Spin the thumb wheel on this radar stick and the radar in the nose of the Tomcat would send its search beams up, down, sideways, or straight ahead. How skillfully the radar intercept officer worked this stick could decide who lived and who died in a dogfight. The challenge was to find the enemy plane with your radar before his radar could find you. The round scope directly in front of my face portrayed in green dots and lines what the radar was seeing. Not only the radar stick —called the hand control unit in the Navy book—but every switch, button, lever, scope, gauge, and key looked terribly important to me as I scanned the cockpit. I felt each might go off like a grenade if I pulled, pushed, twisted, or spun it the wrong way. The lone exception was the clock. Never did the uncomplicated face of a clock look so friendly and so welcome.

Experienced RIOs generously leaned into the open canopy and guided me through the essential procedures I would have to follow once the engines were running on the flight deck. One of the RIOs promised to be on the flight deck just before launch to help me set up most of the systems. But once the canopy closed I would be on my own. I would have to perform several tasks to enable the plane to take off from the carrier. I kept practicing on the parked plane—what we used to call hangar flying in my ancient past as a naval aviation cadet at the end of World War II—until I could go through the essential steps with my eyes closed. The process resembled learning how to work a word processor.

"I'm going to make you bleed," Sammy kidded me one morning by way of announcing I had been cleared to fly with him that day in the F-14. Sharp turns and high speed pullups sometimes put so much gravitational pull on the RIO in the backseat that veins in his nose burst, causing it to bleed. Or he could be knocked out from the G's. A favorite story in the Dirty Shirt wardroom was about the pilot who said, "Good night, Charlie," to his RIO as he went into the break in front of the carrier at high speed. The pilot knew the G's would put his RIO to sleep for a few seconds.

I figured going up with Sammy would not only be safe and exciting but fun. Sammy always managed to make the most of life's golden moments. He had more good news for me this morning of the F-14 hop. We would not be doing the safe old orientation maneuvers. We would try to knock CAG Mazach and his RIO, Lieutenant Commander Ron "Bo" Edington, out of the sky in another F-14 as we rolled around in mock combat. Sammy was one of the hottest dogfighters on the ship. And I suspected the deceptively modest Mazach would show us a thing or two in his F-14 once we got up in the blue. I was ecstatic. Commander Jim Glover, skipper of VA-75, had been right: "The only difference between men and boys is the size of their toys."

It was a picture book Mediterranean day when I walked with Sammy toward "our" F-14. A friendly wind rippled the sea. The clouds were white and benign looking, not a menacing gray. There was endless blue between the clouds. Great viz for a dogfight. We walked around the plane looking for rips in the tires, leaks in the hydraulic lines or junk in the two giant intakes of the twin engines. Nothing. So far so good.

We climbed into the cockpit. The flight deck crew leaned into my deck cubicle and pulled the long pins with red flags attached to the seat and ejection mechanism. The pins were to keep something from going off accidentally, like the ejection seat rocket, while the plane was parked on the deck or in the hangar. Bo Edington, even though he would soon be the "enemy" RIO in the simulated dogfight upstairs, generously came over to me and pushed and pulled those buttons that could be activated before the engines were started.

Sammy asked me over the hot microphone linking us together if I was all strapped in. I was: lap and shoulder harness buckled;

leg restraints snapped in; oxygen and G-suit hoses connected; radio cord hooked into my helmet. I felt wired up enough to receive a heart transplant.

"Canopy is coming down," Sammy said.

The plastic bubble swung down over our heads and locked itself in place with an authoritative clunk. We snapped our oxygen masks on. We were sealed into one of the hottest fighter planes in the world. It looked at that moment that we actually were going to get hurled off the end of the boat in this 30 tons of fuel, magnesium, aluminium, copper, steel, nylon, and plastic.

"I'm starting my engines," Sammy said.

I could hear Sammy's breathing quicken. A hot mike transmits everything that exerts any pressure on it—breathing as well as spoken words. The pilot and RIO go on hot mike during launch and recovery to save what might be a life saving split second in coordinating their motions in an emergency. With engines started, it was time for me to execute the procedures I had practiced in the hangar bay:

Twist the WCS (weapons control system) knob to the position marked STBY for standby; wait until the light beside it lights; reach left and back to flip the all important liquid cooling switch from OFF to the AWG 9 position to cool the electronics so they would not burn out at a crucial instant; tell Sammy the AWG 9 light went out as required; twist the Nav Mode pointer switch to the left of the radar scope from off to Nav; reach to the right and twist the Identification of Friend or Foe knob to standby; turn the radio knobs to BOTH and ON; punch the latitude and longitude of our current position into the computer by pressing the numbered keys on the keyboard off my left knee; look all around for popped circuit breakers; feel for the ones behind you which you cannot see.

"They're breaking us down," Sammy told me between his heavy breathing. The Green Shirts were detaching the chains that had us hooked onto the port side of the flight deck. A Yellow Shirt acting as traffic cop directed Sammy toward the catapult. He had warned me during the briefing in the ready room that the F-14 would feel differently to me when catapulted than the other planes I had been launched in on previous flights. The front wheel would sink down a little bit just before launch, tilting the pilot and RIO to a downward angle. Sammy tensed his head forward at launch so it would not be snapped back by the yank of the catapult. He wanted his eyes locked on the instrument panel. He did not want their grip to be broken in the critical two second catapult yank down the deck. He said I could either tense my head forward like his or keep it pushed back against the head rest since I had no instruments to monitor for him during the dash down the deck. I opted for head back for this first shot in an F-14.

I watched through the plastic bubble at the furious scurrying around by the men on the deck. Each had a key job to perform in these crucial few seconds before launch. A Purple Shirt held up a board showing the fighter's total takeoff weight. The strength of the catapult shot would be calibrated on the basis of our weight, much of which was fuel, so it was important to make sure the deck crew and pilot agreed on how many pounds were inside the plane. Two Red Shirts flew like butterflies from one of our eight missiles to the other, making sure they were ready to fire. A brave Green Shirt crawled under our plane while flames were shooting out of the engine to make sure we were firmly hooked front and back into the catapult gear. Our launch bar went from the front nose gear to a big hook sticking up from the surface of the deck. Under the flight deck and out of sight was a steel wheeled trolley which would haul the hook-shaped shuttle, with us attached to it, down the deck when the fist of steam smashed into the launching piston. I had a ringside seat on the most impressive ballet ever danced on a war machine.

Sammy swept the stick forward, backward, left, and right so the Yellow Shirts outside the plane could see if our flight controls were working properly. Then he pushed the left and right rudder pedals down with his feet. He repeated the words he told his flying students to memorize to be sure they wiped the controls clean: "Father, Son, Holy Ghost" for the four motions of the stick and "Amen" for the rudder checks. Everything looked go.

"George," Sammy said urgently. "We've got a problem. The outboard spoilers won't come up. Have you got a popped circuit breaker back there?"

I looked all around my part of the cockpit. I saw no sign of the white paint which shows when a circuit breaker pops. I could see most of them but had to feel for the others out of my view.

"Don't see anything popped," I replied.

"We can't go unless we fix it," Sammy said. "Shit!"

The Green Shirts unhooked us from the catapult slot. My heart fell. We were not going after all this. I frantically felt behind me and pushed against every circuit breaker I could find. One went in. I told Sammy.

"Shit hot!" he exclaimed. The Yellow Shirts led us into another catapult on the deck. We went through all the last minute checks again. No problems. "Looks like we're going this time. Got your harness locked?"

"All set," I replied.

I looked to the light on the island to my right. It was green. We were go for launch. I pressed my helmeted head against the side of the cockpit canopy so I could see past Sammy. The ocean looked only a few feet down the track. I was anxious to get launched before I had any more time to think of all the things that could go wrong. I saw Sammy salute. This meant we were ready for the jolt of steam which would hurl us down the deck. The yellow-shirted launching officer leaned over and touched the deck. The sailor watching him from the catwalk on the starboard side of the ship pushed the red launch button. This released the torrent of pent-up steam against the huge piston under the flight deck.

Wham!

My head snapped back into the head rest. My eyes flattened. Something seemed to be pushing them deep into my head. I tried to look out the cockpit to my left but only caught a blur of gray ship and blue ocean. I heard the familiar rattle of steel wheels underneath me. Sammy's breathing sounded like short, desperate gasps through my ear phones. Everything was happening too fast for my mind to register each event separately. They were running together. I saw, heard, and felt all at once. Then everything suddenly went into slow motion. We were off the end of the boat.

"Good shot," Sammy said as we seemed to be slowing up for a midair stop. The Tomcat had run out of catapult power and now was struggling to stay airborne with its own two engines. The engines felt pitifully weak compared to the cat shot. The 150 mile an hour dash down the deck had felt much faster than our current speed of 300 miles an hour in the open air. I felt wonderfully free. We had no walls up in the sky. Just endless blue. I snapped off one side of my oxygen mask and looked around. The world was beautiful from our perch in the sky. From our height the ship looked like a tiny barge with a white tail. The clouds were our neighbors now.

"OK," Sammy said, his breathing coming much slower through the hot mike. "What would you like to do?"

"Hey, this is great. Just do your thing."

"OK. Tell me, though, if you feel yourself getting sick. I'll show how a Tomcat can stand on its tail."

Zoom. Up we went, for the roof of the sky. My back pressed hard against the seat as we climbed. My face felt as if it were going straight into the sun. The blue roof could not be reached. Sammy broke off the climb gracefully and let us fall down, down, down. The Mediterranean came up at me and winked with strips of reflected sunlight. Sammy pulled us up again and leveled off.

"You OK?" Sammy asked.

"Fine."

"Sure?"

"Good shape."

"See that A-6 right above us at 30,000 feet?"

I put my head back as far as it would go and scanned the sky. I finally saw the speck of the A-6. "Yeah, I see him."

Whoosh!

We were going straight up again. Sammy got on the A-6's tail and told me how to thumb the wheel on the radar stick to lock him up for a missile firing. I followed his instructions and soon heard a penetrating hum come through my earphones.

"Hear that tone?" Sammy asked.

"Yeah."

"That means our missile is locked on. I could kill him from here. Fox 2," he said to the world, the expression Navy pilots use when they are shooting off a Sidewinder heat-seeking missile.

A tone. A whoosh. A fireball in the sky. Maybe a chute. Probably not. That is how death would come from an air-to-air missile. No rat-a-tat-tat followed by a chivalrous wave from victor to vanquished as was the case in World War I and sometimes in World War II. Just an engulfing fire. I thought it would be better to be shot down the old way.

"This is how you do a guns-only kill," Sammy said as he went into a fresh set of maneuvers.

We twisted back and forth across the sky, something like a big eel on the move. The 20mm gun in the nose would have raked the poor A-6 if this had been a real fight.

Our real quarry for the day came into view. CAG and Bo were below us in their F-14 looking for a Texaco, a flying KA-6D tanker. Pilots refuel after they are airborne when they practice ACM (aerial combat maneuvers). The maneuvers, several with afterburners lit, gulp fuel. Sam spotted a Texaco off in the distance and wheeled toward it. The tanker unreeled into the open sky a long black hose. We headed for the end of it marked by the "basket," the round plug-in spot which looked like the feathered end of a shuttlecock. Sammy's challenge was to fly this 30-ton fighter plane so precisely that he could stick the end of a broomstick-like probe smack into the basket as both planes bounced along at 345 miles an hour. He pulled out the switch that slid the probe out of the right side of the F-14's nose section like a horizontal periscope. He closed the distance between us and the KA-6D. I felt as if the fuel-laden tanker was going to sit in my lap if we got any closer. It was almost within touching distance. We were flying for a precisely timed midair collision of probe and basket.

It seemed to be taking forever to push the probe into the basket dancing in the sky just a few feet from my face. Smack! Clunk! Sammy had rammed the plane forward at the right instant so the probe speared into the basket. Sammy flipped some switches in his cockpit and the crew in the KA-6D flipped others in their tanker. Fuel started flowing down from the tanker and into the F-14. A midair transfusion was under way. I felt grateful for the extra minutes of flying time pouring into the Tomcat but I sure as hell would be glad when the big airplane out there got off my lap. Sammy radioed up to the tanker that he had taken on enough fuel. He slowed to break the lock on the long hose. The KA-6D crew reeled in the hose. Procedures required us to pass up beside the tanker to let the crew know we had looked over the exterior of their plane and found everything in order; that the hose was not still sticking out. We waved goodbye and wheeled away, we were on our own again. Enough of this near-miss flying, I thought.

Sammy and I searched the sky for our quarry, the F-14 sporting the bared-fang markings of VF-11, the Red Rippers.

We spotted it below us starting out on the refueling procedure we had just completed. Oops! The F-14 zigged while the tanker zagged. The F-14's extended fuel probe and the basket trailing from the KA-6D collided. The F-14 probe on the right side of the nose bent like a twisted car aerial. There would be no dogfighting with CAG this day. He could not retract the bent probe. He would have to fly around gingerly for the rest of the flight and then land. Dogfighting maneuvers might rip off the extended probe and cause it to damage the plane. Too bad. We decided to "shoot down" CAG anyhow. It was not a fair fight with his speed and maneuverability limited by the damaged probe. Then again Sammy had something of a no load of a RIO in his back seat. Sammy coached me at zeroing in on CAG using the radar for kills with the long distance Sparrow and close up Sidewinder missiles.

Modern aircraft radars are indeed electronic marvels. By thumbing the tiny wheel on the radar stick I could zero the missiles in on the green water bug of light skating across my scope. I could order the radar to stay focused on this water bug no matter what. The radar-directed Sparrow missile would ride those radar beams right into the enemy plane and blow it out of the sky. With help from Sammy, I ran the radar in its various modes and at distances determined by twisting the range pointer on the dashboard just above the stick. Whenever I thumbed the wheel on the radar stick well enough to pin my dot of light on that of the enemy plane on the scope, Sammy would exult through my earphones:

"That's right. Lock him up! Hear that tone? He's dead."

I learned that killing the other pilot in today's dogfighting at missile distance is indeed like standing at one of those Atari war game machines. Thumb the wheel, jiggle the stick, punch some buttons, fire. Death by computer is as mechanical as typing on a word processor, green-lit screen and all. Again like working a computer, the effective killer is systematic and cool. He is not a pilot with a white scarf screaming, "Kill!" as he fires a machine gun through his propeller. Despite the difference brought on by high tech, trying to kill before being killed in the sky keeps the adrenaline pumping through your body—even in mock combat.

I figured we had been rolling around the sunlit sky for about ten minutes when Sammy radioed back to me that our two hours were up. We would have to return to the ship. We had only one more adventure ahead of us: getting this fast-flying mother down on the deck. Sammy found the ship with no trouble. I could not have told you at that point whether it was to our north, south, east, or west. We caught up to CAG, who was also on the way in, and slid over and under him in an orbiting maneuver that felt smooth but was no doubt quite a feat of airmanship to perform. Then we zoomed over the ship from stern to bow; turned hard left in the break at 400 miles an hour at an altitude of 800 feet; skidded around without losing altitude to a course that would keep us parallel to the carrier on our downwind leg; swept the wings forward; lowered the landing gear, slates, and flaps; descended to about 600 feet, turned left again about two miles astern of the *Kennedy*, crossing her wake at what looked to me like a 90 degree angle; and aimed for the white stripe down the center of the canted flight deck. Sammy's breathing became gasps again as he worked the stick and searched for the ball on the port side of the ship. He was only seconds and three-quarters of a mile from the deck when he told the ship that he had sighted the ball and identified his airplane and the amount of fuel he had left in his tanks.

"One zero three Tomcat. Ball. Three point four."

Sammy tried to keep the ball lined up with the green arms of lights as he plunged down. I looked out the left side of the plane, saw the lights but could not tell how well we were lined up. I was watching instead the flat rectangle of steel coming up at my jaw like a knockout punch. I was not sure we would hit the ship at all, far less catch one of those four threads I could barely see stretched across the deck. Ouch! We hit the steel deck with a bang and a screech. I shot forward like a rocket—for probably no more than three inches as my shoulder harness held me back. I heard the screams of metal meeting metal as the tailhook on the Tomcat grabbed for and caught a wire. The wire let us roll forward for a few dozen feet in what felt like the reassuring controlled skid I had felt in other landings on the carrier. We rolled back to let the arresting wire fall out of the tailhook. We were down and almost safe.

Sammy parked the plane. The canopy opened. We unbuck-led, yanked off our oxygen masks, raised our visors, and climbed out onto the sunshine of the deck. We looked at each other, laughed, and shook hands. It had been one hell of a ride for me.

"Sign me up!" this old bastard hooted as we trooped across

the deck and into the ship. We had just escaped for a glorious 150 minutes.

Captain John "Frog" Allen, the only former Blue Angel pilot on the *Kennedy*, had advised me to forget all about taking off from and landing on a carrier at night. "Walk into a closet, close the door, and feel around," Frog had advised. "You'll get the same feeling." And of course it would be much safer. But I did not see how I could write a credible book about carrier operations without experiencing what pilots fear most: night takeoffs and landings in a hot, unforgiving fighter. So after my day flight in the Tomcat with Sammy, I pressed for a night launch and trap. Pinky landings, landing at twilight which I had already done in the EA-6B, and the night landing in the E-2 Hawkeye would not do. They did not entail the sweaty-palm risk of swooping out of the black sky in an unforgiving fighter plane and feeling for the chip of black stuff on the ocean. It had been scientifically proven that a pilot's heart beat faster while he attempted a night landing on a carrier than when he was being shot at in combat.

It was already dark when I reported to VF-31's ready room for the briefing on my first night flight in the F-14. My pilot was going to be Commander Rick "Wigs" Ludwig, executive officer of VF-31, and considered one of the best pilots in the air wing. He could do it all. Smooth passes on the way to catching the Number Three Wire; highly intricate ACM maneuvers. Wigs was a serious, disciplined, and skillful aviator who looked as if he had been cast for the part by Hollywood. He had the square, ruddy face of an actor and the muscular build of a weight lifter, which he was. He laughed a lot, enjoyed the life of a naval aviator, obviously had great hand and eye coordination for night landings which somehow did not transfer itself to his fingers when he picked up his guitar. I knew this from living in the room separated from his by only a thin, steel wall. I suffered through his unsuccessful efforts to teach himself a second song on his guitar.

I sat in the VF-31 ready room and listened to the briefing all the ready rooms were getting over the closed circuit television from CVIC—the combat information center. The briefer gave the position of ships in the area, talked about the weather and announced "the standoffs"—how close we could fly to the border of each country this night.

"We're going to go find a tanker so George can experience the whole night evolution," Wigs announced to the crew who would be flying on his wing in another F-14. Lieutenant Greg "Road" Streit, one of the hottest nuggets on the ship, would be the pilot and Lieutenant Jim "Mac" McAloon the RIO on Wigs' wing. I had just sweated out having a KA-6D tanker on my lap in broad daylight as we refueled in midair. I was wondering if going through the same thing at night would be better or worse.

" 'Brain Damage' will be flying up there trying to jam us," Wigs said kiddingly of Lieutenant Commander Dan Mazzeo of VA-137, who would be practicing electronic warfare on us from his EA-6B this night. He told Road and Mac that we would be playing "three in a barrel" and flying mock night attacks with our Sidewinder missiles.

"Now George," Wigs said. "I'll want good alignment." This was the expression for informing the inertial navigation system as to the exact spot of the ocean from which we departed.

The navigation system, knowing the starting point of the flight, could tell us where we were in relation to the ship, while up in the night sky—crucial information. I always marveled how pilots could find the constantly moving carrier at night. I had trouble finding my home creek when I returned in my fishing boat from a night outing on Chesapeake Bay. The computer was part of the pilots' secret, provided the RIO in the back seat gave it the right information in the first place.

"We'll go up to 30,000 feet and go supersonic," said Wigs in continuing his briefing of the night flight ahead.

I had not been supersonic, in either day or night flying. I was told that nothing very dramatic happened inside the cockpit when a fighter broke the sound barrier. But I wanted to feel what it would be like.

Wigs then gave Road a series of cautions to avoid collisions in the night sky: do not fly lower than 500 feet; watch out for tankers overhead when you pull up; "when my antismash comes on, be on your merry way." The antismash are warning lights designed to avoid midair collisions. Navy pilots flying at night also use their red and green navigation lights to warn their wingmen what they are going to do next. Wigs said that when he dimmed his lights Road was to consider him the lead airplane, the one Road was to follow through the night sky. "It means

I've got it, and I'll take the lead."

Wigs, the veteran, gave some advice to Road, the nugget, about the night landing staring him in the face.

"Max concentration on the way down. Hopefully you've got needles to guide you back to the flight deck. I don't think we have a whole lot of natural winds out there yet tonight. So watch your lineup coming in toward the angled deck. We're going to be working on an axial wind. It has a tendency to drive you high. Think green!"

I looked up at the night sky as I went through the walls of the carrier to the openness of the flight deck. I could see stars but no moon. Pilots loved a big moon. The more moonlight illuminating the ship and its flight deck the better. With moonlight, the pilots can distinguish between sea and sky. They have a horizon to help fix their spot in the sky. Otherwise, the night is just like Frog had said: the inside of a locked closet.

I climbed into the rear seat of the red-tailed Tomcat. Lieutenant Scott "Stewie" Stewart, the RIO in the spare F-14 which would be launched if either Wigs' or Road's plane experienced a breakdown, climbed up the ladder leading into my part of the cockpit. He checked through the switches that could be set up before the engines were started. I still would have to do considerable punching, pushing, twisting, and flipping once the engines were started. But it was comforting to know everything that could be done cold was already done.

Wigs climbed in, and started giving me instructions for the prelaunch phase. One big difference between my day and night prelaunch preparations was the lighting. Pilots become accustomed to flying with a certain amount of reddish cockpit light. I had the lights on too bright. Wigs wanted them dimmed. I dimmed them. Now they were too dim. Getting ready to fly off a carrier at night takes preparations as fastidious as those of a beauty queen contestant primping for her grand entrance. I finally got the lighting right. Wigs went through the checklist and started the engines. It was now my turn to set up the gadgetry in the back. I twisted the same knobs and flipped the same switches as I had done in the day flight for Sammy. Then I had to punch numbers into the tiny keyboard on my left knee to tell the computer exactly where we were on the ocean. The first set of punching failed to put the proper display on the scope. I erased the first attempt and started over. The numbers took this time. Wigs got his navigational fix. I felt greatly relieved. I dared look outside the cockpit.

Dark! Damn, was it dark! Walking across the deck I had seen pinpricks of light all over the flight deck and on the island to give me a sense of where I was. But just the height of the F-14 had wiped out most of those lights. I felt as if we were suspended in the black air above a black ocean. The noises of the deck force breaking us down confirmed there were indeed other human beings around us, but I still felt cut off from everything familiar.

Wigs taxied toward the catapult slot. I saw the Yellow Shirts waving their faint yellow wands to direct Wigs into the catapult track. I noticed the launch light on the side of the island to my right was red. We would not be going anywhere until it was green. Wigs' breathing was coming through the hot mike in quick huffs. I braced for the slam of steam about to kick us in the tail. I looked left at the launching officer. He was twirling his lighted wand, the signal for Wigs to rev up the engines, including torching off the afterburner. Two giant blow torches of yellow fire shot out our tail and bent up onto the steel dam erected behind us—the jet blast deflector. I looked to my right again. The launch light on the island was green. Oh, Jeez! Here we go. The catapult officer did a graceful bend toward the bow and touched his yellow light to the deck.

Wham!

The old feeling of being kicked in the back and shoved in the face returned with a vengeance. I tried to see the deck fly by as I listened to the now familiar trolley car sound of steel wheels racing along the track under the deck. But I could see only streaks of white, presumably whitecaps, and the silhouette of the catwalk as we went hurtling toward the black hole off the end of the boat.

"Good shot," Wigs said over the mike.

I felt the acceleration of the Tomcat slow up as it ran out of catapult energy. It vaulted over the waves on the strength of the two giant plumes of fire shooting out our tail. We were up and away. We were safely off the boat. We seemed alone in the sky as I looked all around. Above me were the most stars I had seen at one time since lying on my back and staring up at the Wyoming night sky during a backpacking trip through Yellowstone National Park. This night I felt closer to the stars. Wigs aimed the plane right at them. They seemed to get brighter. I then looked down. The Mediterranean had transformed itself into a black mirror. I could see starlight reflected in the water. Starlight, in fact, seemed to be up, down, and all around me. There was a soft milkiness to the night pressing in on me from outside my bubble of plastic. Beautiful! Not scary. Ethereal and beautiful. We were in one of God's special places—a place few people could reach.

Road in the Tomcat somehow found us in the dark. He pulled his F-14 up alongside, off our right wing. Wigs and Road discussed their next joint maneuver as I let myself be distracted by the beauty of the night. Next thing I noticed was fire. Gobs of it poured out of Road's F-14 as he kicked it into afterburner. There cannot be too many more spectacular sights than twin fountains of flame from a seemingly invisible source streaking the black winter sky of the Mediterranean. On the deck the afterburner flames had looked yellowish. The sky somehow had cleansed the flames into a bright white which projected pure power.

We chased Road to the roof, leaving our own twin streaks of white flames behind us. I felt sure we could reach the stars if only we kept going, but I suddenly felt weightless as Wigs flipped us over and down toward the sea. I was lost for a few seconds. I could not tell which was sea and which was sky. Everything looked milky with dots of lights. Was that the sea or the sky below me? I could not tell. No wonder pilots have to rely on their instruments at night. You cannot tell after a few rolls, loops, and turns whether you are upside down or right side up. Confused or not, I was enjoying the hell out of the ride.

Wigs, as promised, went looking for a KA-6D tanker orbiting near the ship. He found one and lined up to plug into it. I saw the circle of light around the basket, the socket Wigs was supposed to spear with the seemingly short refueling probe on the F-14. It took considerable airmanship to plug in bright daylight. How the hell, I wondered as we closed on the dancing basket of light, is he going to get the probe in that little thing without colliding with the tanker? We closed the distance. I could see the black line of hose leading back from the basket to the KA-6D. We looked so close to the basket that I felt I could grab it with my hand if the canopy was open to the night sky. Wigs was good. Very good. He coaxed his warplane forward, up, and sideways at just the right speed to ram the probe into the basket with a thunk on the very first try. We took on extra gas so Wigs would have plenty of fuel to carry out the high-energy maneuvers he wanted to perform.

We unplugged. Wigs pulled up alongside the tanker to look him over. He waved farewell and raced off to an unoccupied area of night sky. I sat back with eager anticipation for the next event when my ears were assaulted by the penetrating buzzing of the jamming radio waves sent out by the EA-6B crew in the plane piloted by Lieutenant Commander Mazzeo. Wigs radioed back to instruct me how to foil the jamming. I think I botched the procedures. I was also having trouble with the radio. I learned later that this particular Tomcat had chronic problems with its radio, but I might have twisted the knob to the wrong channel at the wrong time in the confusion of trying to cope with the jamming. The jamming drill ended after a while, to my relief, and we went back to flying.

"I'm setting up for a supersonic run," Wigs radioed back.

He put the Tomcat straight and level and pushed the twin throttles forward a bit at a time. He called off the speeds as we approached the sound barrier: "Point eight; point nine; mach one. Feel it?"

I did feel a slight shudder in the Tomcat. It was more like a shiver. We were breaking through the turbulence piling up against our nose as we exceeded the speed of sound. We were breaking the sound barrier. It was a historic moment when Air Force Major Charles E. Yeager did it on 14 October 1947 in the X-1. But this night Wigs broke the sound barrier in his F-14 with a shudder he handled with ease.

"One point one; one point two," Wigs called off as we went beyond the sound barrier. There was no more shudder.

"See," Wigs called back. "There's not much to it. But now you can say you went supersonic."

We did some mock combat with Road, shooting him down with missiles, and then it was time to find the ship and land. I looked down and could see absolutely nothing on the water except the reflection of stars. The *Kennedy*'s lights did not stand out from nature's rhinestones. I appreciated how limited the naked eye was at night in trying to find ships on the dark ocean from a fast-moving airplane. No wonder downed pilots clamped strobe lights to their helmets when floating on the sea at night trying to attract a rescue helicopter.

"There's the ship," Wigs called out.

Was he kidding? All I could see was something that looked like a tiny flashlight beam. How the hell was he going to line up with that little slice of light far less drop the Tomcat smack on top of it while all 26 tons of us were falling out of the sky at 130 to 150 miles an hour? Impossible. Put on the damn lights, I thought to myself, as I looked down on that little dab of light which was reputed to be an aircraft carrier 1,100 feet long.

"You call the ball," Wigs instructed as he set us up for my first night landing. I was supposed to tell the ship who we were, how much fuel we carried, and whether I spotted the yellow circle of light on the port side of the ship. Wigs would be busy enough. I did not want to cost him the time of correcting my radio message. So I wrote it down on my pad so I could read it off as soon as I saw the ball.

We fell out of the sky and headed down toward the ship. I could see the black hulk of the *Kennedy* but had not yet picked out the ball. Wigs saw it. He told me to call it. I pushed down the radio button and uttered the message. It did not go anywhere. The radio was not transmitting. Lieutenant Commander Ron "Hawk" Hoppock, standing in front of the ball on the landing signal officer platform with the job of talking us down to the landing, heard nothing. He saw Wigs was lined up fine, ball message or not. He gave him the cut lights. This told Wigs he was cleared to land. I saw the green arms of light, heard the smash on the deck and felt the yank of my shoulder harness all at once. We were down and hooked onto the wire. Wigs had scored a clean night trap on his first pass. I saw the deck crew scurrying around us with different colors of lighted wands. We were safely in the hands of the *Kennedy* men again after a spectacular invasion of the forbidding night sky.

I entered the VF-31 ready room to the hoots of several of my friends there. They had been listening to us on the radio and watching us on the closed circuit television as we came down for the landing. "You didn't call the ball, George," Lieutenant (junior grade) Randall "Hacksaw" Reynolds, an RIO, kidded. "Here is George Wilson calling the ball at night," he continued, moving his mouth but making no sound. The junior officers in the ready room said I had been too frozen with fright to call the ball. My protestations that I had called the ball but the radio did not transmit were met with good-natured jeers.

"Aw, come on, George," Lieutenant Mike "Zone" Jones ragged. "You're learning fast. There's an old pilot's expression:

'Deny, deny, deny.' You don't say 'I forgot to do something.' You say, 'I'll recycle.' ''

Wigs conducted a little ceremony to celebrate my night flight, complete with Polaroid pictures and inscribed log book. A couple of junior officers slid by and quietly invited me to a private party they were going to have in the Me Jo—for marginally effective junior officer—bunk room down the passageway later that night.

When I knocked on the Me Jo door, I found a party in full swing. Pilots and RIOs from VF-31 were laughing and scratching, singing into a broom as if it were a band stand microphone, smoking cigars, and drinking anything that was wet. A problem developed. They ran out of ice. They did not want to tip the brass off to the fact that a party was in progress this late at night by carrying ice from the Dirty Shirt wardroom through admiral's country to reach the bunk room. Solution: Wilson would borrow ice from the enlisted mess below. I did so, returning with a huge bag of ice cubes to keep the party going into early morning. Everybody was done flying. We were going to be home soon. This cruise was going to end after all. So what the hell! Let's celebrate. Sing another song. Four JOs gathered around the broom and sang lustily into it. We were all twenty years old again and back in the fraternity house. I recalled the complaint of Rear Admiral Roger E. Box, who at this moment was trying to sleep through the noise assaulting his cabin down the passageway:

"It's hell to have an ensign's mind in an admiral's body."

The sailors looked at me quizzically. It was 4 A.M. and I was in my jogging suit in the hangar bay.

"You're the guy on here writing the book, aren't you?"

"That's me."

"You work out here this time every day?"

"Not really," I said and jogged off, being careful to skip over the chains holding the airplanes to the deck. I did not dare tell the puzzled sailor that I had found myself taking an admiral's body to an ensign's party and was now trying to work off the head-splitting effects with some air and exercise.

19   Homeward Bound

I DID SOME more flying from the carrier after the memorable
night flight in the F-14, mostly with the Rooks in the EA-6B,
logging 20 traps. But I had been spoiled by the nimbleness of
the Tomcat. The cat shots and landings and the feeling of escape
once in the air never stopped stimulating me, but I found myself
playing fighter pilot in the back seat of the EA-6B, looking at
another plane and figuring out the geometry for getting on his
Six—the kill position on his tail. Everyone in our city seemed
to feel the cruise was over even though we were still orbiting off
Bagel Station and launching planes every day. The marines were
now home. We were still in the Med, treading water. February
and March dragged. The sailors got through the long days by
checking each one off. "Only four laundry days and we're
home," was the morale boosting line uttered in the sleeping
compartments when March at long last gave way to April.
Rumors abounded that we would be breaking off from Bagel
Station and heading to Naples to brief the carrier that would be
replacing us on operations off Lebanon. Captain Wheatley
broke the suspense on the carrier by confirming the mess deck
rumors through this announcement over the loudspeaker system:

"Now is a good time to write home to your family because
free mail service will end as our commitment here in the eastern
Mediterranean ends," Wheatley said. "Free mail will close out
at 0800 tomorrow morning. So let's take a steady strain. We've

got a transit to complete. We've got flight operations today. Deployment certainly isn't over, but we're on our way west. I look forward to seeing you on the beach in Naples. That is all.''

It really sounded this time that we were going west and not coming back. I checked around the sailors' work spaces to see if they were celebrating. I heard no cheers; saw no eyes glistening. The sailors had worked too long and been disappointed too often about where they were going next to hoot or holler.

"They could still turn us around, right?" one sailor said in a typical reaction to the news about our heading west.

Boatswain's Mate Third Class Marty Martell did not want the *Kennedy* to linger in Naples for fear it would be ordered back to Bagel Station. "I'd just as soon skip Naples and keep right on steaming until we bumped the dock at Norfolk," he said.

AD Second Class Michael Navicki, twenty-eight, of Beckley, West Virginia, was afraid to count on getting home. He joined the Navy in 1974 because back in Beckley "all they had was coal mines and I didn't want to be a coal miner." He had already done one cruise aboard the USS *Saratoga,* also an aircraft carrier.

"This one was a lot harder for me mentally because you didn't know day to day, month to month whether you'd be sitting off Beirut; whether you're going to be able to pull into port.

"You're on a ship with a lot of guys. You eat with them, sleep with them, work with them and there's really no privacy for yourself. You look forward to getting off the ship. You count on the port visits on the schedule.

"Then they say, 'You're going into port. No you're not.' This adds to all the frustration."

Navicki said he loved his country and did not mind sacrificing for it by working a seemingly endless seam of days on the *Kennedy*. But he found himself wondering if all the work he did while the carrier stood off Lebanon really accomplished anything.

"I learned that the people over in Lebanon would go to work normally during the day, go home, and eat dinner and spend time with the family. After that they would grab their guns and go up to the hills and start fighting. And it has been going on like this for centuries.

"Then we jump right in the middle of the situation. I don't

know. Seems as if there could of been something else done. As far as me being here, I'm patriotic, and I don't mind doing what I did for my country. It's a hard life out here. We ended up pulling our forces out of Lebanon and the fighting is still going on. So I don't know if we accomplished anything or not.''

I heard similar views from other sailors as I chatted with them in their berthing and work spaces. Some had taken their troubles to Chaplain Doffin during the cruise. Doffin always tried to help the sailors get through their long todays and tomorrows on the *Kennedy*. He had less to offer his flock of 5,000 on the *Kennedy* than the military chaplains on shore. They could offer instant relief by arranging for the troubled soldier or marine or airman to get off base for a while. Doffin and his charges were locked together, for better or worse, inside the steel walls with a moat thousands of miles wide outside them. He had no way to give instant relief to the men on the ship. He could not send them home on a 24-hour pass or even encourage them to get away from everybody for an hour by going into town.

I walked down to Doffin's office to ask him how this cruise—which finally seemed to be ending—compared with the six previous ones he had taken.

"Uncertainty," he began. "That's what made this one tougher on me and everybody else on the ship. Navy people like to be able to count on certain things. It's built into us. It's part of our training.

"When we came over here we knew we had seven months to do, and the places we were going to go to were all written down. Then they said, 'OK, we're not going to the Indian Ocean. We might be going here; no we're not going there.'

"After a while, that uncertain malaise just kind of set in. I think you can see the effects of all this uncertainty right now. Here we are fixing to go home. This ought to be a time of great exhilaration for us, OK? But I personally don't feel that. I'm glad to be going home, but I don't personally feel this channel fever—the excitement of going home that keeps you from going to sleep at night. I haven't been sleeping right the last six months. Everybody is just emotionally drained out, washed out. I hate to use the term burnout because that covers such a wide variety of things. But I think it is just an emotional lackadaisicalness added to the uncertainty which has everybody saying to himself, 'Well, I'm not going to believe it until I see Hampton Roads. And I'll only believe it then because once we get in the channel there, they can't turn us around. We've got to go on in.'

"A first class came in to see me this morning. He had been in the Navy twelve years, been married five years. This is the first time he has ever been separated from his wife for any period of time. He is working TAD (temporary assigned duty) in the brig. We're talking about a guy who has got it pretty well together. He gets no negative feedback from home. His wife writes frequently. They're all encouraging letters, but he says to me:

" 'Chaplain, I've got a certain anxiety. I don't know why. I feel this uncertainty.'

"So I tried to identify this uncertainty for him.

" 'Has there been a change in your marriage, a change in the relationship?' I asked him.

" 'Oh no, no sir. If anything, from being separated so long I really realize how much I love my wife and how much I need her. Another thing, I come from a pretty religious family. My grandfather and grandmother who raised me are very religious. I've really gotten closer to God since I've been on this thing.'

" 'What you're telling me then,' I told him, 'is that there has been some change in your life; a rearranging of priorities in your mind. Change doesn't have to be a negative.' "

Doffin told me he thought he made progress with the first class sailor in focusing his attention on the positive changes, such as discovering he loved his wife more than he realized when he set sail back in September. Still, the first class was filled with dread as we headed home. He was not sure that all the months of not being able to tell his wife where he would be next so they could at least talk by telephone had not frayed their marriage knot for all time.

Doffin told me that all the uncertainty had inflicted deeper wounds on sailors who were not as stable or well supported at home as the first class petty officer. Many had been kept out of touch with their loved ones so long because of the *Kennedy*'s infrequent port calls "that they don't know what they're going to find when they get home." Because a carrier is the heart of the battle group she is sailing in, she cannot swing into a port without suspending the mission. Smaller ships, like frigates, destroyers and cruisers, are less heavily committed. They usually pull into port more often than a carrier and do not stay at sea as long. Doffin said that on his previous six cruises he could cable worried wives that their sailor husbands would be telephoning them from a port at a certain date. He could not divulge the place because of military secrecy but could give them dates to hang on to so when the fateful day came the anxious wives could say "I love you" through tears and ask long lists of questions once they had pulled themselves together in lonely apartments in Norfolk.

"I couldn't do that on this cruise," Doffin said in an anguished voice, "because nobody knew when or where he could make the call home." It was the kind of uncertainty that is accepted in war but is destabilizing for the sailors in the AVF—all volunteer force. They know the country is at peace and cannot understand why they are kept at sea for so long with so few port visits.

"In the Navy," Doffin said in continuing his post audit of the cruise as we sat in this small office under the mess decks, "we live a very orderly and disciplined existence. To say once we get to sea that we're not certain we're going to go here, or go there, goes against the grain of the sailors' indoctrination. I just think we've been out here too long. If we had been out here five months, six months at the maximum, I don't think we would be seeing the same depressing effect we're seeing now. OK. We just stretched the rubber band too far."

Given the fact that unpredictable international developments often dictate where the carrier goes and how long it stays at sea, I asked the chaplain, what would he do if he were calling the shots, to shore up the sagging spirits of sailors on a severely taxed warship like the *Kennedy*?

"What I would do, for example, like Easter Sunday when we told the sailors we were going to have a picnic on the flight deck and then had to cancel it—well, I would have just gone ahead and given them the day off. Why the hell did we go around and look for something for them to do? There are always reasons and things that need to be done, but there comes a time when you should say, 'OK, if you don't have the duty, go do what you want to do. Sleep, play cards, read.' They were going to give them that day off anyway for the picnic. But all of a sudden we couldn't have the picnic, so there's always something to do. They give the sailors days off on the small boys (ships smaller than a carrier, like destroyers). I'd also cut out some of these inspections so you wouldn't feel somebody is looking over your shoulder all the time.''

I left the chaplain to talk with Master Chief Stan Crowley, who worked out of an office next to Doffin's. He said he had heard few cheers down on the hangar bay when the word came over the IMC that the *Kennedy* was heading west. He agreed with Doffin that the uncertainty had been the biggest single drain of the long cruise.

"A guy likes to know what's going to happen next," Crowley said. "We set our lives by schedules and clocks most of the time. Along with the uncertainty, here we are out here, and we don't get any time off. Not because the CNO (Chief of Naval Operations) doesn't want to give us time off, but he's got to keep those planes running.''

How come, I pressed Crowley, despite the uncertainty, the unrelenting work, the mental and sexual frustration of few port calls, the feeling that Lebanon was a loser, the long deployment —the kids on the *Kennedy* kept working so hard and so well that the carrier won the Battle E as the best carrier in the Atlantic fleet? Crowley paused, fixed me with a smile and answered:

"I don't know. These guys have something you don't find elsewhere. Where they get it from I don't know.''

I sought out Commander John Burch of VF-31, the skipper whose squadron had lost two F-14 fighters in three days, to ask him if time had healed the wounds the accidents had inflicted on himself and his men.

"Over a period of time," he said as we reflected on the cruise while sitting in a quiet corner of the Tomcatters' ready room, "time heals all. If this had been a normal type cruise where people had time to dwell on, to think about those accidents, I think it would have been much harder to get through this cruise. The men would have had to live with the stigma of losing those two airplanes for a long time. But because we were flying on a continuous basis for such a long period of time, they never really had time to dwell on the accidents. Now we are almost six months removed from them. I think we got over them as individuals. I was real proud of the way our squadron hung in there after our misfortunes. I am proud of our maintenance people. We didn't offer them a whole hell of a lot. All we offered them was hard work. I have a real good feeling about our enlisted people and our junior officers.

"We paid the price as a squadron when it came to competing

for the Battle E. Those accidents hurt us as a squadron.

"I search my soul for what we could have done to prevent those accidents. But they were just accidents which should not have happened. They were aircrew error accidents. People can do better.

"I would like to think that they're not going to stay over my head. I can rationalize that it was not John Burch who caused the accidents. But I also understand the Navy system. The guy who is the skipper—he is in charge. I have to live with that.

"This is my seventh deployment. We broke new ground out here this time on the amount of work you expected out of a guy. A guy would come in from a flight and have four hours off until he had to get ready for the next one. He needed to sleep that four hours. But how can you get something to eat and then go instantaneously to sleep so you get four hours of rest so you're ready to start another eight hour cycle which will be a night Case Three recovery when the weather is shitty and there's no moon?

"From the standpoint of the professional warrior, this deployment was frustrating because we did not make them pay the price for killing our marines. I had the sense all along that this thing was not going to come out as a military victory. It looked from the start like a Vietnam type operation. It's frustrating to be involved with a no-win operation. It's frustrating to sit out here and see the Israelis go into Baalbek time after time. I don't think the Israeli air force is any better than we are. They just do it more.

"I'm not bitter about it, but I don't think we were committed enough to make a difference in Lebanon. If this deployment accomplished anything, it showed America's resolve to dedicate a lot of people and a lot of money to keep the peace. It cost the taxpayers a lot of money to keep two carriers over here and the marines ashore, even though people directing the operation knew it was a no-win militarily. Reagan did put out the message that he is not afraid to use force but he is a reasonable man about it. I don't think one year from now it's going to matter whether we were here or not. But from a worldwide perspective of how Reagan does business, our adversaries might think twice about doing certain things."

The *Kennedy* reached Naples 12 April 1984. The officers and sailors flew from the ship like starlings leaving an isolated tree in a parched field for the easy pickings of the city. One part of the *Kennedy* flock flew into the officers' and enlisted men's bars at Air Force South. Others went in ones and twos to the bars in the gut to douse their ears with the loudest rock in the harbor. Still more made pilgrimages in Navy buses to the Post Exchange to buy cameras, tapes, VCRs, and whatever else looked like a bargain. Hey Joes hawking sleazy wares displayed on car hoods and on the sidewalk of the street across from the pier did a brisk business. Sailors wanted something colorful to bring home without spending a lot of time shopping for it.

One afternoon I went out to Carney Park, a huge Navy playground outside the city, to play softball on the Red Rippers' team. I immediately demonstrated how six and a half months at sea—to say nothing of advancing years—can ruin the timing of a once sure-handed fielder.

"Hey, there's still time for you to come back," shouted Commander Keith Shean when I finally caught one of those long balls hit to right field.

The last full day of the liberty Chaplain Doffin and I left Naples and drove a rented car into the beautiful Italian hills, ending up in Salerno. I tried to retrace the ferocious World War II battle there. But there were no markers to help us. The vanquished apparently do not want to leave reminders.

At lunch at a waterfront restaurant in Salerno, Jim and I laughed our way through several spectacular courses of Italian food, recalling scenes from the human comedy we had played in during our almost seven months on the USS *John F. Kennedy*. By serving as his rabbi without portfolio, by sharing our ups and downs, we had become close friends. We toasted with what I convinced Jim was nothing more than ceremonial wine our good fortune in having lived the unique experience of the 1983–84 *Kennedy* cruise together. We vowed to keep in touch. All sailors do this of course and then go their separate ways. But I felt Jim and I would continue the special relationship developed in the crucible of our mutual isolation in a benevolent prison.

The last night ashore in Naples, I went to dinner in a big hilltop restaurant above the harbor with CAG Mazach and the Condo gang. We ate well, drank a lot of wine, talked loud but did not burst into song as we had done on our way out during the first liberty in Rio. There was sadness in the realization that this might be our last night together in an exotic spot where we could celebrate each other. We were slowing down for our landing on the world of the ordinary. We, too, soon would be going to the office in the morning, coming home at night to the family, doing dishes and homework, cutting the lawn, paying bills, and worrying about leaky faucets and the cost of living. No more Mr. Irresponsible, or Mr. Unreachable, or—worst of all—no more Mr. Wonderful. We all promised to keep in touch, just as the chaplain and I had done in Salerno. But we all sensed, without saying it, that we would never be this close again.

The *Kennedy* battle group paraded out of Naples in a fancy formation the morning of 18 April 1984. Rear Admiral Jerry O. Tuttle wanted to show everyone on shore how a varsity Navy got under way. Forget about what happened in Lebanon. The U.S. Navy was leaving Naples in style this day.

One mighty gray warship followed the other in a precise circular swing in, through, and out of the storied harbor of Naples. I watched the officers on the bridge sweat out the close quarters and worry about mistakes and collisions which could ruin their whole day. But everybody did it, by God. Goodbye Naples, said the United States Navy in a classy farewell salute before melting down to gray blobs on the horizon of the Tyrrhenian Sea.

The air wing's flying days were over, barring sudden emergencies, as we steamed westward in the Med toward Rota, Spain. Rota would be our last stop before Norfolk and home. Inside the *Kennedy* a "what the hell" feeling took hold. We had done it. The deployment had been completed. We were going home. Impromptu parties broke out in many of the rooms. Time-honored aviator antics which had been pushed to the back of everyone's mind by the intensity of flight operations made a sudden comeback. One such was the afterburner demonstration during a party in a room perilously close to the admiral's cabin. The pilot filled his mouth with lighter fluid, spit accurately in a fine stream to a lit lighter being held by a buddy across the room. The result was a spectacular flame from the pilot's mouth to the lighter. It did look like an afterburner trail. The important part of the trick was to keep lighter fluid off your face so there was nothing for the flame to eat there. Fluid on the face meant suffering a burn.

"Shit," said a fellow aviator, "everyone knows an F-14 has two engines." With that, he stood beside his buddy so they could spit out two parallel streams of lighter fluid to create the twin afterburner effect.

Whooooooooosh!

The two streams of lighter fluid burst into flame. Damned if it did not look like a Tomcat taking off at night with afterburners kicked in.

The cheering stopped when somebody noticed one pilot's face was on fire. He had not wiped it clean of lighter fluid. Somebody smacked a wet towel on the pilot's face. Then, amid the laughter, a worried flier made a discreet call to a sleeping flight surgeon who was a bit of a player himself. The surgeon made a house call to the room. He assured the pilot he would live but would go home with some cruddy rash on his otherwise kissable face. Bad news. The vain pilot had spent hours tanning his face and hardening his body for the triumphant return home. Fortunes of war.

"Hey CAG, I've got to get to the beach to set things up for our Outchop party at Rota."

It was Sammy Bonanno appealing to CAG Mazach for a ride on anything flying off the *Kennedy* to Rota. He hitched a ride there and set about buying for the Outchop party rounds of roast beef and kegs of beer. He also passed mimeographed invitations around to any part of the base where women in the mood for an air wing bash would be working or living. It was to be the final blast with the Bonanno go-for-it touch.

We arrived off Rota on 21 April but could not launch liberty boats because the sea was too rough. It looked for a while that Sammy would have to party all by himself. But helicopters would be flying over the rough seas shuttling supplies from the big base on Rota to the *Kennedy*. Scores of officers from the Third Air Wing hitched rides on the helicopters and reported to the officers' club on Rota for the Outchop party. Outchop means clearing the *Kennedy* of operations duties and releasing it to cross the Atlantic in her transit back to Norfolk.

The party was just beginning to gain altitude when I entered the club. The aviators and ship's company officers were three deep at the long bar, fifty people in the rear party room were sampling the roast beef and rolls. The mixed drinks at the bar were cheap. The beer in the back room flowed cold without much head. And there was music thudding in on us from speakers somewhere. The missing ingredient was women. The word must have gone out at Rota to stay away from Outchop parties where hundreds of men who had been without regular sex for six months or more could grab you.

For want of competition, and also because she was indeed attractive, a waitress named Kathleen working the back room came in for heavy attention. One aviator insisted she get to know Lieutenant Brian Kelleher, one of the youthful looking flight surgeons in the air wing.

"You don't look old enough to be a doctor," Kathleen told Brian.

"Hey, he'll prove it to you," said Brian's unhelpful buddy sitting beside him at the table. "He'll give you a pelvic examination right now."

Kathleen scurried away.

I joined CAG Mazach at the bar in the other room. His last act on the ship had been to call each of the squadron skippers into his cabin and inform them how he had ranked them in the personnel files that would travel with them for the rest of their careers. The Navy required such a ranking. Ties were not acceptable. The rankings had to go from one through eight.

"Call your friends in and tell them how you rated them," CAG winced. "That's a real bitch."

After completing that final, searing chore, Mazach no longer had any more duties to fill as commander of Air Wing Three.

"I just called Pat," he said sadly, "and told her I'm a has been."

"Hey George," Lieutenant Commander Chuck "Mumbles" Scott of the Red Rippers hailed as he spotted me at the bar. "You going to get fucked-up with us?"

I raised my glass and gave him a thumbs up. Mumbles, a congenial aviator, had told me—a baldie—his story of getting hair transplants for the top of his head. The Navy doctor who did the operation did not have the prescribed medical drill for making the holes for the individual tufts of hair to be planted on Mumbles' head. Not to worry. The doc just got a Black & Decker drill from a local hardware store and used that.

"No wonder," Lieutenant Mean Jim Greene kidded when I relayed the story. "One of those drills went too deep."

The alcohol intake rose but the party did not gain altitude proportionally. It got to a certain level of conviviality and hung there. I figured plain weariness kept the party from breaking through to the wild zone of Outchop celebrations. There was some sporadic roll throwing; a few raucous incidents. But on the whole it was a low-key affair.

Several of us were drawn into the dining room of the club by the music there. We spotted CAG Mazach and Potsie Weber eating dinner at a back table and joined them. Two pitchers of stingers mysteriously arrived. The singer with the band, Jamie, sat down with us briefly. She was just about finished for the night and declined the numerous offers to dance with the sex-starved *Kennedy* men. The band swung into a final few lively numbers. Monty Willis left the table and treated us to his attempt at break dancing. He could not spin himself. Potsie went out onto the dance floor to twirl him. Too much back on the floor. No spin. Lieutenant Bill "Sinker" Hays thundered across the dance floor doing some kind of southern dance. CAG Danny Powers, Mazach's replacement, went out and did an artful jig. So did Skipper John Combs of the Red Rippers. The air wing was providing its own entertainment. Sammy had done his entertaining earlier by mooning the back room. I was inspired enough to do a backward somersault. The party gained some more altitude then dipped as exhaustion and alcohol took hold. Officers quietly departed in ones and twos and looked for a place in the bachelor officers quarters to lie down. A few had reserved beds. Most just looked for a flat spot in the lounge. Somebody sprawled out on the pool table. I borrowed a bed in an apartment of an officer I had met early that night in the party room.

The morning light found us outside the Rota BOQ waiting to catch a ride to the airport. The sun pained our eyes. Monty Willis took one look at Lieutenant Abe Ellis and cracked: "Whatever you do, Abe, don't exhale."

Back on the ship, everyone was doing what he could to prepare himself for the homecoming. Most of the officers in the air wing would fly to their homecoming in the planes of their squadrons. These fly-ins were highly ceremonial affairs. Women would drive to the home fields of the squadrons. These were Virginia Beach, Norfolk, Orange Park, Florida, and Whidbey Island for the *Kennedy* squadrons. The squadron would chip in to buy flowers for the wives and girl friends and punch for the kids. As the wives stood out on the edge of the fields watching and waiting, the planes would come into view, flying in tight formation. The families would cheer and tingle, waiting for their men to land, climb out of the planes and run into their arms.

Commander Robert L. "Bunky" Johnson Jr., skipper of VAW-126 which flew the E-2C Hawkeye, wanted his squadron's fly-in to be extra special. He stood at the blackboard in front of the ready room and chalked out for the officers of his squadron how he wanted them to march together out of their planes and up to the gate where the families would be waiting. The junior officers in the back of the room did not like his plan at all. They considered it too complicated; Mickey Mouse. Bunky reconsidered and then insisted on doing it his way. This inspired a coup engineered over ice cream in the Dirty Shirt wardroom. A genius in flight suit disguise came up with the idea of rushing Bunky en masse as soon as they were out of the planes, hoisting him to their shoulders like a victorious football coach and running with him to the gate. This would get rid of the Prussian formation and flatter the skipper at the same time. Great! I learned later that the friendly coup was carried out in great style.

I opted for staying with the ship until she bumped smack into the dock at Norfolk rather than flying off ahead of time. I waited with great anticipation for the sight of sailing into my beloved Chesapeake Bay on the lookout bridge of an aircraft carrier.

Nature was kind. The homecoming day of 2 May was sunny with caressing breezes. I stood on the lookout bridge and drank in the sights. I saw signs on buildings on shore saying "Well Done" as we entered Hampton Roads. Passing ships tooted welcoming salutes. But all eyes were on the dock where we would land. I could only see its outlines as we sailed into the Hampton Tunnel and into the Elizabeth River toward Pier 12. I could see a clot of people on the pier. I could make out shapes and colors but not faces. I strained to find my wife, Joan, and my son, Jim, who I knew would be with her. Still too far. I could not make them out.

We finally swung around to port and headed straight for the concrete pier. Welcome home bands struck up. Signs waved, many of them with sailors' names on them. Cheers rolled out over the water and washed over the carrier. Sailors standing in dress blues around the perimeter of the ship twitched. They wanted off this boat. Other sailors noticed guards on the piers were keeping their eager, straining wives, daughters, sons, and parents behind a rope. They set up a chant:

"Let our women go!"

Somebody broke through the rope. Others galloped through the hole. The guards stood back. A flood of people, many shouting, crying and squealing all at once, broke onto the flatness of the pier right next to the carrier. Men raced down the two brows onto the pier and pulled loved ones against their aching bodies. I found Joan and Jim in the crowd and did the same thing. USS *John F. Kennedy* and her five thousand men were home at last.

Epilogue

No one could spend more than seven months chronicling life inside an aircraft carrier without emerging with strong conclusions about the men, about the war machine, and about the national policy for employing it.

My strongest single conclusion about the men is that the sailors are worked too hard and receive too little in return.

From my time on other carriers and warships, I am convinced that the work ethic for sailors has come down from the top command of the Navy. It is not peculiar to the USS *John F. Kennedy*. Therefore, the change must come from the top.

The United States Navy of the middle 1980s is blessed with the most educated and, as a group, most motivated sailors in its peacetime history. The Navy indeed has a new sailor. But Navy leaders have not trimmed their sails to accommodate him, to maximize his potential.

The admirals at the top do indeed brag about the record number of high school graduates in the ranks. Yet they still let them be worked like uneducated serfs. And they still send to them for entertainment stale, third-rate movies and canned television soap operas. Navy leaders, for failing to respond to the needs and potential of this new sailor, are allowing his young mind, the nation's greatest resource, to lie fallow for months on end while warships steam on distant oceans with him locked inside the steel walls.

The Navy, for its own sake as an institution and for the sake of this new breed of sailor, must break its mindset and treat its help better. The change must come from the top from the Secretary of the Navy and Chief of Naval Operations. Skippers at sea today are doing what they know the command wants done. If the demands from the top require sailors to be overworked, so be it. That is life at sea. But this approach could prove shortsighted from the standpoint of continuing to attract and hold high-quality sailors. Unless there is a change in the work ethic, the Navy may bring back the bad old days of post-Vietnam when the all volunteer force could not fill its ranks with high-quality people. It strikes me as shortsighted and dangerous to overwork sailors as to overfly pilots.

It will take more than messages from the Chief of Naval Operations to break today's mindset. Navy leaders will have to keep track of how many hours sailors are worked on each ship just as they now keep track of how many hours pilots fly on each carrier. I hate to add to the paperwork already plaguing the officers on ships under way, but I see no other way to make everybody from the Chief of Naval Operations in Washington to the skipper of the ship adopt a new value system regarding the American sailor. There is always something more to paint. It is easier not to give every sailor one day off a week while at sea. But I think everyone would do better if more sensitivity about the sailors were instilled in everyone for whom they work so long and hard, especially on a carrier.

I know there are awards beckoning and working sailors overly hard is one way to get them. I also have heard the arguments from Navy officers that productivity would drop dangerously low if every sailor at sea were guaranteed at least one day off a week; that the time goes faster when he works every day; that idle time is trouble time. I read the same arguments when I was growing up as business executives warned about the disaster which would befall the American economy if factory workers were given Saturdays off. They were wrong. The record documents that a refreshed worker is a more productive worker. I see no reason that this would not be true of sailors at sea.

As for the sailors getting in trouble at sea if they were not working, the leadership obligation here is to provide this modern sailor with more ways to make productive use of his free time at sea. My seven-plus months on the *Kennedy* prompt me to recommend that the Navy take these steps:

- Add an antenna to the forest of them already sticking up from Navy carriers and other warships so live television shows could be taken out of the sky and shown throughout the ship. Communication satellites already are whirling around the earth. They could be employed to beam live news programs and football games. If there are legal obstacles—I doubt if there are major technological ones—let the Navy request legislation from Congress to clear them away. I cannot imagine politicians voting against such a measure once they understood who it was for. Such broadcasts would not give away a ship's position any more than the hundreds of messages which currently whip back and forth between land stations and ships at sea. In emergencies or periods of confrontation, the television signals could be suspended.

- Install radio telephones on every Navy ship that stays out for extended periods so the sailors and officers can call home occasionally. A phone call can end anxiety about a sick loved one; strengthen a frayed marriage; alleviate, if not cure, depression, loneliness, homesickness, and heartache. In this age of global communications, radio telephones present no technological problem. There may be a mindset problem, however. But if the morale of the crew means anything, and I think that it can mean everything, then it is time to break this mindset and provide the men a way to call home on occasion.

- Offer televised educational courses for degree credit over a ship's closed-circuit television system or on videocassette recorders. This might require making costly arrangements with colleges on shore to produce courses for which the colleges and universities involved would give academic credit toward a degree. I realize that the Navy is already providing educational courses at sea. But my conclusion after watching the process for the better part of a year is that the educational effort is not broad enough. I recommend an outside review by distinguished civilian educators of the Navy's educational efforts at sea to see how they could be improved and broadened.

- Bring more of the outside world inside the walls of Navy ships by thinking beyond Christmas shows by Bob Hope or Wayne Newton and visits by the Dallas Cowgirls. Again, the initiative must come from the top of the Navy. To cite just one of endless possibilities, it would be stimulating and uplifting for the men at sea to hear from the U.S. ambassador to the country which they are helping to stabilize by patrolling off its coast. This never happened the whole time the *Kennedy* was off Beirut. The ambassador could have been flown to the *Kennedy* for an hour or so to appear on the closed-circuit television. If he had said how the men were helping their government, and why, and closed with a word of thanks, the gesture would have been enlightening and uplifting to the men out on that point. The new breed of American sailor is interested in learning how what he is doing fits in with the nation's policy.

As for the aircraft carrier as a war machine, it is undoubtedly a fantastic embodiment of American engineering and human performance. Archeologists hundreds of years hence will shake their heads in wonder as they piece together its function. They will ask how twentieth-century man managed to snag 30-ton airplanes going 150 miles an hour on a short stretch of steel deck floating on the ocean. But in this age of satellites and smart weapons, carriers are vulnerable. They can be located, however vast the ocean, if enough technological effort is applied to the search. And after a carrier is located, modern weapons could disable or sink it with cruise missiles fired from submarines below, planes overhead, or ships beyond the horizon.

The question is not whether carriers are vulnerable, in my view, but how vulnerable. Vulnerability to modern weaponry does not mean the day of the supercarrier is over. It does mean that its employment must be reassessed. The supercarrier remains in 1986, and for the foreseeable future, a valuable saber for the President of the United States to rattle, partly because in this day of few overseas bases for projecting American military power he has no other visible instrument for displaying support or opposition. Gunboat diplomacy with carriers also helps to deter the madmen of the world from taking rash actions, with Libya's Muammar Qaddafi the leading case in point.

The future of the supercarrier is less clear when considered against the threats posed to them by modern military forces, like those being built by the Soviets. I was not alone on the *Kennedy* when I concluded that the Soviets with enough effort could have penetrated the defenses of the carrier, as good as its men and machines were. As one pilot who agreed with that vulnerability put it, "They can make it rain longer than we can swim."

To assess the vulnerability of the supercarrier in the year 2000 and beyond, I think it is vital too for the President or the Congress to name a commission of experts to address these questions:

- How capable will the Soviets be in locating a carrier on the ocean with satellites and other means over the next 20 years?
- If the carrier can be located, can it be sunk?
- Given the vulnerability of the supercarrier to modern weaponry, does it make sense to build more of the giants?
- Or is it time to switch to smaller, cheaper ones which, through automation, could have much smaller crews than the five thousand men on the giants?
- The switch would be driven by the conclusion that in any war with the Soviets, carriers would be sunk, making it advisable to build two for the price of one if possible. What should be the mix of giant and medium-sized carriers?
- What more needs to be done to bring a new generation of V/STOL (vertical and short takeoff and landing) aircraft into being? These planes would not need the complicated launching and trapping gear aboard the supercarrier. The V/STOL aircraft now in hand do not have enough range and payload for going into combat a long distance from the carrier.

To generate more light than heat from such an inquiry, I would recommend turning to the expertise lodged within retired members of the American military and bypassing the Washington lawyers who so often end up on such commissions. If the day of the supercarrier is over as far as fighting a modern power, the sooner the nation finds this out, the better the chance of saving lives and billions of dollars—and winning any future war. My own mind is open on this key question.

In the meantime, I would recommend a second look by the Secretary of Defense, Navy leaders, and Congressional committees about the way supercarriers are deployed with an eye to reducing the strain on the men inside them without compromising the mission. I could never figure out why the *Kennedy*, for example, was not authorized to stand 100 or 200 miles off Lebanon where there would be less risk of terrorist attack rather than 70 to 80 miles. Preparations would not have had to be so intensive and fatiguing with the wider firebreak. At 80 miles the *Kennedy* was not visible to people on shore anyway, so whatever deterrence visibility buys would not have been lost by going out farther to sea. Another 100 miles would have been only a few minutes' flying time for modern jets. Also, as I flew in jets over Soviet warships at anchor in the Mediterranean, I wondered if anchoring occasionally during a cruise rather than continuously steaming as we had done did not have merit. Why do we Americans have to keep moving feverishly over the seas almost all the time in peacetime?

Finally, I fervently recommend that U.S. decision makers do a mini-version of what I did: live on a warship long enough to appreciate the immense sacrifice the men inside make. I salute them all.

GCW

Spring 1986

Acknowledgments

THERE are so many people to thank for making this book possible, starting with my wife, Joan, who had the far more difficult job of taking care of everything at home while I was at sea.

I am indebted in a professional sense to Secretary of the Navy John F. Lehman, Jr. and Admiral James D. Watkins, Chief of Naval Operations, for clearing the way for me to go out on the *Kennedy* for her full deployment. I am also indebted to the editors of *The Washington Post* for granting me a leave of absence so I could go to sea for more than seven months.

Navy information officers were also supportive and helpful, particularly Admiral (lower half) Jack Garrow, Captain Jimmie Finckelstein, and Captain Brent Baker at the Pentagon and Captain Jay Coupe, Jr., director of public affairs at the U.S. European Command in Stuttgart, West Germany. And the enthusiasm displayed for the project from start to finish by retired Captain Vincent C. Thomas, Jr. was both helpful and inspirational.

I am also grateful for the encouragement several of my journalistic colleagues provided, especially William Greider, Haynes Johnson, Richard Harwood, and Bob Woodward.

On the *Kennedy* herself everyone went above and beyond the call of duty to explain what they were doing and why, to say nothing of letting me fly in every airplane on the flight deck except one which was equipped with highly secret gear. Rear

Admirals Jerry O. Tuttle and Roger E. Box; Captains Gary F. Wheatley, John A. Pieno, John J. Mazach, and James E. Doffin; Commander Ronald Weber; Lieutenant Commanders Fred Major and Sammy Bonanno must go on my short list of people to whom I feel indebted. There were thousands of others, with Thomas Brinson III of the boiler room, Marty Martell of the flight deck and "Ben," the troubled sailor, among the many I will always remember warmly as shipmates during a very special period of our lives. And I cannot end this without a salute to Pat Mazach, an especially classy Navy wife, for sharing her insights into the lives of women left on shore, an important dimension to the story I have tried to tell faithfully between these covers. GCW

Index

Accidents. *See* Mishaps
Adee, PO George, 95
Ahern, Ensign Brian, 141
Air Wing Three, 20
Allen, Captain John "Frog,"
  256, 258
"All hands evolution," 234
Alonso, Mark, 184
Alonso, Radames, 184
Amos, Seaman Recruit
  Nathan B., 97
Anchoring procedures,
  87–90
Andrews, Commander Ed
  "Honiak," 137–38, 148,
  149–50, 151
Antisubmarine warfare
  (ASW), 232–42
  "all hands evolution,"
    234
  helicopters and, 235–36
  S-3 Viking weapons,
    235
  Sosus and, 233–34
APAMs, 121

Balcom, Gertell H., 19
Beach, Lieutenant Mark
  "Sonny," 142, 190 95,
  198–99
  in "The Box," 190–95
Bear hunts, 71–85
  Lieutenant Dan "Traps"
    Cloyd and, 76–83
  defined, 71–72
  example of, 76–83
  Lieutenant Brad Goetsch
    and, 74–76
  Korean Air Lines Flight
    007 and, 76, 81
  patrol geography of Bears,
    72
  rapport with Soviet pilots,
    72, 73–75
  Lieutenant Dave "Tag"
    Price and, 76–83
Belenko, Lieutenant Viktor,
  73
"Ben" (biography of sailor),
  42–44
Benoit, Steve, 67–68

Bernard, Commander Paul, 124, 151–54
Bever, Lieutenant Gil "Beaver," 139, 140, 161–62
Bombing raid (Dec. 4, 1983), 133–54
  aftermath of, 155–67
  comments by fliers after, 156–69
  decision to retaliate, 136–37
  fliers chosen for, 138–42
  incident initiating, 133–35
  officers' comments on, 163–66
  red-shirted ordies and, 159
Bonanno, Lieutenant Commander Sammy, 30, 34, 84–85, 91–93, 236, 240, 248–56, 273–75
  flight with author on Tomcat, 248–56
Boston, Captain Mike, 23, 41
Box, Rear Admiral Roger E., 15, 73, 120, 135, 175, 189, 263
Box, Ruthie, 15
"Box, the," 192
Brashers, Eggie, 67–68
Brauer, Lieutenant Bob, 170
Brinson, Thomas "Daddy B.," 65–70, 89
  biographical sketch of, 68–70
Brown, Commander Greg "Zipper," 222–31
  biographical sketch of, 223
Burch, Commander John

"Market," 5–6, 20–21, 103, 107–08, 112, 114, 115–17, 133–35, 269–70
  memorial service and, 115–17
  reflections on cruise, 269–70
  speech after mishap, 108
Burlin, Commander Dave, 146
Byrum, Lieutenant George P., 19, 34, 94–96

"Captain O. D.," 16–17
Captain's Mast, 5, 53–55, 56–59
Chaplains, 33–34
Checkmates, 233
Christmas 1983, 168–89
  flight over Holy Land, 176–82
  Bob Hope performance and, 186–89
  interviews during, 182–85
  Wayne Newton performance and, 170–72
  Red Rippers' party, 168–70
  Rooks' party, 172–75
CIWS, 211
Clager, Lieutenant Robert "Bo Bo," 170, 200–02
  in "The Box," 200–02
Cloyd, Lieutenant Dan "Traps," 76–83
  Bear hunts and, 76–83
Colage, Aviation Ordnance Man John, 159
"Collateral damage," 126, 136–37

Combs, Commander John, 112–14, 201–02, 275
  biographical sketch of, 112–14
Combs, Tanya, 114
Conley, Larry, 185
Creamer, Parachute Rigger Don, 177, 182
Crosby, Cathy Lee, 186, 188
Crowley, Master Chief Stanley G., 62–64, 65, 168, 188, 269
  comments on cruise, 269
Curran, PO John, 98–99

Damone, Vic, 189
Darvin, PO Larry, 95
Daube, PO Joseph, 14–15
Daube, Terrie, 14–15
Davis, Lieutenant (jg) Peter, 169
Davis, Lieutenant William "Catfish," 131, 139–40, 142, 144–45, 150–54, 160–61, 190–99
  biographical sketch of, 196–98
  in "The Box," 190–95
Day, Commander Steve, 146
December 4th raid. *See* Bombing raid (Dec. 4, 1983)
Dixon, Hospital Corpsman Walter, 102
Doffin, Captain James E., 34, 42, 86–87, 94–96, 115, 160, 161, 185, 266–69, 271
  "Ben" and, 42–44
  comments on cruise, 266–69

painting a school in Rio, 94–96
Drug abuse, 59
Dry, Aviation Boatswain's Mate Robert E., 27
Dulke, Lieutenant Mike "Skimmer," 146
Duntemann, Flight Surgeon Tom "Doc," 91, 93, 100, 101, 102

EA-6Bs, 217–18
Eckhart, Commander Jim, 168, 172–73, 176–82
  flight over Holy Land with Wilson, 176–82
Edington, Lieutenant Commander Ron "Bo," 248
Electronic Sensing Measures (ESM), 83
Ellis, Lieutenant Abe, 275
Engine room tour, 65–70
Ertschweiger, Commander John "Turtle," 222–31
  biographical sketch of, 224
Escamillia, PO Mark, 95
Executive Officer (XO), 48–49

F-14 Tomcat, 246–63
  author flying, 248–56
  night takeoffs and landings, 256–62
Fahey, Commander Mike "Iron Mike," 45–46, 65, 66
Fisher, Marine Lance Corporal R. L., 162
FLIR, 238
Flynn, Captain Sam, 206
FOD, 18

Fox, AW Tim, 236–37
Francis, Lieutenant Scott
  "Spanker," 170, 200–02
  in "The Box," 200–02
Frano, Lieutenant Pete, 147,
  151

Geister, Lieutenant
  Commander Joel, 46,
  56–58, 89–90
Gemayal, Amin, 118, 134,
  232, 243
Glover, Commander Jim,
  146–47, 151, 248
Goeke, Lieutenant Keith,
  146
Goetsch, Lieutenant Brad,
  74–76
  Bear hunts and, 74–76
Goodman, Lieutenant Bobby
  "Benny," 140–41, 146,
  151–53, 207
Goulette, Michael J., 39–40
  biographical sketch of,
  39–40
Granito, PO Mark, 182–83,
  185
Green, Hospital Corpsman
  Gary, 102
Greene, Lieutenant Jim
  "Mean One," 168–69,
  274
Griffin, Senior Chief
  William D., 25, 27
Guthrie, Lieutenant
  Commander "Arlo," 202

Hamilton, Lieutenant
  Commander William, 101
Hayek, Julie, 186, 188
Hays, Lieutenant Bill
  "Sinker," 275

Higgins, Lieutenant
  Commander Tim, 110
Higher Authority, defined, 2
Hilt, Lieutenant Commander
  Jim "Big Jim," 237–39
Holcomb, Vice Admiral M.
  Staser, 136, 164–65,
  166–67
  comments on bombing
  raid, 164–65
Holloway, Commander Bud,
  128, 129–30
Hook runner, 36–37
Hookup man, 36–37
Hope, Bob, 168, 176,
  186–89
  Christmas show
  performance, 186–89
Hopkins, Hospital Corpsman
  Patrick, 102
Hoppock, Lieutenant
  Commander Ronald
  "Hawk," 91–92, 262
Houston, Aviation Ordnance
  Man Dale, 159
Hughes, Commander Kirby
  "Skip," 143–46, 161

Jablonski, Lieutenant Ian
  "Jabbo," 147
James, Airman Apprentice
  Chad, 25–26, 27
Jancarski, Lieutenant David
  Pierre "Frenchie," 1–9,
  81–82, 97–99, 117
  on flying Tomcats, 6
  medical treatment after
  rescue, 100–03
  rescue of, 98–99
Jillian, Ann, 186, 188
Johnson, Commander Robert
  L. "Bunky," Jr., 82, 276

Johnson, Lyndon B., 244
Jones, Captain Willis, 241
Jones, Commander Jim,
    240–42
  biographical sketch of,
    241–42
Jones, General David C.,
    212–13
Jones, Lieutenant
    Commander John, 146,
    147, 148, 150–51
Jones, Lieutenant Mike
    "Zone," 195, 262–63

Kaminsky, Dr. Howard H.,
    101–02
Kelleher, Lieutenant Brian,
    274
Kennedy, John F., 49, 244
Kennedy, Robert F., 116
Kennedy, Ted, 116
Kidd, Commander Jim, 143
Kirby, George, 189
Korean Air Lines Flight 007,
    76, 81
  Bear hunts and, 76, 81

Lahren, Lieutenant
    Commander Jack W.
    "Jocko," 82
Lange, Cheryl, 141
Lange, Jamie, 141, 161
Lange, Lieutenant Mark
    "Doppler," 140, 141–42,
    146, 151–53, 156, 157,
    161–62, 167, 168, 196,
    198
  death in bombing raid,
    152–53
  memorial service for,
    161–62
Lawson, General Richard L.,

136, 164–66
  comments on bombing
    raid, 165–66
Lebanon bombing raid. *See*
    Bombing raid (Dec. 4,
    1983)
Lehman, John F., Jr., 10,
    203–19
  on building smaller
    carriers, 213–14,
    218–19
  on EA-6Bs, 217–18
  on Israeli air force,
    207–08
  Israeli and U.S. Pilots
    compared, 208–09
  visits *Kennedy,* 203–19
  on spotting missions,
    209–10
  on STOL, 217
  on subsonic A–6, 206–07
  on terrorist threats,
    210–13
  Paul Thayer and, 204
  on threats to carriers,
    214–16
Lescavage, Lieutenant Greg,
    102
Lethbridge, Lieutenant (jg)
    Mark, 24, 26
Lewis, Lieutenant
    Commander Steven G., 27
Linquist, Commander Jim,
    146
Ludwig, Commander Wigs,
    108, 114, 116, 256,
    256–62
  on night flight with author,
    256–62

McAloon, Lieutenant Jim
    "Mac," 135, 257

Machinery room tour, 66–68

McCracken, Lieutenant
Larry, 21–22, 24–25, 27

McDonald, Admiral Wesley
L., 16, 17

McNally, Lieutenant Mark
"Mork," 140, 142,
143–46

McNamara, Lieutenant Bob,
177, 180

McNamara, Robert S., 66,
125

Major, Lieutenant
Commander Fred J.,
22–23, 83–84

Marsh, Hospital Corpsman
Victor, 102

Martell, Boatswain's Mate
"Marty," 37–39, 186,
265
biographical sketch of,
37–39

Martin, Aviation Ordnance
Man Billy, 159

Martin, Vice Adm. Edward
H. 136, 164, 167
comments on bombing
raid, 164

Mazach, Commander John J.
(CAG), 87–90, 119,
124–31, 137–38, 144,
146–51, 156, 186, 248,
271, 274, 275
anchoring the *Kennedy*,
87–90

Mazach, Pat, 186, 274

Mazzeo, Belva, 174–75

Mazzeo, Gennaro, 174–75

Mazzeo, Lieutenant Dan,
174–75, 257, 261

Mellema, First Crewman
Mike, 99–100

Metcalf, Vice Admiral
Joseph III, 26–27

Michener, James, 186

Millar, Lieutenant Doug,
21–22, 24–27

Miller, Lieutenant John
"Fossie," 133–35

Mishaps, 1–12, 97–117
Commander John Combs
and, 112–14
death in flying accident, 3
decision by pilot to leave
Navy and, 110–12
morale and, 107–08
Navy wives and, 103–08
Red Rippers and, 112–14

Moore, Senior Chief, 238

Nabours, Lynn, 191

Naples, (port of call),
270–72

Navicki, AD Michael
265–66
biographical sketch of,
265

Neely, Chief Bob, 39

Newton, Wayne, 168,
170–72, 189
Christmas show
performance, 170–72

Nixon, Richard, 244

Noble, Lieutenant
Commander William, 102

O'Neil, Dana, 20–21, 116

O'Neil, Lieutenant (jg) Cole
"Bam Bam," 3, 20–21,
103, 104, 108, 114,
115–17, 221
death in flying accident, 3
memorial service for,
115–17

Pabst, Lieutenant Rick "Blue Ribbon," 147

Paradis, Commander Curly, 80

Patrick, Yeoman Nicholas Eugene, 160–61
as conscientious objector, 160

Patterson, PO Mark, 96

Pena, Kathleen, 117

Pena, Nicole, 117

Pena, PO Fernando "Mex," 117

Pena, Richard, 117

Pericles, 162

Perry, William, 231

Phillips, Airman Mark, 99–100

Pieno, Captain John Anthony (XO), 48, 60–62, 65, 87, 168, 175, 195
biographical sketch of, 60–62

Piorkowski, Lieutenant Joe "Fighter Doc," 93, 94

Pittman, Lieutenant Commander Glenn "Porky," 237–39

Player, A, defined, 73

Powers, CAG, 275

Price, David, 109–12
decision to leave Navy, 109–12

Price, Etta, 111

Price, Lieutenant Dave "Tag," 76–83
Bear hunts and, 76–83

Principles of Naval Engineering, 65

Prueher, Commander Joe, 125, 127, 131

Puritano, Vincent, 18

Qaddafi, Muammar, 122

Reagan, Ronald, 2, 9, 12, 34–35, 119, 123, 136, 137, 155, 162, 186, 232, 243–44, 270

Red Rippers, 112–14, 168–70

Reynolds, Aviation Boatswain's mate Randy, 26, 27

Reynolds, Lieutenant (jg) Randall "Hacksaw," 262

Rio (port of call), 86–96
painting school, in, 94–96

Rizer, Clarence E., III, 19

Rockel, Airman Daniel, 98–99

Rogers, General Bernard W., 136, 166
comments on bombing raid, 166

Roper, Commander Dan, 115

RTB, 83

Scott, Lieutenant Commander Chuck "Mumbles," 82, 274

Scull, Commander John "Belly," 3, 103, 104, 108, 114, 115–17, 221
death in flying accident, 3
memorial service for, 115–17

Scull, John Woodward, 116

Scull, Mary Paul, 116

Shapiro, Airman Recruit, 27

Shean, Commander Keith, 271

Shellbacks, 83–84

Shields, Brooke, 186, 187, 188

Shoemaker, Rear Admiral
James M., 19
"Smart bombing," 220–31
defined, 222
Smith, Aviation Boatswain's
Mate William R., 26, 27
Smith, Commander
"Supo," 187
Smith, Commander Ted, 45
Smith, Joe, 185
Solik, Lieutenant Bob, 147,
151
Sosus, 233–34
Soviet Bear bombers. *See*
Bear hunts
Space (Michener), 186
Steward, Lieutenant Scott
"Stewie," 243, 258
STOL, 217
Stranger to the Ground
(Bach), 75
Streit, Lieutenant Greg
"Road," 135, 257,
260-61
Strickland, Lieutenant Rich,
99
SUCAP, 211
Sulfaro, Commander John,
192

TAD, 183
Target X, 126-31, 141
TARPS, defined, 134
Terrell, Bernard, 184
Terrorism, 118–32
APAMS and, 121
defenses against, problems
in, 121–23
retaliation targets, 124–32
Soviet missiles to Syria,
130
Target X and, 126–31

Rear Admiral Tuttle and,
119–20
Thayer, Paul, 137, 204
Lehman and, 204
Tindle, Lieutenant
Commander John,
146–47
Titi, Lieutenant Richard
"Rick," 19, 30
Turpen, Lieutenant Chuck,
170
Tuttle, Rear Admiral Jerry
O., 119–21, 122,
123–24, 125–29, 135,
136, 137, 138, 158,
163–64, 165–67, 205,
234, 244, 272
comments on bombing
raid, 163–64
terrorism and, 119–20
Tyce, Samuel E., 185

USS *John F. Kennedy:*
anchoring procedures,
87–90
antisubmarine warfare
(ASW) and, 232–42
Bear hunts and, 71–85
"below decks," 65–70
bombing raid (Dec. 4,
1983), 133–54
breakdown of ship's
company, 40–41
chaplains aboard,
33–34
Christmas and, 168–89
deaths in mishaps, 3
departments of, 48
departure of, 13–27
drug abuse and, 59
eating arrangements
aboard, 32–33

homecoming at Norfolk, 276–77

homeward bound journey of, 264–77

initial tour by author of, 28–31

Lehman's visit to, 203–19

as management challenge, 48–49

marine pullout and, 243–45

mishaps and, 1–12, 97–117

in Naples (port of call), 270–72

night takeoffs and landings from, 256–63

racial harmony aboard, 46

in Rio (port of call), 86–87

ashore at Rota, 273–75

"smart bombing" and, 220–31

terrorism and, 118–32

young sailors aboard, profile of, 40–46

Vessey, General John W., 137, 166
comments on bombing raid, 166

Voytak, Dave, 183–84, 185

Walsh, Lieutenant Commander Michael A., 34, 94–95

Watkins, Admiral James D., 10, 136, 137, 166

Watson, Lieutenant Dennis "Sluggo," 177, 180, 182
comments on bombing raid, 166

Weber, Commander Robyn "Potsie," 91–94, 138–39, 185, 275

Weinberger, Caspar W., 136

Wheatley, Captain Gary F., 4, 19, 47–50, 51–53, 65, 87, 88, 89–90, 168, 189, 264–65
at Captain's Mast, 53–55, 56–58
on Mast Chief Crowley, 63
orientation lectures by, 49–52
on "popular" commanders, 52–53
on responsibilities as skipper, 47–49, 51–53
on uncertainty surrounding voyage, 53

Whyte, PO Steven, 24–25, 26

Williams, Lieutenant Commander Don "Rookie," 93, 186

Williamson, Lieutenant Tim, 131

Willis, Katie, 171

Willis, Lieutenant Commander Monty, 171, 275

Wilson, George C.:
approval to report on carrier, 10
"below decks" tour, 65–70
biographical data on, 10–12
Christmas interviews by, 182–85
departure from family, 13–14

Wilson, George C., *cont.*
  equator-crossing ceremony
    and, 83–84
  flying F-14 Tomcat,
    248–56
  flying over Holy Land on
    Christmas Eve, 176–82
  homecoming at Norfolk,
    276–77
  initial tour of ship by,
    29–30
  Lehman interviewed by,
    205–19
  on liberty (Rio), 90–96
  night takeoffs and
    landings, 256–63
  reaction of shipmates to,
    30–31
  recommendations to Navy
    by, 280–83
  ashore at Rota, 273–75
  on ship arrangements,
    31–32
  talks with sailors, 35–38

Wilson, Jim, 12, 185, 277
Wilson, Joan, 12, 13–14,
  15, 16, 36, 185, 277
Wilson, Kathy, 12, 185
Winters, Commander Tim,
  240–41
Withers, Lieutenant Tom,
  98, 99
Witzenburg, Captain Gary,
  88
Wright, Lieutenant
  Commander Ollie, 1–3,
  6–8, 9, 11, 81, 97–99,
  114
  rescue of, 98–100
Wright, Sue, 103, 104–07
  letters to husband Ollie,
    104–07

Yeager, Major Charles E.,
  261
Yellow Shirts, 23–24